Resurrecting Virgil

Dorie LaRue

The Backwaters Press

Winner of the 2000 Omaha Prize

Also by Dorie LaRue

The Private Frenzy, University of Nebraska Press, 1992
Seeking the Monsters, New Spirit Press, 1993

Acknowledgments

Ben-Abraham, Avi. "Putting Death on Ice," *The Saturday Evening Post.* April 1989. Vol. 216: pps. 60-62.

My thanks to Greg Kosmicki and Mark Spencer, the Louisiana Division of the Arts, the Shreveport Regional Arts Council, Louisiana State University in Shreveport, Dr. Jay Toups, and my son, Michael Royce Darr LaRue.

First Printing 750 copies December 2001

This is a work of fiction. Any similarities in this work to any persons, living or dead, or to any nonfictional events, is purely coincidental.

Published by: The Backwaters Press
                  3502 North 52nd Street
                  Omaha, Nebraska 68104-3506
                  gkosm62735@aol.com
                  (402) 451-4052
                  www.thebackwaterspress.homestead.com

ISBN: 0-9677149-6-6

Printed in the United States of America by
Morris Publishing • 3212 East Highway 30 • Kearney, Nebraska • 68847

Many thanks to these supporters of The Backwaters Press without whose generous contributions and subscriptions the publication of this book would not have been possible.

ANGELS

Steve and Kathy Kloch
Greg and Barb Kuzma
Don and Marjorie Saiser
Rich and Eileen Zochol

BENEFACTORS

Barbara and Bob Schmitz

PATRONS

Guy and Jennie Duncan
Cheryl Kessell
Tim O'Connor
Maureen Toberer
Frederick Zydek

SPONSORS

Paul and Mildred Kosmicki
Gary Leisman and Wendy Adams
Jeff and Patty Knag
Matt Mason
Pat Murray and Jeanne Schuler
Carol Schmid
Alan and Kim Stoler
Don Taylor

FRIENDS

J. V. Brummels
Twyla Hansen
Judy Levin
Jim and Mary Pipher

For Mic

and in memory of my mother

Resurrecting Virgil

One

Virgil Matthews sits slumped in the pink Naugahyde platform rocker next to the window in the Harrisonville City Funeral Home and picks his teeth. His jeans pull tight at the seams. He can say one thing for his meemaw—she can cook. Virgil has worn a dent in the Naugahyde watching the funeral home's big Curtis Mathis TV without benefit of antenna or vertical control and eating his good supper she packed for him every night for the three months since he's started work. But then the TV busted all the way and his boss Harvey L. Sloane did not see the need to get it fixed. Virgil still balances his plate on his knees in front of the screen, even though there are plenty of tables around, and stares at it by habit. He misses M*A*S*H especially, but lately he is not really bothered. Without B.J. and Hawkeye to watch every evening at suppertime, his eyes strayed out the window once by chance and fell upon an old classmate of his, Lorna Jean Gibson, as she left the back doors of the T.C. Haynes Construction Company.

Virgil did not even know Lorna Jean worked for Haynes, and since he was in love with her from the first time he lay eyes on her way back in high school, it became his ritual to catch her leaving every evening and watch her walk off down the alley. In fact Virgil is beginning to feel closer to Lorna Jean than ever just because of all the secret watching. He considers it a small price to pay for reruns of M*A*S*H.

Lorna Jean Gibson always walks down the alley to the corner of Ursuline and Crocket, and then disappears into Speed Maxwell's red Bronco parked on the curb. She is better than any actress on TV—her entrance onto the street, her hair floating blonde patterns in the wind. Today, when the double doors open, she is wearing a white T-shirt, a short blue jean skirt and yellow tennis shoes. Lorna Jean and Speed Maxwell are a couple, but Virgil doesn't even try to fight his feelings.

A couple of years ago in civics class at old Jefferson High, one row over from her, Virgil often followed the lines of her ponytail to the back of her tanned shoulders down to the curve between the seat and the backrest of her desk and then on to the perfect perpetually tanned legs. Virgil burns red, just remembering, guilt and the sweet potato from supper sitting heavily for a second until Speed and Lorna Jean drive off. It is unbelievable the stuff he thinks of, the things no one else would guess he was thinking. He looks around the room until he feels the heat burn off his neck and his breathing slow down.

Despite the shiny tables and the instruments stuck in jars, and the white of everything, the evening sun coats the room, mutes it to a pink softness, making the whole space seem edgeless and colorful. Virgil is becoming fond of the place. Beside the broken-down TV is a bookcase where Harvey L. Sloane keeps all his undertaking books and back issues of *Casket and Sunnyside*, a surgical trolley, an ordinary chest of drawers full of sheets and towels and finally the newest addition—refrigerated roll-out bins, one of which at the moment, holds a half-dozen boutonnieres. Someone on the day shift is getting married tomorrow.

Actually the mortuary is only half the business. In addition to owning the only funeral home within a hundred mile radius, Harvey L. Sloane also runs a successful Porta-potty company. The Porta-potties are outside in a cyclone-and-barbed wire enclosure. Harvey has a separate number for this business and separate door and sign. It is almost totally obscured from the street. Most of the customers for the Porta-potties make their inquiries by phone anyway.

Virgil brushes the fried chicken crumbs off his lap. Then he gets up and goes to first floor by way of the elevator, as big as a small room, and walks across the foyer to the double-doors that separate the lobby from the coffin room. "Casket" room, he remembers. Harvey

2

told Virgil when he first started working for him not to say certain words. "Casket" is more polite, than "coffin", Harvey believes. He wants him to say funeral "coach" instead of funeral "hearse."

It is a cavernous room. Each casket has to have plenty of room, fifty or sixty feet, and proper lighting. Harvey has all the caskets in a certain order, on imaginary streets, like Park Avenue, Subaru Street, and McDonaldland to make it easier to remember prices. Virgil turns down Subaru and goes to a bronze-plated and maple half-couch job (which shows the person from the waist up) and lifts the lid. Virgil uses this one for a hiding place. He reaches in and takes out a heavy, spiral-bound book. He puts it under his arm and heads back to the elevator.

Back in his chair on second, he takes off his shoes and gets comfortable. Virgil is taking a taxidermy course by mail and he studies at work because he knows his meemaw would hate the idea. One day, when Harvey's present assistant is gone, Harvey is going to move Virgil up. Virgil had sent off for the course before Harvey told him that but since he has already paid for the stuff, he still reads the books. Probably it is a little like being a mortician, anyway. Virgil puts his socks up on the nearby trolley of syringes and kidney bowls and settles in to read. He's barely had the second volume a week and he is already whipping his way through chapter eight: "Choosing the Glass Eye and Headform."

Presently Harvey L. Sloane comes in. Virgil makes a little show of stumbling his feet to the floor and closing his book but he always has the feeling Harvey barely notices him and has his thoughts fixed on something in the far future.

"S-s-s. I'll tell you what," Harvey says as way of greeting. He always has this hiss to his words. Not a stutter exactly, but a little sibilance sort of to announce the word. He looks at Virgil with his little pop eyes. Harvey has a conveniently sad, froggy face, and he wears the same style clothes all the time. There is something dashing about them that Virgil admires. Tonight he is wearing a checkered coat of indefinite colors, a pale double-breasted vest, and gray shoes with black suede uppers. Once he told Virgil that he was a showboat operator on the *Delta Queen*, and Virgil suspects that he gets a lot of his ideas of style from the stage. Harvey rubs his hands together like he does when a body, a beloved one, is about to be delivered. But Harvey says, "S-s. Go ahead and knock off early, s-son. I got an order for the toilets-s-s and I got a little work to do."

His eyes glint.

"All right," Virgil says. He closes his book not-too-enthusiastically. It is only eight-fifteen. His meemaw and his daddy, Shelby, will still be up watching the end of *Unsolved Mysteries*. Tonight is a feature on unclaimed fortunes.

As he walks toward home slowly down Ursuline Street, Virgil realizes he has a problem. With Harvey there he has not been able to return *The Art of Taxidermy* to its casket. Now he has to sneak it into the house under Meemaw's darting eyes. It isn't so much that Meemaw would hate the idea of his learning taxidermy, but she would make him hate it. Virgil's meemaw is a trial. She wears long home-made dresses with old-timey bibbed aprons and big floppy sunbonnets and she carries on in town like she is living on a thirty-acre farm. She raises chickens and vegetables and fruits right in the back yard. Their property is only a quarter of an acre, but Meemaw has learned about tiered rows and intensity planting from gardening books she's found in the library. Meemaw also has a little yellow-eyed Chihuahua she talks baby talk to and that attacks Virgil crazily every time he comes home, like he didn't live there. Meemaw named him Mike Hammer after some old favorite TV character. Besides his yipping, he has a weird habit of humping against the furniture legs at odd times. Virgil hates Mike Hammer. But Meemaw is sure Mike Hammer has cured Virgil's daddy's asthma. Chihuahuas are known for that. Meemaw believes that Mike Hammer has taken on the disease. And Mike Hammer does look a little under the weather all the time, despite his energy and yippiness, with his runny nose and weird little eyes.

Even without Mike Hammer, Meemaw would have been a pain in the neck to Virgil and would have probably been a pain in the neck to Virgil's mother if she hadn't died when he was only one year old. Shelby, Virgil's daddy, has lived with Meemaw so long he has learned how to put up with her.

Shelby lives in some kind of dream world, anyway. He has invented a lot of things that have not paid off because there is no call for them: a portable electric sock dryer suitable for travel, a smoke alarm that plays "Great Balls of Fire" when it senses smoke, and a toilet seat that glows in the dark and reminds people to leave the lid down with a genuine police whistle sound. Some of them Shelby has even gotten patent numbers on, like the self-tester for halitosis, a complicated contraption of rubber bladders and tubes and straps. None of them ever made a buck, though. About three years ago, Shelby gave up his small engine repair service, where he worked on most of his inventions between customers, and took a nine-to-five at KILLER FOR HIRE CITY PEST CONTROL.

As Virgil walks along going over in his mind the various places he could stash his book— beside the garbage cans, in the junked washer in the garage Shelby has yet to haul off, in his Meemaw's pea patch— something right off a television show happens. With his head down he bumps, literally bumps, into Lorna Jean Gibson who is turning onto Ursuline Street from Baker. Virgil is stunned. It is the last thing he's ever expected, even though he's survived on just such fantasies for years.

"Oh, says Lorna Jean Gibson in-person. "For heaven's sake. I didn't see you."

Virgil swallows hard and forces his lips to move. "Well, hey, Lorna Jean," he says. He realizes with horror his voice is raised three octaves. Then he can't think of what to do next.

Instead of hurtling on past him as Virgil expects, Lorna Jean stands squarely in front of him, blocking his path. "Say," she says. "I know you. High school. Old Bitch Tanner's civics class?"

Virgil nods, suddenly aware of The *Art of Taxidermy* under his arm. He pushes it up higher so that the title is good and hidden.

"Aren't you..." Lorna Jean pauses, "Vernon?"

"Virgil," says Virgil, dizzy. Lorna Jean has almost remembered his name. He feels like he is about to burst out of his skin. Lorna Jean's v-neck, white T-shirt exposes her throat and her tan seems to go on forever. He tries mightily to raise his eyes.

"Well, Virgil," she is saying. "I wonder if you'd do me a little favor."

Virgil would kill to do Lorna Jean a little favor, but all he can do at the moment is stand there and try to pull his eyes off her neckline and onto her face. When he finally is able to keep his gaze up for more than a second, he can see that her mascara is smudged slightly and that her nostrils are flared and so lovely that he feels a tear in his eye.

"I need to borrow a quarter," Lorna Jean says in a honey voice. "Do you think you could give me a quarter?"

"Sure," says Virgil. He reaches in his pocket to pull out his change, but there is nothing but a handful of pennies, a lint-covered aspirin, and an old washer that belongs on his reading lamp at home. "Here," he says, magnanimously pulling out his wallet and handing her a dollar bill.

"Oh!" Lorna Jean acts as though something has just made her mad. She looks mad but at the same time bored. "I need it for that." She points over at the pay phone hanging by the entrance of the Kiwanis Club.

Virgil is stunned by what he says next. "I just live a little way," he hears himself saying. "You could use my phone if you want." Then it hits him. Back home Meemaw is sitting in her chair in front of the TV with Mike Hammer in her lap, and Shelby is snoring by now in his new Home Shiatsu Massage Recliner.

"Oh, could I?" says Lorna Jean even more sugary than before.

"Well," Virgil stammers, thinking of Mike Hammer's little T-shirt his meemaw has bought him at T G & Y. Across the front of it are the letters, *"I'm the boss!"* Then he says, "It's not too far. But if you're in a hurry—"

He is about to suggest they go back to the funeral home to use that phone, but Lorna Jean seems to take offense. "Look, if you don't want me to use your phone, just say so." She tosses her head and the flame of gold-melded hair causes Virgil to hold his breath a second. He shifts his book helplessly to the other arm.

"Oh no," he says, doomed. "Sure. Sure you can use my phone."

And there they are walking down the street towards Virgil's house, Lorna Jean beside him taking her floating steps, the occasion he would have killed for in high school. He seems to be walking to his execution. And then they are turning into the driveway, with Shelby's Hyundai sitting in it with its giant plastic cockroach tipping his derby hat on the roof and the doors' painted KILLER FOR HIRE CITY PEST CONTROL letters gleaming up at them, and then they are passing the junked washer and the collection of odd lawn mowers Shelby takes parts off of to keep the good one going.

Virgil can hear tinkly music and a salesman's hard-sell voice before he opens the door, and through the window and the dining room's entrance arch, he can see that *Unsolved Mysteries* is over and Meemaw is watching the *Home Shopping* channel with Mike Hammer curled in her lap. All he can make of Shelby are his slippers suspended in mid-air on the footrest of his recliner. He opens the door as quietly as he can and holds it for Lorna Jean.

Mike Hammer comes barreling out, his red T-shirt flashing, yapping all the way through the kitchen-door, catches sight of Lorna Jean, cranks up even higher, and goes ballistic into Virgil's ankle. Virgil tries to push him back with other foot, gives up and tumbles toward the kitchen, Lorna Jean following. In the kitchen, he points at the phone for Lorna Jean. Then he limps out toward the dining room dragging Mike Hammer like a ball and chain.

Virgil tries to position himself in the dining room out of sight of both Meemaw and Lorna Jean, but he hears the rocker squeak.

"Here y'are," Meemaw says, coming in. She is dribbling brown drool out of one side of her mouth. Meemaw dips snuff.

"Meemaw—" Virgil begins, over Mike Hammer's growls.

"Meemaw, what?" she says. She peers around him, catching sight of Lorna Jean's little skirt in the kitchen. "Eh?"

"Somebody to use the phone's all," says Virgil, desperately.

"Phone!" snorts Meemaw. "Well, ain't nobody stopping nobody I can see." She peels Mike Hammer's little needle teeth out of Virgil's ankle, picks up the Crisco can she uses to spit in off the dining room table, and goes back to *Home Shopping*.

Virgil stands stupidly in the dining room until he hears the receiver click into its cradle, then he edges into the kitchen. Lorna Jean has taken a compact out of her purse and is attacking her eye shadow.

"Would you like some coffee?" he hears himself say. The words sound so almost normal, like he knew what he was doing, he gets light headed for a second.

"Oooooh, I don't think I do," Lorna Jean says into the mirror. She tilts her head a minute at her reflection, then clicks her compact closed. It occurs to Virgil that Lorna Jean is supposed to be out with Speed Maxwell.

"Hello," says Lorna Jean, looking over his shoulder.

Meemaw is sidling into the kitchen still holding Mike Hammer, bug-eyed and rigid. Soft dangerous growls rumble from his little throat.

"Humph," says Meemaw. "Who are you, girl?" Virgil feels his

spine draw up into his collarbone.

"I'm Lorna Jean Gibson," says Lorna Jean after a second, and then smiles a little. She raises one of her eyebrows.

Mike Hammer quits growling, yips once, and starts panting excitedly with his tiny, animated gulps. His little T-shirt rises up and down with each breath.

"Humph," says Meemaw, as though she doesn't like Lorna Jean. Then she says to Mike Hammer. "Oo going to bee-have?" She puts Mike Hammer down and looks at Virgil. "You get fired?" She cackles like a wicked witch on the Saturday cartoons.

Virgil says, "I got off early, Meemaw."

"At Box City?" she cackles again. She always thinks referring to the funeral home as Box City is a fine joke.

Lorna Jean is moving for the door, Mike Hammer in a dead calm, slowly advancing on her, delicately extending his little nose to her yellow shoe.

"Can I drive you somewhere?" mumbles Virgil, forgetting for a second, he doesn't have a car. If he is ever desperate enough for wheels, he has to take Shelby's cockroach.

"What?" says Lorna Jean, tugging at the door.

It occurs to Virgil, suddenly then, that Lorna Jean Gibson is standing in his house, in his meemaw's kitchen, just inches from where he eats his breakfast every morning, just a few rooms from where he sleeps, and, Virgil thinks crazily, just a few feet from where Shelby cut his toenails that morning over yesterday's newspaper.

"Boy says can he drive you somewheres?" bellows Meemaw, snapping Virgil out of it. Meemaw can yell louder than a truck driver.

"Oh! No! I'll just wait for my friend at the corner," Lorna Jean says. "Thank you all very, very much," she adds loudly and really clearly, as though the two of them, Virgil and Meemaw, are both stone deaf. Then she gives a little hop, dislodging Mike Hammer, who, Virgil notices with horror, has been in the process of attaching himself to her leg in an amorous hump, and runs.

Virgil stands with his meemaw in the kitchen staring at the door, which has closed after Lorna Jean Gibson. Behind him he can hear the opening strains of an old *Gunsmoke* rerun from the direction of the living room, and a sudden giant volley of snores from Shelby.

"Tee hee," says Meemaw. "Matt Dillon." She looks at his book still under Virgil's arm. "What's that?"

Two

irgil doesn't have to be at work until three in the afternoons. Shelby comes home for lunch, then leaves immediately afterwards, and Meemaw and Mike Hammer go to their bedroom off the kitchen and take a two-hour nap. Both she and the dog snore to beat hell. Other than that, the house is peaceful at that time of day. But every morning until then it is noisy enough because vegetable and egg customers come and go and in between customers Meemaw cooks a big, hot meal and it is a production: stewed okra or peas, fried chicken, pork chops, or smothered steak. Virgil's pawpaw had been a soybean and cotton farmer who wanted a hot meal on the table at noon every day, and Meemaw had never bothered to break the habit of cooking a big dinner at noon with the result that Shelby's belly strains against the last hole on his belt and Virgil, who eats heartily himself and also gets the leftovers to take to work every evening, has the beginnings of a little paunch. Though Shelby gave up his shop downtown when he started work at KILLER FOR HIRE, he still putters with something or another in his spare time. His big dream is a squirrel-proof bird feeder, but he also has odd machines all over the house. An electric coffee grinder made out of an electric can opener. An electric can opener made out of an electric knife sharpener. He is always changing one thing into another, and then having to make something to replace the original. Virgil doesn't see why everything can't be what it starts out to be. But Shelby has built Meemaw a miniature guillotine for her chicken production that Virgil admits is one of his better ideas. It is a hundred times better than the ax. Virgil doesn't mind eating fried chicken but he hates all the activities that go into the preparation. He especially hates catching the chicken for Meemaw. First he gets Shelby's bass net out of the store room, then he scatters the feed, while nonchalantly holding the net behind his back before he spots a good shot and pounces. Half the time, he misses. By then all the chickens are on to him, especially the condemned one. It is twice as wily as the others.

Go get 'em, boy! Meemaw cackles as Virgil lopes around the chicken yard with the bass net. He always prays nobody happens by, or is watching in secret. Then after Meemaw decapitates it, the little feathered body dashes for a while in circles like some silent chicken horror movie, its bloody nub sticking up out of the gore. Virgil always tries to avert his gaze until the chop and the mad dash are over, but it is like his eyes are pulled to it all. *Hoo, boy,* his meemaw shouts when it finally runs down like a Christmas toy with shot batteries. Then she grabs it and picks the big feathers off. After that, Virgil puts on thick Rubbermaid gloves and plunges the carcass into scalding water to loosen the pinfeathers so that he can scrape them off.

❧

It is Friday, D-day for some unlucky bird, and over the steamy pink bath, Virgil's face heats up and rivulets of sweat run down his arms. He is picking out the big feathers and splashing his gloves in the water so that they float off. Mike Hammer sits nearby in a state of rapture, his little tongue lolling hopefully out of his grin.

Once Virgil figured out what shorts and corn chops cost and realized they could buy eggs and chicken fryers all cut up at the Winn-Dixie for almost half the price, but Meemaw hadn't appreciated his figuring. She just has to farm. It is in her blood. Right now, in the back yard, peas grow in all the flower beds instead of flowers like in their neighbors' yards. Blue Lake runners climb out of half-barrels and onto the patio's trellises. Meemaw has laid landscaping posts down in the St. Augustine and planted squash and butterbeans in tiers. Cucumber vines cover the cyclone fence. Tomato plants stuck with stakes and tied with Meemaw's old nylon stockings grow next to the central air and heat generator. And always is the incessant clucking from the chicken yard.

Virgil sometimes wonders what Lorna Jean would think if she could see the decapitation scene. He pictures her again and again as she stood that night, one foot thrust in front of the other, staring into her little mirror. Just remembering makes his throat ache.

Virgil finishes the back and legs and starts working on the breast. When he is finished, Meemaw will singe the carcass with a match, gut it, and cut it up and fry it. Once Virgil tried his hand at cutting up a fryer and he made a mess of things. It was strange, at the supper table that night, eating the weird, unidentifiable chicken parts. Meemaw never let him try again.

After a while, Meemaw puts her pea pan down and takes the fryer from Virgil and holds it up to judge the amount of meat on the bones. She buys a few spare pullets every year to fatten for eating. Most she keeps as layers though. Those that bite the dust do so only when they quit laying. But at one time, when Virgil was a baby, Shelby said, she kept thirty or more barred rock pullets; then she would slaughter them all in one day and store them in the freezer. Both Virgil and Shelby are glad those days are over. Shelby says that when he was a boy on their farm outside of Winnfield, if some relatives from out-of-town turned into their driveway, Meemaw would swoop down on the nearest young rooster (all named after Confederate generals) and start wringing its neck before the people got out of the car. If she could, Meemaw would put a cow in the garage, pigs on the patio, and lord knows what else. Luckily, or unluckily for Virgil, they live in the unzoned section of town known as Dixie Gardens, which is why Meemaw can have chickens.

Meemaw comes over and looks at the fryer. Humph," she says. "What did I tell you, Virgil. Ready for the pot."

Mrs. Zelma Wade comes over from next door through the back gate by the squash vines. She is one of meemaw's biggest customers. Her people were cotton farmers in the Delta Country and in Texas. "Let me see that fryer, Addie," she says to Meemaw, "if it's bigger than I got at the

A & P yesterday."

"Take a look," says his meemaw, holding the bird up by its legs like Virgil has seen doctors holding up newborn babies in the movies. De-feathered, it looks oddly human.

"I thought you was busy over here," says Zelma. "Why, it looks fat's a old hen."

Zelma's daughter, Daisy Wade, sticks her head over the gate. Daisy had been two years ahead of Virgil at Jefferson High. She is Lorna Jean's first cousin, but they are nothing alike. Virgil ducks his head and starts scooping water out of the tub.

"Hey, Mom," Daisy yells. "I got ten minutes to get to work—if you still want a lift to pick up your car."

"Coming, coming," says Zelma and goes right on talking to Virgil's Meemaw.

"Yoo-hoo, Virgil," Daisy calls. "How'd it go?"

Virgil looks up and nods his head, but he goes on scooping water out of the tub. Daisy has on her Burger King uniform and is leaning on the fence with her hand under her chin like she is posing for a picture. Daisy always goes out of her way to holler at him when she sees him around, but she bugs Virgil. They have lived next door for six years, and whenever she comes near him, he feels like she is making fun of him. She says things he doesn't understand why they are supposed to be funny.

"How'd it go, Doc?" Daisy is calling to him now. "How did the operation go?" Like that. She says things like that to him.

"Hoo, Virgil," Meemaw says, picking up her pea pan from off the ground and sitting down in her plastic lawn chair. "Get Zelma a dozen eggs."

Virgil picks up one of the egg cartons Meemaw is always having people save for her, and counts out twelve eggs from the basket he collected that morning and put by the picnic table on the patio. He's forgotten to wash them. "They not washed good," he calls over his shoulder.

"That's OK, hon," Zelma says. She is busy counting out eighty-five cents to Meemaw.

"Do you think that chicken will ever be able to play the piano again?" yells Daisy.

"I hope these taste good," says Meemaw.

"You know they will," says Zelma.

Virgil watches them go and thinks about Lorna Jean. In addition to all the spying he does at the funeral home, whenever he's seen Lorna Jean at Daisy's house, Virgil hides behind the chicken house and watches, in case, for instance, they decide to come outside to sit in the grape arbor swing in Daisy's back yard and paint their toe nails, and drink iced tea or something. They sometimes do that, sit on the swing until dusk among Zelma's yard decorations she is always setting up, and chatting in low laughing tones, their heads bent, their long swishy hair falling over their bare feet, which have little cotton balls between the toes, the insertion of which drives Virgil slightly crazy.

Virgil could stand for hours, among the rooster Braxton Bragg's and the barred rock hen's sleepy mutterings and the dusk fading to dark. From a distance, Lorna Jean and Daisy look like twins. They both have long, long hair, except Daisy's is red, and Lorna Jean's—Lorna Jean's hair is the shade of golden rod. They both have skinny bodies about the same height. But Lorna Jean has a sweet face, and Daisy always wears a double-dog-dare-you look.

Of course, they are really very different people. What makes them so totally different, her and Daisy? Lorna Jean has a easy, dreamy way of moving, like she is just wandering around on the beach somewhere.

Daisy Wade, former Miss Poke Salat, former Miss Chicken of Tomorrow, star of Jefferson High's stage and marching field, is no bigger than Lorna Jean, but she is tough and scary. She had the lead in every school play and she turned every one of them into a smash with wild maneuvers like improvised dance routines in the middle of the acts. She's been a majorette, and she's even mastered twirling fire, a lost art in Harrisonville. She used to practice for hours with an unlit baton on the other side of their fence. The only visible way Virgil knew she was there, was the sight of the silver cylinder, the ends wrapped in tape, as it shot up by the hour over the chicken house roof. Sometimes she brought out her boom box for company and drowned the backyards in Eric Clapton.

Daisy Wade is a noisy neighbor, and a nosy one. Once she stopped her baton tossing to hang over the fence about the time Meemaw was trying out Shelby's guillotine for the first time. "'Tis a far, far better thing I do," she whooped mysteriously, "than I have ever done."

"See you in O.R., Dr. Death," Daisy calls to him now as she closes the gate.

"I reckon I better get this fryer cut up," says Meemaw.

❧

After Shelby eats, and he and his cockroach disappear around the corner, and Meemaw and Mike Hammer go to their room, Virgil goes to his room to get ready for work. Actually all he has to do is brush his teeth, wet down his hair, and clip off a hangnail that has been bothering him all morning.

But first Virgil stares in the mirror at his pale, moist face, and his hair curling around his ears. He wishes he'd had time to get a haircut this morning instead of chasing hens around the yard with a bass net. Harvey mentioned earlier in the week that he is going to talk to Virgil. Virgil hopes Harvey is going to take him on as apprentice. If he does, Virgil's hours will change and he will be learning the trade. He will also be free at night to—to what? His only friend, Booger Beall, always told him what he really should do is hang around with guys who at least talked about doing it with girls, but Virgil never had a lot of friends. He didn't even have Booger now. Booger Beall up and joined the Navy right after graduation.

Besides, Virgil loves Lorna Jean. He doesn't want anyone else. One of his daydreams is to picture himself ten years from now as a successful funeral home director, owner of a good car, with a condo, and a spectacular sound system maybe, and of course, married to Lorna Jean. Virgil lies down on his bedspread designed with pictures of football pennants of all the major teams on it even though he has never been interested in football in his life. Shelby bought him football equipment, football pennants, and the pennant spread for him one Christmas because, Virgil suspects, sometimes Shelby woke up out of his dream world where he was always thinking about what to invent next, and bought him things he thought Virgil's mother would have bought him if Virgil's mother were alive. Virgil closes his eyes then and dreams another daydream, the one in which his and Lorna Jean's lives become intertwined step-by-step, until they were old folks, but as sometimes happened, he gets only as far as the wedding night. Virgil sighs and his sigh catches in his throat and comes out ragged, like he has a stuffy chest or something.

ℰℴ

     Virgil often wonders how Lorna Jean feels about morticians. The boy that had Virgil's position before him quit because he said that people started giving him The Look, and girls especially, once they found out what he did for a job. They did not want to hang around him any more. Of course Virgil does not know if people are less eager to be around him or not, now that he works for Harrisonville Funeral Home, because people, with the possible exception of Booger, have never been eager to be around him in the first place.

     Virgil knows it is highly possible that what the former night shift employee suspected could very well be true. Once Virgil did a Social Studies Fair project on "Funeral Customs of the World," the only time he has ever got close to having an *A* on something, and he learned quite a bit about how all kinds of people felt about other people who dug graves or handled bodies. A lot of ancient tribes thought those people were just dangerous. Among the Maori people, for instance, any one handling a corpse, carrying it to the grave, or touching a dead person is cut off from all communication with their folks. Sometimes as much as a year. They are like social outcasts. And in the Philippines, those poor people could only come out at night, when they were not likely to meet anybody because whosoever looked upon them died a sudden death. They thought. To prevent fatalities the body washer, or body carrier or whatever, had to bang on trees and stuff with a stick as he goes along, warning everybody he is coming, like he is a leper or something. He has to shout, "Beware!" And the trees on which he bangs are supposed to die. Legend has it. And if he sees or hears somebody who hadn't had time to hear his warning, he has to hide himself behind a tree or brush thicket. Of course, Virgil doesn't believe any of that stuff himself. Some of that thinking could have filtered down, through evolution or DNA or something. Lorna Jean should know morticians make plenty of money, everyone knows that. Harvey drives a new Mercedes Benz that he trades in every year, so that he is always driving a new car.

The funeral profession is just Virgil's thing. That is the only sure thing in his life. Watching Harvey, hanging around a place actually doing something about death...such important stuff. And Harvey L. Sloane raises undertaking to an art. Harvey has this eternal look, totally serene, in his eyes, so concerned is he at all times with the sorrows of the Bereaved Ones. He knows everything there is to know about preservation. He has a way with words, too. He calls death "the late great leveler," and "the icy hand." It "cometh soon or late," he would say. And Harvey makes the services of Harrisonville Funeral Home sound all rich and golden and noble for people, like the funerals used to be for the Egyptians and kings and stuff.

The dead never bothered Virgil. Of course, he has only known one dead person, and that is his mother.

But death is a special interest to Virgil. All his life, Virgil has stooped to look at flattened squirrels, two-dimensional frogs, and armadillos squashed on the highway out near the school. Not in a morbid way, but in a scientific way. Where did the living spark go? In English class he had to read *Frankenstein* and sometimes he feels like that English doctor did, like there should be a way to put the spark back in. For a while, back before high school, Virgil got so interested in figuring out what happened to dead things, he collected little killed animals for observation. He stored them in Meemaw's freezer, mostly birds, a snake, frogs, and a couple of mice. Little bitty things, not too noticeable in a 150 cubic foot state-of-the-art Amana freezer. But one time he went too far. He'd put in a few bigger specimens than usual and Meemaw discovered them. She made Virgil dump all his collection. What happened was she thawed what she believed to be a good-sized package of stew meat for supper, and instead unwrapped Mrs. Eloise Thompson's declawed Siamese cat who'd been cornered earlier in the week by Leroy Otley's rottweiler. At the barber's shop once Virgil read an article on cryonics, storing people in super cold storage tanks until modern advances in medical technology could fix whatever it was that had killed them. Doctors could simply thaw the suspended body, like a package of Meemaw's frozen butter beans, and cure the disease. Virgil wishes that his daddy suspended his mother so that he would have a chance of knowing her one day. When Virgil's mother died, Virgil was the only one with her, but he couldn't remember what happened because he was only been one year old. Virgil and his mother were driving back from Mt. Ida, Arkansas, where they were visiting his mother's relatives, and the accident happened.

Shelby hadn't come on this particular visit because he had been working then as a traveling aluminum siding salesman. It was late in the evening, about dusk, and Virgil's mother didn't see a parked log truck. She was killed instantly. In his car seat, Virgil had not got so much as a knock. It was morning before they were found.

8

That evening at work Harvey comes in and tells Virgil that one of his assistants is finishing school and going away to Memphis. He wants Virgil to come in on the morning shift, to be a real apprentice.

Later, Virgil looks out the Lorna Jean window and catches a glimpse of himself reflected in the glass glazed by the air conditioner. He stares, trying to imagine himself as a successful mortician. His face looks old and patient. Virgil is reminded of a dream he had once about his mother emerging from a giant Thermos bottle of liquid Nitrogen in some kind of mummery of wind and mist. She had the same patient look, but she was smiling in a knowing, quiet way. Just then, behind the image of himself, and the remembrance of the dream, he sees Lorna Jean, emerging from her cocoon of work.

Three

Virgil's first real assignment on the daytime shift at the Harrisonville Funeral Home is to watch Harvey handle a Beautiful Memory Conference. First Virgil and Harvey go to meet the Bereaved in the funeral home lobby.

The first floor is much different than the rooms upstairs that Virgil has become used to. His main job upstairs has been to answer the phone and to tidy up the tables and drawers and equipment, but especially to keep the white tile floors clean of, not so much dirt, never much of that, but messy stuff from work.

Downstairs the floors are not tiled but covered with two-inch Aculan and with gold and cream-colored Chinese rugs on top of them so that each step is like sinking into banana pudding. Floor-length draw drapes match the gold colors, and from somewhere concealed lights slide softly down the walls. In one corner is a chrome-and-tile coffee bar.

For his new position Virgil wears his only suit and one of Shelby's ties, which is red and designed with little gold screwdrivers. Shelby thinks it is real snappy.

Harvey is wearing his suit with the thin lapels, shoulder wings, and vest, string tie, and the trousers with the little pleats. He nods, almost half-bows when the Bereaved Ones come in the door. The Bereaved

Ones are a couple that looked more perturbed than bereaved.

The man is slightly stooped and beginning to gray at the temples and he keeps mopping his face, even though Harvey has a temperature control set on the optimal setting, which he has explained carefully to Virgil earlier. The woman looks solid, but shapeless, like an overstuffed sofa. She is smiling in a tight turned-up line and nodding and clutching a big straw pocketbook with both hands. For some reason she looks familiar to Virgil.

Harvey speaks more softly and sibilantly than he usually does. He introduces Virgil as his fine, young assis-ss-stant. Then he says, "S-s-s, let's-s get you folks a cup of coffee before we go to the conference room." He motions towards the coffee bar. "S-s, care for a Danish? I believe we have cheese-ss-sss and apricot today."

One of Virgil's new duties is to stop by Burger King on the way to work to pick up a few boxes of Danishes every morning to microwave. This morning he'd been unfortunate enough to be waited on by Daisy, who sang the funeral march to him, "Tum Tum te tum, TE tum, tum, te TUM te Tum." Then she said, "See you later, undertaker." Daisy is weird.

Harvey loads the Bereaved up with cups and plates before they make their way to his office.

"S' lovely," says the woman to Virgil, who also says her name is Mattie, and her husband, who she introduces as Lamar, says nervously, "Good, real good." Mattie explains that they both missed breakfast this morning during all the excitement. They all settle themselves around the table in the conference room that is also Harvey's office.

On the big round table near the windows Harvey has put out a stack of brochures in three different folders.

"My sister is coming," says Mattie. "She's always late. Be late for her own, er..." and her voice trails off.

Just then Zelma Wade bursts in the door. She is wearing a wildly flowered Hawaiian dress and one of those wrap around hats that women stick all their hair up in for some reason, so they could just as well be bald and no one would know. It is purple. The effect of her dress and hat is naturally totally absurd.

"This here's my sister," says Mattie pleasantly. Then she turns to Zelma and says in a lower voice, "For heaven's sake, Zelma. We said we'd pick you up if you needed us to so's we could all get here at once."

"Well, I'm here, anyways," says Zelma. Then she sees Virgil. "Well, hey, Virgil," she adds, and reaches over and ruffles his hair like he is a little kid.

With supreme effort, Virgil resists the impulse to duck away. He is floored. Zelma Wade is the last person he expected. Then Zelma plumps down between Mattie and Virgil, and Virgil knows why he thinks Mattie looks familiar. Both women have the same wide faces and barrel figures. And then Virgil has another thought: since they are sisters, that makes Mattie Lorna Jean's mother. He stares at Lorna Jean's mother's face, round as a melon's. It's a shock.

Then Zelma says, "Well! This is just so sudden. I had no idea Ronald was in such a bad way. Why, I was just telling Daisy, my daughter Daisy? Before she went to work? Why, this is just so sudden.'"

"Hmph! A seventy-seven-year-old alcoholic? What's so sudden about that?" says Lamar, wiping his brow again. He has a huge white handkerchief, and when he finishes he stuffs it in his suit pocket so that it sticks out like a clown's.

"Oh, hush, Lamar," says Mattie, biting into her apricot Danish. A huge blob of it squishes out the end and drops on her chin but she doesn't notice.

"Lord!" says Zelma. "I've completely forgot to call Crystal and Janice!" She pulls her chair closer to the table. "Is that apricot?"

Virgil wishes Zelma would lower her voice a little and stop looking so cheerful, like she is at a party or something. Then he tries to think who Crystal and Janice are. Crystal and Janice. Crystal and—oh, yeah—Virgil believes they are Daisy's real old sisters who are married and everything. The ones Virgil has heard Daisy refer to as *The Stepford Wives* or some such thing. Virgil has seen those two ladies in and out of Daisy's house in the last three years.

"If I could just interest you in these materials for a s-second, folks, perhaps we could get started," says Harvey. "Of course anything you select, casket, linen, and so on, we'll just understand that the real product will be shown to you before anything's final."

Harvey looks calm and wise sitting in the captain chair at the head of the table. His sibilance is hypnotic. "Your uncle didn't have no pre-need plans, ssso looks like we going to have to sstart from sscratch."

Harvey opens up one of the spiral notebooks with the glossy, colored pictures in it. He takes them out of the binder and spreads them on the table.

Virgil leans forward and stares at the brochures as if he is a part of the Bereaved. So that's who it is—Old Mr. Turberville. Daisy's and Lorna Jean's uncle. Virgil remembers Mr. Turberville has come once or twice to get tomato plants from Meemaw. A thin, loud old man with a wild pink nose. He and Meemaw hit it off. They had used some similar technique on growing watermelons in the past. Soaking the seeds in sugar water or something.

Lamar clears his throat and leans forward too. "I'm thinking the old man has all together a little over five thousand bucks of burial insurance. Wouldn't have that much if he weren't a vet."

"Of course—" Zelma is staring at Mattie's Danish. "There's the savings bon—Ouch!"

"Yeah!" Lamar interrupts her. He glares at Zelma. "Yeah, five thousand bucks range is all we need to look at."

Zelma shuts up. She frowns.

Harvey stares at Lamar for a second and gathers the pages up. He picks up another one. "This here is plan B," he says. He leafs through pages. "Here are your choices of caskets. Here now, your linings." He deals the laminated colored pages like a deck of cards. "This here, is your choice of vaults. This—"

"Vaults! Do we need a vault?" says Lamar.

"Lamar!" says Mattie.

"Heaven's sake," says Zelma.

Harvey looks hurt. "S-s certainly," he says, sitting up straighter. "It's the law. Now this here Wilbert Burial vault you wouldn't want to do without. It has your outer receptacle to protect the casket and Mr. Turberville with your choice of pre-asphalt lined, copper lined, aluminum or fiberglass lined. They just getting more lovely ever year with your choice of s-sstripes or forevernesss ssymbols, like this here tree, or this here ssetting ssun."

Virgil leans back. Just off the top of his head, he thinks the vault is the most important thing. Why, the better the vault, the longer the preservation, it stands to reason.

Lamar looks at his watch. "Look," he says. "Why don't you ask us all the questions in the $5000 range, and that might make it easier on everbody."

"Why, ss-scertainly," says Harvey, and he whips out a typed list. "Now, first off," he says. "The casket. Open or closed?"

"Closed," says Lamar.

"Open," says Zelma and Mattie together.

"Open," says Harvey and checks a blank on his sheet.

"So you need the Slumber Room and the half-couch. Now. Valley Forge, Futuristic, or French Provincial?"

"French Provincial," says Lamar.

"Hold it," says Zelma. "Uncle Ronald was a veteran, right? What exactly is a Valley Forge?"

"Ah," says Harvey. He reads off another sheet. "Masculine courageous qualities related to the American Revolution. It brings to mind the rugged, intrepid ideals of Valley Forge."

"Ain't that nice?" says Zelma.

"Valley Forge, then. Valley Forge," says Lamar.

"Beautyrama-adjusta Soft-foam Bed, or Sealy Innerspring?"

"Sealy," says Lamar.

"Well, now," says Zelma.

"Next," says Lamar.

"Will you be bringing clothes from home? Or do you prefer a hand-made designer ensemble with a faux linen suit front? And shoes? You'll just have a hissy over our Fit-A-Fut Oxford, or our newest Ko-Zee soft slipper, but with a fashionable authentic street shoe kind of look."

"Home," wheezes Lamar. He takes out his handkerchief again.

"Taupe silk, with traditional European designed panels?"

"Yeah."

"Now the vault. Aluminum, copper, asphalt, concrete—"

"Concrete!" says the women together. Lamar just swallows.

Virgil sits politely in his Montgomery Ward suit, which is beginning to pull tight across the shoulders. Zelma's thick, babyish chin with the dot of apricot on it squeezes up against her throat several times as she listens to Harvey. Mattie finishes her Danish and her breathing becomes slow, regular, contemplative. He looks away from them. Not one of them seems to want to ask the questions he would want to ask, say if it were his mother, or somebody. How long does a vault protect? What are the advantages of the different types of materials?

Virgil considers the big oak cabinets of the conference room. He tries hard not to listen. He squints his eyes and notes the dark grain, the way the dark stain has blended its oak grain. He pretends to unscrew the fancy brass screws, lift off the handles. He studies the holes, the dented places that the handles have left. Then he gathers up the screws, replaces the handles, and puts everything back like it was.

Zelma and Mattie and Lamar are choosing the most inexpensive service they can. Of course, even some Egyptians had to do that. Virgil moves his fingers a little, counting up the prices of what they are choosing. So far, Mr. Turberville's Egyptian day comparative worth—less than $2000. Which for the Egyptians would have been a quick immersion in a natron solution. Or an awful molten asphalt substance, which coated the body to provide at least some kind of protection. Or a procedure even worse, tanning. Virgil stifles a shudder. Even drying the body in the open air is better than that, thanks to the hot old dry Egyptian climate. For the medium price, some embalmers would have spared a little cedar oil after so many days of natron solution depending on how much the relatives could afford. But even with medium prices, you could forget the full twenty days immersion, the bathing of the eviscerated stuff, and the four sacred Canopic Jars: Imset, the human head, which protected the liver. Duamutef, the jackal's head protecting the stomach. Hapy, the ape's head protecting the lungs. Qebeh-Snewef, the hawk's head, protecting intestines. Leaving the heart and kidneys in the cavity. Do God knows what with the pancreas, the little stuff. But at least you have what you could say was a decent funeral. Of course, even the cheap Egyptian funeral is better than what the Mongolians did—throwing their dead to hordes of dogs, which for some reason a picture of jumps vividly in Virgil's mind.

Virgil has always heard the Wades were rich, but tight. And the Gibsons he always assumed were rich because Lorna Jean wears such pretty clothes. Now, he just doesn't know.

Suddenly, Virgil remembers that Harvey wants him to be able to discuss what he's learned when the Beautiful Memory Conference is over. He makes himself tune in to the present again. He watches Lamar laying out a Visa card.

Harvey is ticking off buttons on his new IBM desk calculator.

Its melody rises pleasantly into the air. "Ah," says Harvey, "Five-thousand-forty-three dollars and twenty-three cents."

சு

Harvey wants Virgil to witness a complete funeral service from the beginning until the departed one is lowered into the final resting place, so later on that day, Virgil peels his jacket off and slips into the pile of plastic Harvey hands him-- new shower curtain smelling coat, pants, a hairnet, mask, gloves, goggles, and shoe covers.

Then Virgil follows him, his plastic crackling with each step, up to the preparation room and through the old familiar double doors with the Day-Glo sign: DANGER! POTENTIAL CANCER HAZARD. FORMALDEHYDE. AUTHORIZED PERSONNEL ONLY. The second floor room is changed from the muted, shadowy place Virgil had known nights when he watched M*A*S*H and waited for Lorna Jean to a bright and clamorous place. Taps gurgle, and the usually silent duotronic injectors hum. The heavy smell of formaldehyde has increased considerably.

"S-s, I'll leave you two to get acquainted," says Harvey, after introducing him to Douglas, the assistant whose place Virgil will take one day soon. If Virgil has the stuff, Harvey says, he will send him to Mortuary Science School like he has sent Douglas. Virgil looks at Douglas over the china-white slab and what he takes to be Mr. Turberville's remains. Mr. Turberville is completely naked.

"Pleased to meetcha," Douglas says. Then he looks at Harvey and waves a stainless steel tool toward Mr. Turberville's head. "Can't do a thing with the subclavian vein, here, Harvey. It's solid as spaghetti. I had to go for the carotid," says Douglas.

"Oh, I knew you could handle it," beams Harvey. "You'll have some shoes to fill here, Virgil. Douglas is a virtual genius. Just ask him anything. Anything."

"Fire away," says Douglas, as Harvey leaves them. Douglas wears only gloves and an open plastic coat over his clothes. He has a jauntiness about him that reminds Virgil of those old movies, like he is James Dean, or somebody. His hair is even slicked back like James Dean.

When Virgil couldn't think of anything to ask, Douglas jerks his head at Mr. Turberville and says conversationally, "I've got what you call Flextone in here. In a minute I'll hook him up. Makes 'em soft."

Virgil peers down at Mr. Turberville. Suddenly he feels hot and stuffy under his plastic. Mr. Turberville's long line of a body looks like a toppled, pale mannequin from some store window, not like a person at all. He is so thin he might have starved to death. His boniness reminds Virgil of a picture of Mahatma Gandhi from his social studies book at Jefferson High. The only thing that seems untouched by his whiteness is his big red nose. Dying makes it even redder than Virgil remembers.

As if reading his mind, Douglas taps Mr. Turberville on the nose lightly with the tool, which resembles an auger. "They won't have any trouble with this baby," he says. "If the Flextone don't get it, the tints will."

He tosses his auger-thing into a tray. "So you want to be a derma-surgeon, huh? Well, it's steady work. Hah! And Harvey won't steer you wrong. When you go on to Mortuary tell 'em you know me.

"Now, right here is the injection needle for the stuff to go in. Over here is the drainage forceps for the vein. I prefer the subclavian vein, but this old guy's arteries are all pretty slippery so the carotid was the way to go. You can use your femoral artery, or your jugular vein, too—either one."

Douglas points to Mr. Turberville's right thigh. "Femoral vein's here. It's easy for a beginner. Everybody has their own favorite place, though. S'long's there's a vein and a artery within shouting distance of each other, you OK.

"What this is is a solution of formaldehyde, glycerin, borax, phenol alcohol and water. This procedure comes after the trocar." Douglas lapses into a formal text book tone, which reminds Virgil for a second of his biology class, and also that he flunked biology in tenth grade. Of course, Virgil thinks defensively, he will be glad to study hard now. Now that it has to do with some purpose in his life.

"Ha," Douglas says, turning on more humming, a higher pitched humming, by flipping a switch in what Virgil thinks is a dashing way.

But as interested as Virgil is, all the humming now reminds him of the dentist's office. In fact, his stomach he notices is fluttering like he was about to climb into the dentist's chair.

"Now," Douglas is saying, "trocar." Out of a machine, he pulls an impossibly big needle that is attached to a long tube. "This is your trocar," he says, tapping it with his finger. "This is to suck all the stuff out of the cavities." Suddenly, Douglas jabs Mr. Turberville right in the stomach, hard. Then he begins poking around.

Behind his mask, Virgil blinks. The trocar must be the equivalent of the Ethiopian Stone, a sacred stone knife the Egyptians used. The Egyptians just made one expert cut though, and took everything out neatly and respectfully and put it into the nice, sacred jars. Douglas looks like he is torturing Mr. Turberville. Suddenly the cold Beanee Weenees Virgil had brought for lunch rise up in his throat. Mr. Turberville looks like he is reacting to all that poking. His unbearable whiteness begins to turn color.

"This old guy's a little on the emaciated side. Sometimes are, this old," Douglas is saying. He stops the trocar and looks at Virgil. "You okay, kid?"

"Sure," says Virgil, unable to tear his eyes away from Mr. Turberville—like when he is watching one of Meemaw's beheaded chickens.

"Now, the Duotronic. I'd guess about three gallons'll do the trick. He's pretty skinny and all." Douglas pushes the end of the duotronic hose into Mr. Turberville's neck, and turns a knob that makes the humming louder.

Virgil stares. He blinks and stares again. Every cell in Virgil's body freezes. Mr. Turberville's fingers are twitching. Virgil feels his jaw drop: "YIIIII. YIIII." He can only point. Douglas looks at the twitching hands and frowns.

Virgil's pulse rattles in his ears at about a million decibels. He clutches his own hands. "He's alive! You embalming somebody alive!"

Douglas is looking with mild interest at Mr. Turberville. "Well, ha! He ain't now."

Then Douglas says, "It's just some old nerves and stuff. Happens some time. Don't you worry. We always get a death certificate. It ain't possible that anybody's alive when they get to this table."

Virgil feels stupid. He of all people should know about nerves and twitching bodies. He has watched Meemaw kill enough chickens.

Then he remembers reading about how heads, which have been chopped off during the French Revolution, would continue to blink their eyes for several minutes.

Before Virgil can completely get a handle on his own jumping nerves and the odd bits of historical facts accosting his brain, he sees something else. The man is turning yellow. Virgil stares as Mr. Turberville grows mustard yellow, then a faint green. Virgil keeps staring, but doesn't move. He isn't going to yell this time. At least the hands have stopped twitching.

Then Douglas sees what Virgil sees. "Hell! Jaundice! Never mind. It'll just take a little extra paste in cosmotage." Douglas picks up a smaller needle and a tube. "I'm loading this hypodermic with massage cream. We'll just fill in the sunk-in places. Here, under the old chinny chin chin. On the back of his hands and fingers. Yep, that'll do it." He sticks the needle into Mr. Turberville's chin. "Now. The Smile. Not a smile actually, but as pleasant a look as you can fix without actually smiling. Lips might drift apart, so... Sometimes we have to break the jaw. But, nope." Douglas squints his eyes speculatively. "This looks OK."

Then Douglas clasps his needle in both hands in front of his chest and says in a high, funny voice, "Now don't he look like himself?"

Virgil makes his voice casual. "So how long do they last?" he asks, thinking about the Egyptians again.

"You mean, how long do they stay pretty? Through the funeral—if we're lucky. Few days at the most."

"Huh?" says Virgil. The phrases from the Beautiful Memory Conference Harvey used echoes in his mind: "peace of mind protection," and "eternal preservation."

"Oh, we could make `em last years," Douglas says. "Like the cadavers they have over at the med school in Shreveport. But they look awful. Like old shoe leather."

Douglas hits the switch and the humming stops. He presses his thumb on Mr. Turberville's neck and swiftly removes the tube. Then he picks up another needle and begins threading it with what looks like dental floss. "I just need to sew this one thing up."

"Jeeze," says Virgil. He looks down at Mr. Turberville and his eyes blur. He can almost imagine him dissolving right there on the table. An ache starts up between Virgil's shoulder blades. "Jeeze," he whispers.

"OK!" says Douglas after he makes three expert stitches where the trocar has been. He snips off the thread by cutting it with what looks like a pair of Shelby's toenail clippers. Then he pulls a tube from his pocket and dabs a little of something on the suture. He screws the lid back on, hands the tube to Virgil to hold, and begins pushing his thumbs around the stitches like Virgil mashes his pimples sometimes. Then he bends over and studies Mr. Turberville's neck critically for a few minutes. "Looks OK," he says finally, straightening up. He gives an army salute to Mr. Turberville. "Yep, you come a long way, baby!" He reaches over the body for his Pepsi on the surgical cart, pops it, and takes a long swig. "Now to Cosmotoge, and you'll really see some interesting stuff." He sets his can by Mr. Turberville's ear, begins pushing him toward the double doors.

Virgil looks down at the tube Douglas handed him. He peers through his goggles and reads the label: OSSA TRU-SEAL. DISCRETE. INFALLIBLE.

೮

In Cosmotage, the cosmetician takes one look at Mr. Turberville and throws up her hands. "Green!" she says. She picks up the Pepsi and hands it to Douglas. Then she looks at Virgil. "And who is this?"

"This is Vir-jul," sings Douglas, like he suddenly thinks Virgil's name is funny or something. Then he says, "Maisie Connors. Virgil Matthews."

"Please to meetcha, Virgil," says Maisie. She is an older woman about forty or fifty with a very long, gray-streaked ponytail.

"Hey," says Virgil, politely, but Maisie's eyes are following Douglas as he leaves.

"I thought I told you to get me some arms and hands!" she yells at his retreating back.

"Yeah, yeah, yeah," Douglas calls in a bored voice over his shoulder.

Jesus, thinks Virgil.

Maisie looks at Virgil. "Arm and Hand Positioners. Is what I mean."

"Right," says Virgil, breathing carefully.

"OK, let's see what we got here," says Maisie. "Hmmmm. Needs a shave. Shampoo. Any clothes, I wonder? Manicure..."

Maisie begins pushing some tubes of stuff around on a tray.

"Something cream based for this green...Number 12. A number 12 should do it." She holds up one of the tubes near Mr. Turberville's face. "The lid is the color, see?

"Well, hon. It's good to see a new face in this place. Or one that can talk back at least. You going to Mortuary?"

"Not yet," says Virgil, watching Mr. Turberville's nose turn back into a normal color.

"But you want to?"

"Yeah," says Virgil, a little louder than he intends. He wishes he could sit down. Douglas has let him take off his bee-keeper-looking head covering, but he still feels stuffy underneath his plastic suit. Maisie only has on a long pair of rubber gloves and an unbuttoned doctor coat over her clothes.

"Eighteen months. Eighteen months of school. But then you'll be all set. Well, this is the color. But before we get it on—shave and shampoo." She turns on a tap that Virgil used to get water out of to make his coffee.

When Mr. Turberville's hair is all clean and free of soap, Maisie parts the thin hair and combs it. Then she picks up an old-fashioned razor, like Virgil's papaw used to have, and lays it to one side. She begins lathering shaving soap on Mr. Turberville's newly filled-out cheeks with a brush.

"See the procedure with Douglas?"

"Yeah," says Virgil.

"Well, he's the best. Smarty-pants, though. I hope you stay sweet and don't pick up his bad habits." Maisie is busy with her razor.

"You won't, probably, have to do this. Harvey will keep you in the embalming room—except, never say *embalming* around Harvey. He prefers *procedure*. And so do customers. One kid was fired. He said something like "stiff" around Harvey one time." Maisie gives Mr. Turberville a last few swipes and picks up a brush. "And Douglas does all the cremations—what few Harvey don't talk 'em out of."

Virgil is horrified. He hopes he never says the wrong word. But he is glad he never has to do cremations. He never wants to do one of those.

"OK," says Maisie. "Let's get rid of this awful green."

A few minutes later Maisie is patting some fine detail around Mr. Turberville's eyelids with a brush.

Harvey appears beside them holding an armload of clothes.

Welllll!" he says. "Almost ready for casketing. You are watching an art, Virgil."

Virgil nods. But Harvey is already leaving, padding happily away.

"Is this your first job, kid?" says Maisie.

Virgil stands up straighter and shakes his head. "Naw," he says.

"Well, ha! It's almost my first job. Mr. Connors and me had our own beauty shop for twenty years, but when he passed on, it just wasn't the same." She holds up the trousers Harvey has delivered and looks at them speculatively. "No. Just wasn't the same. The Hair Today Shop we called it. I always say I went from the Hair Today Shop to the Gone Tomorrow Shop!"

Virgil tries to smile at Maisie's joke. But how is she going to get those clothes on Mr. Turberville? It looks impossible. It looks like just an impossible job.

Then Maisie whips out a pair of scissors out of her pockets and starts cutting. "Cutting it down the back, see?"

She snips for a few seconds, then says, "I tried staying at home. Tried taking courses—aerobics, tole painting—but then I'd met Harvey when Mr. Connors passed over and he knew I was a beautician. One day he called, after the last funeral home cosmetician quit, and said he heard I'd shut the Hair Today down and wanted to know if I was tired of the leisure life. `By God, yes!' I said. And here I am."

Douglas comes in wheeling a Valley Forge. "Room service," he says.

"Just in time, sweetie," says Maisie.

By the time Virgil moves out of the way so Douglas can position the casket, Maisie has tilted the table, guided Mr. Turberville in, and she and Douglas are bent over the lowered casket, arranging clothes.

"Harvey likes the right shoulder pushed down a bit..." says

Maisie, "so it don't look so unnatur...Stop it! Stop it!" She slaps Douglas' hand. "I'll handle the buttons, Mr. Know-It-All. You left two undone yesterday with Mr. Leonards. Now who gets the blame?"

"Wellll, exscuuuuse me," says Douglas. "Say, this lipstick is an odd shade, if you don't mind me saying so."

"Dang," says Maisie. "Turned on me." She reaches into her pile of tubes and sticks. "Ah, #7." She elbows Douglas out of the way. "Move it or lose it, honey."

Finally they are both bent over the Valley Forge, fussing with the creases in Mr. Turberville's pants.

Mr. Turberville reminds Virgil of a big doll, and Douglas and Maisie remind him of parents fussing over a baby carriage. He shakes his head to get that ridiculous image out of his brain.

But, finally satisfied, Maisie says, "Now. Take Baby to the Slumber Room, Daddy."

Four

aisy Wade, former Miss Poke Salat Festival Queen, former Miss Chicken of Tomorrow, star of Jefferson High School, wiggles her Burger King uniform down, and then kicks it aside. In six seconds flat she pulls on a skin-tight pair of turquoise jeans, her white silk western shirt with the fringed yoke, and a pair of high-heeled suede Ropers.

Daisy permits herself a second to stare into the wobbly cheval mirror, which looks like an antique but is really one she bought unassembled in a box at Wal-Mart after renting *The Last Time I Saw Paris* at Star Video. She wishes she had a mink coat to wear. A mink coat, a cigarette lighter, and turquoise jeans—that would shake up this town!

"How long are you going to stay sober, Charley?" she says to the mirror, lifting her chin the way Sandra did to Van Johnson.

Daisy is not a raving beauty. Her hair is not blonde, she is not winsome, but she has her compensations: a tight, gymnastic body, which is *in* at the moment, and more guts, as her mother puts it, than an Army mule. She can also dance, sing, pantomime, and make an accordion sound like a twenty-piece orchestra.

On impulse Daisy grabs a turquoise-eyed peacock feather that is stuck in her dressing table mirror and braids it carelessly through her hair. She picked it out of a workman's pocket two years ago who was standing near the railroad track at Grant's Farm in St. Louis as the miniature train loaded with the graduating class of Jefferson High whooped and huffed along. To this day she doesn't know what made her do it. He was standing there talking to another workman, she had been admiring the peacocks and wanting a feather all day but hadn't found one, and there it was sticking out of his pocket, just the perfect distance for Daisy's fingers to reach down effortlessly and filch it. She could remember it now, the whoops from the other seniors, and shouts of "Isn't that just like her!" The man's beginning look of surprise as his face momentarily flashed by, the too-late gesture of his reaching behind him, the tip of the feather slipping through his fingers. Then it stayed stuck in her dresser mirror for almost a year, reminding her that she had committed petty larceny in broad daylight, in front of God, the graduating class and their sponsors: Coach Hilburn, who'd moaned, "Oh, Daisy!" and Mrs. Lou Ellen Perkins, the home-ec teacher, who shook her head until her hair stuck out like a wingnut. Mrs. Perkins, already miserable because her hay fever started acting up on the trip, pursed her lips and wheezed, "Daisy Wade, you ought to be ashamed of yourself." Now here is the reason for it all. Fate. The reason she'd taken it. The feather perfectly matches her jeans. It brightens up her long, dark auburn hair. It gives her the touch of "exotica" she needs. Anyway, who else in this dreary old town would think to wear something so unusual?

"You got to eat," her mother says suddenly from the door, "before you go traipsin' off Lord knows where. And, young lady, I expect you to be at the viewing tonight."

Daisy starts grabbing her make-up off the dressing table and shoving it into her little flowered make-up bag. "I already ate, Ma, and I'm gonna be late as it is," she says matching her tone and syntax as though it had come out of her mother's mouth. Daisy can talk as southern as Scarlet O'Hara in one breath and in the next, as New Yorker as Barbara Streisand in *What's New Pussycat?* She can sound so much like Marilyn Monroe that she almost looks like her, despite not being blond. She can do Mae West. She has Katherine Hepburn's entire script, and bodily gestures, memorized from *African Queen.* At school Daisy's speech teacher, Mr. Johnson, wanted her to go to college and major in drama or in linguistics, but Daisy only lasted one semester at Louisiana State University in Alexandria. Then she took up with a thin, sad faced, though rich cowboy whose noncommittalness seemed to fit her mood at the time, and while Zelma had kittens in Harrisonville, they went on a trip to Hollywood. When she came home Daisy told Pee Wee and Zelma that she was moving to California, or New York, or some place where there was some LIFE as soon as she got some money together.

Her mother doesn't understand this desire Daisy has to be rid of Harrisonville. The longest trips Zelma has ever been on were to Graceland with Pee Wee on their anniversary once, and on the Azalea Trail every spring with her church group. All her mother ever understands is decorating their old house and "prettifying" the yard, as she calls it.

Zelma is always packing home something to liven up their surroundings: knickknacks and crafts for the inside, but especially junk for the yard: pink plastic flamingos, bird-baths, a painted plywood cut-out of—and this is the worst—a fat lady's behind—she is supposed to look like she is bending over tending flowers—and then the plaster items: two huge lions, a life-size deer, a two-foot chipmunk, a duck and half-dozen waddling ducklings. High school boys hate to cut their yard. Her latest additions are a seven-foot replica of the Statue of Liberty standing opposite the jockey at the end of the drive—the jockey Daisy had long ago painted white to her parents' complete bafflement.

Daisy will never have a yard like this, in what she thinks of as her real life. Her real life begins somewhere in the hazy future, when she goes to film school somewhere—somewhere good, and big, and famous.

Of course Zelma and Pee Wee have been, have always been dead set against any talk at all about Daisy's future outside of Harrisonville. A long time ago, after high school, Zelma and Pee Wee laid down the law. If Daisy didn't want to go to the University of Mississippi like her sisters, like her mother, and her Aunt Mattie, and Grandma had, then she could just stay in Harrisonville and commute to LSUA. Daisy had gone one semester, batted out straight A's, and then quit. Sending Daisy to LSUA had been, what looked like to her parents, her ONE LAST CHANCE. Ha! It was Daisy's sisters who had to carry on the Southern Belle routine with their four years at the University of Mississippi and being in the Kappa Alpha Thetas and all. And then coming home and marrying people they knew in high school!

Pee Wee and Zelma had given up a long time ago trying to get

Daisy to follow in her sister's footsteps and stop acting like a movie star and running around with anything in pants, as they put it. But Daisy knows she has the right ideas about love and romance.

Daisy's two considerably older sisters, Nora and Janice, are tall, homely girls who'd married well (in Pee Wee's and Zelma's eyes) and are, despite their degrees in home ec and interior design, housewives and mothers first—and Mary Kay Cosmetics and Amway salespersons second.

Pee Wee often tells her mother that he thinks his job is responsible for a lot of Daisy's personality. He is the manager of the Princess Theater and Daisy has seen thousands of movies in her lifetime. And up until a few years ago, Daisy's birthday present from Pee Wee and Zelma has always been a day's worth of old films she picks out and Pee Wee orders just for her. Pee Wee thinks people like Rita Hayworth has just warped her mind.

A long time ago, when Daisy was about thirteen, and after about a jillion movies, she decided she is never going to let a man fool with her mind, dump on her, or be completely in charge. It is one thing to watch that in movies and another thing to let it into your life. In modern movies women get beat up, raped, treated like stupid dolls, and hung on men's arms like decorations. Just like real life, like Daisy's poor old dumb cousin, Lorna Jean Gibson.

The old movies are better—women back then had more...well, balls. For a long time, Daisy's philosophy has been to treat men like sex objects before they can treat her like one. Something she forgets with Owen, her current fellow. When Daisy first started meeting Owen, she'd gotten that old high from the thrill of the chase. Men chase her until she catches them, of course. Every time, it is like that: Every man is just some exotic high country with mysterious, wild mountains to climb and deep, dangerous rivers to ford until finally Daisy has conquered the whole wilderness and realized she has been there before. And it is time to move on.

But Owen gives the impression he couldn't be fully explored. And Daisy doesn't want to move on. Owen is different, all right. For one, he isn't as easy to shock in bed as most men.

The only bad thing about Owen is that Daisy can hardly wait to get back in bed with him. Before Owen it was bad enough—Daisy could hardly go a week. With Owen, she can hardly go a day. She's just got to remember to make him wait some times. Just to keep her old hand on top. She'd hate to know she is becoming another Lorna Jean Gibson.

Daisy firmly believes that when she lost her virginity it was not to J.T. Adkins in the eighth grade, as J.T. probably still thinks, but to Marlon Brando. Not Marlon Brando in *The Godfather*, of course, or even in *Last Tango In Paris*, or *A Streetcar Named Desire*, but Marlon Brando as Mark Anthony in *Julius Caesar*. Marlon had been clad only in brief purple shorts, and his toga, which ended high on his thighs. Between takes he had draped his round-muscled, bare-chested body across Daisy's and her virginity had been history. Daisy has the movie poster of *Julius Caesar* still over her bed, not over the headboard, but on the ceiling, and she is quite willing to conjure Marlon up again at any time. Talk about a high. Talk about perfect. See it with someone you love. Like in her case, Owen. Daisy looks in the mirror. Good heavens, is her mother still here?

Her mother is peering around her, her chubby face moving slowly closer to Daisy's, clearly not knowing what to say to anyone who has a peacock feather sticking out of her head. "Hmph," she says. Zelma has on her shopping hat, the rolled brimmed number that is deliberately squashed together on one side and culminates in a wide, fat bow that jiggles when she moves. Daisy smiles generously at her mother in her mirror. For all her faults, her hat, which really cracks Daisy up, is kind of, well, cute.

Zelma looks at her daughter worriedly. She isn't sure if she wants to go take her after Sunday dinner nap now or to wait until after Daisy leaves the house. She frequently snoops in Daisy's room when she finds the opportunity looking for evidence of drug use and premarital sex: cassette disks of reggae artists, new underwear, strobes, birth control vials, incense, slick magazines featuring androgynous figures, sandwich-sized baggies, tweezer-looking instruments known as roach clips, and ash trays that are always clean. Zelma knows about drug use because she reads the *Home Journal* and *McCall's Magazine* and listens to her hairdresser, Delbert, who once lived in New York City. So far she has never found any evidence--just overdue library books on the film, overdue videos of movies as old as Daisy was, and letters from colleges that are too far from home. Still, Daisy just plain scares the hell out of her. Like right now. Zelma eyes her daughter's peacock feather, and remembers she forgot to lecture Daisy on the way she talked in the Winn-Dixie the other day when her old Sunday School teacher Mavis Fortenberry stopped to say hello and ask Daisy what she was going to do with the rest of her life. "Be a porno queen," her own daughter said. Zelma liked to have died. This is just the kind of stuff Daisy has done all her life that has driven Zelma crazy, and given Pee Wee all his gray hairs. But Zelma looks at the peacock feather and then at Daisy's dreamy expression reflected in the mirror and only says, "Don't forget the wake. Seven-thirty. On the dot." She has never been able to fuss at her daughters good, like her sister Mattie had fussed at her child. Even the older two tune her out occasionally. And Daisy is permanently tuned out to practical suggestion. After high school she took off on a three-day trip to Hollywood with a boy! Zelma doesn't ever want to push her too far—knowing she has that in her.   Then Zelma adds, what she hopes is conversationally, "Even though the poor thing has been on display all day! I've never heard of such a thing—a viewing before five o'clock. Never, never go to view before seven. When I called the funeral home to complain—they so much as told me to mind my own business!"

Daisy is staring into her cheval mirror pretending she is Debbie Reynolds in *A Summer Place*. She looks at her flat turquoise tummy and imagines it growing, growing. Growing a Troy Donahue baby. Just for amusement, of course. One thing that makes Daisy laugh is the Debbie Reynolds-Doris Day type, good-girl movies. And actually anything about the birth process disgusts Daisy. Back in high school one of the cheerleaders found out she would never be able to bear children. While the other cheerleaders commiserated in hushed tones for days on the subject, Daisy just thought to herself, *what a break!*

Daisy catches her mother's eye in the mirror. What is she still hanging around for? Daisy guesses it is time for her mother to go through her stuff again. And she knows there is no getting out of going tonight.

Daisy picks up her make-up bag. "*Au revoir,*" she says, brushing past her mother. "So long. Catchya later. Be seein' ya. *Ciao.* Y'all take care."

Zelma listens to the sound of Daisy's Volkswagen Bug zipping out of the driveway and into the street. Then she turns toward Daisy's armoire, and opens the doors.

Five

Virgil and Harvey stand beside the open doors of the Little Chimes Slumber Room Number 3 and nod people through the door. They both nod at the same time. They both fold their hands in the same way. Virgil, though, keeps craning his head back behind Harvey at the people in the Slumber Room. He has just seen Lorna Jean come in between her mother and her father. Right now Mattie has her off to the side and seems to be lecturing her.

Harvey's usual sad face looks even sadder today. You'd think every beloved one was his own. When he hears a phone ringing faintly down the hall he says to Virgil morosely, "Take over, sson," and then he goes toward his office. Virgil takes the opportunity to step inside the doors of the Number 3 Slumber Room and merge with the guests. He strains his ears in Lorna Jean's and Mattie's direction.

"Only thing to do, Missy," Mattie is saying.

Mattie is wearing a shapeless black dress. She looks like a huge, black hole about to swallow Lorna Jean up. "And another thing, if you hadn't stayed out so late..."

Lorna Jean tosses her hair and seems to say something, but Virgil doesn't catch it because just then Daisy and Zelma come in. Zelma nods her head at him. "Virgil," she says. Then Daisy steps on his foot deliberately.

"*Scusi*," Daisy says. She gives a fake double take at his suit as if he has forgotten and left his pajamas on or something that morning. She is wearing a long baggy black thing that must have been some kind of dress and is carrying an enormous purse. Virgil forces a little smile. He never knows what she is going to do next even though he has lived next door to her for six years.

Mr. Turberville has a thin but steady stream of visitors through Number 3. Maisie's and Douglas' skills have rendered a beatific expression on a tanned, outdoorsy-colored face with no hint at all of green. The visitors form a line around the bier, study the handiwork briefly, and move off in small groups and chat. A few older women are sniffing together in the corner. A bottle-bright blonde woman with orthopedic shoes comes over and weeps loudly with them for a few minutes. "Who the hell is that?" Virgil hears Zelma say. Virgil is trying to keep his eyes off Lorna Jean. He can hardly stand to see her this close. Virgil has an ache that started in his upper lumbar region in the preparation room yesterday, snaked along his spine, and is now making his head ring like a steeple. He wants to get away from the Slumber Room and Mr. Turberville's visitors and the orthopedic shoes that keep trailing Kleenexes in the deep carpet.

He wants to get away from the sight of Lorna Jean whose face is as shut as a door. Lorna Jean who obviously doesn't know him.

Virgil goes out into the hall and looks around for Harvey and when he sees his office still closed, he pads across the foyer's spongy carpet and goes to the casket sales room. He listens a second outside the doors, then he opens them as quietly as he can and steps inside. He waits for his eyes to adjust to the dimly lit landscape of caskets on trolleys, each with the muted light coming seemingly from nowhere. Harvey hides the lights behind a little panel near the ceiling. He likes the lights to slide down the walls and onto the caskets to make the trolleys sort of unnoticeable.

Then Virgil makes his way down Suburu Street and sits down on the floor behind a Bronze Metallic Classic Beauty. He rubs his eyes. The low lighting eases his head. He leans against the wall. What a weird thing it has been to see Lorna Jean. First, all morning looking for her, then the shock when he finally sees her and the realization that when she looks at him, she doesn't see anything. Like he is invisible. Did he dream it, or did it really happen that he walked four blocks with her? That she stood in his kitchen. That her eyes took in Meemaw and Mike Hammer. And not died. That her hand held his doorknob. That she looked straight at him and said, "Thank you very, very much." She didn't even speak to him today. She has not noticed, nor has ever noticed the strange way she stirs him. His heart in some wild acid rock rhythm, his palms slippery with sweat. How could she make him that way?

Suddenly he hears a low voice. Virgil peeks between the legs of the trolley. Two elderly women from the Slumber Room, one apparently leading the other, have strayed in. They walk hesitantly down Park Avenue, peering at the merchandise. They stop in front of the bronze and maple half-couch where Virgil remembers he stored *The Art of Taxidermy* and in all the excitement of his new duties, completely forgotten about.

Oh no, he thinks. Shoo. Get away from there. One of them, the spryer of the two lifts up the half-lid and peeps in.

"Well, this is a lovely color, Hazel. And look at all those sweet little tucks."

"Ooooo! I'd like to have that pillow at home," says the one named Hazel. "But mercy, I'd hate to sew all those tucks."

Then the first lady makes a little noise, hesitates, and reaches into the casket. "Well, what's this?" She picks up Volume 2 of Virgil's taxidermy course. They both adjust their glasses and look down at the cover. "Good heavens!" says one, and the other one makes a low sucking sound, drops the book, and they do some kind of speed hobble toward the doors, and out.

Virgil settles back against the wall and shuts his eyes again. He thinks it would be a good thing to stay here forever. He can not think of a thing he would ever want but to stay here in this dusk and half-light with his eyes closed making his mind blank. The carpet underneath him is as good as his bed. He leans his head back and feels his breathing becoming slower and slower.

Suddenly he blinks his eyes wide open. He realizes he's drifted off to sleep. But what has woken him? Maybe he is dreaming, but for a second he thinks he hears a voice. He peers between the legs of the trolley again. At first he doesn't see anything but gradually a mass of shadows near a Danish Modern Dream appears to move for a second. Virgil blinks at the shadows.

Then Virgil, plain as day, hears Lorna Jean Gibson say, "I can't."

"You can," says Speed Maxwell.

Virgil goes stiff as a Beloved One. He stops breathing and strains his ears to hear.

"I can't. They're already mad because I didn't want to come. I can't just up and take off."

"Little baby," says Speed. He sounds real mad. Virgil leans over to one side behind one of the trolley legs toward them. His heart is beating so loud it is an effort to hear their voices over it.

"What are you doing here, anyway?" Lorna Jean says.

"Business—I got to talk to Douglas on business—and pleasure." Virgil hears a smacking noise.

"Oh, stop it. You and Douglas! How come you know him so good?"

"I met the old boy somewhere. No. Listen. You just come on home with me. You goan be sorry when I'm gone. Come on."

"Can't."

"Then here," Speed says.

"Stop that," says Lorna Jean. "You are <u>so</u> gross."

"Come on," Speed whines. "Just give me a little kiss."

"Not here, dummy. Ick." Lorna Jean starts laughing a little. "This place gives me the creeps."

Virgil shudders. Rat ran over his grave, Meemaw would say.

"Why you always givin' me a hard time?"

"Maybe I *like* to give you a hard time." Lorna Jean's voice sounds like Virgil has never heard it sound before. Kind of like Daisy's when she leans over the fence in the back yard and says something totally unfathomable.

Then Speed says, "Well, it seems a shame to waste a whole afternoon you off work hanging around this place."

"I tell you my mama's on my case from last night."

"Well, tell Mama to get off your case." There is a silence.

"Stop that." Suddenly Lorna Jean's voice sounds real serious. It has a note in it that sounds almost scary to Virgil.

Lorna Jean seems like a ventriloquist, with different voices, the sweet one Virgil knows, the Daisy one, now this other totally different one.

Then, Virgil hears sounds of scuffling.

The Danish Modern casket shakes a little. Good lord. Maybe Speed is molesting Lorna Jean. He looks down. His hands are trembling. Then he hears another voice. "I got to go," says Lorna Jean. This voice has lost the dangerous note. It is not a voice Virgil could even try to identify. It is not a voice that belonged to someone who felt in danger.

"Just a second," pants Speed.

"Ohhhh, baby, I got to go," breathes Lorna Jean. "Come on. Behave."

No reply from Speed but a little groan.

Virgil tries to imagine what they are doing. He shuts his eyes and leans hard against the wall like he is trying to hold it up with his back.

Lorna Jean says in her newest voice, "Please, Speed. Don't. You know I—" Then she stops what she is saying and there is nothing but the sound of their breathing.

"Babe," says Speed like he is real pleased with something.

Despite himself, Virgil opens his eyes. Their shadows are mushed together and are pressed against the wall. He could see Speed moving Lorna Jean's clothes around. His hand pushes up her skirt. Virgil feels something hot squeeze out of the corner of his eye.

"Not here," says Lorna Jean like she is real sure about something.

"Yes, here," says Speed. He is breathing like he is running a race.

Then Lorna Jean lets out this low moan. It is a sound like Virgil has never heard before. He would never in a million years be able to describe it, but it makes him feel weird, and sad, and excited, and breathless, too. Virgil leans back harder against the wall like he is trying to push his head through the plaster. He feels his new Montgomery and Ward suit tighten up around him as a picture jumps into his mind, of Lorna Jean running for the bus after school, her breasts moving and shifting under her cheer leading uniform. JESUS CHRIST! He reaches down. He has the biggest boner in his life.

"Oh-oh-oh," says Speed.

"Oh, baby," breathes Lorna Jean. "Hooks in the front."

"Bingo," moans Speed.

"Oh, baby."

"Oh, baby."

Oh lord, thinks Virgil, their duet noises sinking him and his inflamed nerve endings into a sweet hell as precisely the first luxuriant, humiliating drop slides into the folds of his Monkey Ward's finest and Virgil's mind is inundated with a rushing river. There comes cat yowls and curled tongues. A crowd's cheers. Sunlight and pennants wave. Footballs explode into jubilee. And in the distant, a long, drawn-out Tarzan yodel. Virgil's head tilts back like a Beloved One whose repose block has been ripped out from beneath his head.

Then he is falling the deepest abyss he has ever known. Lorna Jean and Speed are doing it. They are really doing it. All this time, he thought maybe, just maybe, by some miracle they didn't, but he can see how wrong he's been. They do it all right. They probably do it all the time. Virgil feels the carpet shifting and falling out from under him. He lets himself slide slowly over until his big stupid body lies on the floor.

"Yiiii," says Lorna Jean and Speed together.

Then a winding down kind of breathing, and silence. Virgil's chest expands like a tight, new balloon, then freezes and begins to choke him.

"Good for you?" says Speed.

"MMMmmm," says Lorna Jean. "Better hurry."

"Yes, Ma'am!"

Rustling sounds of clothes. Silence.

A blade of light sweeps the room as the door opens, then closes. "Lorna?" Daisy's voice floats down the street.

"Uh. Yeah?"

"Aunt Mattie's looking for you, mad as hell."

"So what else is new!" Lorna Jean says like she is real disgusted. Shadows weave.

"You better not go in there with Speed."

"Oh, all right!"

"Have you seen Virgil?" Why is Daisy looking for him?

"No!" The light blade slices again.

"Well, now," Speed's voice.

"Well, now," Daisy says in an even more sarcastic voice than she ever uses on Virgil. "If it isn't Speed Maxwell. God's gift to women!"

Then Virgil hears Speed say, "You better believe it, honey."

Virgil hears Daisy snort and Speed say, "Daisy! You looking goooooood!"

"You just keep your hands off the merchandise, jerk, or you're goin' to be talking a lot higher in just a second."

Then Speed sounds disgusted. "OK, OK!" The light slices open. "Women! I be dogged. They drive you nuts."

Dark again. Virgil hopes Daisy has gone out the door behind Speed. He holds his breath a few seconds more, then relaxes and starts breathing again when he didn't hear anything.

"Virgil?" whispers Daisy.

Virgil groans and crawls away on his hands and knees.

"Twelve hundred sixty-three dollars and no cents," Daisy's disembodied voice floats over his shoulder. "One thousand ninety-three big ones! Jesus! What a rip-off." A shadow wanders down Matchbox Lane, magnifies, wavers, then turns into Daisy who sits down beside him. "Hey, want some coke?"

"No," says Virgil hopelessly. "I'm not thirsty."

They sit under the Classic Beauty, Daisy cross-legged and Virgil hunched over, his legs crossed high and clamped tight. Daisy opens her feedbag-looking purse and takes out a little amber-colored glass bottle with a cork in it. She says, "Not that kind of coke, dumb ass."

Daisy fishes around in her purse again and takes out a straw, a little mirror, and then a razor from behind a zipper. Virgil looks closer. Daisy has the cork out of the little bottle and is pouring out little white rocks. Virgil stares. Jesus Christ! Daisy has that kind of coke!

"Here hold this," Daisy says, busy with her razor. She is chopping and crushing at the rocks.

Virgil looks at the vial in his hand, then at Daisy's chopping, and thinks to close his mouth, which has fallen open some time in the last few seconds.

"Now, here. Hold your nose like this," Daisy orders. She puts her finger up against her nose.

Virgil leans closer and stares at the pulverized rock powder Daisy has arranged into four lines. He feels his hand coming up from somewhere, touching his nose. He feels himself breathing in a little. He hears Daisy say, "Easy. Just one side. One side! Suck. Suck it up! Easy! EASY!"

Virgil breathes in, vacuuming tentatively, vacuuming harder, vacuuming up one of the lines.

"Whoa! Half a line. Half a line! Careful! DON'T SPILL IT!"

The stuff is going down his throat. It is awful. Awful! It tastes like Meemaw's ear wax solution, only worse. His eyes tear up. He gags. He thinks he is going to be sick. Then it strikes him. Good god! A Dangerous Substance. Virgil Matthews is doing dope! Oh—this is what it is all about! Those lectures in assembly which never applied to him. And those exclusive advertisements on TV—"This is your brain. This is your brain on drugs." And here, the coolest, the scariest girl in the world is showing him how to do it.

A few minutes later Virgil leans back against the balloon tires of a Glide Easy casket carriage. He feels it noiselessly slide away and he falls back, his legs sticking up still in their cross-legged position as a warm, bright-winged feeling takes him over. I'm stoned, he thinks, with that word he knew but has never had the right to use. "I'm stoned," he says out loud.

Daisy is leaning against the wall in some kind of bluish haze, bending her head over the coke. Her rather nice reddish brown hair starts to shimmer in the dull lights. It starts to be beautiful. Virgil can see that it is not red at all, but brown, and gold, and black...and indigo. Virgil's hand reaches out to touch a stray strand but stops, and takes on remarkable properties. It seems an incredible hand, curiously disarranged, yet lovely, the veins lying just below the surface of his translucent skin, the bones melting, moving into different shapes, into trapezoids, into parallelograms. Daisy is whispering something. "Do you know," she says, "This is the first time I have ever gotten stoned in a funeral home." That seems to strike her as funny and she starts giggling.

Virgil takes his eyes off his hand and studies all the caskets glowing in their mysterious dark and light patterns. Two black isosceles triangles under one are so exquisite that Virgil has to swallow. His throat feels numb.

"Well, look at this, " Daisy is saying. "Virgil Matthews. Stoned. Ha!" She looks at Virgil and smiles fondly, it seems to him. Yes, fondly. "So how's it going?"

"Fine," says Virgil. It really is. He feels calm and sleepy and at the same time as though his every cell is alive and zinging. No wonder people become dope heads! Say, didn't he just have a dream a minute ago? Dream. He'd dreamed he was doing it with Lorna Jean. It was so real! He'd dreamed she was moaning and holding him close, saying "Virgil! The hook's in the front." Oh, wonderful stuff.

He has to hand it to Daisy. He knew she was bad but not this bad. How did a person get to be bad? Maybe it is just opportunity after all.

After the fourth white line is gone, Virgil decides to sing a song, "On the Wings of Love." But he can't remember the words so he can only hum, "La, la, la, la, la." In fact, he can't remember the last fifteen minutes. Or hour? He'd fallen into a lovely black hole. Space.

"Pretty cool," says Daisy. She stands up, "Better get back." Gotta to go to work." Then she sings too, "Burger Kinggggg. We do it all for you-oo-oo."

"That's McDonald's," says Virgil. That takes a great effort to say. He stands up and sways beside the Classic Beauty.

Then Virgil remembers Lorna Jean.

He peers beside the Danish Modern Dream where she sat with Speed. The light there seems to have gone foggy and far away. This stuff is OK.

"I'm stoned," he says again. He looks down at Daisy.

She stands up and gives him a salute. "May The Force be with you," she says. That seems to make perfect sense to Virgil.

"Daisy," he says and forgets what he was going to say.

"That way, Doctor Death," says Daisy, pointing him toward the door.

Virgil touches all the buttons on his suit, then floats out and across the lobby to the entrance of the Slumber Room where Harvey is standing, his hands folded.

Harvey looks at Virgil. He widens his eyes and blinks at him.

Virgil smiles beatifically. He folds his hands over his rumpled suit.

The crowd in the Slumber Room has picked up. There is hardly any space for anybody else to go in. He hears a little commotion behind him. He turns around. It is Meemaw come to give her last respects to Mr. Turberville. Her little round pigeon eyes dart at him.

"Boo!" she says.

Six

M r. Turberville lies in Harvey L. Sloane's tenth best casket with an unfurrowed brow and the subtle beginnings of a smile that is Douglas Dornbusch's signature. He is surrounded by dozens of flower sprays, some that Virgil and Harvey transported from the Slumber Room to the Chapel of Cherished Arms, and some that have been unloaded by some guys from one of Harrisonville's flower shops, Rosie's Forget Me Not Florists. Pee Wee and Zelma Wade are talking to the minister, the Rev. R.M.V. Shackleford.

Rev. R.M.V. Shackleford has been asked to preside over the funeral service but there is a little problem. Rev. Shackleford arrives at the church under the impression that Mr. Turberville is Mrs. Turberville and he has prepared his sermon with phrases like "loving wife and helpmate," and "hand that rocks the cradle". Luckily, it is open casket.

Rev. Shackleford is busy with a little pencil.

Pee Wee peers over his shoulder. There is a razor scrape on his cheek. "Mother—" he says.

"I know. I know," says Zelma. "There's not much to say. Let me think."

Virgil straightens up a carnation and rose spray with gilt letters that reads: "Gone Home." It smells like cold, grape Kool-Aid. This particular bouquet is helping hide the cord for the microphone which Virgil has just finished placing on the podium.

Zelma is actually telling Rev. R.M.V. Shackleford that Ronald Turberville has been an old reprobate that the family had not had much to do with for over ten years because of repeated drunkenness and she did not know exactly what he should say. Virgil wishes she would lower her voice. Rev. Shackleford brightens at her words and sticks his pencil back into his pocket. "Just leave it to me, Mrs. Wade," he says.

The mourners drift in and sit down. For an old guy who lived in a boarding house, Mr. Turberville is getting a pretty big crowd. In the back is a line of three wheelchairs, Mr. Turberville's old buddies from Colvin's. Virgil decides to sit near the rear of the chapel. He wants to be first out of the funeral home because he is going to go with Douglas in his van ahead of the procession to make sure the Steril Chapel tent, folding chairs, and the Lifetime artificial grass mat are arranged properly. Virgil walks back to the last pew, sits down, nods to the old wheelchair guys, and slides over next to a stained glass window. Underneath the window, a plaque glows dully: "In memory of Margaret O'Neill who was employed at Harrisonville Carpet Works for thirty-five years. Erected by her fellow workers as a token of esteem."

Virgil looks at the stained glass. It is a picture of Jesus, in white, driving the moneychangers from the temple. The moneychangers wear rose-colored robes and they all have the same hairstyle and the same face. Staring at the scene reminds Virgil of all the times he had sat in church, gazed at the windows, and suffered. For a few years, Shelby insisted on them going every Sunday. It was one of those times when Shelby came out of his own private world and thought of something his mother might have done.

An organ starts up. It is Mrs. Charles Montgomery, pumping away, who used to teach him Sunday School. The song is familiar. "On a hill far away/stood an old rugged cross—" Virgil remembers that song.

Mrs. Montgomery looks like she has gained weight. Her husband is the deacon of their church. Then Virgil remembers something. One Sunday Mrs. Montgomery made her class a promise. It was that on the next Sunday she was going to bring them something that they had never seen, and that they would never see again. Virgil tortured himself with that puzzle all week.

The next Sunday morning Mrs. Montgomery held up a peanut. "You have never seen this particular peanut," she said dramatically, "and you will never see it again." Then she popped the peanut into her mouth. Virgil was floored. He was hoping for some kind of miracle like water into Coca Cola or something. Mrs. Montgomery had been trying to get a perfect attendance record.

Reverend Shackleford steps up to the pulpit, but continues to thumb through his notes. Pee Wee and Zelma sit down next to Meemaw and Daisy and Lorna Jean. Virgil tilts his head back and lowers his eyes until he is looking through little slits. The sun reflects through the moneychangers' robes and the light in front of him glows in a long, misty shaft.

Earlier, when Virgil woke up that morning, it was hard to tell what happened to leave him with a hollow-wound feeling in his stomach. He'd gotten that feeling before when he'd been in trouble. Once he and Booger Beall got caught stealing rum from Booger's daddy's liquor cabinet and Mr. Beall threatened to tell Shelby, and once he had out and out flunked biology. But after a few seconds he'd remembered yesterday with a needle clarity. He hadn't lost his job, that was something. Harvey had given his rumpled clothes a few odd looks but that was all.

It is something else: this morning, just glimpsing the back of Lorna Jean's head intensified his eternal hollow-pain feeling. He is also beginning, now that he has time to sit down and think, to get a kind of light-headed, flu-feeling. Virgil tries to not look over there, but Lorna Jean's golden, halo hair keeps sneaking into his perspective. Next to her Daisy sits with a black veil on that looks like a lacy black tablecloth. He stares at it. Virgil sometimes gets the feeling that Daisy is dressing up to act out some kind of part, just for the hell of it. Parts she's seen in movies, probably. Last year, her own father fired Daisy from being an usherette at the Princess Theater. She watched more movies than she ushered. She is some kind of movie nut. That is why she works at Burger King, and not for Pee Wee.

"Let us—to the Holy Wor-r-r-" Reverend Shackleford intones something in a far-away, muted voice that makes Mrs. Montgomery's organ trail off. Reverend Shackleford is taking his text from the New Testament, a story about a woman who used a little something-- Virgil couldn't hear—when making bread. Virgil strains his ears. Then the bread did something—oh, raised, not one, but three whole loaves, ready to be put in to the oven and baked. Reverend Shackleford says that it is just like a man's whole line—line?—oh, life, a little amount of spirit could make a whole man do good deeee... and his voice trails off again.

Virgil wonders what Reverend Shackleford is getting at. And why can't he hear? Is Virgil losing his hearing? Then shoot! It hits him. He's forgotten to turn the mike on.

Virgil feels something push on his arm. He looks around. One of the boarders is looking at him.

"Say, sonny," the old man says through gappy teeth. His voice is too loud. "You Shelby Matthews or his son?

"Son," says Virgil, turning back around. He pretends to be interested in Reverend Shackleford's sermon. Some of the members of the congregation lean forward and turn one ear toward the pulpit.

"Told you," the old man behind him says to somebody.

"Is that you Delores?" another old voice says.

"Naw, Toby. We in a chapel."

"He does look like his daddy," a third old voice says. "I thought it was him. Pest control man. Good one."

"Delores?" the one named Toby says.

"It's them ears. He has the same ears."

"Delores--meet me back of the courthouse," says Toby.

"Hush, Toby."

Virgil has never been mistaken for his daddy before. He focuses his eyes straight ahead. The people in the congregation have stopped leaning forward. People are even whispering to each other like they were at a ball game. Everybody has relaxed and are not even bothering to decipher Reverend Shackleford's faraway sermon. Where did all these people come from? A family in front of him with little kids and a baby. An old faded couple that looks like they've driven in from the country. Why, there is even old Beansie Stewart's parents. Oh yeah, Beansie is Daisy's second cousin. He is the brother of a famous, former defensive tackle—famous, not because he is so great, but because he drove to New Orleans one weekend and got caught buying anabolic steroids. Steroid Stewart. Beansie is sitting between Steroid's parents, but Virgil can't see Steroid. One time too, he had been arrested for breaking and entering a restaurant. Steroid Stewart, before he got expelled, used to stand around with Daisy in the gym and goof around. There has always been a wildness about Daisy that made her popular to a lot of people but it is probably the same thing that bugs Virgil. Yesterday, though, she was pretty OK. Now Lorna Jean has mystery and...gentleness. Virgil feels those different voices he heard yesterday were just some abnormal kind of behavior triggered by that jerk, Speed. Virgil is still in love. In fact all the pain he suffered yesterday makes it more intense somehow today. He has a lot of pain and fantasies and feeling invested in that girl.

Reverend Shackleford appears as if he is getting excited about something. He loosens his collar and waves his arms around. He looks like a TV program that somebody has turned the sound way down.

Daisy's veil shakes a little. Virgil bets she is giggling at Reverend Shackleford.

A few years ago, Old Daisy kept Jefferson High jumping all the time. She did things like piercing her ears in several places and wearing two or three pairs of earrings at a time. She started that fad. And she was the first rollerblader in Harrisonville and the first to own a DVD. She was also the one person who caused the Dress Code at Jefferson High to be rewritten every year. She was the first, too, to come to school plugged into a portable CD player, and to bring a cell phone hooked onto her waist on one side and a pager on the other. It was also rumored Daisy had a tattoo and at least one pierced body part, both in places, of course, people wouldn't normally see. Once Daisy cut the top of her hair in some weird crew-cut, but that was grown out now. That style was definitely awful. She was something though, Virgil had to admit. Right now, wearing her tablecloth veil, she stands out as the chief mourner. But it is Lorna Jean beside her who has the class. That delicate neck, that skin the color of a pale apricot.

છ

Daisy sits between her mother on her right, wafting the smell of Estee Lauder, and her first cousin, Lorna Jean Gibson, on her left, who seems to have taken a bath in Shalimar, in the creepy chapel of the

Harrisonville Funeral Home. To keep from going crazy, Daisy concentrates on the way Reverend Shackleford's Adam's apple quivers under his rat face whenever he prays or reaches a certain pitch in his sermon. She can't tell. The mike is dead, thank the lord for that.

Daisy moves her jaws at spaced intervals so that no one will know she is chewing gum. Right next to her, Lorna Jean, alias Snow White, stares, eyes fixed, as if she is hanging onto every word. Probably thinking about Speed's dick or something.

Lord! Is this thing never going to end? Daisy stifles a sigh and almost swallows her gum. Oh, cigarette! If she just had a cigarette. Boy, wouldn't her mother die if she lit up right now. Daisy almost smiles thinking about the faces around her if she even pulled one out. But they would probably not be too surprised. Now if Lorna Jean, Miss Butter-Won't-Melt-In-Her-Twat, would light up any place at all, they'd faint. And what a joke that was.

Last year at least a few people found out Lorna Jean isn't as pure as everyone thinks. After New Year's, Lorna Jean came crying to Daisy, saying that she had got herself in trouble. Daisy knew right away what she meant, but she said, "How can you get *yourself* in trouble? Spontaneous combustion?" But anyway, Daisy ended up driving her into New Orleans to the Delta Womens' Clinic for an abortion—a secret enterprise, or so it started out to be. But Pee Wee found 300 extra miles on the Bug's odometer and in so doing put another bar on Lorna Jean's prison—is the way Lorna Jean puts it. Daisy had to tell because Pee Wee and Zelma thought it was Daisy up to something. Of course, she was, but only to help Lorna Jean, the ninny. She just hadn't had time to adjust the mileage meter, a complicated procedure that involved jacking up the bug and running it in reverse for a while, as had always proved useful around Mardi Gras season in high school. The problem was Pee Wee and Zelma told Aunt Mattie, and for a while Lorna Jean was mad at Daisy. For about a month. And that's the thanks she got for all that whirlwind driving to make it there and back in a day.

She'd driven one hundred and twenty-five miles straight. Then wouldn't you know? It had been St. Patrick's Day and the place was crazy. The streets were jammed. The clinic was on the seediest street in New Orleans, and all the foot-washing Baptists or something had turned out to protest abortion. Right-To-Life signs were a solid wall. When they got out of the car, some woman in this tacky polyester pantsuit came right up to them and said, "Jesus is watching you!" and stuck this baby-doll covered in red paint right in their faces. And Lorna Jean started screaming. But Daisy howled right back at them. "Do we take pictures of beat-up kids to O.B. clinics? Hi-yi-i!" she yelled, assuming a karate stance—not that she'd ever had a karate lesson in her life, but how would those crazy Bible bangers know? Well, Lorna Jean had to admit—Daisy got her through that. What good did it do though, she complained, if the next day Zelma was on the phone with Mattie? She might have just told her mother herself. Of course, all that was water under the Lake Pontchartrain Bridge now. Lorna Jean pretended it was her previous boyfriend she met up with briefly right in the middle of a relationship with Speed. Which goes to show parents will believe anything. Her previous boyfriend was Joel Edwards whose mother and Mattie were friends in the Harrisonville Welcome Wagon Committee. *Were* friends is right, because after Aunt Mattie found out what she thought was the truth, she ran her shopping cart into Mrs. Edwards at the A & P and pushed her over into a ceiling high stack of Kennel Ration dog food cans. All this without a word. In fact, Aunt Mattie never said *another* word to that woman to this day, which probably made it a little awkward when they ended up on the same Wagon to welcome somebody. Only Daisy knows the whole truth. Lorna Jean, acting just as stupid as she could be, got pregnant on purpose just so Speed Maxwell would marry her. And then he had just given her money for the abortion and taken that champion Chesapeake Bay retriever to Mississippi to qualify for their state fair finals and not even gone with her. Lord, he is a jerk. Lorna Jean thinks half the time Speed loved his dog more than her. That's right! Speed Maxwell, the sleaze ball of the earth, hadn't even been there to hold Lorna Jean's hand when she went under the knife. He was out of the state with said dog. Which makes Lorna Jean the dumbest woman alive.

Lorna Jean just refuses to look at Speed Maxwell for the prize scuz he is, always off by himself, when he isn't showing his own dog, to throw ducks or judge in one of those dog trials himself. And he only does that judging to suck up and get to know the other judges. He is just nothing without his guns, caps, and cars, and his dog. After he started winning with Rocky, he sold all his other dogs and stopped keeping Rocky in the steel-and-concrete air conditioned enclosures at his Mom's house, and let Rocky move into his apartment. Which was one of Lorna Jean's frequent complaints.

Daisy looks over at Mattie who just happens to turn to look at her, too. Daisy gives her a friendly smile, knowing full well that just her presence irritates her aunt. Mattie smiles back in an uppity way and turns back to the preacher. Aunt Mattie always believes that Daisy is a bad influence on Lorna Jean! Which is as far from the facts as you can get. Well, if there is one thing Daisy and Mattie agree on, it's the worthlessness of Speed Maxwell.

Speed Maxwell doesn't even have a steady job but takes on what he calls contracts here and there. That is the main reason Aunt Mattie and Uncle Lamar don't like him. Daisy knows a lot about Speed, because for a very brief time, during a particularly dry spell, when she had nothing better to do, and probably because of some kind of temporary brain dysfunction, she and Speed had got it on. But Lorna Jean doesn't know that. And Daisy is not going to tell her.

Lorna Jean believes all that romance and marriage stuff. Old movies, where men like sweet, dumb women at first, but end up going with smart, independent women, are over her head. And she actually thinks when she gets married she can change Speed Maxwell into staying put and getting a real job! On top of that, she calls Daisy at least once a day to complain.

Lorna Jean is dumb! Dumb! First she masquerades like she is the sweetest, purest, little thing in Harrisonville! Even when they were children she always thought her naturally curly blonde hair was her ticket to the world. If Daisy had blonde hair, she would try to be like Grace Kelly, under whose iced down demeanor lay a spark of fire ready to be fanned. Lorna Jean is more like Marilyn Monroe trying to be Jean Harlow. She is available at a price, but can never quite pull off the deal.

Lorna Jean is just one of the last of the left over people from another age, who can't quite get the hang of what she is intended to be, but doesn't have sense enough to do different. The age Mattie and Zelma are from—that age in which Daisy's sisters are the last of a dying breed. With all those rituals and rules! Lorna Jean still uses gallons of hair spray and even has a trousseau complete with a Wallace International Rose Point silver pattern and a deviled egg plate, among other weird boring things. But her college career, that halfway house before marriage, had come to an abrupt end because she freaked out when she didn't get pledged Theta. Plus she is so dumb her grades were terrible. So here she is in Harrisonville. It is getting harder and harder to be a Southern Belle. Thank God.

Daisy has had to go to extreme means to survive in this town with people like Lorna Jean and Aunt Mattie to put up with. Even her own parents—just wrong-headed. Both of them convinced that Daisy is going to wind up on skid row if she does not marry some local yokel and live the rest of her life in Harrisonville taking aerobics and collecting casserole recipes. Two parents who use words like *skid row*. And *what a card!* And *she's a mess!* They still aren't as bad as Lorna Jean's parents who write cheery Christmas newsletters with bunches of exclamation points and Xerox them and send them to tons of other boring relatives. Who put things in it that they think look impressive but are actually awful. Like Nora winning that goofy pink Cadillac from selling Mary Kay Cosmetics, and R.C. and Crystal taking a cruise to Europe where they probably played shuffleboard with people just like them wearing Bill Blass wrinkle proof cotton duck with sporty sailing motifs and who belonged to Kiwanis Clubs back home. So what else can Daisy do but entertain herself with men, the few halfway decent looking ones there are in this town? You can't watch movies all the time.

Movies are more real to her than life, she always knew that. The old movies with Brando, Clark, Dean, Peck, Tracy! The men around here are not even pale imitations. But then she met Owen.

Owen lives on Olive Street and fixes cars from time to time, but only if somebody just begs him to death after his friend J.R. sends them over. He does it to give himself something to do. He has an iron pipe slung between the forks of two pecan trees in his backyard where he can even lift out a motor if he needs to.

On the next street over from Olive is what is known as colored housing.

Next door to Owen is Mrs. Holly, who lives on Social Security, and is always watering her begonias and watching him suspiciously. Mrs. Holly spends a lot of time being suspicious of everything, but where Owen is concerned, she is doubly conscientious. Mrs. Holley once told Owen she lived in terror for years that his house would be rented to blacks, and was so glad when Owen moved in. But then J.R., the black guy who pumps gas at the Exxon and his friends started to come over all the time to get their cars fixed and she probably heard the false rumors Owen had J.R. spread so that folks would leave him alone, that he had killed babies in Vietnam and that he stalked high school girls at night. Owen is hardly bothered by her at all—except for the glares over the boxwood. What strikes Daisy about Owen is that he doesn't fit in with the usual type of men in Harrisonville. Maybe it was the war. Owen is an old guy, a Vietnam war veteran. Maybe the war makes people more observant or sensitive or something. She knows awful stuff went on, like in *Platoon*, but Owen has never told her much about the stuff that happened to him. He says nothing bothers him any more, but he would just as soon not talk about it, thank you. Daisy always tries to find men who at least try to act like Bogey, Joseph Cotton, or Spencer Tracey. So, theoretically, what she sees in Owen Flowers is even beyond her. He is more like George Peppard in *Home from the Hill*, or the guy in *Written on the Wind*. Or Jesus! *Random Harvest!* In *Random Harvest* Ronald Colman is this shell-shocked World War I veteran who has amnesia and marries Greer Garson to settle down for a simple life. And that guy in *Paris, Texas*, what's-his-name, who refuses to speak for a while.

Because when Daisy first met Owen he was a real hermit. A sign on his door said: WARNING/ AIDS AND PIT BULLDOGS, which J.R. said was just a joke.

J.R. told her she wanted a cheap transmission, he knew somebody would do it. He told her this when his boss wasn't looking, and he told her directions on how to get to Owen's house. The sign wasn't exactly a joke—it had a purpose. It was just that Owen used to not like a lot of people coming around. But Daisy had got him over that. Thanks to her, Owen quit being so reclusive about stuff and started going out and around town.

The first time she asked Owen out he wouldn't go. He didn't like to go anywhere in public. She'd never tried being the pursuer, not an obvious pursuer, anyway. But finally, after a full campaign on Daisy's part, they had gone out—to Caney Brake, eating moon pies and drinking Royal Crown Colas and throwing crumbs to the ducks.

They sat and ate moon pies and fed the dumb-shit ducks and skimmed rocks across the lake. Daisy was a champion rock skimmer as a child and when one of hers flashed one, two, three, four, not five, but six times across the root beer-colored water, the luckiest, the best she's ever done, she got this scary, horrible feeling that this was the best time she'd had in a while. She could have been walking around the mall with somebody, for heaven's sake. She could have been in New Orleans at Brennan's.

They didn't even sleep together right away, too. Owen had plenty of opportunity, but for a long time, nothing happened. And since Daisy liked to do *everything* on the first date, get it out of the way—somehow things felt awkward until then—the situation almost got out of hand.

One Wednesday night, after a late shift, she'd come by Owen's house with a look fixed on her face that she used to practice at home in the mirror and which she called *sultry*. She thought she might loosen him up a little by surprising him so late at night. How, she figured, can she decide if she liked this guy if they never slept together?

But Owen smoked her dope and drank beer and asked her a weird question—if she had any other boyfriends or not.

Owen has the teeniest beginnings of a paunch, he only owns about three shirts, and Daisy never truly liked red hair, her own is auburn, not red—but the man, for reasons beyond her, floors her. So what was she doing there? The men she usually preferred were cool dressers (with the exception of one who seemed to have the same tailor as J.R. Ewing), and who usually could not care less if she had a different boyfriend every day of the week.

"I've made a career of frivolous sex," she'd said to see if she could rattle him, sitting in her most seductive position on his old, beat-up couch.

"Mmmmm," he said, sitting down beside her. He turned on an old *Gomer Pyle* rerun.

Then Owen ran his hand through his shaggy hair and said, "Is TV OK?"

"TV?" she said. "Oh, sure. Why the hell not?" Third or fourth date. Daisy figured the guy must be gay.

"You mad or something?" Owen said, at least putting his arm around her. Daisy just looked at him.

Then Sergeant Carter yelled, "Ah-tennn-SHUN!"

"Listen to that," Owen laughed. "Nobody ever says, Ah-ten-SHUN! It's Ten-Hut!"

"You know," Daisy said, after a good long damn while, "you're so square. Don't you want to kiss me?"

Owen looked at her then. "I just like to go slow," he said. "I like to think about things, get it right the first time. And anyway, you're the one's square."

"Me!"

Then Owen picked up a piece of her hair off her shoulder. He was wearing that awful faded palm tree shirt that he'd worn the day Daisy had brought her VW, on its last leg, into his yard and asked him real cute like if he had metric tools.

"You square but you don't know it," said Owen. Then he kissed her a little and put his head back on the couch and settled back to watch Gomer. Daisy stared up at the ceiling, just floored.

"Shucks," Gomer Pyle said to a woman in a tight, polka dot dress and red high heels, "I know Sergeant Carter wouldn't want me to go against my conscience. No siree."

Oh, good grief, Daisy thought. Later, she remembered that what Owen said was what that crazy vet had said to Jodie Foster in *Taxi Driver*.

But eventually things got cracking between them. They'd just started doing it one time finally. For a while, Owen still hated to go out and stuff, though.

So Daisy had got out the only book she kept from college, *Intro to Psychology*, and learned how to do behavior therapy. Owen had some kind of real aversion to crowds and places and stuff. What she did was simple—just paired those pesky fear responses to pleasurable stuff. Real pleasurable stuff. ("Here?" Owen would say, looking at the feet that passed by them under the bleachers at Homecoming. "Here?" he'd say, in the dome tent of a camping display at Service Merchandise.) Agoraphobia and going down, just do not mix. So, everything between them at the moment was cool. In fact, when Daisy decided where she wanted to go to film school, Owen had promised to come with her.

෨

Reverend Shackleford's sermon is getting involved. The sound of it, devoid of sense, begins to take on an evangelical tone. Virgil stares at the hymnal rack in front of him. It is better than watching Reverend Shackleford do a pantomime of a hell-fire sermon. He's obviously decided to turn the opportunity into a chance to save a few souls. Just as well Virgil forgot to turn on the mike. He hopes nobody complains though.

Virgil hears the old man named Toby behind him say hopefully, "We in the Blue Moon?"

"No, hush, you blind bastard. We in church. Ronald's dead."

"Who?"

"Ronald!"

Several people turn their heads to look. They look at Virgil. Daisy, veil and all, gives him the high sign. Zelma bends her head to Daisy and her lips move. Lorna Jean doesn't budge.

The organ cranks up. "Let the lower lights be burning," sing the people. They get up to file around the casket and say good-bye to Mr. Turberville. Virgil can hear Daisy's voice above everybody's, "Let it beam across the seeeeeeea!" She can belt it out as good as Madonna, for heaven's sake.

"Roll out the barrel," sings Toby in a weak, tin-can voice.

Virgil feels like he has known Toby for a long time. He hears a swish and sees that Harvey L. Sloane has opened the doors from where he's been waiting in the lobby.

Virgil means to be first out of the chapel but the wheelchairs hold everybody up. The people in the aisle come to a standstill. The old blonde with the Kleenexes from the Chapel of Cherished Arms is there. She begins sobbing what seems like to Virgil, big fakey sobs.

Virgil catches a glimpse of Lorna Jean's face. He slows his breathing to meet the knife-blade thrusts in his chest. She looks pale and artistic, and filmy somehow. Daisy is behind her. She gives him a mock dramatic look. She winks at him. Meemaw is behind Daisy, calling to people she hasn't seen in a while.

In the lobby, one of the guys from derma-surgery meets him with a funny look on his face. "You hooked up the mike wrong, Virgil," he says. The next door chapel had gotten a hell-and-brimstone sermon for an elderly, retired minister. Twelve members of the congregation had come forward to be saved. Harvey, standing by the door, looks pained. "S-s-sshit," he says, walking away.

Outside the hot air hits Virgil like a sledge. Douglas is in the van waiting for him, his patent leather hair gleaming in the hot sun, a toothpick hanging out of the side of his mouth. Beside him is Speed Maxwell. "Hop in, kid," says Douglas, gunning his motor.

Seven

The backhoe has done its job. Virgil sidesteps the canvas-covered disembowelment and peers into an ocher pit. The corrugated wall of the gorge looks shocked clean as far as he can see, then descends into a square of matte black. The peculiar chill that set up in Virgil since morning ripples like a polar current down his spine.

Ka-snap! Virgil jumps, as a blinding emerald green flash bursts from his peripheral cloud and then floats down over the black. He gasps, then shuts his mouth quickly. It is only the Astroturf being thrown over the open grave. He ducks his head and steps back. "Sorry, fella." A boy Virgil has never seen before kneels and adjusts a corner of the grass.

Virgil looks up towards the dark line of trees on the horizon. He sees the coach on its way, and the chain of cars, their headlights like pale eyes, moving toward them. Harvey, motioning Virgil with him, goes to meet the coach. The first car holds the immediate family, or what has to do for Mr. Turberville's immediate family. Gibsons and Wades. The second car exudes Son Williams and Doyle Lanier and Lamar and Pee Wee and some other man Virgil doesn't know. Harvey starts giving them instructions in placing the casket on the tapes. Reverend Shackleford gathers with the mourners at the graveside. At the funeral the crowd is half as big as at the viewing in the Slumber Room, and now it has halved again.

Reverend Shackleford starts intoning something. From where he is, Virgil can see Lorna Jean real well. Her delicate, doe-like stance beside Mattie's squatness almost seems funny, but for some reason, looking at them, Virgil's eyes start to water. It is impossible for one thing, for him to go up afterwards and to say, 'Hey, how are y'all?" Or strike up any kind of conversation. For another thing, even if he has the guts to do it, Lorna Jean probably will look at him, expressionless, or with that half-bored look she has.

Reverend R.M.V. Shackleford launches into a few words. He is holding a container full of dirt that he will throw down on the casket once it is lowered. Virgil wonders if Reverend Shackleford heard the effect his funeral service had on the congregation next door. Virgil flushes red for the thousandth time in the last thirty minutes. Harvey gave Virgil a hurried, pissed look as he is getting into the van. This dream of Virgil's, to be a mortician, is beginning to seem like a crazy delusion. He should have gone to the Navy with Booger, maybe.

Somewhere in the distance a car's muted backfire pops. Virgil raises his eyes and sees a familiar Chevy nosing along toward them. It parks at the farthest edge of the other cars, and Zelma Wade climbs out. Virgil can tell it is Zelma because of the hat. She begins walking, not along the winding drive, but on a short-cut, through the older memorial section. That woman is always late.

Virgil idly follows the bobbing hat as it weaves in and out the monuments. Suddenly, right in front of his eyes, Zelma disappears. Virgil blinks. He shakes his head slightly. No. She is gone. Is he dreaming? She is there one minute, then gone the next. Virgil squints at the place she disappeared. Where could she have gone? It's like she dropped into the earth. Maybe she tripped. But no, she just vanished all at once. Maybe she fell into a hole. Jeez! Maybe she stepped onto one of those old graves where the casket had finally disintegrated and it had caved in with her. He's heard talk about things like that happening. Why, Douglas has said so. He has a million stories about weird things happening in the business.

Grave collapsing! But what to do? If he can get Pee Wee's attention, maybe they can sneak out the service and go see what happened. But Pee Wee is so short Virgil can barely make out the top of his head behind the other pallbearers. Virgil tries to signal Harvey by waving his hand at his side. Harvey doesn't look for a while and then when he does, he just frowns at Virgil. Virgil jerks his head toward where Zelma has disappeared and mouths, CAVE-IN! Harvey stares at him without changing his expression. Virgil makes his face into a look of horror, CAVE-IN! Harvey's gaze narrows, then freezes like he's real mad.

Virgil sees Douglas looking at him curiously. He tries the same thing. CAVE-IN! Douglas stares back at him, and then he rolls his eyes. He waggles his eyebrows up and down. He punches Speed and nods at Virgil. He thinks Virgil is fooling around!

Virgil is dumbfounded. Maybe he should interrupt the service. Maybe he should shout CAVE-IN! He takes a deep breath but he can't open his mouth. And maybe he is even mistaken about Zelma Wade. But maybe he isn't.

Virgil peers around at the faces. They all seem to have fallen into this meditative trance. Even Douglas falls into this kind of staring with a far away look in his eyes. Daisy is standing with a kind of motionless, easy indifference. Lorna Jean stands beside her. Lorna Jean! She looks like one of those famous statues or something. Immovable. At least she isn't standing by Speed Maxwell. All the faces, the people he didn't know, are staring wide and unblinking and dreamy. For a second they remind Virgil of something he saw one time on the *Twilight Zone*. Some overworked housewife found a medallion in her garden and by holding it and saying "Shut-up" she could make the whole world stop. She'd freeze her yelling kids at the breakfast table, stop the whole world to shop for groceries. Virgil looks around. Reverend Schackleford has stopped talking. For a second everything, even the traffic on Highway 9, seems to halt. And it seems in that second, that single second before Reverend Schackleford reaches down for the symbolic cup of dirt, that this is the way it has been all his life, like he has something to yell, and he can't make his voice work, and nobody will look at him, really see him. Then it hits him! Zelma. How long has he been standing there trying to think what to do? What if she is suffocated? Is suffocating. Virgil feels his own breath leave him and a sick sensation start in his stomach and work its way up. Then he makes his legs move.

Virgil works his way backwards, steps behind one after the other of the Bereaved Ones. His heart is beating steady and hard. One of the

Bereaved Ones, a man in a colorful sports shirt and a light blue leisure suit, like he is on vacation, raises his head from a bowed position and frowns at him slightly. Virgil realizes he is moving around in a prayer.

Then he is far enough away to start picking up speed. He dodges between the memorials, the fancy old ones with lambs and scrolls and stuff, away from the newer section with its flat plates that can be mowed over. He slows down to a good brisk walk. No sense in looking too stupid. Zelma could be just fine for all he knows. He passes by a memorial with an angel poised for flight that somehow looks familiar.

When he was a kid, Virgil played hide and seek here with Booger, until Booger leapfrogged one of the stones, knocked it over and broke it. He remembered some of the old stones pretty well even though he hadn't been here in a long time. He and Booger were afraid to come back.

The ground under his feet is still spongy from last night's slow rain. The graves are so close together he can't help stepping on some of them. Oops, sorry, sorry. Sorry, lady. Sorry, Mister, whoever you are.

Over here the ground seems even more spongy. Virgil tries to keep in as straight a line as he can so he won't lose the spot he thinks Zelma is. Then after a trio of close-together family tombs, he suddenly sees Zelma Wade's head, sitting on top of the ground. He stops short and stares. It is so weird he can't call out. It looks like one of those Apache tortures he's read about where they buried their enemy in the ground and left their honey-covered head sticking out for the ants. Lord!

Zelma's face, for all her trouble, looks more thoughtful than scared. Her hat is still on, a little to one side, and the feather on it is broken and hanging down in her face. When she sees Virgil, she lights up in a big smile.

"Virgil!" she says. "Thank the lord you're here. Oh, saved! Thank you, sweet Jesus!"

"Good lord," Virgil says. "Mrs. Wade!"

"Can you give me a hand?" Zelma says, like she needs him to help hold a package or open a car door or something. "You know, I've always heard not to step on graves. Grandma Bee once said it was bad luck to step on them, but I thought it was just superstition. I guess there's a good reason behind every old wives' tale, huh? Ha! Life's funny, huh?"

"Lord," says Virgil again. "I'll go get help. You just sit tight, Mrs. Wade."

"Oh no!" says Zelma. "Can't you just give me a hand? Pee Wee will have a fit. And everybody will know. Give me your hand! We can do it!"

Virgil comes closer and eyes the ground. Zelma is sunk up to her chin, one arm out still clutching her pocketbook. "Oh, my," he says, "I've just got to get help."

"Virgil," Zelma whispers in an urgent hiss. "Please don't go. Don't tell. Oh, you don't know how much trouble this will cause. I stopped off from the procession, because Dawson's was having this sale, see? Petit-point bathroom seat covers? You know how much they cost. They were half-price? Then Mabel Manning, Mabel Manning at the check-out counter has to go on and on about how Leon's gotten off coke, and going on to trade school and all, and then about her sciatica, and then I got this awful feeling—this awful late feeling. And sure enough I'd made myself real late. Mr. Wade just won't understand! Please! Please. Just pull me out."

"Oh, me," says Virgil. He walks up tentatively and squats down. Slippery. Virgil gets up and squats on the other side, so he can halfway wrap his arm around the stone. He grasps Zelma's plump, out-stretched hand.

He pulls. No, no. He can feel her chubby sticky fingers slide through his, and his wing tips slip underneath him. He clinches his teeth. "This is not working, Mrs. Wade."

"Try once more!" says Zelma. "Please, son." Her warm, chubby fingers won't let go. "Come on," she says. "Heave. Give the old home-town try!"

A second later, Virgil's head is sticking out of the ground too. He'd tried to leap up, jump, when he felt the earth giving way but it had been too late. Virgil's legs, thighs, and shoulders are pinned tightly into the mud and dirt on one side, and Zelma Wade on the other.

"Oh, my goodness," Zelma is gasping.

"Oh, good lord," says Virgil. He strains, pushes, but it only makes something under his left foot give way more.

"Stop! Stop!" hisses Zelma in his ear. "You making us cave in more!"

"We're going to have to holler," says Virgil. But in that second he sees the look on Nora Jean's face when she arrived with the rest of the crowd and so when Zelma says, "Just give it a minute. At least until they're through. Let's us wait 'till everybody leaves and call the grave diggers," he shuts up.

Zelma goes on in a chatty voice, "These grave side services are usually short, if I remember Grandma Bee's correctly."

Virgil groans. When he does that, his left foot drops another couple of inches.

"Now just don't panic. It's just like I told myself--don't panic. It's just dirt and somebody's fifty-year old or so dust. Bones in here aren't bones any more, just dust. Dust to dust, as they say." Zelma lifts up her chin to engage the bifocal part of her glasses. "Who have we fallen into, anyway? Why, look at that!" She is staring at a fat, mumpy-cheeked cherub face on one of those real old-timey tombstones. Zelma reads out loud:

> "Mrs. Margaret Penneybaker
> who departed this life
> March 16, 1893
> Aged 63 years 3 months 5 days
> Forever thin.
> Er-rat-um, for thin read thine."

Well, thank heaven for that! For a second I thought Mrs. Margaret Penneybaker was like all those foolish young things trying to outdo one another to stay thin."

Virgil sighs. He has this horrible feeling he is stuck for eternity with Zelma and Mrs. Margaret Penneybaker. And now, he just has to think about Lorna Jean. Go away, he thinks as her face floats up in his mind. He can't deal very well with the thought of her right now. If she comes and sees him like this, he'll just die. He'll make himself die. He might die anyway. For one thing it is hot as hell. For another thing he is about to get smothered by Mrs. Wade's chest. He has fallen deeper than she is and the left side of his face and nose is stuck right in her bosoms and the lack of enough air and the smell of talcum powder is about to asphyxiate him.

"Mrs. Wade," says Virgil. He realizes his voice is muffled. "Mrs. Wade, try stepping on my knee and hefting yourself out."

"No, sir!" says Zelma Wade starchly. Her feather flops in Virgil's face. "And push you to the middle of the earth? You just keep your shirt on, young man. When folks leave and the grave diggers are doing their thing, we'll give them a holler. My sister there and all. Oh, she'll just love it!"

"But Mrs. Wade—" he says.

"Tick-a-lock!" says Zelma. "In a few minutes they'll leave and then we'll just call the grave diggers."

"Uh, Mrs. Wade?" says Virgil, making his voice real calm. "We don't use grave diggers any more. It's all mechanized."

"Oh, come on, son," says Zelma. "Be a good sport. I have this very critical family. You just don't know what I go through."

Virgil thinks of Lorna Jean again. Already she has seen Meemaw. And Meemaw's snuff can. And Shelby's feet. Now this. He sighs. He guesses he can stand it for a little while. As long as they don't slip any further.

Then Zelma starts talking about everything under the sun. The problem, she says, is that her whole family looks upon her as this clumsy person who never gets anything right. A kind of clown, who is good for nothing but shopping and decorating. Not that they appreciated her flair for that either! What did she care for new houses and fancy vacations? Go! Go to the Grand Canyon! All she wants is some odds and ends to make her happy. But does Pee Wee appreciate that? No! "Listen, son, listen," she interrupts herself. "Isn't that a whippoorwill? Law, I haven't heard one of those in years. But isn't it a little early in the day for them?"

Shut-up, Virgil thinks. *Please, please shut-up. Or don't shut-up. Talk. Scream for help.* And then he remembers what happened to that housewife who found the medallion. At the end of the story she stops a nuclear missile seconds before it hits the ground. She has the whole world, her family, everybody frozen around her. But if she says, "Talk!" the missile will blow the world away. No, better to keep them frozen in ignorance, everybody, Lorna Jean, Daisy, Harvey, and wait for a miracle.

Nightmare, Virgil thinks. "Nightmare," he whispers into Zelma's talcum powder, like, he realizes, a crazy person. Zelma must have some kind of strong perfume on, too. He believes he is getting a headache. He hasn't eaten all day come to think of it, if he doesn't count a little microwaved can of Dinty Moore Beef Soup. Virgil is used to bigger lunches, but because of his new work hours he doesn't get them any more. Today is Thursday, scrambled egg sandwich night, because Meemaw heads out to Bingo early in the evening. He and Shelby normally eat four or five sandwiches each to make up for it being a sandwich supper. Virgil's stomach begins to rumble.

Zelma's powder and perfume reminds him of the Chapel back at the funeral home. Fragrance of spring flowers and death. Jeeze, buried alive! What a horrible fate. Just like the Jijians. The Jijians used to bury their elderly relatives alive. They thought if they went that way, before they got feeble, they could keep the same faculties. Only Virgil is already losing his faculties. What if it were days before they are found? Virgil imagines the police and police photographers gathered around their crowded grave. Police laughing. Reporters' leering eyes. Jokes. *The male died of asphyxiation by perfume. Or hunger. Or bosom suffocation.* Lorna Jean will probably not even come to his funeral. An embarrassing funeral. An embarrassing death. Douglas can add to his collection of funny deaths. The folder of unusual and amusing deaths he collects as a hobby. The man going under an overpass and a truck carrying two tons of frozen meat turns over and falls on his car, crushing it. The guy in Florida who falls into a giant rinse cycle at a commercial laundry. "Can you imagine explaining how your husband died?" Douglas whooped. "Crushed by two tons of ground round. Didn't make it through the rinse cycle! Ha!" What will be said about Virgil's death?

"—almost peaceful," Zelma is saying. "Listen, haven't they finished yet? We should hear the cars start up soon. Lord, I'm trapped in a grave, with my best dress on, and my pocketbook's full of mud, and my good handkerchief's where I don't know."

Virgil listens hard but all he can hear is an occasional car whoosh up on the highway and the birds' chatter from the line of woods at the top of the hill. He is dizzy, so dizzy he wonders if he will be able to yell loud enough now for anybody to hear.

"Yessir, Pee Wee will have a lot to say about this." Zelma is beginning to sound less perky than she had been. "He thinks me and my whole family are flighty, and why? For the simple reason I am from Texas instead of Louisiana like him. To tell the truth, Pee Wee is prejudiced against Texans. And my whole family comes from Blessing, Texas, so too bad! And Mattie will just die!"

Zelma seems to be at least realizing the seriousness of their predicament. Virgil decides to encourage her. "Mrs. Wade. Shouldn't we call for help now? What if the back hoe people don't hear us?"

She cocks her head, Virgil deduces, because the perfumed mass surrounding his face rippled.

"Voices!" says Mattie. "Off to the north. Coming closer. Oh, thank the Lord! We are going to be saved. And by strangers, too. We are going to be out of this mess and not have to make complete spectacles of ourselves with those Gibsons and all!"

Virgil strains to listen. A male voice calls, "Ethel May, please."

With the one eye on sea level, Virgil sees skinny legs attached to tennis shoes come into view. "Ethel May, please. Let's don't fight. Let's discuss," a boy's voice says.

A second pair of legs appears. With great effort Virgil lifts his eye higher to long tanned legs, cut-off shorts. Butt-length flaming red hair, almost the color of Daisy's. "Tube top," Virgil hears Zelma murmur. Virgil squints. The girl is wearing one of those things called a tube top that Virgil heard Daisy and Zelma have a big fight about one day before Daisy drove off squealing her tires. The other skinny legs belong to a kid about his own age.

"Can't you just listen a minute?" the kid says.

"You go to hell, Ed," the girl says. The boy grabs her arm.

"And let go of me," she says, jerking away. She turns her back on the boy.

"You don't have to do anything you don't want to do," she says to flower pots on a monument. "Just get off scot-free. Go anywhere. Oh, you damn man!" she says over her shoulder.

"I didn't mean it," says the boy. "Please, Ethel May. I want it. I swear."

"Like hell you do. I'm going tomorrow. Before it's too late. Think I'm going through this hell while you're out doing what you want?"

"No, don't do it," says the boy. "I promise. I'll never do what I want. I mean, you're what I want. I'll get a job. I'll take care of you!"

"Oh, yeah? Are you going to get fat too?" says the girl.

"Yes! Yes, I will!" the boy says hysterically. (Virgil believes him.)

Zelma is clearing her throat. "Uh, excuse me," she says.

They both look down.

"We need a little help down here," says Zelma in a voice that seems a little upbeat considering their circumstances, Virgil thinks.

"Yiiii!" says the couple, grabbing each other.

Virgil groans.

"If you could just give us a hand," Zelma goes on hurriedly. "We seem to have fallen in a grave? You know my grandmother Bee once said it was bad luck to step on a grave, but I thought it was just superstition. I guess there's a good reason behind every old wives' tale, huh?"

"Yiiiiiiiiii!" yells the couple, and they bolt.

"Well, for heaven's sake," says Zelma. "Young people!"

The faint sound of motors cranking up come through the monuments.

"Mrs. Wade!" says Virgil. "I think the grave side services must be over. Want to try to call now?"

"Well, OK," says Zelma. "I can only take so much you know." Then she takes a deep breath, "Oh, Mr. Grave Diggers! Yoo hoo. We need help now! Yoo hoo. (Come on, son, try to yell with me.) One, two three: YOO HOOOOO!"

∞

Daisy relishes the trail Virgil's crazy meemaw makes, as she winds her way around the Wade's living room. Meemaw has a high cackly laugh and a way of zeroing in and bothering the very people it seems wants her company the least. Right now, she has Daisy's sister Crystal and her husband R.C. cornered against the buffet. R.C. is a dentist, for God's sake, but no matter, Meemaw has her shoe off and her stocking pulled down showing the perverted swelling around the ankle of her little scrawny chicken foot, and asking medical advice. Crystal looks steamed and as pink as that Mary Kay Cadillac she drives.

Daisy almost has to laugh out loud every time she sees Crystal's pink Cadillac. Crystal sells Mary Kay Cosmetics when she takes time off from being a dentist's wife and the mother of two obnoxious teenagers and she has really made a killing.

But you'd think Crystal would repaint the thing at least, or trade it in on a BMW. But no, she is as happy with it as if she had received an Academy Award.

Daisy looks around and groans out loud. Their living room is stuffed with hungry mourners. Somehow Daisy's family has been chosen as headquarters for the funerary food. Tons of it has been arriving all day. People keep drifting in from the service and chawing down. Crystal and R.C. and Meemaw are joined by Janice, Daisy's other sister, and Roy, her husband. Roy is a chiropractor, and Daisy's mother often revels in the fact that both her daughters have snared doctors. Daisy snorts. Janice and Roy and Crystal and R.C. hug and slap backs and shake hands and kiss as if they didn't live in the same town and didn't see each other every week.

Crystal and Janice are as slick as owl shit Daisy thinks. Pee Wee and Zelma believe they have the perfect lives—their medical husbands, their aerobic classes, their recipe books, and their part-time jobs. "Look at them, sister," Pee Wee is fond of saying. "Your sisters live good, decent lives. They know what it's all about. They don't want the moon." Daisy has to laugh whenever he says that. Daisy believes her sisters are bored to death and don't know it.

Daisy looks at the spread of dishes so close together the top of their buffet is completely hidden. She passes everything by, however— the fried chickens, tomato aspics, potato salads, deviled eggs, the mystery casseroles—her sisters and their drippy husbands who call out to her, "HEY!"—and goes into the kitchen for a celery stalk.

Daisy sits down to eat in the breakfast nook that Zelma had built last year. She is bushed. Work schedules at Burger King and funerals just didn't mix. She leans back and bites into her celery. The seats in Zelma's nook are soft enough, but Daisy always feels a little spacey here— the curved, modish style in what is supposed to be cotton candy pink— Daisy wouldn't tell her mother this—remind her of Burger King booths. She feels like she is still at work or something. The breakfast nook job cost over two thousand dollars too, quite a price, Pee Wee likes to remind Zelma, for a family who never eats breakfast. Daisy's parents are always fighting about money.

Daisy runs a hand over the pink fake leather seats. The main problem with the kitchen is that the modern style corner is out-of-place in Zelma's old-fashioned kitchen. Pee Wee was too tight to buy a built-in oven, new appliances and everything. So Zelma just painted—the refrigerator, the stove, the cabinets. Pink.

Daisy's mother has the whole kitchen in Pepto Bismol pink— pink walls, pink curtains, pink refrigerator, pink and white tile floor, pink dishes in the pink cupboards, even pink Hefty garbage bags under the sink.

The noise from the living room is becoming louder. More people must be coming in. If there is one thing this town loves it's a funeral, because, except for Founder's Day, entertainment is scarce. Which is why Daisy herself has always had to go to extremes to keep herself from going batty. And which is why she can hardly wait to get her hands on some of Grandmother Bee's money her parents are sitting on and take off for a real college.

After Daisy refused to go to her mother and aunt's alma mater, and after she came home from Louisiana State University's branch, she had a big job convincing her parents to finally let her go to a school that taught the film. Finally they were reconciled, but only after it looked like to them Daisy was going to make a career of Burger King. Hard head parents! Daisy is applying at all kinds of places, but the place she wants to go to the most is in California—UCLA, where Vincent Price's son teaches. UCLA is on the other side of the moon to Daisy's parents.

Staying in the kitchen Daisy has been thinking maybe she can avoid boring conversation with everyone, but here Mrs. Lee is sticking her head in the door, brightening up, fakey fashion, when she sees Daisy. She comes on in, followed by her drippy daughter Terry.

"Well, here's DAY-ZEE, Terry SUE!" she sings. Women in Harrisonville always sing their words.

"Welllllll, girlllllll, how are youooooo?" Terry Sue is sort of an off-key soprano.

Daisy smiles what she calls her don't-fuck-with-me grin while they deposit two big Tupperware bowls in the pink refrigerator and sing their way out. "Your Uncle Ronald certainly looked good, Sweetie. They did a nice job, didn't they? Now, you'll have to come over to the house sometime, girlllllll."

What a class act those two could put on. Daisy has been up late watching old movies with Owen and she is a bit sleepy and in no mood to encourage any of these people even so she could laugh at them privately.

Last night she watched *The Philadelphia Story*, and *To Have and To Have Not* for the zillionth time.

Daisy and Owen plan to head out soon. She wants to register get going on her screenplay education and she imagines herself one day in a cozy bungalow like the one in *Play Misty*, somewhere on the California shores after she graduates and starts making money. She and Owen making Vietnam movies and other cool stuff. Owen, whose job—none—can be relocated anywhere, has a dream too. He believes there is a fortune in the Snow Cone business. And after years of thought, he also believes Snow Cones are the only business he can get into that doesn't plunder the planet. Owen's funny that way. How he'll worry about stuff like that, but, say, smoke cigarettes. The main thing is that, luckily, his dream, can be relocated anywhere.

Daisy is not exactly crazy about the thought of Owen being in Snow Cones. It's not that she sees anything intrinsically wrong with the business—Owen's explained it all, and showed her the figures and talked about the peanuts of start-up capital. It's just the whole enterprise reminds Daisy of the summer in her sophomore year after she got her driver's license and took a job driving an ice cream truck. That job was just a traumatic experience Daisy would just as soon forget, thank you.

Daisy had driven all summer in that ice cream truck, in 110 degree heat and at the top speed—fifteen miles per hour—listening to "Pop Goes The Weasel" eight hours a day. And now Daisy hates frozen confections of any type. Just looking at a fudge bar makes "Pop Goes the Weasel" start pounding in her brain.

She wouldn't tell Owen, of course. What is important is having a dream, and Snow Cones is his.

Besides, Owen will start with a stand, not a truck, and end up owning lots of stands, and after a while, Daisy will be in the film business anyway, and Owen can go into that with her, if he wants to, after he sees how successful she is.

Zelma's pink phone rings, but before Daisy can get up, it stops. Someone must have gotten it upstairs.

Lord, there must be people all over their house.

Just then Gloria Pettijean comes into the kitchen.

Gloria Pettijean is one of those curious people around

Harrisonville who is stuck up with absolutely no discernible reason to be. Oh, Gloria did think she was a fashion expert, but only someone from Harrisonville with such a big horsy face, who would just as soon strip herself naked in front of the First Baptist Church at high noon on Sunday as wear white shoes before Easter, would think spectator pumps, a matching pocketbook (as she called it), and double-knit, for God's sake, was high fashion.

In school Daisy distinguished herself by being sent home on a regular basis to change clothes. Daisy single-handedly introduced mood rings, gangland laces and clunky shoes to old Harrisonville Middle School. In high school, she was solely responsible for the addition to the Dress Code banning Spandex. As a senior, she made numerous black friends after she embraced the style of dressing known as hip-hop.

Daisy pops the last of her celery stick in her mouth. What is Gloria doing here anyway? It is spooky in this town, the way huge crowds show up for a funeral.

"Well, hey-ay, Daisy," sings Gloria. Gloria is famous for her theme parties and for being chosen to be the maid of honor at more weddings than anyone in the history of Harrisonville—a real honor these pathetic folks believe. Gloria always invites Daisy to her parties no matter how rude Daisy makes a point of being to her. But Daisy always gets the feeling Gloria enjoys looking at Daisy's clothes—for the wrong reasons. Gloria is staring at Daisy's long black T-shirt dress over her Burger King outfit right now with a now-what-are-we-wearing-today? expression.

"Gloria!" says Aunt Mattie, suddenly sweeping into the kitchen, carrying a piece of Chess pie as big as a Buick. "How ARE you, sweetie?"

"Just fine, I'm doing just fine, Mrs. Gibson," Gloria sings back.

"TELL me about your new job!" says Aunt Mattie. "I hear you're the new home extension agent?"

"That's right." Gloria flashes a proud look at Daisy from Burger King.

Oh, puh-leeze, thinks Daisy. Aunt Mattie and Zelma both, are obsessed with people who have college educations, boring jobs, and who plan to marry dull-ass people and live and die in Harrisonville.

"Hold on, dear." Mattie looks at Daisy and frowns. "Daisy? Have you seen your mother? No one saw her at the cemetery! Is she upstairs?"

Daisy thinks a minute.

"No, Aunt Mattie. I don't believe I have," Daisy says slowly. She doesn't tell Aunt Mattie, though, that it wouldn't take much to figure out what would make a good guess. The last time Daisy saw her, Zelma was talking about taking her own car to the cemetery so she could stop by Dawson's and look at some petit point on sale. Zelma is a compulsive shopping nut, but she never buys anything expensive, except for that once when she talked Pee Wee into the breakfast nook, so a sale is real hard for her to resist. Sales are a kind of a compromise to Pee Wee's being so tight. And Zelma is known to shop at the weirdest times, so Daisy isn't worried. Her mother had gone shopping when Janice was delivering her first baby. She went shopping when Grandma Bee was sitting in a lawyer's office donating her old Arkansas home place to the Hare Krishnas and the rest of the family was going crazy. She even went shopping when Janice's sons, Darryl and Jamie, on a visit to their aunt and uncle in Texas, were arrested at a souvenir store on Tasmanian Devil Street, and put in the Six Flags Over Texas Jail, and Janice and Roy had to drive to Texas to bring them home. Shopping is her mother's answer to anxiety. Probably Zelma just made herself so late that she was standing at edge of the funeral crowd, and then she went out shopping again.

Then Pee Wee bursts into the kitchen with, of all people, Courtney Wilson, Daisy's old best friend from high school—second cousin by marriage to Van Cliburn—of which she never let you forget. Courtney Wilson is carrying a fancy looking camera in one hand and a quart jar of something green in the other. She is the editor of the women's section of the *Harrisonville Times*. It is creepy the way everybody in Harrisonville insists on pictures of their families' funerals. Somebody must have prevailed upon her to record the event. As if poor old forgotten booze hound Uncle Ronald was a major part of the family.

Pee Wee looks upset. "Have you seen your mother, Sugar? Courtney here said Marilyn Biedenbeau was wondering why her car's still parked out at the cemetery. And Virgil Matthews's missing. Shelby said the funeral home called looking for him and now they just called here."

"Gee, I don't know, Pop," Daisy says. No use telling anyone now about her shopping theory.

"Somebody should go out there and look." Courtney has a low, business-like voice, one of the few women who didn't sing in Harrisonville, and at one time, she and Daisy used to knock around together all the time, but Daisy didn't like her now. Once, the summer of their junior year, Courtney accused Daisy of sleeping with her boyfriend, Randy Baker, while she was away at Space Camp. A thing that Daisy positively never did. But Daisy got mad at Courtney for her accusation—Randy Baker was not even good enough for Daisy. Courtney never forgave her for something that never happened.

"Well, let's go," says Pee Wee. "We taking Courtney's van 'cause Shelby and Addie are going. Wait! Hold it, everybody! I got to tell Lamar where we going. You out back, hon? Meet us out back, Daisy, if you going with us."

Courtney puts the jar on the table in front of Daisy. "I got to get my purse." She shoots Daisy The Hurt Look, and follows Pee Wee.

"Good heavens," Mattie says. "I do hope everybody's all right." Then she lowers her voice. "Is that Courtney's mother's chow chow? I'd throw it out, Precious. I love Lele, but her refrigerator's just filthy. You wouldn't believe."

The back door in the kitchen bangs open. It is Lorna Jean, looking all well fucked and Speed-guilty and then real dismayed that the first person she sees when she comes in the door is her mother. "Well, hey ever body." Then Lorna Jean turns pinker than Zelma's stove. "What's going on?"

ℂ

It is almost dusk and the locusts have come out louder than Virgil ever heard them. Their sound seems to be in the grave with them. Nighttime pulses somewhere just out of sight over the horizon and at least half of Virgil's body is completely numb. A persistent mosquito is buzzing in his left ear, and in his right, Zelma is saying, "It's really peaceful, you know. Look! Look! Lightning bug! One little lightning bug. There he goes again. Lord! When I was a child we had thousands of lightning bugs every night in our front yard. But where are they now? Pesticides got 'em probably. I believe that. Why, we used to put fifty of 'em in a

Mason jar and have a lightning bug lantern. Oh, pretty! It was really something."

Virgil blinks his eyes slowly and methodically, a habit he's picked up in the last few hours because his eyelashes seems to be the only part of his anatomy that he can still move. Except his mind seems to be moving around, like a panorama, focusing in on odd facts. Like the one that comes to him now: In China, at a funeral, when the coffin is about to be lowered into the grave, all the people lean back, scared their shadows will fall into the grave because that would be bad luck. The grave diggers and casket-carriers even tie their shadows to themselves with a cloth. And sometimes they bury folks at high noon in case one of the mourners, taking one last look or something, might fall in. And here Virgil was, right smack in the middle of a grave. Bad luck is right.

Virgil tries to move his numb left foot a hair, while stifling a groan. "Listen, son!" Zelma suddenly whispers fiercely.

A disembodied voice floats down to them, "Zellmaaa! Zellmaa!"

"Pee Wee," Zelma sighs. "Well, I'm not too picky right about now who saves me. Pee Wee! Oh, PEE WEE!"

Virgil calls out, "Help! Help!" but his voice sounds puny.

"Zelma! Zelma! Where are you?" It is Pee Wee all right.

Virgil has the feeling of dark shapes following him. In a second a crowd of faces are bent around their grave. Pee Wee. Harvey. Then Mattie. Lamar. Daisy. Shelby.

"Step back, step back!" Pee Wee hollers. "It could cave in any minute."

"Good grief!" Daisy's whooping.

"Ma'am? Mr. Matthews?" an unfamiliar female voice calls, and there is a flash blinding him. He almost doesn't catch the shadow of someone, coming up behind Daisy, whose face, behind the bubbles of light, is Lorna Jean's, all right.

Eight

"Ho! Virgil!"

Virgil looks down at his breakfast. His meemaw has fried him two lacy, sunny-side up eggs and three strips of well-done bacon. This was the way his Grandpa liked his breakfast when he was alive, Meemaw says, and although Virgil likes his eggs over-easy and his bacon limp, he has learned to eat it this way.

"HO! VIRGIL!"

Virgil puts his knife and fork on his plate. He sighs. Daisy is calling him. After yesterday, he is going to make it a point to avoid everybody. What could she want anyway? Why can't she leave him alone?

At the cemetery she laughed herself silly to see her mother's and Virgil's heads sticking out of the ground like that. Harvey explained later what happened and it was just what Virgil first suspected when Zelma disappeared. The old casket underneath deteriorated leaving a hollow cave. Then the right kind of rain and something heavy, like Zelma for instance, stepping on it at the right time caused it to cave in. "Happens more than we like to think," Harvey said. Though Harvey didn't come out and say it, Virgil gets the feeling Harvey blames him for the whole catastrophe.

"Hey, DOCTOR DEATH!"

Meemaw looks at him. "Listen to that," she says, waving a wooden spoon at him menacingly.

"OK, Meemaw," says Virgil. Meemaw's mole-colored eyes gleam at him.

"Virgil," Shelby calls from the patio. "Daisy's hanging over the fence hollering at you."

Shelby is working on a new version of his squirrel-proof bird feeder. He has been working on it for years, and for years they have the fattest, healthiest squirrels in town. And the most squirrels.

Virgil goes out and passes through the patio where Shelby is sitting in the middle of pieces of Plexiglas and wooden shingles and springs and sprockets, muttering to himself, something like, "Squirrel A pokes nose in here, see. Then he disengages point B. Point C drops, automatically resetting..."

Daisy is waving at him over the honeysuckle. She is wearing a burgundy vest and what looks like one of Pee Wee's dress shirts.

"Did you see this?" She waves the morning newspaper at him, and then holds it still for him to see. He reaches slowly for it. On the front page, the feature story's headline: MAN AND WOMAN TRAPPED IN CAVE-IN. Underneath that is a picture of Zelma suspended in midair as she is being hoisted out of the grave, and Virgil's own head sticking out of the ground, as a small crowd looks on, the most recognizable face, his own, banjo-eyed, staring in dismay. One of the Gibson's cousins, a newspaper reporter for the *Times*, had joined the search party. She just happened to have her camera with her. Virgil groans. Harvey will love this.

"Ho, what a trip!" Daisy says.

Daisy obviously thinks the whole thing is entertainment. Virgil stares at the picture, too gutless to read the story. He imagines Lorna Jean bending her blonde head over the morning paper, too. He sees her laugh. Virgil, beyond mortification, sighs.

"Don't worry about it, Virgil. You'll live it down."

Daisy's eyes look like they are outlined by a Black Magic Marker. She waggles her eyebrows like Groucho Marx. Then she sticks a purple running shoe up on the gate and starts retying a lace. What does she mean by that? Like she knows about his craziness for Lorna Jean. Like she is reading his mind or something.

It is too early in the morning for Daisy Wade. It is too early for anything today.

"Look," says Daisy. "Don't sweat it. Besides, Lorna Jean doesn't know funny from Adam."

Virgil stares at the girl who is famous for turning an ordinary softball into an impossible hardball for four years and striking out more hitters than in the whole history of Jefferson High. Good grief! How—?

"If you want my advice, I'd drop it anyway."

Virgil swallows, hard. "Daisy," he says, carefully. "What are you talking about?"

"Lorna Jean. You in love with her, right?"

"Naw!" he hears himself squawk.

"Ha. Just as I thought. I knew it! I knew it because I see you looking at her all the time. At the funeral, the wake—all the time. And every time she comes over, you hide out behind the chicken house and spy on us," she adds, shattering him.

Virgil tries to smile. Then he tries to smile harder. He tries to smile like he is humoring Daisy. Like he has not felt his face turn into the death gray of stone. Funny how he thought he was miserable earlier. It is nothing like this! God! Behind the chicken house! Cool!

Virgil turns his head to see if Shelby is paying any attention to them. He is peering into his squirrel feeder, scratching his head. "I'm not—I mean—" Virgil has lost his breath. "Aw," he manages. "You crazy."

Daisy hops up on the fence that Meemaw and Zelma has told her hundreds of times in the last three years to stay down off of. Then she says, "Give it all up, Virgil. Lorna Jean honestly thinks she's going to marry that clown Speed. Listen. I know this jerk. Lorna Jean just refuses to look at Speed for the scuz he is. Always gone—to show that dog, or to throw ducks for somebody, or to watch a dog trial—only does that so he can suck up and get to know the judges."

Virgil tries to look uninterested. "Why," he says, in what he hoped is a mystified voice, "are you telling me all this?"

"Not interested?"

"Well, naw. I guess not," Virgil lies. Almost true. He feels so flattened from yesterday's interring, he is not as interested as he would have been, say, last week.

"Well, my cousin is just too stupid. So forget her. If she marries Speed, Aunt Mattie's going to have kittens, I'll tell you that. Know what he does for a living?"

"Naw," says Virgil, adding in his mind, Lorna Jean is not stupid! Daisy can irritate the devil.

"Neither does anybody. He used to drive people to Mexico for Laetrile treatments or weird operations like hair transplants or sex changes. Experimental stuff."

"Ha!" says Virgil, like he believes that is funny. But poor Lorna Jean!

"And once a traveling circus paid him to drive a truck load of white leopards up to Fayetteville and abandon them downtown. Publicity stunt. Lord knows what he does now!

"Old Lorna Jean's problem is she never knows what's going on! HA! Every since we were kids she always thought her naturally curly blonde hair was her ticket to the world. If I had blonde hair, I'd try to be like Grace Kelly—" Daisy puts her hand on her forehead dramatically. She drops her hand and snorts, "Lorna Jean's more like a dumb Doris Day or is that redundant?"

Virgil knows Lorna Jean's parents believe old movies have warped Daisy's mind. Has made her weird. Right now, he thinks they are right. A lot of times, Daisy may as well be speaking Ancient Sanskrit to him.

"What I want to know is, how does he know Douglas? How did they get up each other's ass?"

Come to think of it, at the funeral home, Virgil has seen Speed what could only be called a lot lately. "I don't know," he tells Daisy, depressed, suddenly real tired even though it was just morning. "Why do you care?"

"Just curious. Lorna Jean wanted to know. Well. If you don't know, you don't know. I told Lorna Jean you were in another world, anyway. Got to run. Ta." Daisy hops down.

"Virgil!" bellows Meemaw, who has slipped out into the yard behind him. "Would you look at this. We got some little tomatoes on these vines!"

After supper, Virgil sits with his meemaw and Shelby and watches the *CBS Circus of the Stars on TV.* Sarah Michelle Gellar, as the ringmaster, wears a cute top hat and a little bitty tuxedo with her boobs taking up most of the screen. Virgil hates it if anything sexy happens on TV when Shelby and Meemaw are in the room. Meemaw always snorts, "Haw, haw," and Shelby just sits there with the same blank expression on his face as if he is watching *Gunsmoke* reruns or *The Wide World of Sports.* It just seems so bazaar to have Shelby and Meemaw in the same room with Sarah and her breasts.

Like right now, Shelby has his feet stuck on his automatic foot massager. It makes a low noise, barely audible over the circus music, like a weak, faraway dentist drill. The massager softly hums and moves around Shelby's feet, which have huge, clear-yellow, big toe corns that Shelby often tries, but never ultimately succeeds, to saw off with his pocketknife. Shelby's foot massager can be used for other parts of the body, too. Sometimes Shelby puts it on his head for a headache, or on his back. It looks like a cloth bag with giant snails in it trying to figure a way out. When Virgil stares at it too long, with the humps rising and falling, and squeezing and humming, it starts to look a little obscene.

After *Circus of the Stars,* the old *Cheers* rerun comes on when everybody in the bar thinks Cliff has murdered his mother. Carla wants to break into his house to look for clues. Virgil has already seen that one.

"I don't get it," Meemaw says, every two minutes like she always does during comedies, but nobody bothers to explain the jokes, which really aren't too funny to Virgil, either.

It seems to Virgil life is like a situation comedy. But nobody doing the laughing is in the comedy. They just do all the suffering for someone else to laugh at. Virgil guesses it is pretty strange for a grown person to hide out behind a chicken house and spy on people. He guesses it is pretty laughable. Lorna Jean probably sees him as a stupid kid.

Virgil turns over in his mind the things Daisy said about Speed. He wishes Daisy would go on over and explain to Lorna Jean what a jerk Speed is. What is she waiting for? Virgil has no doubt what she tells him today is true. Not many people know this, but Daisy has dated Speed. Virgil knows because he saw Speed pick up Daisy a few times. Of course, that was a long time ago in high school. Virgil sighs out loud and turns it into a yawn. Not that Meemaw and Shelby notice.

After a while, Shelby, Meemaw, and Mike Hammer are snoring. Virgil gets up.

He reaches over and flicks the switch off to put Shelby's snails out of their misery. Then he goes upstairs.

In his bed, Virgil rolls over, punches his pillow, and deflowers Lorna Jean a few times in a circus setting. Behind the lion cage. He is the star bareback rider of the circus, even though Virgil has never been on a horse in his life. Lorna Jean is the tightrope walker. Her costume is so skimpy, it is nothing to get off.

Nine

Hugging the shoreline between the Clyde Fant Parkway and the river, Virgil steers along the bike path with one hand, the other helping steady an old briefcase on his knee Shelby had once attempted to reinvent with a couple goofy amenities. It is more bulky than heavy—Virgil having ripped out Shelby's improvements, an ice-crusher and a shoe-shine kit from the false bottom. But even with only a notebook in it, on the bike, it is still hard to handle. And Virgil is hot. Meemaw's outdoor thermometer read 86 degrees at seven that morning. Probably it is closer to a hundred right now, in the middle of the day's raw sunshine. Or maybe over a hundred with the heat index. In his suit, Virgil sweats, blows out his breath, pumps methodically, and prays. He always prays that nobody he knows, especially Lorna Jean, of course, will see him on a bicycle.

Next to the bike path are dead cottonwoods and giant pines, smothered to death by the tangle of kudzu, which cover every inch of them. They rise like huge green monsters, their arms waving tatters of leaves and vines in some way-up half-assed breeze, not a speck of which drifts closer to earth. As he pumps along Virgil spots stuff like beer bottles, oil cans, candy wrappers, an armless baby doll in the still, dusty Johnson grass. A drop of sweat worries the end of his nose, but every time he jerks his head to make it fall, another one starts down from his scalp to take its place. The sweat drips down his suit sleeves, and onto his palms and fingers, still sore from yesterday's stitching. The sweat stings, and Virgil moans under his breath, for more reasons than that. Harvey has given Virgil yet another responsibility—collecting the monthly burial insurance policy payments from the insured around town who couldn't or wouldn't mail them in. He is on his way now to call on a future Beloved One.

Gradually, the path crowds with taller weeds and then altogether poops out—first the thin macadam goes, then the narrow thread of packed dirt, until Virgil is pedaling over alligator brambles and sticky weeds. Finally the river veers to he right and Virgil pumps out of the woods onto a decrepit old street. Shotgun houses line both sides. Some have boarded up windows and more than one has advertisements nailed up for siding: RED MAN CHEWING TOBACCO. BLACK DRAUGHT. Virgil has to squint his eyes at one real old faded one: IMPEACH EARL WARREN. Now where has he heard that name before? History class? Somewhere.

Old cars begin to line the street with jacked-up chassis. Nobody is in sight. Virgil gets off and begins pushing his bike. A stickiness in the air makes him dizzy, that and the gray and green street shimmering with heat waves.

None of the houses seem to be numbered. Some are boarded up where nobody could be. But down a piece, a half-starved dog slinks under one's pilings, a pots-and-pans' noise comes from a second, a set of new bamboo fishing poles lean against another. Virgil takes a deep breath and counts the houses on the left. The street address is useless. No wonder Harvey says the fourth house on the left after you turn pass the first intersection.

Virgil stops at the fourth house. He takes a deep breath and walks into the yard. He leans his bike up against an old refrigerator and climbs onto a porch which gives under his weight. Next to the door is a washtub full of Coke bottles, and a three-legged dining room chair. What puzzles Virgil is that somebody from here is buying a burial policy from Harvey. Douglas says there has never been a colored-person Beloved One at the Harrisonville Funeral Home except for the porter's great uncle. Usually black funerals aren't for a week or so after the death, because the wakes are so long. Just isn't good business, as Harvey sees it, to tie up the staterooms like that.

Virgil knocks lightly on the saggy screen door, and the inside door creaks open so quickly he jumps. Through a rusty screen, an Arawak shrunken head regards him. "Are you Jehovah's Witness?" a high old voice says.

Virgil stares. It isn't an Arawak. It is a white woman—living in an old half-abandoned black section of town. Then it strikes him. Ethel Mae Landsbury! It is *the* Ethel Mae Landsbury that has come from being a rich lady in a big house to a poor lady that had to move in with her maid. Virgil has heard about her all his life! For heaven's sake. The maid died and Ethel Mae still lives in the old falling down house.

"Naw," he says. Ethel Mae is about Meemaw's size, a little old shriveledy lady with fuzzy patchwork-colored hair. She clutches a frazzled pink bathrobe around her and squints at Virgil. "Naw," says Virgil again. "I'm just looking for Ethel Mae Landsbury."

"Who's asking?" the old woman says with spunk. Virgil moves closer to the door. A cicada has hung its skin on the screen, and Virgil peers around it.

"Virgil Matthews, Harrisonville Funeral Home."

"Oh, come on in, sonny." The screen opens. "Y'all a little late this month, aren't you?"

"Guess so," says Virgil, stepping inside. Some oily-sweet smell clings to the air.

"Are you Harvey L. Sloan's son?" says Ethel Mae Landsbury. Behind her a faded Mardi Gras Queen of Rex flag hangs on one wall.

"Naw," says Virgil. "I just work there." In her pre-need plan, Mrs. Landsbury asked that she be buried facing the direction of New Orleans.

"Keep your job!" says the woman, suddenly, startling Virgil. "Because you don't know when you're going to get another one!"

"Right," says Virgil. He puts Harvey's briefcase on a chair, a mate to the three-legged one on the porch and takes out a notebook. Actually he doesn't need a briefcase at all, but he thought just carrying a notebook around makes him look like he is still in high school. Virgil says, "Ten dollars and eighty-three cents, please." Then he picks out the receipt from the back and makes it out.

Mrs. Landsbury is already ahead of him. She hands him an envelope out of the bureau that stands right in the living room.

"It's always ten dollars and eighty-three cents."

Virgil hands her a receipt.

"Harvey Sloan sick?" she says, taking the slip.

"Naw," says Virgil. "He's just busy."

"Too rich, you mean," says Mrs. Ethel Mae Landsbury.

In a few minutes he is pedaling down the street, the briefcase bumping on his knee. Two oldish fat women in T shirts and short shorts stand at the end of the street exchanging the time of day.

"Hey, Honky," yells one. "You Jehovah's Witness?"

"Naw," says Virgil, pedaling away, "I ain't."

ဆ

The next person Virgil has to collect a pre-need payment from was Mrs. Bristol, who lives downtown across from the courthouse. Virgil doesn't know Mrs. Bristol, but he knows about her. He parks his bike in front of an iron gate and walks up the path to the front door. Mrs. Bristol lives in a raised-piling house, flanked with latticework and an old timey porch, which wraps around three sides. Shelby told Virgil that she is the governor's second cousin. Mrs. Bristol has KILLER FOR HIRE every month and Shelby says that she once told him her family history while he was burning catalpa worm nests—not normally a KILLER FOR HIRE job—out of her catalpa trees.

Virgil rings the bell for several minutes before he finally notices a little penciled sign tacked up that says the bell is out of order. The door opens after he knocks another good five minutes.

"Ha," says a voice from a cloud of platinum hair that is standing straight up in a crazy way, the way Virgil remembers how a picture of Einstein looked in his science book. "I told you—I'm canceling that blasted paper. Nothing but crap. Sheer crap. So buzz off, sonny. You're not getting my $11.35 cents again."

Virgil stares. He is floored. "Ah, ah, ah--" he says, "I'm not—not—uh, the paper boy."

"Oh, selling magazines, huh? Well, you can just get out of here too. Are you the same young man who couldn't find my tulip bulbs?"

"No, ma'am," says Virgil desperately. "I'm Virgil Matthews. Harrisonville Funeral Home. Harvey Sloan sent me. For your pre-need easy payment plan?"

"Harvey Sloan! That ghoul!" says the crazy hair. "Well, come in, sonny."

Virgil steps into a dark foyer, and before his eyes adjusts to the dark, Mrs. Bristol seems to have disappeared.

"I'll be right back," her voice calls from the shadows.

Virgil looks around. The foyer is crammed with wicker furniture and chests and ferns and old photographs, like maybe it is some storage room or something. The photographs are brown, in round brown frames of olden times people. They are all over the walls, and all over the wicker tables. Mostly they are couples or plain single people, but one is of a pilot who is wearing a flying cap like Snoopy's. He goes up closer to look at that one.

"You like caps?" says Mrs. Bristol, so near his elbow that he almost jumps.

"Caps?" says Virgil, thinking she means the cap in the picture.

"CATS! C-A-T-S! CATS!" hollers Mrs. Bristol.

"Yeah," says Virgil. "Yes, ma'am."

Mrs. Bristol hands him a check. "Come on, then," she says. "Come see my baby."

Mrs. Bristol tugs open some French doors.

In a bedroom off the hall is a huge old yellow cat lying on a bed who takes one look at Virgil and jumps onto a dresser and into an open closet--two bounces and there he sits up on the highest shelf.

"Mr. Whiskers!" yells Mrs. Bristol. "Dang. Here, son," she says handing him something.

Virgil sticks out his hand and when he looks down he sees a huge oblong yellow pill.

"Mr. Whiskers!" yells Mrs. Bristol again. "Here's a nice boy to give you your medicine." Then she says in a loud whisper to Virgil, "If you could just pop this into Mr. Whisker's mouth before you go, I know an old woman who would truly appreciate it."

"Well, gee, I don't know," says Virgil. He has a feeling he has been in this house a long, long time.

"I'll go get the step ladder," says Mrs. Bristol, like she doesn't even hear him.

She comes back hauling a step ladder which she opens and sets down on the floor of the closet. The ladder seems to lean to one side.

Virgil steps on the bottom rung tentatively. Mr. Whiskers looks down from his perch. He looks Virgil right in the eye and lifts his yellow cat lip and slowly curls it over his top teeth.

Virgil steps up onto the top rung and grabs hold of the clothes bar for support. "Here, kitty," he says weakly. He can feel the ladder swaying underneath him.

"I got the ladder," Mrs. Bristol says from below. "Go ahead, Sonny. Shoot."

Virgil reaches up. Mr. Whiskers lays his ears flat against his head and bares his long yellow cat teeth. This real ticked-off moaning snarl comes out of him.

Virgil reaches up higher. "Here, kitty, kitty," he whispers. "Open up, kitty."

"Yowwwwww," says Mr. Whiskers. His yellow eyes turn dark amber.

"Kitty, kitty," Virgil says louder, reaching up. "Come on, nice kitty."

Then Mr. Whiskers springs right on top of Virgil's head, and sinks his teeth into the hand Virgil reached up to grab at him with, and using one side of Virgil's face for traction, bounds away. At that second the ladder gives way and Virgil falls in a heap of clothes and coats and mothball smells.

"Lord," says Mrs. Bristol, who must have managed to jump out of the way. "I do hope you planning to put all that back."

❧

"The truth is," Harvey is saying, "folks are less interested in Passing Over than they used to be." Then he reads from his clipboard, "Bra-molds, Post-Mortem Form Restoration, twenty-five."

Virgil peers at one of the stacks of boxes and starts counting. "Twenty-five," he says, a few minutes later.

"Good," says Harvey. "Let's see...Vari-Pose Head Rests, fifty boxes of ten each."

"Here," says Virgil. "Edwards Vari-Pose Head Rests." *For the discriminating dermasurgeon,* he reads to himself before he begins counting. *Dermasurgeon!* Virgil thinks Douglas has been saying *demi-surgeon all this time.*

They are in the large storeroom, where shelves of stuff line the walls, and where, during the week, new supplies are unloaded and counted. A large shipment arrived yesterday and Virgil and Harvey are checking it in—something that is supposed to be done before the deliveryman leaves, but that someone has neglected to do. Actually, that person is Virgil, but Douglas forgot to tell him, so Harvey is helping him get it all straight. Harvey seems to have forgotten about the cemetery incident. Virgil is glad because he worries Harvey is having second thoughts about him being an apprentice.

Harvey is in a talkative mood today. He bends over and moves some Plaster of Paris around on one of the lower shelves to make more space. "The problem is," he is saying, "Harrisonville is getting too large to respect Passing On. Can you imagine that, son? Twenty years ago, when farming and church was all folks had much, a funeral had a, ah, certain respectful quality. I'm afraid that's beginning to be a thing of the past. It's a ssssad thing..."

"Fifty," says Virgil, hoping he's counting right. Harvey is in a talkative mood, and philosophical mood, too, ever since a double cremation that morning. By his own admission, cremations depress Harvey. Virgil knows just how he feels.

"Fifty. Check," says Harvey. "Now. Repose Blocks, thirty boxes of fifteen each." Harvey goes over and sits down at the big metal desk, a lot different than his huge old, executive walnut desk in the plushy office upstairs. Above this metal desk hangs a weird pin-up calendar from Echols Cosmetic Tints that Virgil hates: A young woman Beloved One, completely naked, lies on a heart-shaped bier above the advice: "Each month completely review your stock. Order your supplies!"

Virgil always tries not to look at the Echols' lady in full repose, with her unusually long blonde hair at least attempting some kind of cover-up in places, but it is hard. It is worse than the one in the laundry room. That one, from Primero Chemicals, shows a picture of a little boy, Edward P. Walker, age five, at play. Underneath the picture the information is, "Perfect appearance for as long as two months. Primero is tops." Edward is embalming a doll. Edward creeps Virgil out.

Harvey rattles a few papers and then he says, "If you ask me, the problem lies in the fact that disease is beginning to be so efficiently taken care of. Folks just live longer than they used to and they expect to live longer. Live birth rates are up. Children survive normal childhood diseases. Nobody has to think about Passssing Over on a daily basis."

Virgil loses his count.

"And folks are getting into newfangled ideas about Passing Over and dying. Wanting things ssensible and low-priced—like they don't even care about the Beloved Ones. Showing respect, I mean. And those Living Wills, and putting everything in writing. Talking about rights for the dead! The Bereaved Ones always following along with their wishes more times than not. Then this business of finding cheaper caskets on the Internet. Shipped to us COD overnight! And we have to take them. Like heathen. And this trend toward cremation!" Harvey shudders. "Ain't natural."

Virgil wants to mention that actually primitive societies had quite elaborate rituals, and sometimes totally effective preparation, but he doesn't want to interrupt. Harvey rarely talks to him longer than to give him instructions, except he did fuss at him a little about the microphone. He still isn't real happy with Virgil's and Zelma's live burial, either, which, Virgil thinks, in all fairness, isn't at all his fault.

Harvey usually just moves quietly through the halls and chapels of the Harrisonville Funeral Home like the High Priest of the Necropolis—the only person allowed to come and go when he wants. In ancient Greece, everybody else who works there has to live in the Necropolis for life.

"Rights!" says Harvey, disgustedly. "A Bereaved One has only the rights the living give him."

Virgil thinks about that. Harvey can sound so profound. He would have been the very highest High Priest of the legal tribunal in Egypt that decided if the right to burial should be granted. "Weighing the Heart of Anubis," was what it was called. If the Beloved One was of good character, everything worked out and he got a rich, decent funeral. If not, if the weighing went the other way, the unfortunate deserved burial in a common grave pit. Virgil wonders what kind of funeral he deserves after making so many mistakes. He sighs and starts counting over.

"*All* the Beloved Ones deserve the finest, Virgil. Remember that. All funerary service is art, all the Beloved Ones potential artwork, and everyone deserves the finest art. But not an easssy medium. Oh no, Virgil. You know that by now. But the mossst rewarding... Ready?"

Virgil nods. "Thirty," he says, knowing he is screwing up. It is hard to think about so many things at once. The legal tribunal, thirty Repose Blocks...Then there's the pain from yesterday's cat scratches making his face stiff...

"It's rewarding because we hold the key to it all. Eternity. Resurrection. Because of that, any damage must be rectified. We are not, any of us, at the mercy of violence, of aging, of natural flaws. But too, too much is changing. No one really cares about the sanctity of the reposing body. Now human tissue is invaluable simply because of what it can reveal. And what it can do. Now then, thirty Throop Foot Positioners."

"One," Virgil begins, after he finds the stack.

"Even," Harvey—

Oh no, thinks Virgil.

"Even the clothing of the mourners, for instance. They used to wear heavy black with hats, in the very old days, that is. For the funeral— sashes, hat bands of lovely black crepe. Today, it's leisure suits, and God knows what else. However, I'm thinking of some kind of uniform, for the staff..." He interrupts himself, and says as if he just remembers it, "All our new coaches, those we buy from now on, will be replaced with dove gray, powder blue, even a rather giddy green—ah...keeping up with the times, but..."

Twenty. Twenty-one. Virgil can't help thinking of funerary colors of the world—black for Christians, white for China and Japan, blue or violet in Turkey, a few sorrowful grays and browns here and there—but he doesn't know if Harvey will be interested, so he keeps quiet. Harvey probably knows all that stuff anyway. Privately, Virgil thinks cheerier colors might be a nice touch though, like the new casket linings coming in lately. Five-six—

"And!" says Harvey, so wrapped up in his subject he isn't noticing how slow Virgil is. Harvey turns in the swivel chair, and drops his voice confidentially. "Some overly practical consumers are actually setting up Memorial Co-op Societies with their own facilities." When he says that Harvey looks a little giddy green himself. He also looks really sad. Then his face hardens and he whispers, staring into space over Virgil's head, "Restrictive legislature. It's the only answer."

"One—"

"How coarse to be concerned with money at a time like that! How crass!"

Virgil couldn't agree more. One— On the other hand, there is old Mrs. Ethel Mae Landsbury over in the Bottoms. With what she is paying, she is only going to get a bargain brand funeral. Poorer Egyptians, Virgil remembers, had to use the awful tanning process similar to leather treatment. That fact always makes *him* sad.

"And cremation!" says Harvey. "I do it, of course, for the depraved individuals who insist. And if their Beloved One's shells are one day sought by divine powers to live another life, their prepared whole bodies summoned, and there *are* none, what will they do for the Divine Recall, for that Great Recycling Center in the Sky? That is my argument to them, anyway."

"Thirty Foot Throop Positioners," says Virgil, giving up. "I mean, thirty Throop Foot Positioners."

"Check. Check." Then Harvey starts to choke on his words for a second. "Some—some totally deranged ones actually envision an enormous human compost heap where Beloved Ones will be plowed under, after being planted like naked seeds, unretouched by the advances of science, the comfort of ritual. Where they'll become, eventually, compost for gardens in parks and public places—first will be ground into powder, then stuffed into paper sacks, and merrily sped on their way—not only to parks and such, but even to this godless nation's farmlands. And hospitals will be the worse! Hospitals with their very own incinerators. No period of bereavement. The newly deceased will be thrown into chutes! Like laundry, dropped immediately, without fanfare, when the ceasing of all vital signs is ascertained, into—Harvey paused and then almost chokes again, "conflagration. What a waste, my boy. A waste. It is up to us, even if most families don't care to buy respect any more, to keep this great industry operating, however we can, so that the few who do want the palatial ceremony, well, will be able to do so."

Suddenly Harvey looks over and glares at Virgil like he is mad at him. "I've heard one day bodies might be launched to the moon in regular deliveries and unceremoniously dumped. Then after decomposition, the sacred, enriched moon dust will be used for, for—" and here Harvey almost spits, "food production!"

Virgil is horrified. He dreams the wave of the future will be cryonics. Or at the worse, keeping the body preserved well enough until, he hopes, all that religious stuff comes true.

"It's the immediate present, though, that one has to contend with, Virgil. We must rise, must we not, to the demands of the times? And the trend is away from the fancy funeral, the custom-made casket, and on toward—what? Uninterested relatives and the economy service! Human tissue for DNA testing! Eye banks! Blood, hair, placenta collected for research! The seeds of change have been sewn! Developments in biotechnology have pointed the way for today's sad but true path!"

Harvey starts talking in his normal voice. "It was a good, good profession, Virgil. It was lifetime security. To say that it was a lucrative profession would be a grievous understatement. More importantly, the funeral administrator was a leader in the community. He was a force against the darker forces—but—oh, well, never mind. We must do what we have to do. If we, the funeral industry are called to be a link between the immortality of our Beloved Ones and the genetics companies or whatever, we must answer the call! And if some can benefit others who wish to carry on a fine tradition, well, here, here!" Harvey pauses and clears his throat. "Ah, are you...are you aware, Virgil, of Douglas' position on the matter?"

Virgil looks up. Matter? What matter? "Uh, I ah, no, that is— What did you say? Excuse me?"

"Commodifying the body. That matter. There is no, at this time, constitutionally protected property interest in a dead relative. Is this good? Or do we know?" Harvey sighs. "Ah. Well. You should talk to him sometimes. Fine young man, Douglas. Perhaps you need some reading material, Virgil, so that you can see the drift of this great art of ours. Now let's turn to the brighter moment, shall we? Virgil? Fifty Armstrong Face

Form and Dental Replacers?"

Virgil leans over the last pile of boxes. His head, his cat chewed hand are on fire. Harvey sounds as though the funeral profession is what has died. As though it is already dead. Poor, poor Harvey. *One-two-three*—The main desire of the early Egyptian had been to keep the body from touching the earth. *One-two*—early Chinese could not die peacefully unless they had their coffins—caskets—built already and they were sitting beside their deathbeds. *Three. Four.* Clay sarcophaguses for some. Reeds. Mats. Skins. Baskets. Anything, but dirt.

Ten

C-c-collateral," says Harvey L. Sloane. "Pure and simple." Virgil is easing the camcorder into its box for its resting-place in Harvey's office closet. He doesn't know how to work it right and is always half-afraid he is going to break the thing. Today he has taped a Beautiful Memory Souvenir Video at the Moose Lodge out on Highway 167 where a Beloved One spent most of his time before his last hour. The background music for his video had been the theme from *Rocky*. Videotapes are Harvey's latest idea. In addition to taping the Beloved One's favorite places, the video includes snapshots of childhood interspersed with pictures of national monuments such as Niagara Falls and the Grand Canyon.

"The h-h-hell I will," says Harvey. He is talking to his lawyer on the phone. "The body is ssstill in the basement of my business and will stay there until I am paid."

Harvey is suing the family of James McDavid, 80, who died February 28, 1995, on the charges his family owes him $6,506.95.

"I'm prepared to keep him for eternity if I need to," says Harvey. Virgil has seen Mr. McDavid, who has lain, Douglas said, the last thirteen years in the old refrigeration of the basement now turned down to meat locker freezing that used to be used before Harvey got the new roll-out drawers on second floor.

It seems odd to Virgil the Bereaved Ones couldn't scrape up the money somewhere, but in a way it is a little exciting. It is almost like cryonics.

Virgil shuts the door of the closet and picks up the clipboard for his next assignment. Autopsy! Just his day. Then Virgil stares. Wait a minute. He had the last autopsy! What was Douglas trying to pull here? He was giving himself all the closed caskets and Virgil all the open caskets and autopsies. For every one autopsy Virgil does, Douglas does three un-autopsied. Why is he hogging everyone easy? Maybe Virgil should ask Harvey. Of course, it is too late, anyway. He saw Douglas leaving with Speed Maxwell just a few minutes ago.

"I told them I would but that they'd have to pay me before I buried him because they had absolutely no insurance in any shade or form for the deceased," Harvey is saying. "I have made enormous efforts to gain my remuneration both before and after the services, but it became gradually apparent to me they never had no intention of paying." Then the lawyer must have said something that Harvey liked. He laughs in kind of a mean way, Virgil thinks.

"Good," says Harvey. "I'll see them in court, then." He hangs up the phone, notices Virgil, and looks up at him impatiently. "Problem?"

"Naw," says Virgil, changing his mind suddenly. He goes on out.

∞

"STAND BY YOUR MAN," Tammy Wynette belts out over the duotronic hum.

"Don't forget I get $150 extra for an infected body," Douglas is saying over his shoulder to the morgue person when Virgil looks up.

The morgue person is dressed in green scrub pants and shirt and he is holding a Vlasic pickle bucket that Virgil knows is probably intestines and stuff. He is flashing the bird behind Douglas with his other hand.

The morgue person sets the bucket down. "I don't fool with

paperwork," he says. "Y'all have to remind somebody else, dude." Virgil looks back down. Morgue people are mean.

Virgil bites his lip because the Beloved One, who he thought he'd aspirated thoroughly, makes one last little sigh when he leans on him just a bit to replace the trocar. Unnerving, Virgil thinks. Virgil is constantly being unnerved in this place.

Beside him, in identical mask and gloves, is another apprentice who started a few weeks after Virgil was moved to the daytime shift. He is humming along with the radio and stitching a mile a minute. Austin.

Austin is a college guy, a pre-med student, and he has this confident, slap dash way of doing things that bothers Virgil sometimes. He likes to turn up the radio loud and race, for instance, to see who can finish stitching the fastest. And he isn't as good as he thinks he is. To be honest, his stitches aren't as little as they could be. And when Harvey is not around, Austin copies Douglas by not suiting up. Douglas doesn't suit up because he is so good he never makes a mistake, but if Harvey catches Austin he will be mad. And last week, in a procession, Virgil riding shotgun, Austin turned the coach down the wrong street, and they went down some little side street and then onto another, a long, round-about way to the cemetery about five miles out of the way. The whole procession followed at this kind of faithful, snail-crawl. Virgil had been shocked. If he'd known Austin didn't know the way around town, he would have directed him, but suddenly Austin hung a left, and you just can't turn a procession around in somebody's driveway. They went about twenty blocks out of the way. Through neighborhoods. With people gawking. Pointing. Yelling. Just thinking about it makes Virgil turn red. And Harvey yelled at who? Virgil. And Austin hadn't even been bothered by any of it. Or made it clear that he'd been driving. "Bummer," he said cheerfully. Austin is kind of a younger Douglas, but not as smart or something.

Worst of all, yesterday, when Virgil comes in the two had run out of stuffing for an autopsy and were filling a Beloved One with stuff they took out of the Lost and Found: gloves, galoshes, a raincoat, old empty embalming fluid bottles—even a sack of chitlins and the funny papers. And laughing about it. That kind of stuff just burns Virgil up.

Right now, Virgil's throat feels scorched like it always does but usually not until the end of the day. Autopsies are the pits. For an autopsied

Beloved One, real fine stitches have to be made so nothing will leak. If you do it right, it always gives you blisters. A thing about autopsied Beloved Ones is that they were, or were supposed to be, packed. For absorption. This particular Beloved One has PVC pipes in his legs too. He is a bone tissue donor. Virgil notices they have been getting a lot of bone marrow donors lately. The synthetic stuffing had come in early this morning, thank heaven. Using birdseed was good only in a pinch.

Douglas comes over to them and says above the radio, "Y'all just wasting yall's time sewing them two up." He rattles a paper he is holding. "Crematory. All y'all have to do is take the pacemaker out of Mr. Nobles. And make sure you don't forget and leave it in and blow the whole place up."

Virgil looks down at the work he has already done. An hour wasted. He rubs his sore, cat bit fingers. Virgil has never removed a pacemaker. It is real dangerous to leave them in before they go into the retort. Douglas already told him how lithium batteries could blow a place up, and to be real careful about finding out that kind of stuff.

"Shit, man," says Austin. "Some jerk put 'burial' on the cock-a-doody clipboard!"

Virgil looks at Austin. Sometimes he does have a way of putting things.

Douglas walks out whistling to KQAJ.

"Would you believe that joker?" says Austin. He throws his needle down. "Well, nobody else better die today. No, sir. I'm through. No dying! I double dog dare you! The kitchen is closed, man. Got that?" He leans down over his Beloved One's ear, a university professor, who had come home recently to live with his mother after he found he had been carrying around a brain tumor. "Understand Rubber Band? Kaput. Finis. I've had it."

Austin straightens up and rips off his mask. "In fact," he says, "I'm going to take a little break." And he walks out, leaving Virgil among the Beloved Ones, and the PVC pipes, and the stuffing.

Virgil sighs and bends over his task. Just then, Harvey appears.

Stop, Virgil," he calls. "Change of plans. Both the families are reconsidering their crematory plans. Just knock off for the day, son."

Two weeks later, Virgil stands under the concrete canopy of the Harrisonville Funeral Home and watches one of the funeral coaches disappear down the street, trailed by a procession. Virgil is keeping his eyes carefully averted from the back property of the funeral home where he knows, above the line of magnolias, a fine trail of white smoke drifts up to the heavens even though at present he knows the retort is empty. It still creeps him out. When he first came, Virgil was given a tour and lecture on the crematory. He hadn't ever had to do one, a fact for which he is profoundly thankful.

Virgil is waiting for Daisy Wade. She has called him just as he was knocking off for the day and said she just had to talk to him. Daisy has never *had* to talk to him before. It makes him nervous.

He sighs in the late afternoon heat. Another day like the last few days and Virgil doesn't know if he is going to make it. Every day lately, it seems like there is some kind of unpleasant surprise at work. It is always something, no matter if the night before he'd scoured his brain, dreamed of the worst possible thing, he would have ever been able to predict and prepare for. Mistakes he made, or just stuff that happened he has no control over. Yesterday, for example, just about did Virgil in.

He and Douglas climbed into the black van used to transport Beloved Ones to the funeral home. They arrived at this big, old two-story house, in this fancy neighborhood, but with weeds sticking up in the yard like it hadn't been mowed in a real long time. In the messy foyer was a narrow staircase, and Virgil and Douglas had found the Beloved One at the top of the stairs—in a bathroom smelling like bath oil and soap at first—in the tub! Douglas sank into that look that Virgil had come to know as one that masked a real pissed-off mood. First came his half-lidded eyes, the jaws working, and then this kind of steely politeness.

"No, no trouble at all," Douglas said between clenched teeth to the Bereaved Ones, two elderly ladies from Baton Rouge, who'd happened to be visiting, then had their cousin die on them. They looked bereaved and embarrassed and relieved at the same time to see Douglas and Virgil.

"Mr. Matthews," Douglas said after the ladies had gone downstairs. He always called Virgil Mr. Matthews whenever he was around customers. "Would you do the honor of letting the water out of this tub, while I measure the stairwell?" Because the Beloved One was enormous.

Virgil reached gingerly with his now infected cat scratched hand over the head, a woman's whose hair was dried to a frizz. He could see her pale scalp, with its tiny flakes of skin and as he bent over closer to feel for the tub lock, he could see all kind of horrors—the unbearable liver spots, the melanoma looking moles, the pores, all waterlogged and huge. He slipped his hand in the water, which felt oozy and thick somehow, and cold, but which he imagined oddly burned at the same time like he was sticking it in hydrochloric acid. He slid it down the greasy ceramic, taking care, so much care to stay away from her, from that enormous *her* in the water. He found the lock, flipped it, caused the water to start gurgling out somewhere underneath that mass.

What a huge body! Her tits emerged from the gurgling milky dishwater color like two huge puddings, orange-skin and mottled; the nipples circled and re-circled with huge frozen goose pimples. The upper part of her body was flushed with a baby blue rash, and the bottom half, where the water was disappearing, was a glowing bronze. A clump of flesh hung from her body on both sides—her belly!—almost touching the bottom of the tub, all mushed up to the sides. Virgil gagged as some smell, sour and sweet at the same time, began to assault and re-assault his senses.

And then the journey downstairs, her enormous, slippery body about to come off the gurney at any second, like an enormous dumpling, hanging off the sides, waiting to slither, the sheet sliding off again and again, refusing to stay put. Then the gurney got wedged when the stairwell angled and Douglas' jaws worked even more furiously, and he said, "Turn her a little on her side, please, Mr. Matthews. Let's turn her and the gurney sidewise," and Virgil grasped the gurney and the sheeted feet and they half hefted her over at more of an angle because that way she was a tiny bit smaller, enough to get her down. But then the wheels locked against the wall, began tearing the silver flowered wallpaper and Douglas sneered, "Reach underneath the gurney, Mr. Matthews. Lay the wheels flat, Mr. Matthews, if you will, please, Mr. Matthews."

And Virgil did and finally they were out in the yard, rolling this carcass to the van and Virgil's back sagged, the whole left side going elderly and numb in one second, gone soft-cored and alarmed. Then, on the road, half way back to the funeral home, they heard a crash and they stopped and looked in the back and the gurney had just collapsed, cracked under the weight. They got out and stood looking at this mass, that ton of toneless jellyfish flesh, lying on the floor of Harvey's van. They couldn't just leave her there— "we could get sued," said Douglas, and sweat popped out on his forehead and then he let himself start cussing. Virgil looked and looked and his back started sagging again. The sheet, too small anyway, had come off that gray-blue-bronze again, and Virgil just could not bring himself to get in the van with it—and it was an "it" too. Certainly not a Beloved One. It was a Very Much Disliked One, it was a thing to even those old ladies, who had hovered in the foyer and were only glad to be rid of the thing.

And then Douglas made him get in and Virgil got the head that time—and he'd stared into that blank, empty face, the dazed eyes staring and dry and unfocused. The head seemed too big even for that big, profound body, so mottled a face, studded with pimples, blurry moles and with its curiously amazed expression. Why, it was not a face at all. It was a mask, a monster mask.

"Virgil! Virgil!" Douglas shouted, because Virgil went into some kind of frozen state, a trance, and Douglas yelled again, and Virgil felt pulled to that thing in the van that had been living and growing and swelling and dying all those years for just this moment, for this moment in Virgil Matthews's life.

Virgil choked back something in his throat and reached under the tumorous flesh of her armpits, under the mess of blue and orange and purple that felt like cold Silly Putty and he pulled and heaved. The milky blind eyes stared up, and he wanted to press those eyelids down, down, but that would come later, in Preparation, and he tried to believe that this thing, this thing was not coming slowly to life, that it was not about to reach up and hug, press him, Virgil Matthews, into her monster tits.

Before they'd gotten back in the front of the van, Virgil had to upchuck, had to lean over in the gutter, right on Maple Street, in front of somebody's neat restored historical home, some kid tearing down the sidewalk on a Hot Cycle, veering around him, yelling, startled, "Gross, mister!" This was a thing that happened that for some reason seemed to restore Douglas' good humor. He'd cracked up, whooped—like Daisy when she'd seen Virgil's head sticking out of the grave. Weird senses of humor—both of them.

Douglas is even worse, if possible, than Daisy. One day before The Fat Lady In The Bathtub, which is how Virgil calls that day, Douglas watched and waited till Virgil almost finished an autopsied chest—watched him do the dozens of fine stitches it took to assure the fluids would stay put—then he'd laughed and Virgil looked up, his puffed, sore fingers zinging, and Douglas was waving a scapula at him. "Apprentices always forget this," he said. It was a lesson he taught Virgil, a part of a tradition, because that was how it had been taught to him. Virgil felt like everything connected to the funeral home was a lesson.

Virgil shakes his head and forces himself back to the present. He stares at the cottonwoods on the edge of the parking lot and tries to make his mind go empty, empty.

A clunking sound of heavy shoes against concrete makes him turn his head. For a second he squints his eyes—the light is awfully bright—and then sees it is the old blonde that he had first seen at Mr. Turberville's service.

"Hello, Virgil," she says. Her name is Doris. They are on a first name basis. "I'm running late, aren't I?" She dabs her eyes and heads to an old black Plymouth parked on the curb.

Virgil is so glad to be back in the present, for a second he is almost relieved to see her. Besides, Virgil really is getting used to Doris' face. She attends services as a hobby. Today Doris is wearing a black polyester pantsuit, and black beads that bounce on top of her bosom when she walks. Virgil can smell a puff of perfumed powder as she goes by him. Her pile of yellow hair hovers around her head in a dramatic, shining helmet, winged, like the god Thor might have. Doris is a fixture around the funeral home. Virgil thinks she is some kind of lesson too, but Virgil hasn't figured out what kind yet. Sometimes, just looking at her teary old face, for people she doesn't even know, makes him sadder than he is for any Beloved One... any Bereaved One.

As Doris bounces towards her Plymouth, Virgil wonders where she gets all of her energy to come to just about every funeral. Right now, it is five o'clock and Virgil wants a nap more than anything. Under his tiredness is a cold dead spot too, as though some part of him, on a subcutaneous level, has been removed.

He isn't sure when he started feeling like that. Maybe it is all the stuff he has to do and see, or maybe it is all of Harvey's new ideas for updating the funeral home. Harvey has a new idea every day and Virgil has a hard time keeping up with him in addition to all the other stuff he has to know and do. Virgil has taken up writing himself notes on the back of his hand to remind himself to do things. If he writes it on paper he loses it. He looks down then and checks his list. TK SD PO, take special delivery letter to the post office. He did that all right. ALF. Virgil pondered. Sometimes he can't remember what his abbreviations mean. Sometimes he had to get Maisie to help him decipher. One day she'd noticed him staring at his hand list and said, "What is that, Hon. Have some allergy tests?" and he had to explain his method.

Virgil stares at ALF. Then he looks up to where the procession has long disappeared. American Legion Flag. He was supposed to put that in with the Beloved One. Virgil blows out his breath. He scrooches his aching toes inside his new wingtips and wishes he were walking home.

Virgil has spent most of this morning assembling material for another video of a Beloved One's most cherished moments. The option of buying a keepsake video made with pictures and testimonials and shots of the Beloved Ones' homes and favorite spots on earth and the final ceremony all to the tune of the Beloved One's favorite song is going over real big. Even better than Harvey's Dial-A-Eulogy, $2.19 a minute. Today, the video has been made to the background music of "Vibrations" by Marky Mark and the Funky Bunch, and Harvey and Virgil shot the testimonials of apparently a girlfriend, the football field at Harrisonville High, half the football team, dozens of still photographs of baby to prom pictures, and finally the mother and the father, both who gave two speeches each, at the beginning and at the end of the video, on the dangers of steroid use.

At least this is working out better than the idea Harvey had last week. Actually it was the owner of a north California funeral home who had the idea and Harvey was making plans to copy him--something no other funeral home in this state offered—a drive-through window. It seemed someone in California converted a restaurant into a funeral parlor that allowed motorists to view caskets and sign a guest book without leaving their vehicles. Harvey likes the idea. He says that other people just pester the Bereaved at times like these, and this provides them a chance to be alone with the Beloved One. Also, he reasons, it benefits those on a tight schedule, the elderly, or physically challenged folks. The guy in California, Clyde Morrison, said they were already doing it in others parts of the country--up north. Harvey is even going to get a sign to put out front saying what time a Beloved One would be on view. Like a movie marquee. Or if they want to see someone not displayed, Harvey thinks he might get a phone at the window, and then they can ask to have a particular casket rolled up to the window. Even Douglas likes the idea. He thinks Harvey should include a tilting device to make it easier for motorists to see the Beloved Ones. The only problem as Harvey sees it is that City Hall wants the viewing area screened from passersby. They want a concrete wall to shield the drive-through from those less hot to the idea. That was adding another five thousand dollars to the project.

Harvey is always looking for ideas to offer customers the very latest. Harvey is already involved with a place called GeneLink that provides a little kit for funeral homes to get DNA from the Beloved Ones. The kits costs Harvey $100 each and then he gets Douglas to retrieve the DNA and store it—for twenty-five years. It's for people who want to save their Beloved Ones' genes for whatever reason: sudden inherited diseases that might crop up in the family, paternity testing, and whatnot. This is interesting to Virgil, but he is still hoping for cryonics to catch on.

Presently Virgil hears the cartoon "beep, beep" of Daisy's Volkswagen. He looks up to see her make a dashing turn around the corner and zip up the driveway. She weaves her way around the coaches and comes to a quick stop in front of him.

Daisy sticks her head out of the window. "Well, come on. Hop in, Virgil," she says.

Eleven

In Daisy's Volkswagen, Virgil's knees come up to his chin. He reaches tentatively under the seat, touches a lever, and the seat shoots backward. Roger Dodger, KQAX's loudmouth disk jockey blasts from the dashboard, "Okay, Roger Dodger fans—here's your next hot hit." Daisy fiddles with the dial and tunes RogerDodger down to a dull roar.

Daisy drives along at a good clip. She puts her head against the backrest of the seat as if she were relaxing and hums along with Marky Mark and the Funky Bunch.

Virgil wonders if Daisy has her little amber bottle. He wonders if she will open her purse and offer him some. Those moments under the Classic Beauty has given him a taste for the stuff. And it may help the way he is feeling now. Virgil sniffs the air inside the Volkswagen. He thinks he detects The Smell. Maybe Daisy has grass in her purse, too.

One little hit of something may take the edge off the situation. Since, in the last few days, Virgil feels as though everything that can go wrong, has gone wrong, when Daisy'd called, he figured he'd go ahead and see what she wanted, because what more can happen to him? But now speeding through space and time with her, he is not so sure.

"I wanted to talk to you about Speed Maxwell and Lorna Jean," says Daisy, interrupting her humming.

Virgil is floored, of course. He waits, but Daisy starts humming again.

Daisy heads on down Highland and turns onto North Main. Virgil stares out the window. They pass by the Princess and Daisy blows the horn at somebody in cut-off jean shorts and a red cap who is changing the marquee. The kid stops what he is doing, recognizes Daisy, and waves an "R" at them.

What in the world would make Daisy ask him about Speed and Lorna Jean? Even if Daisy has figured out that Virgil is in love with Lorna Jean, (which, in all fairness, would probably be a lucky guess—what could hiding behind chicken houses really tell you?) how would he possibly know about Speed?

Just then Daisy passes by a stand of chinaberry trees that Virgil had an experience in once. It always makes him feel bad just to pass by the place. What happened was he'd gone with Booger Beall and a group of guys from his high school to bash mailboxes with rocks and push them down. But when everybody was making their way down this street, Virgil, suddenly nauseous, found himself trailing behind further and further and then, without any conscious planning, he darted behind this stand of chinaberry trees in somebody's yard. He stood there for a half an hour, just feeling awful, but not sick any more, trying to breathe normally and watching the way a half dozen fat, pumpkin-shaped clouds worked their way through the ribs of a tree in front of the light of an old full moon. When he was sure nobody was going to look for him, he beat it home. Booger ragged him for years. Just thinking about it now made Virgil feel red hot on his neck.

Booger had always been up to something, and Virgil was always screwing up with whatever his part had been. Once Booger and his cousin from Mobile planned to sneak out in the middle of the night and go find a car to hot wire. Virgil worried all evening, and then he decided to forget to show up. But he lost face for nothing. Booger and his cousin found a Dodge Ram parked at the Conoco station, but weren't able to figure out how to hot wire it.

Virgil has this horrible feeling he is off on one of Booger's schemes again. Come to think about it, Booger and Daisy have a lot in common. Love of risk.

Then Daisy suddenly wheels into the library. She pulls into a parking place and hops out. She goes to the front of the car, opens it, and begins taking something out. With an armload of magazines, she dashes up the steps. "*Varieties*," she says, when she returns. "Overdue." She cranks up.

When Shelby took his job at Killer For Hire, they had been so far behind in bills, they'd moved out of their nice, brick house on Ockley Street that had a pretty little yard to the old-fashioned frame house with the big yard, and Daisy on the other side of it. They only lived there six years, but for some reason Virgil was beginning to feel like he's lived next to Daisy forever. Virgil watches Daisy gallop down the steps of the post office the same way she galloped down the steps of the library. Her red-brown hair blazes in the sunlight. She sees him watching her and gives a funny little hop. She bounces back into the car. "At last. Let's stop by Duck Pond on the way home."

Duck Pond. For heaven's sake. This is taking forever. Duck Pond is not exactly on the way home, either.

Duck Pond is not officially Duck Pond, but that is what everybody calls it. It is really Harrisonville Confederate Memorial Children's Park, but it is overrun with big white ducks and greedy geese, that quack and honk their way around the pond and the playground equipment looking for handouts. So it is hard to think of it as anything else. Somewhere along the line there has been a duck and goose population explosion.

When Virgil was little, Shelby used to remember to take him there sometimes. But he hasn't been in a long time.

The place is still full of kids on roller skates, bikes. Swinging on the swings, monkey bars. Obviously, Daisy is not going to offer Virgil any grass here.

Daisy parks near a beat-up old Toyota wagon where a couple with a bunch of kids is getting out with a picnic basket. "Marylee," the man calls, "How you going to do the shrimp?"

"Boiled," calls the woman.

When Virgil opens his door, one of the kids, a little boy with messy black hair pushes out his tongue at him. The kid shoots Virgil the bird and runs.

As a rule, kids make Virgil nervous. For one they are just too lively—bigger acting than their small size sets you up for. For another...well, they just make Virgil nervous, that's all.

Daisy finds a bench under a big cypress, but the duck poop smell is so bad, they have to find another.

"Shoo, you old shitter," says Daisy to a duck coming out from under it. The duck sticks out his beak and neck in a straight line and heads for the water.

"Well, Virgil," says Daisy, sitting down and fishing in her bag. She pulls out her cigarettes and lights up.

Suddenly, Virgil panics. He just fully expects her to say something awful, something born of her psychology books, and smartness, and Daisy ESP or whatever it is—something like, "Virgil Matthews, I know you are in love with Lorna Jean Gibson. I guess you think Speed Maxwell is just going to disappear. Well, he's not. And what makes you think you can fantasize about my cousin, laying, as you do, on your football pennant bedspread, playing with yourself all the time? Don't you know that everybody knows that? Don't you know the whole world knows you beat off pretending you're Lorna Jean's lover?"

Daisy takes a long puff and blows out a pretty good smoke ring. Then she says, "Do you know anything at all about what that jerk Speed Maxwell has been up to lately?"

Virgil feels his inside's crazy feeling rise up, go up in the air along Daisy's slightly whopsided smoke ring. His back sags in relief. It is a second before he can say anything. "Naw. What? What do you mean?"

"I mean that he has been up to something and Lorna Jean has come, as usual, whining to me. She's trying to marry him. But he keeps going out of town more than ever, or working up at the funeral home weird hours, and she's suspicious. Do you know why he's hanging around Douglas so much? The funeral home?"

Virgil's mind is stuck a minute on the word "marry." Course, it is to be expected. He sighs. He *did* think that Speed is hanging around a lot. Even though in Harrisonville if you are friends with somebody it is not unusual to go to work with them and help if it is OK with the employer. Booger drove around a whole summer with Ron Ford who was working for Harrisonville Animal Control and had not got paid a cent. But Speed was in the Preparation Room the other day. Nobody, but nobody, from the public, is supposed to go in there. Harvey says, and everybody knows he says, that if they fainted or something there might be a lawsuit. "Well," Virgil says finally, "I guess he *is* around a lot."

"Well, why?" says Daisy. "If you know something, please tell me. Do you know, is he fooling around with somebody else up there at the funeral home? I know he flirts with everybody, but if it's another woman besides Lorna Jean—"

"Naw," says Virgil. "There's nobody else to fool around with that's young like him."

"Well, is he doing something he shouldn't?"

"Like what?" says Virgil.

"I have no idea!"

The duck Daisy shooed off is creeping up on them, watching Virgil out of one side of his head. It is covered in irregular black and white feathers and his beak has a big red growth looking something on it. Kind of obscene up close.

"I mean I know this guy," Daisy is saying, "Speed is always up to something, and it always involves fucking, or making a buck with something that is going to put him in Angola for a good while—if ever he would get caught. I don't even buy stuff from him—he's just dangerous. Lorna Jean worries, since she caught him in a few lies, that it involves another woman. If you know, Virgil—if he's got somebody else, one other special person, that you know of, that he sees a lot of, you better tell us. And why does he go out of town all the time? Is he selling Laetrile trips to Mexico again?" Daisy leans close to Virgil and looks him in one eye like the duck did, "He got a señorita?"

Virgil leans back. How would he know this stuff? "Naw. I don't know. He hangs around with Douglas. But that's all I know."

Then Virgil remembers something. When he caught him in the preparation room, Speed was carrying a body bag. It was empty of course, but why would he be carrying that? And headed for refrigeration? But that is nothing to tell.

"Well, all right," says Daisy, "but if you see anything let me know. OK? I just wouldn't mind him getting caught in something to tell you the truth. The last thing my ditz-brained cousin needs is a guy like him. I mean, like last year she comes to me. Says she's got herself in trouble. Anyway, I ended up driving her to the New Orleans Delta Women's Clinic to get her unknocked. What a trip!"

Virgil is horrified. "You shouldn't be telling me this."

"Oh, everybody always thinks Lorna Jean is so good." Then Daisy goes on. "She is not, I'm telling you. I could tell you stuff! And the things I do for my cousin! And where was Speed while we were fighting all the Right To Lifers in New Orleans? Up on Lake Bistineau, throwing ducks for Rocky. Practicing for a dog show for heaven's sake."

"Jeeze," says Virgil. Lorna Jean has been going through all of this and he hadn't even known. When he thinks of Lorna Jean he remembers her like he's known her for years. Cheerleading and running around in convertibles. Flashes of thigh. Tan arms. That Speed Maxwell! Weren't lovers supposed to be miserable together? Poor Lorna Jean. "Poor Lorna Jean," he whispers.

"Aw, she's over it. Squally babies make her nervous, anyway. Is the way she puts it. But this guy is just poison. Really. Keep your eye on him."

"OK," says Virgil dully. Here Lorna Jean has had an abortion, led this whole other life, and he hadn't known any of it.

"Keep your eye on both of them. Douglas and Speed."

Virgil nods. Then Daisy stands up and makes a throwing motion out over the duck's head at the water. The duck makes a run at nothing. "Ha! Stupid duck!" says Daisy. "God! This place is ass-deep in ducks. Owen and me used to come out here all the time. When I was desensitizing him to open spaces."

Virgil looks out at the dishwater colored pond. Nobody knows why this place is so popular. It is smelly. Clumps of beheaded cattails line the sides where kids have broken them off. On the other side of the pond is the Bunny Bread factory, hardly a scenic part of nature. And the ducks and geese are overwhelming, their incessant honking and quacking, like something out of a horror movie—like Ray Milan in *Frogs* only it should be *Foul*. Or Alfred Hitchcock's, *The Birds!* Where a whole species turns on the humans. He should say that to Daisy, her being a movie buff and all. But he is still floored about Lorna Jean, and Daisy is walking away, ready to go home.

As he gets up, Virgil sees two boys wading around the cypresses, slogging it toward shore. Maybe it is good out here because there is nobody official to make you mind the rules. Like not lighting fires to boil shrimp, not wading in duck shit and broken glass. Telling you something is dangerous when you already know.

"Hurry up," calls Daisy. "I got to get Owen a six pack."

OK," says Virgil, but he suddenly he feels real, real tired.

The boys make it to the shore.

"Hey, J.T.," says the taller boy, when they go by him. "There's the man that gives us the sweet potatoes for Halloween."

Virgil ducks his head and follows Daisy. He wishes Meemaw would let him give out candy for Trick or Treat, like normal people do.

Twelve

Daisy sets her fingernail polish down on the arm of the swing and watches her mother and sister, arms loaded up with Wal-Mart sacks, getting out Crystal's car. Daisy simply fails to comprehend, as she has a jillion times before, why any sane person in the world would want to drive a titty-pink Cadillac with the words, "Mary Kay" swirled on it in big letters, in broad daylight, clear across town, or anywhere, for that matter.

"Whew," says Zelma, puffing up the steps. "Hot!" She is wearing a polka-dot skirt and a frilly sleeveless blouse. The thin nylon features broad sweat rings under the arms.

"Here's the plan," says Daisy's brother-in-law, coming out of the house. "I'm going to buy me a six pack, sit down in front of the TV and not move until it's all gone or this heat wave has broke, whichever comes first. What do you think you can pull together for supper, Crystal, honey?"

Crystal has just given Zelma a ride shopping because Zelma's car is in the shop again. It is in the shop again, because, Daisy thinks, darkly, Zelma has never once, to Daisy's knowledge, ever taken her foot off the clutch. Why Pee Wee doesn't buy her a new automatic Daisy didn't know. And the thing must be ten years old. The problem with her parents is that they have a mixed marriage. Zelma is from some kind of crumbling Theta aristocracy, and Pee Wee is from a tobacco spitting, still-got-the-first-nickel, farming class strain. But from Pee Wee's side came the money. Unfortunately, Zelma loves to spend, and Pee Wee loves to save.

"I'm not cooking," says Crystal. "It's too hot."

Zelma starts trying to talk Crystal and R.C. into staying for supper. "Y'all can eat with us. Beans and rice! Stay! We'll have a big time—"

"Mama!" says Crystal. "You don't need to be cooking either, in this weather. Sandwiches are good enough for anybody."

"Oh, foot," says Zelma. "I've got a crock pot full of beans going right now. If they not burnt up. I'm just going to throw some rice on. You can drink beer just as easy from my couch as yours. Roy's coming home with Pee Wee. It'll be a party."

Daisy takes in all this information. Inside, Janice is talking on the phone, hot to trot. She is Junior League's Fourth of July's dessert chairwoman this year. Daisy groans to herself. The last thing she ever wants is to be in the house when Janice and Roy and Crystal and R.C. and Zelma and Pee Wee are all together. They simply bug her to death. Especially Crystal and Janice—how much can you talk about fashion, hair, and Oprah Winfrey? But looks like, at the moment, Daisy doesn't have much choice. She is off work tonight herself, and wouldn't you know, J.R. from the gas station has picked up Owen to drive out to Haynesville to rebuild somebody's faulty ignition. So she doesn't even have a date.

Good grief! Crystal and R.C. may even have Daisy's old accordion in the trunk—taken up long after Daisy had mastered it—and they may decide to take it out and have Crystal play like they do sometimes. Crystal is an awful accordion player and she only knows one song, "Love is a Many Splendid Thing." R.C. plays the spatulas, that is, he thumps a couple of rubber spatulas against his stomach in time to Crystal's chords. Daisy picks up her Passionate Peach nail polish and walks into the house.

"Good Lord!" Janice is saying into Zelma's pink Princess phone in the kitchen. "We couldn't possibly ask her. She's the one who brought those frozen peach pies and slice and serve canapés you buy at Sam's

Warehouse to the Spring Arts Festival!

"What about Thelma Beard? She still bakes those good cheese straws from scratch—Well, I know that, but the point is that she could at least have the decency to bring—Hold on, Tootie." Janice buries the phone receiver into the shoulder of her lime green B.H. Wragg.

"Daisy! I saw Lorna Jean at the Dillard's this morning. I forgot to tell you. She wanted to know if you were working tonight, and if not, to please call her. She sounded upset." Janice puts the phone back in her ear. "What? No, no! Everybody knows Martha Anne Foster uses a lot of canned marshmallows, Cool Whip, cake mix, and all!"

"Thanks," says Daisy, blowing on her nails. On the Formica of Zelma's breakfast nook is a stack of college catalogs. Daisy blows harder on her nails. She better pick them up before something gets spilled.

Sure enough here comes Zelma. She is saying, "Let's make some Rotel Dip. R.C. and Crystal are staying for supper. Do we have any Velveeta, Daisy?"

"I wouldn't know," says Daisy. Rotel Dip is the official appetizer of Harrisonville—a can of chopped up tomatoes with enough Velveeta to stop up an elephant.

"I saw some Rotel tomatoes last month in New York." said Crystal, coming in behind Zelma, followed by R.C. "They were $2.75 a can." Crystal never misses a chance to remind everybody she could how she and R.C. fly up to New York every now and then to shop.

"Lord! At the K-Mart they two for a dollar," says Zelma, opening the crock-pot Pee Wee and Daisy gave her for Christmas one year. Sausage and bean and spice smells baptize the air. Daisy's family could eat hot sausage during a heat wave and drink iced tea during a blizzard.

"Just as I suspected," R.C.'s head is inside the refrigerator. "All Pee Wee has is Miller Light."

"Oh," says Zelma. "You know somebody at work told him about fat grams, Hon."

So we having red beans and rice, thinks Daisy. That makes sense.

"I'm gone," says R.C., heading for the door.

"Bring some Fritoes," Crystal says.

"The big ones," adds Janice, Miss Do It By The Book Too Good For Packaged Pudding Chairwoman, hanging up the phone.

Daisy gathers up her catalogs. Time to retreat.

ಬ

The funny thing about both her sisters' educations is that the money comes from Grandma Bee, Pee Wee's mother, whose folks are from the hills of Arkansas and who, like most of that side of the family, have never even made it through high school. But that's where the money came from. All the good taste had come from Zelma's side of the family— through Grandma Lilah, who'd had money once, but died poor—though fashionably correct, one of the last living authorities on Harrisonville bloodlines. Of course, nobody on the outside really knew how poor Grandma Lilah had been. She lived in a kind of genteel poverty in a big old two story house at the edge of town that, after her death, had been sold for debts, and turned into, with considerable remodeling, a chic furniture store. Grandma Lilah was the kind who'd say, whenever she met any of Daisy's friends, "Now, who are *your* people?"

Nobody knew how rich Grandma Bee had been either. Grandma Bee had bought Wal-Mart stock early, ("I knew that Sam Walton," she said once. "He was a good boy to his mama."), and lived in a skinny little shotgun house she and Papaw had bought when they first came to Harrisonville. At Christmas time, she gave all her grown kids and grand kids alike five-dollar bills. The thing Daisy and Grandma Bee like to do best was give garage sales.

Poor as she was, Grandma Lilah would have never stooped to have a garage sale. That's where Crystal and Janice got all their notions. And why, watered down as all that wisdom has become, and fuzzy with lack of early enough money to support the habits, Lorna Jean never does quite know what to do. She has never had sense enough to break tradition, like Daisy. Even after the Gibsons did get their share of money, Lorna Jean never quite got the hang of Harrisonville society, or making the grade at Mississippi State. And she has fallen for a guy Grandma Lilah would have never stood for—Speed Maxwell. She is supposed to marry someone like R.C. and Roy. Lorna Jean will never be a Janice or Crystal, but she admires those two beyond reason—especially Janice.

What is really funny was that Janice was actually Roy's second wife, which makes it hard to belong to the same country club, and stuff. Roy's first wife, who had won the preliminary in the Miss Louisiana

Beauty Pageant by twirling a double-fire baton, (and if it weren't for Daisy, now almost a lost art in Harrisonville) is a realtor in Baton Rouge. After she and Roy married, she started selling Avon on the side, but one day she took all the money she made and left Roy and went to real estate school in Baton Rouge. Then Roy married Janice and they eventually had two big old teen-age sons, sons who came as close as possible to chipping the permanent smile off Janice's face. Right now, those two were mercifully away at the John Newcombe Tennis Ranch near San Antonio for the summer—or this whole house would have been chaos.

Crystal does not appreciate how lucky she is—she spent most of her life trying to get pregnant but with no luck at all. Instead, she and R.C. had to resort to raising Yorkshire terriers, of which they have four. Crystal always followed Janice's pregnancies real close. The perfect aunt. She drove Janice to the hospital the first time when her water broke early on during the second half of the last LSU basketball game of the season where her husband sat in the bleachers, having conveniently forgotten his cell phone. Crystal drove Janice to the hospital again for the second baby, after Janice's water broke at the A & P as she was standing getting her groceries checked, had just politely waited until the clerk finished, then put her checkbook back in her purse, gathered up her bag, smiled her famous smile, and walked out the door. She bumped into Crystal in the parking lot, who was coming in to get some salad makings.

Suddenly Pee Wee yells from downstairs. "Day-Zee! Supper!"

∞

"Good beans," Pee Wee says, scarfing it up.

"If it was me," R.C. is saying, "I'd go on to LSU. Does this UCLA have a decent basketball team, Daisy? Crystal, honey, how about some chopped onion over here?"

"I thought you liked jalapeños, hon," says Mattie.

"I do like 'em. They make my head sweat."

"These keep you up," warns Crystal, pushing the Tupperware bowl of onions toward R.C. "Did you call Lorna Jean, Daisy? Janice said she was looking for you to call."

"I will," Daisy says, mincing her salad around on her plate, making little crosshatches on the lettuce. Good grief. A basketball team! Then she thinks about Lorna Jean—she had simply forgotten to call her. Daisy hopes it isn't another problem that will cause a trip to New Orleans.

"USL's coming on strong this year," says Roy, between bites of the red beans and rice spilling off his spoon. "The Ragin' Cajuns."

"I wouldn't give you two cents for the Ragin' Cajuns," says R.D., still sprinkling onions. R.C. only had eyes for professional football—he had been loyal to the New Orleans Saints through decades of losing.

"And look at LSU's basketball still coming on strong. That Chris Johnson's got a lick."

"I hear that," says Roy.

Then Zelma says, "Daisy's not interested in colleges in Louisiana. And she does not want to go to the Mississippi State where Mattie and I and Grandma Lilah were all in the Thetas. Daisy is a modern girl. She wants to go way off from home. I will never feel right about it, but that is her decision."

Then Pee Wee says, "We already said she could go, now, and she's going."

"Are you still dating that Owen fellow?" Janice asks, innocently. Being a second wife made her a little mean.

Daisy looks at her sister and smiles a forged Theta smile, matching her sister's, sunbeam for sunbeam. "Yep," she says. Daisy has long given up fighting with her sisters or rising to anything they might consider bait. After all, there but for the grace of God, and Rita Hayworth and others, goes Daisy.

"You should have this Owen over some time, dear," says Zelma frostily, as Daisy knew Janice knew she would.

Daisy can picture Owen right now at this table. Oh, yeah. Right.

Crystal says, "Well, if Daisy goes off to school, she'll meet lots of new men. No telling who. Right? There's always a bright lining? Right, Mama?"

Crystal and Janice are so much alike, Daisy forgets which one is who half the time. Both their houses look like Tara in *Gone With The Wind* except for the modern appliances, hot tubs, water sprinkler systems and such. And their husbands could have even worn each other's clothes. And sorry men! Neither one of those boys could change a light bulb. Or could fix a car. They had made so much money they didn't have to. Owen, on the other hand, could and would fix anything. He could rebuild a carburetor with a pocketknife.

"Let her alone, Sisters, both of you," says Pee Wee.

"Sorreee," Crystal and Janice sing together like a demented Greek chorus. "We was just trying—" says Crystal.

"—to point out the—," says Janice.

"Bright side," finishes Crystal.

Daisy would have liked to point out a few sides for them. Like how Crystal has come so close to divorce one time. Crystal spent the first three years of marriage cooking Martha Stewart fancy dinners. Then, after a particularly trying menu, R. C. had come to the table in his jock strap, and Crystal had cut out to a Holiday Inn for two weeks. But then she had "come to her senses" as she put it and returned. To Daisy, that had been the only lucid moment in her sister's life. And Janice—whose idea of heaven was to go shopping for another cocktail ring for Roy to pay for. Lord!

"Good supper, Mom," says Daisy, picking up her cigarettes, and heading out. Zelma does not let her smoke in the house. Thank god!

"How 'bout something sweet," says Zelma, opening the refrigerator door and taking out a dish wrapped in Saran Wrap. They are still eating funeral food.

"No, no, thanks," says Daisy. She doesn't have to help with the dishes because she is the only female to have A Job. Mary Kay and Amway are just hobbies for her sisters.

"You didn't eat much," calls Zelma, lifting up the wrapper on a lemon pound cake and sniffing it thoughtfully as Daisy breezes by.

∽

Daisy sits on the porch smoking her cigarette. One day she is going to quit, in fact, she has already almost positively decided to definitely quit, but then she started going with Owen, with his Lucky Strikes eternally rolled up in the sleeve of his tee shirt, and that plan had just never materialized. Out in California, they can both quit, soon as they get all the wrinkles ironed out in their new life.

Around Daisy in the bleary stuff that passes for dusk, the yard is just a smear of dark green, and Zelma's colorful decorations have transformed into a petrified charcoal army. Daisy can hear the mutters of Barred Rocks from Virgil's back yard as they go in to roost. One day someone is going to complain about those people having livestock in their yard. Though there isn't an ordinance, pretty soon somebody will probably create one.

Daisy takes a last deep drag and tosses her cigarette into the direction the pink verbenas grew. If Zelma had seen that she would have bitched. Daisy usually tries to hit one of the potted ferns, so thick they'd hide anything, but they are too far away and she is just too hot to get up. Suddenly, two black forms explode out of the verbenas and race across the street. Mrs. Biedenbeau's cats. Mrs. Biedenbeau's son, Dwayne, four years ahead of Daisy in school, who Daisy dated briefly, named them Trojan and Ramses. Dwayne and Daisy used to think it was funny to see which people those names could make stop and think.

Just then Lorna Jean's Ford Escort turns into the driveway and Lorna Jean hops out.

"This is important," says Lorna Jean, as she made her way through the Six Dwarves—a few years ago, someone had stolen the Seventh—Grumpy.

"What's wrong?"

Lorna Jean sits down on the swing and hitches up her purple tube top. "Why didn't you call? I've waited for you all day."

"Busy," says Daisy. "What's up?"

"Speed. You know he keeps disappearing and won't tell me what's going on? He is so secretive! Yesterday, in his Bronco, I found a plastic cup that said, 'Dallas-Ft. Worth, Your Do It Now Cities.' Why would he go to Dallas without me? He knows I love Dallas."

"Aw," says Daisy. "Is that all? He probably drove someone somewhere for a hair transplant and picked up a souvenir."

"But he goes in the middle of the night. It's got something to do with that funeral home. I followed him last night and he went there and I waited as long as I could and he didn't come out. A truck drove up I've never seen. Florida tags. Kissimmee Tissue Bank on the side."

"Daisy?" Zelma is calling from inside. "Is that Lorna Jean, hon?

Ask her has she eaten supper yet."

"Yeah," says Daisy, "yeah, she has, Mom."

"Maybe we should go upstairs." says Lorna Jean.

"How about in the swing?" says Daisy. She likes it outside at night. A breeze has come on and the crickets are cranking up.

"No. Vernon's probably spooking around back there."

"Virgil," says Daisy.

Then Lorna Jean puts her head down in her arms and starts snuffling. "If we could just get married."

"I don't think you're ready for marriage," said Daisy. "And him neither—hold it down, will you?" She didn't want her mother to think Lorna Jean was preggers again. "What did you say? Kissimee Tissue Bank?"

"We are so ready for marriage," says Lorna Jean. "If Speed would just stay put. How—how can we find out what he's up to? It's that Douglas he's hanging around with all the time—do you know him at all?"

"Nope," said Daisy. "Maybe we could try Virgil again. Maybe he's found out something by now. Maybe he knows about this tissue bank."

"That geek." Lorna Jean stuck a Nike on the swing. "Do you think Speed's into devil worship, or something?"

"What makes you ask that?" Daisy says, startled.

"I read something last year in the paper about it. Teenagers and all."

"Speed's not a teenager. And he doesn't worship nothing," says Daisy. Except himself, she adds privately. "Let's ask Virgil again. Maybe he's seen something by now. He's not so geeky he can't be useful."

Daisy feels a little guilty saying that. Despite herself, she always manages to drum up a little pity for Virgil, Virgil in his eternal weenydom. She looks over in the Matthews's yard—equally as strange as their own— the dark splotches where its dewberry vines, persimmon and fig trees, tomatoes, peas and cabbages are. The shadow that was that ridiculous chicken house. How would it be to be a Virgil? All soft and strange and worried.

"Come on," Daisy says. "It'll be fun. We'll go over now. Give him a thrill."

"No," says Lorna Jean, pulling up the other Nike. "I most

certainly will not. Besides, I got a better idea.

"You and I will follow Speed. Just stick with him until he comes out from whatever he's doing in the funeral home and follow him wherever he goes."

"He'd see us. He'd know who we were."

"We can take Laurene's car. He doesn't know Laurene's car."

"But he knows us! Besides, what if he's gone for a few days. What would we tell our folks?"

"Well, we could say we're going shopping in Dallas."

Shopping in Dallas was a feasible excuse—one big problem though.

"What if one of them wants to go with us?" Daisy says. "You know how they love to save money on gas. We going to follow Speed with your mother or mine or Crystal or somebody in the car with us? In Laurene's car? You know that's what they'd want to do."

"Well—you think of something."

Just then R.C. and Crystal come out on the porch. R.C. is carrying two large spatulas.

"Hey, girl," sings Crystal, and heads to her Mary Kay Cadillac. For her accordion, Daisy figures.

Thirteen

You owe me," says Laurene Haynes Tinsley, sliding the key into the door of J.R. Haynes Construction Company. Laurene is a real interesting case, a person who has made and lost a fortune in emus and wound up working for her daddy. "I'm going to wait downstairs in my car 'till I see you both leave. Just mash this button, hon, see? And it locks again. Be sure you close those curtains when you get through." She looks at Norma Jean. "Men! I hope you find what you looking for. But, oh lord, the woman is the last to know." She reaches for the light switch.

"Don't!" hisses Daisy and Lorna Jean together.

"Oops, I forgot. Sorry 'bout that. Don't touch nothing now. And don't smoke. You know Mr. Swanger has stopped. He don't want anybody smoking around him, and he can smell it from a hundred yards."

After Laurene leaves, Daisy and Lorna Jean pull up a chair to the big window behind Mr. Swanger's desk. Then Daisy steps up on it, opens the heavy windows, and Pee Wee's binoculars swinging heavily against her chest, climbs out on the fire escape. "Come on," she says to her cousin.

By sitting on the first step and craning their necks they have a shot at a decent view of Virgil Matthews' workplace. But across the street, the old-fashioned Victorian Harrisonville Funeral Home with its cupolas and gingerbread window scrolling is dark and shut-up looking in the upstairs part, and Daisy figures all this is just a waste of time. They both rummage for their cigarettes.

"What do you expect we'll see?" Daisy asks her crazy cousin. The moon gives out just enough light for Daisy to see the outline of her nose and mouth. "Even if those two do get beside this particular window on this particular floor, we won't be able to hear anything."

"Oh, I don't know," sighs Lorna Jean, taking a drag. She smokes Eve cigarettes, not because of the taste, but because she says the package is pretty. "You're probably right. But I don't know what else to do short of following him all the way to wherever he goes. And I guess you're right. It'd be hard to do that."

Lorna Jean sighs again. "Laurene Tinsley had a lovely wedding, didn't she? Wisteria in bloom. Sugar love birds on top of a ten-tiered wedding cake—"

"Oh, give me a break," says Daisy. "Now she's divorced and working for her daddy." Laurene's marriage could not stand up to a crisis. Their emus had developed a leg fungus, and the Tinsley's had lost their shirts.

"Still," says Lorna Jean as though that settled something.

"Truthfully," says Daisy, "I don't know what you see in old Speed."

"Good. Let's keep it that way." Lorna Jean leans over and looks straight down into the street. "What a drop!" Then she says, "Well, OK. Sometimes, I don't know either what I see in him. It's just I got so much invested in that boy. What about Owen? What do you see in Owen?"

"He's really sexy," says Daisy. She didn't even have to think about it. "He looks like Robert de Niro. He was wounded in Vietnam and he's got this little ridge of scars on his back. He's tough. He's smart. He, well, he tells it like it is."

"How old is he?"

"Fifty-one."

"Wow!" Lorna Jean presses her face to the hand railing. "That's old. Come on, Speed. Where are you? Maybe I should have stayed pregnant."

When Lorna Jean had seen the ring the little take-home

pregnancy kit made in her piss, she called Daisy at work. The manager told Daisy there was a family emergency. Looking back, Daisy believes Lorna Jean has always been a walking emergency looking for a place to happen. Later, after all the dust had settled down, Daisy decided to have a tubal ligation herself, an out-patient procedure which she read about in a woman's magazine so she would never, never be in that kind of jam. But the hospital was booked for the next six months so she was supposed to wait. All this in secret, because if Zelma ever found out, it would be worse—almost—than having a baby. Daisy looks out the window and decides not to even reply to Norma Jean's stupid remarks.

Once when Norma Jean and Daisy were little, Daisy saved Lorna Jean from a fire they both started playing with matches in their Papaw's hay field. They pushed hay bales together for a house and lit a fire in the pretend fireplace. Daisy ran but Lorna Jean just sat there staring in horror, unable to move. Daisy had to run back in and pull her out.

"I am having to keep that damn dog for the weekend," Lorna Jean says, after a while, suddenly, in the dark. The tip of her cigarette glows.

"We should put these out," says Daisy, but she didn't. "Who you talking about? Rocky?"

"Yeah, you know his parents won't keep him. Speed won't board him at the vet's. I am so sick of this! He won't come when I call. He growls at me!"

"Just say *no!*"

"He doesn't understand English."

"No. I mean to Speed."

"Oh, that dog is his pride and joy. I pretend to love him. I'd sure hate for Speed to decide between me and that dog, I'll tell you that! And you know last year, after him and a couple of other dogs were dognapped before the Holiday in Dixie Trials, Speed just won't let him out of sight, unless I've got him."

Last year, to keep Speed from competing, some old boys from Oak Ridge kidnapped Speed's dog and a few others owned by other competitors. They gave them back of course, but Speed is paranoid now.

"Look—look!" A light comes on in the upstairs window.

It isn't Speed or Douglas though. The dark figure looks lumpish and familiar. Daisy raises Pee Wee's binoculars.

"It's just Virgil," says Daisy, after a minute. "I guess they had a customer come in."

Virgil moves over near the window. Daisy and Lorna Jean duck, even though there is no need to. After a second, they straighten back up. Daisy raises the binoculars again. Virgil has disappeared. Then a gurney with a sheet over what could only be a dead body comes into sight, followed by Virgil pushing it. "He's got a customer, all right."

"Jesus," says Lorna Jean. "That is so gross. That boy is so weird!"

"Oh, he's weird, but harmless," says Daisy. Now that she had spent three years teasing him and making him uncomfortable it is like she is a little fond of him. And he *is* sort of interesting to observe.

"Well, there are a hundred better jobs than that one. And he was weird before this job. Always spooking our behind that hen house and spying on us."

"Well, duh. He's in love with you." Daisy lowers her binoculars. "You know he's in love with you."

"Oh, yeah, right. Yuk!"

"He just needs to be laid."

"Well, don't look at me! Debbi Porter said he collects dead animals and keeps them in his refrigerator."

"Yeah, I heard that. He was trying to be a scientist or something once. He doesn't do it now, though, now that his Meemaw found out," says Daisy, feeling guilty. She helped spread that information.

"Her mother buys yard eggs from his grandmother. And all that vegetable stuff around their house! And those chickens! It looks like a stupid farm or something."

Daisy raises her binoculars again. Virgil has taken the sheet off. Beneath was a body, all right! Then Daisy's next-door neighbor goes over and opens a drawer from the wall. He comes back to his customer.

"What's he doing now? " Lorna Jean says.

"Shhh," says Daisy, even though there is no way Virgil can hear them. Virgil *is* weird, all right. But Daisy guesses somebody has to do this stuff.

Then Virgil moves down to what Daisy sees as the feet of the dead person. Virgil starts taking off the person's shoes. When he finishes, he sets the shoes on the dead person's chest. Well, somebody had died with their shoes on!

"What's he doing? Let me see," says Lorna Jean.

Then Virgil starts unbuttoning stuff. He starts pulling on the pants legs.

"Good grief," says Daisy. "He's taking his clothes off!"

"Let me see."

"No, wait—"

Just then one of the shoes falls off the dead man's chest. Virgil finishes the pants and bends down underneath the gurney. He completely disappears under it. The gurney moves and rolls a bit. Virgil must have hit one of the legs. The dead man's hand falls off. It falls right on top of Virgil's head as he is surfacing. Virgil Matthews jumps straight in the air and falls back against a tray of stuff, spilling whatever it is on the floor. Then all she can see is thrashing arms and legs.

Daisy puts her hands over her mouth to keep from laughing out loud. Then she bends double. "SSSHHH," says Lorna Jean. "What? What's he doing?"

"The dead guy's hand fell on his head and he jumped a mile." Then Lorna starts giggling. They lean against the window casing. "Oh ho. Oh whee," they can't stop. They hold their cigarettes up in the air and lean against each other, convulsing. Then Daisy falls through the window into the building. Lorna Jean comes after her, tumbling ashes and little sparks when her cigarette hits something. Inside, they fall onto Mr. Swanger's desk rocking with laughter.

"Oh, hee, hee," Daisy really can't stop. "Shhhh. Hee, hee. Sh-he heeee. Shhhhh. Heeeeeee."

Framed pictures of Mr. Swanger's family hit the floor.

"Oh, ho, ho," wheezes Lorna Jean, trying to hold her broken but still smoking cigarette up out of their way.

"Girls!" says Laurene Haynes Tinsley from the door, making them both jump higher than Virgil had jumped. "Speed Maxwell just pulled out of the parking lot with a load of Porta-potties on the back of a big old pick-up truck!" Then she looks at Lorna Jean's cigarette in horror. "Hey! What's this stuff?"

Fourteen

Monday afternoon Virgil leaves work early. Harvey says he can because he'd worked late the night before. Besides, his hands were infected from Mr. Whisker's bites, a fact that got back to Harvey because in Restoration Douglas spotted the awful purple medicine that Meemaw painted on him. "Harvey says, go home. You look like hell," Douglas said to him. But anyway, Virgil is off early.

It feels strange leaving early, before three. He is walking, because he is fed up with being mistaken for a religious person on a bicycle. "Hey, moron!" kids yell at him. You just leave yourself open for abuse pedaling around in broad daylight wearing a suit and tie.

Virgil's purple fingers are throbbing and the cold spaghetti out of a can he had for lunch boinks around in his stomach. He misses Meemaw's good left over dinners.

How strange the living and the dead are to each other, he thinks, as he walks along. Everybody encased in this sack of flesh and skin around this little, possibly extinguishable life spark or something. Then suddenly, boom! Dead as a cockroach.

Every day Virgil stares at all kinds of stuff, stuff he never knew existed, waiting to feel...professional. But he just has this stupid feeling that he is about to make a mistake every minute. About to do something...irreparable. Something to add to a whole life of screw-ups. Virgil Matthews screwing up again, and walking around the world unloved by any other human being. Why? Why is everybody just so unaccessible? And unreliable. It is as though everybody, everybody around him is unreliable. Harvey, even sometimes. Making Virgil copy the guest register for potential customers! Taking down license plate numbers at the cemetery so he can find out names and call and sell them a pre-need plan. Of course, Douglas. Daisy can be counted on to be off the wall. Shelby has always been vaguely unreliable. Meemaw is downright crazy. Lorna Jean, now. If only he could get her to at least talk to him some time, everything would be—well, better. And how does this happen, that he needs her so bad. In high school, he knew she was out of his league, but through some kind of cosmic comedy, her getting a job across the street from his job and him spying on her leaving work everyday, he's become addicted to her, to the idea of her. And his addiction has been so sneaky. Every time he sees her, he wants more. To see her more. To have something back from her. Is this love? Like nose drops. He used them once or twice, and his nose started producing more congestion to offset the decongestants. For a while, he had a chemical addiction to nose drops, and a psychological addiction to Lorna Jean. Lately, not getting to see more of her is really making him sick. Right now his normal mild uneasiness has doubled to total dis-easiness. His pulse feels rapid, his panic level is overwhelming. And something about the funeral home business makes it all seem worse. Like it has something to do with his rejection by Lorna Jean. That part of himself wanting Lorna Jean feels like him seeing the wormy side of death, the side nobody admits.

As Virgil walks along, he decides just not to think about it all. The further he gets from the funeral home, the less scared he feels. He isn't doing so bad, is he? He hasn't been yelled at lately or anything. Virgil tries taking deep breaths. Give the old brain some oxygen.

Then, reaching the intersection of Johnson and Thirty-second, the block where Dunkin Donuts and Baskin Robbins sit side by side, a weird thing happens to Virgil. A situation, for heaven's sake, like the time he ran into Lorna Jean and she used his phone.

She, Lorna Jean Gibson, comes running out of Baskin Robbins holding a giant ice cream cone. She looks frantic. She runs straight to a

136

red Bronco, Speed's, of course, and starting running around it, looking into all the windows. "Oh, damn," she wails.

Virgil stands stock-still and watches her—his feet just will not move. Then Lorna Jean starts yelling, "Oh, Rocky. Rock!" and looks up and down the street. She looks up one way and when she looks down the other she catches sight of Virgil.

"Oh, Virgil," she calls, waving her arms. "Oh, Virgil. Yoo hoo."

Whoa, breathes Virgil. Whoa. Lorna Jean is waving at him, waving. Striped pink T-shirt. Short shorts. Waving.

"Come on," she is saying. She appears to be waving Virgil into Speed's vehicle.

Virgil takes a deep breath and fills his chest with the sweet, sad flavor of Dunkin Donuts. The hot, thick air, with all the limitless possibilities of summer which have not yet been fulfilled suddenly comes alive—and he floats to, climbs into, Speed Maxwell's Bronco.

Immediately Lorna Jean hands him the double scoop ice cream cone and starts up the motor. "Speed's damn dog has got out of the jeep!" she says, flipping a piece of twenty-carat gold hair over her shoulder. "Can you help me catch him? I left the windows down so the old thing wouldn't suffocate and this is the thanks I get! He's always doing this to me. Always! Always running away! And he never comes when I call!"

Virgil nods his head, but Lorna Jean is already gunning the motor and wheeling out onto the street.

"You look on the right," she says, "and I'll look over on this side. I swear. Speed will just kill me if that stupid Chesapeake gets lost. Three thousand dollars, he's worth on a bad day, Speed says. Damn Speed Maxwell, anyway. He leaves me this damn dog to baby-sit and doesn't even tell me—oh, look—look!"

Virgil peers out the window. He can make out the form of a big brown bearlike creature heading towards Kentucky Fried Chicken.

"Wait'll I get my hands on him." Lorna Jean gives Virgil a sidelong glance. "Do you think you could grab him? Maybe he would like you. Maybe he just hates women."

"Sure," says Virgil. The ice cream, something green with sprinkles, pistachio, he guesses, is beginning to ooze between his fingers, melting together with Meemaw's purple medicine, making little rivers of purple and green. God, he is holding Lorna Jean's ice cream cone, something destined for her mouth. Jeeze!

"There he is!"

Virgil looks up just in time to see Rock disappear behind a hedge. Then Lorna Jean mutters something awful coming from so pretty a mouth. Virgil is shocked. She really steps on the gas then.

Finally at Kentucky Fried Chicken, they both spot an earth colored brushy coat floating between the garbage cans. Lorna Jean slams on the brakes.

Out on the pavement, Lorna Jean and Virgil move in opposite directions around Kentucky Fried.

Rocky pauses from his sniffing to give a short bark when he sees Lorna Jean. Then he does this stupid dog bow, like "Let's play!", and runs off. But he is running toward Virgil.

"You dumb dog!" shouts Lorna Jean. "Give him the cone, Virgil! Give him the cone!"

Rocky starts to detour around Virgil but slams to a halt when he sees Virgil bending down, holding out food. He gets a whiff of the ice cream. He does his silly bow, wagging his tail, and zeroing in on the cone, sniffs, and eats it in two chomps, coming down in the second chomp onto Virgil's sore fingers.

"GRAB HIM!" hollers Lorna Jean, and Virgil does. He lunges, circles the thick hairy neck in a swoop, and winds his smarting fingers under the collar.   Then he half hauls, half drags Rocky to the jeep.

"Thanks, Virgil," says Lorna Jean.

She climbs into the driver's side. "Thanks a million. You saved my life." She leans out the window for a second and stares him right in the eye, moving a polished piece of hair back over her shoulder. "Really. Thanks." Lorna Jean's gaze stops a second probably on the purple medicine on his face. Then she smiles at him like she sees purple faces with claw marks across the side every day of the week, and drives off, leaving Virgil in the parking lot of Kentucky Fried Chicken rubbing his sticky, smarting fingers.

Virgil blinks. It all happened so quickly. If he did not have ice cream stickiness all over his hands he would think it is a hallucination— barely five minutes passed since he first saw Lorna Jean come hurrying out of Baskin Robbins. But he stands there, three blocks out of his way now, transported by a few minutes of time, by Lorna Jean Gibson, dreaming of things dazzling and miraculous. He stands there in the sun, feeling almost alive.

Fifteen

*O*verhead the heavy cloud banks part. On the plain, nervous Brahma cattle lift their heads, sniffing the seawind. Virgil's bare feet press into the hot dust of the road. The road leads from the city, past the empty, double-tiered rows of buildings with their reed mat shades unrolled. Near the sea, Virgil crouches near a wall as six bearers appear dressed in white, carrying a large shrouded bundle. Overhead shadows move. Virgil follows. The Bearers ascend steps. The Beloved One is placed at the top of the steps and the bearers descend. Virgil flattens himself on the wall, but the Bearers walk right past him, as if he is invisible. They disappear and Virgil sprints up the steps. The shadows have become the vultures they are, busy picking the Beloved One clean, garbling and slashing. With the shroud shredded it appears to be a woman. Virgil tries to yell, but at first he can't make his voice work. Shoo! Shoo! he finally gets out. Virgil looks over the wall. Come back, please come back, he yells to the bearers. He shuts his eyes. They won't be back for several days, until it's time to gather the remaining bones and cast them into a pit. Footsteps make him open his eyes. The vultures are gone. Speed and Douglas are bending over what is left of the bones of the Beloved One. Douglas appears disgusted. "Virgil got to this one," he said. "Aspirated." "Douglas!" yells Virgil, but he doesn't hear him. "Douglas! Speed!"

Virgil opens his eyes in his own room. Good grief! He is dreaming about the funeral customs of the Parsis people in Bombay. Not as bad as the dream the night before with Mrs. Oliphant yelling, "Help! Let me out!" from a casket shoved into the crematorium. But bad enough. Virgil sits up. His brain aches. His face is very hot. After eating Meemaw's black-eyed peas with Louisiana Red Hot he never sleeps well. Neither does Shelby. Virgil can hear him in the next room tossing restlessly and farting in his sleep between his snores. But what an awful dream. The Seven Towers of Silence! Douglas and Speed! That reminds Virgil. He has seen those two today with a Beloved One on a gurney, and they look in a hurry and not happy to see Virgil who has come back early from his break. Virgil thinks about that Beloved One. Who the heck was he?

∞

Virgil sits under his old post, the bronze, metallic Classic Beauty. He never felt so low. Yesterday he saw Daisy with her boyfriend, Owen, and it reminded him of all he didn't have, mainly Lorna Jean. Daisy and Owen have taken to sitting out on Daisy's back porch in the evenings, busy with some kind of project involving books and papers and ledger looking things. Daisy says they want to open up their own business. A Snow Cone stand or something.

Virgil's gone really weird and he knows it. In the day he's so tired he can hardly make it. At night he has bad dreams. And every time he sees any couple having a good time, it makes him even more depressed. Even advertisements on TV like those dang Mountain Dew commercials—everybody with somebody fooling around on a rope swing and drinking cold drinks. But he can't help it. He just can't stand to see people together. Why has he ever let himself believe he can have a life with Lorna Jean? He would never even have a date with her. And it seems so long ago that he was in the Bronco with her, that close to her.

Virgil hasn't sat down under the Classic Beauty— he'd collapsed. It is five o'clock, and he has a right to be exhausted. Harvey is in Memphis, and Virgil has been through two Beautiful Memory Conferences and helped Douglas reconstruct the face of a twelve-year old who took her brother's three wheeler out for a spin. Douglas molded on her face only a faint semblance of the Smile because just getting the face together was a big enough job. Next, at a viewing, the wife of a suicide climbed into her husband's casket with him and refused to get out for a real long time. Her children finally talked her into climbing out. Then an autopsy came up on the elevator, the Beloved One on the gurney and his intestines in the familiar Vlasic pickle bucket. At first Virgil just flat refused. When Douglas saw Virgil was serious, he just snipped the large, sloppy temporary stitches the morgue always did, and dumped the contents of the bucket back into the Beloved One, then sat and read the racing form. Virgil eventually had to do the stitching, because he needed the table himself for the next Beloved One, which was legally his. Virgil's fingers, finally healed from cat clawing, were bumpy with blisters. And despite the things he does all day, he hasn't been able to get Lorna Jean out of his mind. Lorna Jean. Lorna Jean. Sometimes Virgil feels just like one of the Bereaved Ones. When he looks in a mirror it is like he has a long old sad bereaved face himself. Sometimes he thinks he hates his job. But he knows that can't be so. It is just old Douglas. And the way he lets Speed Maxwell hang around. Speed makes Virgil totally nervous. And the way Austin messes up. And Virgil keeps getting the blame. Virgil suspects Harvey doesn't even like him any more. If he ever did.

Daisy probably sits around all the time with her boyfriend, just like Lorna Jean and Speed. All of them sitting in some warm, erotic daze. The only thing Virgil has is memories. That night when Lorna Jean used his phone. That day when he helped Lorna Jean catch Rocky. It all seems like very old daydreams. Memories! Nothing but memories! At work his eyes have begun to ache. Instead of enjoying his work, he constantly feels light-headed, even dizzy with all those bereaved beings whose Beloved Ones have been summoned by what Harvey calls sometimes, the Great Equalizer. (Harvey sure has a way with words.) But some of the Bereaved Ones: hazy, filmed over eyes, uncomprehending—their connections for the Beloved reaching beyond death—seem like the dead walking themselves.

"Yo, Virgil!" A voice is calling him from the other side of the double doors. "Phone!"

Virgil struggles to his feet and walks into the lobby. Not another customer, he hopes.

In the office he sighs as he sits down in Harvey's deep leather chair.

"Virgil Matthews," he says into the phone.

"It's Daisy." Daisy's breathless voice fills his ear.

"Lorna Jean's with me and she's got a little problem."

At the sound of "Lorna Jean," Virgil catches his breath, his heart changes, suffers, grows, shivers.

"Whah?" he croaks out.

"Yeah, listen up. We need your help. Can you get into the morgue tonight?"

"The funeral home?"

"Whatever," says Daisy, impatiently. "We just need to borrow some refrigeration for a while."

Virgil takes the phone from his ear and put it on the other ear. "What do you want?"

Daisy says, "Can you help us—"

Just then the light on the phone came on. "Wait a minute," Virgil says. "I don't understand what you want. Let me answer this other line." He puts her on hold and stares at the other light for a few seconds.

Then he punches the button and says, "Virgil Matthews."

"Harvey?" a voice on the other line says. A giant wind follows the words into the phone. "This is Austin Pederson."

"This is Virgil," says Virgil.

"No, not Virgil. Austin!"

Virgil can hear, *whoosh! whoosh! whoosh!* It sounds like traffic, and then sure enough, he hears a horn blast.

"I need the address again. Could you repeat it?" Austin is yelling.

Virgil has a brief picture of a coach parked at a Circle K while Austin uses the pay phone. He can see all the Bereaved Ones, with their car lights shining, parked waiting on the highway. He decides not to ask any questions.

"One eleven Hundred Oaks Drive," says Virgil. "Off Exit 39." If he remembers correctly that funeral is going to the big churchyard cemetery near the interstate.

"Thanks, Harvey," yells Austin, and he hangs up.

Virgil releases Daisy from her red blinking light.

"So, could you?" Daisy doesn't even know she's been on hold.

"Could I what?" says Virgil. The other line lights up. "Hold it, again," he tells Daisy.

He punches the button. "Virgil Matthews."

A staticky car phone sound. And then, "Douglas? Well, I got all the arrangements we need, you old vampire, you."

Virgil stiffens. Speed.

"Now listen up. They want hearts, lungs, pituitary glands, aortas. Eyes! Kidneys, spleens, and brain parts. It's like a great big clearin' house here. We on to something bigger than we thought. We got it made, boy. Douglas? Are you there?"

Virgil reaches over and punches the button that cuts Speed off. He sits for a moment listening to the dial tone. He goes back over what he thinks he's heard. Naw! He has been working too hard or maybe he is really losing it. Eyes? Spleens? He must have really misunderstood something. Oh, hell. They must be kidding around! Yeah! He looks down at the light blinking on the phone. Maybe that is all code for something. Like LSD. Coke. Jeeze!

Oops! He almost forgets about Daisy. Virgil punches Daisy's button.

Daisy is saying, "—you meet us at the door. What time is that? About midnight?"

"Huh?" says Virgil.

"I SAID, Lorna Jean and me will be there at midnight."

"Yeah, OK," says Virgil. Lorna Jean? Was coming? "OK, OK." He didn't want to take a chance on them changing their mind by asking too many questions.

Virgil hangs up. He puts the crazy things Speed said in the far corner of his mind. Yeah! Must have been code for something. Those old boys probably selling serious stuff and are using some kind of code. But Lorna Jean is coming! Now don't get excited, he tells himself.

In front of him is some paperwork that he has put off all day. He picks up a pen and finishes it off. Don't. Don't, he says to himself. Don't. Then he walks to the lobby and tidies up the coffee cups and spoons and crumpled napkins. "Don't get excited," he says out loud, softly.

Five hundred gallons of Pierce's Cavicide Fluid arrives.

"Jeeze," says the delivery man pushing the overloaded dolly. "I didn't think I was going to make all my deliveries today."

"Don't get excited," says Virgil, showing him the elevator.

Finally, Virgil can hear the day shift knocking off.

An hour later, at midnight, he walks down the hall, back to the service entrance. When he opens the door, Daisy stands there already.

"It's about time," she says. She is wearing black jeans, and a black T-shirt, and a black baseball cap. She reminds Virgil of a cat burglar.

Virgil doesn't see Lorna Jean.

"Come on," says Daisy, and she turns and sprints toward the horseshoe drive side of the building where the coaches park.

When Virgil turns around the side of the building he sees Daisy trotting over to Speed Maxwell's Bronco where Lorna Jean waits behind the wheel. Suddenly he feels shaky, as though he were wildly hungry and forgot to eat. He starts taking deep breaths.

Lorna Jean looks at him out of the window of the Bronco. Her hair is loose around her face in the way that he likes it. But—she's been crying! Her eyes have little red cross-hatching marks around them and black makeup smudges.

Lorna Jean is wearing two pullover sleeveless T-shirts and the top one sags and shows the beginning of her cleavage and the other one's strap had fallen off one shoulder. Lorna Jean!

Then Daisy says, "Listen up, Virgil. Speed's dog has met an untimely end. We need to store him for a couple of days in one of those refrigerator whatchamadiggles."

"Whah?" says Virgil pulling his eyes from Lorna Jean's straps and letting them travel over the back seat. He focuses on a huge brown form. A bear. No, a dog. Rocky. A dead Rocky.

"It was an accident," says Lorna Jean. Then she opens the door and gets out of the Bronco.

"Look, the guy's going to freak out when he sees this," says Daisy. "Ugly temper. We figure if we could keep the mutt from going bad for a couple of days until Lorna Jean finds a good time to tell him. Preferably after a trip to Marshall, Texas."

Marshall, Texas! Virgil's eyes blurs. That's where everybody goes to elope!

Daisy opens the back door of the Bronco. She reaches in and

146

wiggles an out flung paw like Meemaw does when she checks to see if a turkey is done. "He's already pretty stiff," she says apologetically. "We were hoping you could do something about his face too," she adds, picking the dog's ear. Rocky looks like he has been scared to death.

Virgil forgets about Marshall. He is floored. "Are you crazy?" he says. "This is a funeral home, not a pet cemetery." This is the craziest thing Daisy had ever come up with. "Absolutely not. No. No way."

He feels Lorna Jean's hand on his arm. He knows it is Lorna Jean's because Daisy is beside him and he can see both of *her* hands. He breathes once and looks around as Lorna Jean's hair catches in some stray breeze and lifts off her face. Her lip quivers. Her eyes turn sort of darker blue.

"Please, Virgil," she says. "For me?"

§

Virgil heaves the hundred pounds of fur and rigor mortis onto the gurney and throws a sheet over it. Then he and Daisy push it towards the service entrance while Lorna Jean trails behind.

Virgil pokes his head in the door. When he doesn't hear anything he props it open and they push the gurney into the hall and toward the service elevator.

On second floor, Virgil backs out of the elevator dragging the gurney.

"Come on," he says. "We made it." Just then he bumps into something solid. He whips around. A thin kid with a Sony Walkman on top of a spiky doo stares at him.

"Oh-h," says Virgil. That is the last thing he expected to see.

The kid takes off the Sony and lets the earphones hang around his neck. A thin, far-away sound of Reggae wafts into the air.

"Hey," he says.

Virgil realizes he is staring at his replacement for his old job. How can he have forgotten somebody would be up here?

"Oh, hey," Virgil chokes. The kid looks vaguely familiar and then he remembers him--Brock Thomas, who's been the paper boy on the block. Daisy calls him Brock Strap.

"You Virgil, ain't you?" Brock is looking at the gurney suspiciously, Virgil believes.

"That's right," says Virgil. Then he has a thought. "You know you could go downstairs and check the back door. I think I left it unlocked."

"OK," says Brock. Then he gets a good look at Lorna Jean and Daisy. "Well, hey."

"Just stay there until I get back down there," Virgil says in what he hopes is an authoritative voice.

"OK!" says Brock, like he is pissed. He puts the Sony back on his ears and steps into the elevator.

In Preparation, Virgil chooses the lower, farther right drawer and pulls it out. Daisy and Lorna Jean wheel the gurney over.

"I'll never be able to thank you enough," Lorna Jean says.

"This may just work after all." She looks like she has cheered up. "See?" she says when Daisy pulls back the sheet.

"There's not even any blood. The old fool thing had a heart attack or something. Scared to death by a Mason on a mini-bike."

"That sounds reasonable," says Daisy.

"Do you think you could get him to curl up?" says Lorna Jean. "And wipe that horrible look off his face? I want Speed to think he died in his sleep."

Virgil looks at Rock for a minute. "Naw. You'd have to break his bones to make him curl up. He looks OK. And you'll have to leave his face like that, unless you wanted some major stuff done to him."

"When Speed finds out, he's going to come unglued," says Lorna Jean.

"Screw him," says Daisy.

"He looks like he's scared out of his wits," says Lorna Jean.

"Don't worry," says Daisy. "Virgil, here, can fix him. Relax, why don't you?"

Lorna Jean makes a face at Daisy. When she does that, it is so new, so cute, so different than the way Virgil has ever seen her, he is overwhelmed. Somewhere off in a distance, like in some other unimportant place, a phone is ringing.

"You better go," Virgil says reluctantly. He'd hate Brock to come back and find them all hanging around Rocky's drawer.

"Will anybody open it?" says Daisy.

"Nah," says Virgil. "We use this one last because it's kinda hard to get to without being in a strain. It's only good for a backache." Then he adds, "Not unless there's an epidemic or something."

"Let's go. This place is creeping me out," says Lorna Jean.

"Meet us at Shoney's for a Coke?" says Daisy.

Virgil looks at Lorna Jean and Lorna Jean looks at Virgil full in the face. "Can you, Virge?" she says.

Virge! Virgil feels himself flush. "Sure." he says. He doesn't believe it. He walks with her into the hall. He steps into the elevator beside Lorna Jean Gibson. He has a date! Sort of.

Downstairs Daisy says, "I'd better call Owen. He'll have a hissy fit if he doesn't know where I am." Then she adds, "Well, he won't, but he should."

Virgil shows Daisy the phone and when he goes back to Lorna Jean, Brock Thomas is standing next to her, and close.

"I ran the four hundred meters in high school," Brock is saying.

"OK," says Virgil. "Thanks, Brock."

"Say," says Brock, shooting Virgil a dark look. Then he turns back to Lorna Jean. "I jog almost every day. If you ever need somebody to run with, I run early in the morning. Don't you live near Stoner?"

Virgil tries frowning at Brock. He clears his throat, meaningfully.

Daisy comes up behind them. "See you at Shoney's?" she says. Virgil nods.

Then she says, "Got the car?"

"Naw," says Virgil, embarrassed. "I can walk."

"Igmo!" says Daisy. "It's twelve blocks. We'll wait in the Bronco."

Then Lorna Jean turns to Virgil and does something incredible. She reaches over and squeezes his arm. Virgil feels his insides crash together, something take possession.

"Thanks, Virge," she says, and follows Daisy.

Virgil and Brock watch her leave.

"I'd like to get at those leg veins," says Brock.

Virgil stares at Brock. "You better go back upstairs, now," he says, murderously.

80

After Daisy and Lorna Jean and Virgil settle into a booth at Shoney's, Daisy says, "Well?"

Lorna Jean snuffles a little bit and twirls the straw in her diet Coke. "It was just awful! Speed told me to take care of Rock today because he had a job—"

"Ha!" Daisy. "What *is* his job?"

Lorna Jean sticks her tongue out at Daisy. "Do you want to hear this or not?"

Virgil pretends to suck on his straw, but he cannot take his eyes off Lorna Jean. He wishes Daisy would be quiet.

"That Rock does anything for Speed, but not for me," Lorna Jean is saying. "Deaf! I told him to get in the back seat. Would he? NO!"

"Cut to the chase," says Daisy, taking out a cigarette.

"What I'm going to do is," Lorna Jean takes a sobby breath, "just tell him he's lost."

"Deep shit. You in deep shit," says Daisy. She lights her cigarette and looks at it meditatively.

"This will work. I know it will! When Speed comes back, we're supposed to go to Marshall. I told you! I told you we were getting married! When we get back, I'll tell him. By then I can tell him. We'll be married and all. If I tell him now he'll be so upset he won't be able to do anything."

"You ought to just tell him as soon as he gets back. Don't you think he's going to look for him? What happened anyway?"

Then Lorna Jean tells her story, "I was in Bunkieville, on the main street. Lord, if there weren't these orange sawhorses everywhere! Well, you know Lydia Madock? Well, I was taking her shower present to her mother's and I had to drive down a back street and it was crammed full of cars and people and then I finally stuck my head out the window and asked what was going on. There was this couple crossing the street, wearing matching purple jogging suits (can you imagine? Tacky!) and they yelled "Corn Festival Parade!" A damn parade! And then I noticed all these corn shocks around in people's yards and things and I just had to proceed at a crawl until finally I came to this intersection and I just quit trying. I mean I pulled over because of all these cars and people—I was just trapped. Here come some high school band playing, "It's a Grand Ol' Flag" and then come the Shriners next with those upside-down buckets on and riding those silly little minibikes. Then stupid Rock barked in my ear, permanently damaging my eardrum, and then he started to whine what Speed calls his pee whine. Jesus H. Christ! I just turned my motor off. I was blocking the side street, but I didn't care, and I opened Rock's door to let him out. And then I realized I should have put his leash on him." Lorna Jean took a deep breath.

Virgil is just floored. He just heard her talk more just then than he had heard her all his life.

"I mean this dog with a ten-mile pedigree running around, peeing on the camellia bushes and corn shocks and all and snuffing and barking. Then I jumped out and started calling, and he came back, but he wouldn't let me catch him. Just kept grinning up at me, and then here comes this troop of Boy Scouts hup two-ing in these crooked lines around this corner, and then these palomino horses and cowboys and all, and Rock gets so excited he runs after them. And here I am running after *him*. I had to cut right through the Boy Scouts, and this little fucker with these big thick glasses and fifty million merit badges hanging off his scrawny chest said, 'Whoa! Look at the tits on that!' Can you imagine that? Can you believe?"

Daisy is whooping. Virgil ducks his head. Lorna Jean'd been hanging around Daisy too much.

"And then this stupid clown on a unicycle almost ran me down and I was about to die! I yelled 'Watch it, Stupid!' and took another step right into a pile of horse shit and then this moron of a clown beeped his horn and said, 'Up yours, honey.'

Daisy slumps in the seat, choking, but it all just sounds so awful to Virgil. "Then—then?" gasps Daisy.

Lorna Jean goes right on, not even caring that Daisy is laughing, "And then the Grambling State Band starting playing, 'Oh, When the Saints' and did this fast turn around and started marching right toward me, and then they just marched right around me and did another turn around and I got whacked in the ass with a trombone. And then this black guy with this pointy little beard and little round glasses says, 'Stay cool, Mama.' What a day! OOoooo," fumes Lorna Jean. "I was about to lose it. Can you believe what that dog has put me through? And didn't have the decency to stay alive?"

"Speaking of the dog," says Daisy.

"And then, and then," says Lorna Jean, and she starts crying—"that damn dog was in the middle of the street—dead! And this horrible Mason was yelling, 'Wait'll I find the owner. I'll sue. I'll sue!'—But after he saw it was me he started coming on to me—and ever body started coming up and this other fat guy in the crowd yelled, 'Hey, honey, make your dog do that again.' And this woman with these two little bitty old squally babies said, "Hey, is that your dog? He's dead!" And it was all just awful. I mean if Speed finds out the truth—he is just going to kill me. He loves that dog—"

Virgil realizes that he has put his arm around Lorna Jean and is patting her shoulder. "Awful. Just awful," he hears himself saying.

"Aw, dry up," says Daisy. "It wasn't your fault."

"Speed won't see it that way," sniffs Lorna Jean. "I just about had him talked into marrying me, too."

What in the world does Lorna Jean see in Speed? Virgil thinks about that day when he came on to Daisy in the casket sales room at their Uncle Ronald's funeral. Why doesn't Daisy tell her that? Desperate times call for desperate... something.

"There, there," he says awkwardly, like a dope, but he doesn't know what else to say to Lorna Jean. He wishes Daisy would act nicer to her. Over her shoulder, Virgil can see the Shoney's waitress, a woman with pale skin and a curious blondish Afro, with a teddy bear pinned on her uniform, staring at them curiously.

"Explain it to me again. Why don't you tell him as soon as he gets back? Get it over with. He's going to be just as upset when he hears the thing's lost. When does Speed get back, anyway?" says Daisy.

"Day after tomorrow. And no! I can't tell him until, until...after we're married. I'll tell him we can look for Rock on the way to Marshall."

Virgil stops patting Lorna Jean. His arm falls back weakly on the greasy vinyl behind her.

"In a hundred years, you mean."

"No. He's asked me. As soon as he gets back. We're going to Marshall, I tell you."

"Well, heart attack for Aunt Mattie," says Daisy. "And what about your dream wedding you been talking about all your life? With your lime green bridesmaid dresses that match the punch? With the sparklers in your ten foot wedding cake?"

"Oh, hush. It's better this way. And if I tell him his dog is dead before we go, it'll just mess up everything."

"Well, you crazy!" says Daisy. "Isn't she, Virgil?"

"Naw. I don't know," says Virgil, from his own private hell. Marshall!

"What a way to start a marriage," says Daisy. "Why anybody wants to get married anyway is a mystery to me—"

"You just sorry you don't have Speed. Jealous!" Lorna Jean sits up real straight and looks really mad. "You jealous old thing!"

"This happens to be the stupidest thing you've ever said, cuz," says Daisy evenly.

"You just crazy," says Lorna Jean, jabbing her straw into her ice. "And jealous."

"Remember what Speed got you for your birthday? Think I'm jealous of that? It's about damn time you woke up!"

"Shut up!" Suddenly, Lorna Jean turns and throws herself on Virgil, sobbing. "Make her shut up, Virgil." Virgil goes from doom to the closest he has ever come to feeling good. He looks at Daisy over Lorna Jean's heaving T-shirt straps. Tell her, he thinks. Tell her Speed Maxwell is a two timing...Virgil can't think of an awful enough name.

"Mercy," says Daisy, disgusted. "Some folks have just got to learn the hard way. Aw, come on. I got to go see Owen."

Outside, off in the misty distance, the moon rises over what is the Red River, and Virgil, walking to the car, his arm around Lorna Jean, takes a deep breath of the bleary night air. So this is what it is like to be up close to Lorna Jean. He thinks of Rock, then, small price, in his cold drawer, hanging Virgil's small future in a secret balance. How worth it, it all is.

Sixteen

irgil pops Jesus and his cross off the wall above the altar and reaches for the Star of David he's brought out of storage. He is having to hustle because of the nature of the next service: Most Jews don't believe in preparation, so Harvey has to schedule this service within forty-eight hours and things are always a little tight. Harvey doesn't care for Jewish funerals, even though they get so few of them—there are hardly any Jews of any type in Harrisonville. But since the nearest Jewish funeral home is in New Orleans, Harvey has to know how to do them. The main thing is that Harvey has to special order the plain wood French Provincial. But just the funeral in general makes him nervous. "One second past forty-eight hours and it'd smell like a hundred pounds of mud cat left in a closet for two weeks," is the way Douglas puts it. Douglas is getting so bad Virgil doesn't even want to think about him. Mean! Shirking! Disrespectful! Virgil walks over to the west wall and reaches for a picture of Jesus and the apostles. He dumps them in the empty Star of David box. The easiest funeral of all is the nondenominational folks, what few they have. The hardest of all is the Assembly of Godders, especially the ones who are real comfortable about meeting their makers. They just practically enjoy a funeral, with their big, noisy wakes, and hate to see them end. Which reminds him, he has one in the casket sales room right now waiting for him. He beats it out to the sales room. What a rat race!

Inside, all he can see is the interminable lines of caskets. "Mrs. Grafton?" he calls.

"Yes, sir!" a voice calls. "Over here, young man."

Virgil turns down Subaru Street in its direction. Mrs. Grafton is standing over by Dreamy Dreams. Mrs. Grafton seems to be standing by Dreamy Dreams with a person inside it. Good grief!

"I declare," says Mrs. Grafton. I think this looks just fine on me, and that mattress looks right comfortable."

Virgil walks over and stares down in the person in the coffin.

The person is clothed but headless! He looks closer. No feet!

"Haw, haw," says Mrs. Grafton, sounding just like Meemaw. "It's just a dress form, sonny. I just wanted to see how I'm going to look. This lining is perfect with my dress, don't you think?"

"Oh, me," says Virgil. "Gee, Mrs. Grafton, we need to get that stuff out of there."

"The peach color is just perfect with this pale green polished cotton. You like this material? Two dollars a yard on the Wal-Mart sale table! Don't it go well!" She reaches over and tugs at her collar.

"Mama!" shouts a voice from the door. "What in the world are you doing?" Virgil almost jumps out of his skin.

A tall angular sort of man is striding in. He has the same tight Assembly of God face as Mrs. Grafton's.

Mrs. Grafton says, "Well, I caught sight of this newfangled thing in peach when I came here last week for Sadie Gilbert's funeral, and I thought it would look so good on me, and I wanted to see how I looked in it."

"You beat everything, you know," says her son, in a disapproving voice. "I wondered why you insisted on putting that dress form in the trunk. I should have known you were up to something."

"I said, I wanted to see how I'd look," says Mrs. Grafton.

"Well, still, Mama," says her son, lifting the dress form up. "This is just too much."

Privately Virgil sympathizes with her. Assembly of God women dress like brown mice, with their hair all weird and tied up funny. And Dreamy Dreams is a pale green on the outside, the inside like kitchen wallpaper with pretty green ivy and white trim against a pretty peach background and a mattress cover that matches. He wishes the son would take the dress form back to the car but Virgil has seen Assembly of God children all over town selling peanut brittle for their church. They look all sad and sanctimonious.

Virgil turns to leave, deciding to let Mr. Grafton handle his mother. He has a few more things to do before the Jewish funeral.

"Virgil!" It is Austin, poking his head in the casket room. "Come see."

Virgil sighs and follows Austin. What now?

Back in the Little Chimes Chapel Austin jerks his head towards the bier. Virgil looks over at the casket. "What?" he says.

"Open it," says Austin, in a funny voice.

"Open it? Naw!" Virgil says. This is a Jewish funeral. "We don't open them for Jewish funerals, didn't anybody ever tell you that?"

"I know that. Maizie and me put him in, and she told me. But I had to open it for a second. I couldn't find my Pocket Play Station."

Good grief! "You couldn't find your what?"

"I thought it fell out when I leaned over getting him in. But it's not in there. Guess what else is not in there? Open it. Open it, go on."

Pocket Play Station! For heaven's sake. Virgil moved the wooden bolts on both ends and lifted open the lid.

The Beloved One lay slumbering within one of the last remaining Jewish old school practices, the wooden casket. Virgil stared hard. He sucked in his breath, hard. This person was not Mr. Fishbein. "What happened—where's Fishbein? This is not Mr. Fishbein! This is not him!" Virgil realized he was babbling.

"Well, man. I don't know. It wasn't me who screwed this up. Fishbein is only about 30 or 40. This is an old, old man, the one you and Douglas did."

Douglas had prepared Mr. Dubose. He had told Virgil to take off, and he would finish up. No one had prepared Mr. Fishbein. Hardly any Jews ever did that. Before he started working at the funeral home, Virgil thought they even sent their own SWAT team or something to wash the deceased and dress it in shrouds, what was it called? *Chevra* Something. And he thought they left a family member to be with the body until burial. But Harvey told him the younger generation was leaning more and more to regular folks' funerals. Where are old school traditions when you need them? "Go get Harvey," Virgil told Austin.

A rabbi is entering the chapel. Virgil closes the lid hastily. Jewish folks do not want anyone looking at their dead. Well, he has not done that for sure. Good God! Mr. Fishbein must be on his way to the cemetery to be buried in Mr. Phineas J. Dubose's casket. "Go on, go get Harvey," says Virgil, as the horrible doomed feeling that he is beginning to know so well engulfs him. How in the world does this happen? He watches Austin leave the chapel. No, not him. He is a screw-up, but Douglas was on duty when the two had been brought in last night.

By the time Austin gets back with Harvey the chapel is half-full with Bereaved Ones. Harvey seems strangely cool. "Ssssssss," he hisses quietly. "Mr. Fisssshbein must be on his way to the sssssscemetery right now, Mr. Matthews. In the meantime, just act natural. By the way, do you know there was a lady in the sssales room earlier putting a dress form in various caskets? Was that your idea, Mr. Matthews?"

Then Harvey turns on his Bereaved smile for the rabbi, who is coming over, frowning, and peering at them nearsightedly.

అ

Douglas, Virgil and Speed Maxwell are sitting over their beers at Squeaky's Lipstick Bar. The bad paint job on the outside reads GIRLS! GIRLS! GIRLS!

"Jesus Christ," Speed is saying. "That red-faced queer bait crap ass piece of shit. Austin's probably crawling with AIDS cooties right now."

"Naw, he ain't," said Douglas. "I ain't worried. Harvey made him get tested, though. All this thanks to Maisie. She saw him right after it happened. All soaked in fluid and everything. Then she tells Harvey. Harvey reads me the riot act for not having the kid suited up."

Virgil sits on one side of the booth. Speed has slid in next to Douglas.

Virgil stares at his beer mug. He has been taking hundreds of sips from it, but the beer, which is a little warm by now, has not even decreased down to the mug's handle.

"Well, neither one of us had on nothing. Not even gloves, man. And then I hit the damn femoral aorta and next thing you know Austin is covered with fag blood. He yells and then Maisie runs in." Douglas changes his voice to sound like a woman, "Oh, my god! Oh, my god! You goin' die! You goin' die!' Austin, the fuck-up, ain't worried though. It was the doctor that turned Harvey in when Maisie made Austin get tested. Would have been too early to know anyway."

Virgil looks at Douglas. He is so good Harvey never even makes him wear protective covering, but now there is this big mess with the Beloved One with Aids and Austin. Even though Douglas isn't worried, Harvey is, and that makes Virgil worry, too. It is all just too awful. All this happened last week, right after the Fishbein-Dubose incident but Virgil is only just now hearing about it. And now Harvey may get fined. And on top of this other strange thing with the mixed-up Beloved Ones, which has yet to come out, if it ever does. After the funeral, Harvey just said something like, "Leaving well enough alone." Not only did that blow Virgil's mind, he is not sure he's right. His social studies project, "Funeral Customs of the World," had taught him that respect for the dead was real big with Jews. Even if they didn't have watchers for the body day and night any more, chanting and reading from the Book of Psalms, and even if they didn't tear their clothes, that family would probably have a conniption if they knew the truth. And Phinneas Dubose's family too. Plus it's another awful secret he has to keep. It is an off-limit topic for them to talk about Harvey has decreed. He made Austin and him swear, for the sake of the families, he said, not to even talk about it between themselves. Disinterment was just too disturbing and could be psychologically damaging, he said. But whose mistake was it? Nobody got yelled at that Virgil knew about.

"Austin took the first test. It was negative. Then he'll have to take another one in six months," says Douglas, waving at the waitress, who pretends not to see him.

"Well, tell him to study hard, then," says Speed.

"Honey!" yells Douglas. "Sitting on empty here."

The waitress, whose name is Darlene, turns around. "OK, OK, keep your pants on." Darlene is kind of a controversial person around Harrisonville. She once made everybody in the bar sign a petition to recall Governor Edwards before she served them drinks, and then, after she'd been fired, she got her job back, it was said, by threatening to report building code violations on Squeaky, owner of the Lipstick. The fire chief was her uncle. Plus, Darlene was kind of like Daisy, real tough. Unlike Daisy though, she dropped out of high school in the ninth grade.

"You want another beer?" Speed is looking at Virgil.

"Naw," says Virgil. He looks down at an addled fly that is making his way across their table, something the matter with its wings. Virgil can't look old Speed in the eye. Speed has spent the last few weeks looking for old Rocky. Putting up flyers. Riding around, calling. But all the while unmarried. For which Virgil thanks whatever gods there be. The fly stops suddenly as if realizing the huge plane that he is traveling on might not be as empty as he thinks.

"Well, Jeeze, Virgil," says Speed. "You sure must like your job."

"Huh?" says Virgil, startled.

"You wear your uniform all the time?"

Douglas snorts.

Virgil looks down with horror. He has forgotten to take off the new blazer Harvey ordered for everybody. The blazer is an *M & M* candy green with a fancy gilded *H* on the pocket. The first time in his life he has gone out for a beer with somebody! The first time in his life when he has done something normal—even considering the fact that he has hidden this man's dead dog from him (and he wishes even more misfortune on him: mainly that he would lose Lorna Jean)—for once in his life he is having a drink with some guys in a bar. Not like with Booger, out behind Booger's daddy's garage. The beer doesn't seem to taste any better though.

Virgil ducks his head. At first, because of that secret, he felt not so separate from everybody, not so doomed to that feeling that he is the one who never knows what is going on all the time. Keeper of the dog. For Lorna Jean. But Rock is causing problems at Harrisonville Funeral Home. Big problems.

Douglas is still snorting. "Man! Harvey! Making us wear uny-forms. We all look like a bunch of Century Twenty One Realtors."

Just then Darlene walks by with a tray full of empty glasses.

Speed sticks his mug out in front of her and turns it upside down. "Well, what you want me to do now, Darlin'?"

"Well, I don't know, Sweetheart, what you big enough to do?"

says Darlene, neatly sidestepping him and beating it.

"Wooo-oo-woo!" says Douglas.

"What a dog!" says Speed.

Virgil looks down again. He wishes Speed had thought of another animal insult. In a minute Darlene is back, with three beers.

Virgil lines his new beer up with the nearly full, warm one and groans to himself.

"You a jewel," says Speed to Darlene.

But Darlene is staring at Virgil's side of the table, narrowing her eyes. She reaches out in one smushing, swiping move and takes care of the fly, which has begun its unlucky journey around the other side of the ash tray. Then Darlene sticks out her tongue at Speed and leaves.

"Classy joint!" says Speed.

"Now, now," Douglas says.

Then Speed said, like he has just thought of something, "Say, Douglas, have you talked to Virgil about YOU-KNOW-WHAT?"

"Why no, I ain't," says Douglas, in an innocent-sounding voice, and winks. "But I ain't so sure now's the time. Maybe we better get to know this old boy a little better before we say too much. He might not like our extra business."

"Huh?" says Virgil. They were both smiling at him in this real friendly way.

"We just may let you in on a little side business we have, Virjull, in case you'd ever like to make some extra money."

Virgil can't help be a little flattered, even if Douglas did say his name in a funny way. Even if it is Speed Maxwell, who is probably the only person in the world he hates. Then something strikes Virgil. Maybe this is what Daisy and Lorna Jean want to know. Virgil says, "What is it? What kind of thing do you two do?" He hopes it's not drugs. He hopes it has nothing to do with that strange one-sided conversation the night Lorna Jean and Daisy brought Rock over.

"Well," says Douglas. "Maybe Virgil knows more than we think he does." He takes a big swallow of his beer and says, "Have you ever heard of DNA, Virgil? Genetic testing? Genomes? Replication? And stuff like that?"

"A little," says Virgil. Well, DNA, he had.

"Well, let's just say our side business is on the cutting edge of all this new genetic research. If you can just think of the human body as a factory. If you can just think of everybody as ah, just well, raw material, just potential raw material for a second."

"Raw material? How so?" says Virgil. "Does this have anything to do with cryonics? I'm real interested in that. I'm hoping Harvey might one day add that to his services. Is this what you getting at?" Virgil got a little excited.

"Mmmmm. Naw, not exactly," says Douglas like he is talking to himself. Then he says to Speed, "Virg-jull here, thinks old Harvey is some kind of goo-ru. After he talked to me on the way over here, I wonder if he's our boy, now."

Virgil takes a gulp from his beer. He wishes he hadn't told Douglas on the way over about Weighing the Heart of Anubis and the High Priest and the Legislative Tribunal. He was just trying to make conversation. He mainly wanted to interrupt Douglas as he started giving all the details about his afternoon chloroforming the cat. One of the Beloved Ones wanted her cat and bulldog buried with her. Douglas put the cat in a bag with a chloroformed rag and drove around Harrisonville until it passed. But he drew the line, he says, with bulldogs. Virgil has mixed feelings about the Beloved One's wishes. He knows burying possessions and all was a respected custom with all kinds of societies at one time—the Egyptians, for one. But he is glad the bulldog escaped his fate. Harvey ended up calling the Animal Shelter.

"Harvey? A guru?" laughs Speed. "That fat mother! He's a goo-roo, all right."

"Quiet, boy," says Douglas. "Virgil here believes all Harvey's bullshit." He smoothes the side of his James Dean hairstyle and gazes off into space like Virgil is all beyond him. Then he says, "Virgil here knows all about the Ee-gyptians, and spirits and stuff. All summer he keeps askin' me, 'How long do they last? How long they going to last?' He's real interested in making everybody last a long time."

"Naw, I ain't," Virgil tries to say good-naturedly. Then he makes an attempt to steer the conversation away from the Egyptians and back on to their sideline. "That was just an old social studies project I did once. I was just thinking about stuff—sort of—Now what kind of side business you talking about?"

"Man wakes up wondering about exhumation! Happens to me

every day. Have you ever, boy," says Douglas, "seen a ex-hoo-mation? How long do they last? Ha!"

Virgil leans over his warm beer and the cockroach smudge. "Naw," he says, trying to sound casual. "What's it like?"

"Oh, God," says Speed. He tells Douglas to move so he can get up. "Y'all goin talk shop all night."

Virgil watches him make his way through the crowd.

"It ain't a pretty sight, son," Douglas is saying. You can just forget all that art talk."

Over Douglas' shoulder Virgil can see Speed has come to a stop in front of a vocalist in a red spangly cowboy shirt, who is taking a break. She has long hair except the hair on top which stands up like a boy's too-long crew cut. It looks kind of cool on her. Now he can see what Daisy was trying to do when she tried the same haircut in the eleventh grade. Then Virgil stares at Douglas. He can also see right away that those two are standing just way too close together. In fact, Speed leans up against the bar in a way that kind of traps the spangly blouse, who doesn't seem to mind. Speed's gold necklace glints at the open throat of his Native American print shirt. At that second the girl's arm reaches out and comes to rest on Speed's arm. Virgil hates him! While he is hating him, Virgil decides to go out soon and to try to buy a print shirt like that.

"An exhumed body," Douglas is saying, "is the most dis-gusting, moldy, foul-looking son-of-a-bitch you ever saw. You know that old song 'John Brown's body lies a-moulderin' in the grave'? That just what it does."

Virgil stops staring at Speed and stares at Douglas. In grammar school he hated that song. It always sounded sacrilegious or something.

"You may have a intact body," Douglas goes on, "but I'm talking gross, man. Even after a week, it's pretty sorry. And after two months? Mr. Roger Sinclair—sposed to have a three hundred dollar gold watch in his pocket? Well, let me tell you, Mr. Walk-Like-The-Egyptians, the casket is busted, the pretty silk is all stained and polluted with body fluids. We got your rotten wood—I don't care how much you spent on it. We got your body mold—body *covered* with mold. Mold everywhere. Long whiskers of penicillin mold on your face. And putrid? Picture what a million pounds of the worst trash buffalo fish would smell like laying out in the hot sun in the middle of the Gobi Desert on the hottest day in

August, multiply it times a million, and you got it."

Virgil stares down at his drink. He just hates the way he talks some time. Not like Harvey, all mysterious and reverent and everything. But he guesses Harvey was right about the body mix-up. It would be too upsetting for the families to exhume Mr. Fishbein and Mr. Dubose.

Behind Douglas, Speed Maxwell, who Lorna Jean loved more than anything in the world, bends his head and kisses the lady in the spangly blouse on the mouth.

Virgil picks up his mug and downs half of the warmish stuff. He immediately feels a surge up into his brain.

"Sorry to tell you," Douglas says, like he is happy about something. "But you got such a thing for all this. But get real, kid! Hey—look at Speed!"

Virgil puts his mug down and looks. Speed and the lady musician have moved out on the dance floor and gone into a clinch, moving in time to piped-in music: "My Achy Breaky Heart."

Virgil picks up his mug again, downs the rest of his beer and reaches for the other one. The second one, not quite as room temperature, seems to go down better. Virgil looks around the room and his eyes start blurring, so that with the flashing lights it looks like everybody's face has penicillin mold whiskers.

An hour later Virgil is slouching in the back seat of Douglas' Monte Carlo. His very breathing seems to increase his nausea so he lies down, turns his head, presses his face against the cool glass, tries to breathe shallowly. In the front seat, Speed leans over and adjusts the radio.

Everything on the paved road is glowing with moonlight, so light it hurts his eyes, so light that when they turn on the streets through town Virgil can make out the hair-do pictures in the window of the beauty college as they speed by. It is so light, drunk as he is, he can read the blurred grocery store sale signs, *Hamburger! $2.59 A Pound!* He sees the Livestock Exhibition, the red striped bucket upon the top of Kentucky Fried Chicken, the package liquor store, all closed and shut down beside Harrisonville's rolled up sidewalks. All shiny and clear and magnified and flat white in the moonlight. *Achy Breaky Heart* lays a-moldering in the grave, Virgil hums along with Billy Ray beyond caring about anything.

Seventeen

Virgil has come by himself to the Harrisonville Livestock Exhibition barn. It was built by the Dixie Lumber Company and the Modern Masonry, Inc. about the time he was in middle school. The town had hopes of enticing the home of the state fair from Shreveport to Harrisonville with its fancy new arena and stalls. The plan has not worked though. Now the big domed hall is used for auctions and is rented between times to places like the Jackson Parish Community College for various functions. Today there is a showing of artifacts from Poverty Point, a famous archeological dig in Louisiana.

Virgil wears his work clothes—brown dress pants, tie and the Century 21-looking blazer that he has started to hate. But earlier, at the funeral home, Virgil split his shirt down the back lifting a Beloved One out of a casket, so he is stuck with wearing the blazer all day. The caskets are designed to put Beloved Ones in, not to take them out. But the Beloved One hadn't fit in his casket. Harvey called the widow to choose another casket.

Another thing happened when Virgil and Maisie were settling another Beloved One's head down upon his egg-shell rucked pillow. The Beloved One had been a biker. He was being buried in an open vest, studded jeans, and boots. Maisie washed and trimmed his beard and tied a bandanna around his head, according to his friends' instructions. Nearby, leaning against the wall, were the biker's handlebars from his Harley-Davidson. The handlebars were supposed to go into the casket. Actually, the whole bike was supposed to go into the grave with the owner, but the cemetery just flat wouldn't do it, and told the biker's friends that burying a motorcycle in a grave was against the law. Then the bikers said they would be satisfied to have the handlebars put into the casket with the Beloved One. But the handlebars were too wide. After the handlebars were in, the lid wouldn't close. When Douglas told the bikers the bad news, they just came on back into Cosmotoge, and everybody was so afraid of them with their muddy boots and tattoos, that nobody would point out the *Personnel Only* sign and tell them to leave. Then the bikers took the handlebars and stuffed them into the casket and jumped up and down on top until the lid closed. Virgil just stood there—Maisie had long run—and watched and heard the crunching and smushing and thought he was going to faint or something! Things like that just blow Virgil's mind.

Inside the dome, the heat waffles and wavers. Virgil's skull feels like it is cracking apart with the slightest sound, and nausea, moving in little quantum leaps and bounds, is producing a sort of roll to his walk. Virgil has a hangover. He moves himself determinedly around the giant-sized, plastic-covered sketches showing the sectors, ridges, mounds and locations of evacuation cuts at Poverty Point, Louisiana. He has been looking forward to this all summer and he isn't about to miss it now, headache or not. He already knows some stuff about that area, from the eighth grade, Miss Goff's Louisiana History class. Poverty Point is almost as famous as the massacre site of Bonnie and Clyde over by Arcadia. The traveling show—all the pictures, maps, slides and glass-cased artifacts—are arranged to create a display almost as good as if you are really standing in person by the Bayou Macon at Poverty Point, Louisiana.

Actually Virgil *has* visited Poverty Point in person. In the fourth grade Mrs. Sullivan arranged a school bus to cart the whole load of them—both sections A and B of the fourth grade—to the site itself. But their miserable lot drew Mr. Fortenberry for a driver, notorious for safety and slowness. Mr. Fortenberry drove forty-five miles an hour all the way from Jefferson to Poverty Point for a record run of two-and-a-half hours. By the time they got there it was raining so hard it sounded like a machine gun opening fire on top of the school bus. The fourth and fifth graders, Mr. Fortenberry (who everybody, including Mrs. Sullivan, was ready to kick off the bus), and the teachers and chaperons sat on the bus in claustrophobic depression waiting for the rain to stop, and eating their peanut-butter-and-jelly sandwiches the cafeteria had sent along for a picnic. By the time the weather cleared up it was time to start home. All Virgil got to see was the vague shape of the museum through the gray sheets of rain and the dark outline of pecan trees and levee—where the mound was—lit up in one glorious lightning flash. So when Virgil read about the display in the paper he marked it on his calendar to make up for what Mr. Fortenberry and the rain had done. Funny it is raining today. Something about Poverty Point and rain.

But today, when Virgil looks at the sixteen-foot murals hanging from the Exhibition ceiling, right away he is reminded of his least favorite thing—advertisements. Among the 1000 year-old amulets and tools, the conjectured figures drawn like cartoons hang in bright primary colors. They have no depth. They seem to be drawn for little kids with their ancients smiling unmysteriously, like they are ready to step into a Chevrolet commercial on TV. Virgil hates all advertising. And this is one of the things he privately disagrees with Harvey about. Harvey, thanks to the pressure of a few new funeral home businesses that have cranked up around Harrisonville, now resorts to advertising: TV, radio—he is even considering a billboard. All geniuses have a blind spot, Virgil knows, and advertising is Harvey's.

Everything in a glass case is depressing anyway, Virgil thinks, peering at some fingernail decorated cooking balls. No way to touch the stuff, or pick anything up, make it real. He may as well be looking at more pictures. Not arrowheads, blades, scrapers, teeth and antlers—just flat shadowy rectangles, triangles, trapezoids, and tetrahedrons. And there is no ceremonial burial stuff at all, that Virgil can see. In a private pressurized space of his own, Virgil stands among the maps and the baked clay balls, the stone grinding tools, the polished atalatl weights, and with a reminiscent, distressing hint of peanut butter in his mouth.

It has been two weeks since Daisy, Virgil, and Lorna Jean hid Rock, essentially giving Virgil at the same time a moveable nightmare. A totally nerve wracking last two weeks it has been. The weather is clear and dry and so hot—up in the high nineties—old people are passing on all over town. Especially those in poor neighborhoods where they keep the windows boarded up out of fear of burglars and stuff. Mrs. Landsbury came in the brown van. But the worst is that every day at work, Virgil is always worried somebody is going to open a drawer or a door, depending on the last place he has stashed Rock, and find him. It is not easy hiding a one-hundred-and twenty-pound Chesapeake Bay retriever in a very busy funeral home. Twice he has taken Rock out of his drawer, and moved him down with Mr. McDavid—where he virtually is a sitting duck—then move him back. In addition to the heat, a three-car pile up on the interstate and a separate church bus accident claimed all the drawers two different times. Virgil is a nervous wreck because there is just no place to really hide him in Mr. McDavid's freezer.

The truth is Rock has become a big, cold thorn in Virgil's side. It is crazy. As long as Virgil has Rock, it means that he has some connection, some semblance of a connection with Lorna Jean. Of course, that is good. But keeping Rock on ice is the biggest problem in logistics that Virgil's ever had. That is horrible. When he did screw up his courage enough to call Daisy to call Lorna Jean and get some kind of time line on the keeping of the dog, she told Daisy that when she'd told Speed that Rock was lost, that some maintenance men had let him out of the apartment by accident (she'd been working under the reasoning that lost was not as bad as dead), Speed blew up with just that. He has postponed their elopement. So everybody is just in limbo. Speed out every day, looking. Lorna Jean said she didn't have the heart to tell him now after she's told all those other lies. She is just convinced Speed won't forgive her unless they are married.

Just thinking about the mess now makes Virgil's headache worse. Sometimes he thinks he should let Douglas know about Rock and then Douglas will tell Speed and Speed will break up with Lorna Jean permanently. But Lorna Jean may find out Virgil planned that and then she will never forgive him. Deep down inside Virgil knows he is prepared to keep the Chesapeake forever, if she needs him to. And sometimes he thinks it is kind of sweet that Lorna Jean sees keeping Rock around as important. Not just tossing him away like an old dirt clod. Even if it is for old Speed's ultimate sake.

"Excuse me, sir?" A little girl with goggle-looking glasses, and in a tee shirt with Bart Simpson on it is looking at Virgil politely. "Do you know where the rest rooms are?"

"Sorry," says Virgil, turning back to the cooking balls. He must look like he works here or is sort of official or something, with his blazer and insignia and all.

He moves to a case of untempered pottery shards where a couple of high school kids are holding hands and popping their gum glumly. "This is borrringgg!" sings the girl. Virgil moves on. Even though the kids are unappreciative of pottery shards, Virgil can't help envying them. He still finds just any couple in general painful to see. And they seem to be everywhere. An old couple in matching tee shirts and baseball caps walk hand in hand in a kind of aimless direction. A middle-aged couple is laughing by the display of hand axes and flake tools. Everybody seems to have somebody.

In the part of the dome that is used for an auditorium folding chairs are set up for the slide show. A few children and parents are sitting in them, staring at the blank screen. Virgil sits down near the front where he will have a good view of whatever it is to be shown. A loudspeaker opens up somewhere with a piercing echo. The children put their hands over their ears and giggle. Then a bowel-deep, enthusiastic Voice comes on and tells them they are about to view a slide show about Poverty Point, Louisiana in the year 1030 B.C. The first slide flashes on the screen and the Voice says, "*The Bayou Macon site was a tiny village of about two hundred working families. Their uncovered artifacts reveal no interest in ornamental display nor religion.*" The Voice tells them they are viewing women's culinary objects and men's lithic tools. Then the next slide clicks on and the stuff in it looks exactly like the stuff before. After the Voice, the next slide looks like the same stuff again! Several minutes later most of the parents and children get up and leave. After a few more slides, the rest file out. Virgil sits there all alone. He feels silly being the only person in the audience. But he figures it probably looks a lot sillier to leave, like he cares or something. Besides he is tired, tired, and his head is pounding now as though a hundred pound safe has been dropped on it.

In the semi-dark like that, the slides of the excavated tiers bring the dream of the Seven Towers back to him. Last night, on Daisy's back porch, Daisy told him that the Towers represented a *penis* (she actually said the word to him and in front of Owen) and that the whole dream was about sexual frustration. Virgil can't get over how Daisy will talk about stuff like that whenever it occurs to her.

Virgil is totally embarrassed that his private life was so crystal clear to Daisy and that she felt free to share her analysis in front of Owen. But Daisy is probably right. Frustration is a good word to describe his sexual life since it is nonexistent. Whatever hope he ever had of being able to declare himself to Lorna Jean seems more remote now than ever. Even though he daily risks his job, his whole future, in protecting her. It just seems impossible to love someone that long and that hard and not have the woman realize it after some time. But all women have always totally dumbfounded Virgil in every way. What did they want? What were they, anyway?

"The female objects were at first believed to be constructed of a rare and totally unfired clay."

All he really has of Lorna Jean were memories. That one kiss burns in his memory like a bright candle. Her flinging her arms around him, her breath on his face, the way she hugged his neck. Walking to the car under the moon—later he pretended Lorna Jean's distilled tears were for him. He had that day at Baskin Robbins memorized the lines of her short shorts, her striped pink tee shirt, semaphoring arms. A few times after that he has dropped by Baskin Robbins and ordered pistachio, the weird green ice cream he's avoided since a child, and sat near the window licking it, imagining that day, his movement through heat and time to his surprise of Lorna Jean, her precious metal hair surfing through the air in anxious fury over Rocky. What did that day mean? Wasn't that fate?

"The amazing beginning of solid clay figure discovery in the Lower Valley is a powerful indication of Meso-American contact."

Rocky has become a curse. The bleak truth is Lorna Jean is just using Virgil. He knows that. But it is better than nothing. Though the dog, the fear of discovery, is always in Virgil's mind no matter what he does. But if he just refuses to do it any more, just tells Daisy to tell Lorna Jean to pick Rocky up as soon as possible, he will lose the only contact he had with her.

"These stone female forms are problematic. Did they serve a talismanic function? Was there some use indicating an incipient spiritual inclination? Some rare later ornaments suggest their possible use as religious effigies."

Lorna Jean must really love Speed. That in itself should be
enough to cool Virgil's feelings for her. But he has known about that
forever, and even after that day he hid under the Bronze Metallic Classic
Beauty and heard them, their lovemaking, he just filed it in a separate
part of his brain. It is all so confusing. How did they do it? All of them?
Daisy and Owen. Lorna Jean and Speed. How do they figure out what
to do? What language do they speak? The fact is, Virgil has no real
relationship in the world, he has nobody. Nobody to see, to share his
time. He has more time accumulated with Rocky, carting him around,
hiding him, than he has with any human form.

*"The totemic method was prevalent. It consisted of a ceremonial
association. One theory reveals a connection between certain privileged tribal
members and special designated animals."*

Virgil moves in his folding chair. His head jumbles with dark
pain. Hangovers are not at all what they were cracked up to be. They
always sound so exotic to Virgil. And last night having a drink with the
guys was awful. Speed's hands, his mouth on that singer. Imagine! Having
Lorna Jean and not wanting to be with her every minute. And Douglas'
awful exhumation story! All that—for a $300 dollar gold watch! Virgil
cannot imagine a watch or anything being worth more than the peace of
mind of a tranquilly resting Beloved One.

*"It is believed that when a member of the tribal organization dies,
he or she appropriates another societal level. This position is notable in that it
is believed that the dead continue to have a sociable personality as long as he
or she remains in the tribal memory of the family unit."*

Suddenly two bony claws attack Virgil's eyes, and blinded, he
almost falls out of the folding chair.

"Guess who?"

"Good grief," says Virgil, turning around and pulling the claws
away. In the gloom and with the stars from the pressure it is a second
before he realizes who it is.

"Oona?" It is Oona Willard. Oona Willard from old Jefferson
High. Who won the Science Fair in tenth grade with her collection of
animal skeletons. Who is the only person in the world who used to say
"Hi" to Virgil in the hall.

Virgil says, "Well, hello, Oona." He is flattered she'd stuck her
hands in his eyes. He can never remember anyone ever doing that. He

peers through the foggy pain of his head and the fading stars, and smiles. He always remembers her skeletons fondly.

Oona says, "I thought that was you. Boy, would I have been psyched if it hadn't of been. What are you doing here?"

"Well—" says Virgil.

"Do you work here?" says Oona, peering at his blazer.

Suddenly, Virgil doesn't think he can bear it if Oona gives him The Look, like the teller at the bank recently gave him when he was opening his saving account, after she found out he worked in a funeral home. "Yeah," he hears himself saying. He will never see Oona again, anyway, if she does ever hear the truth.

Oona looks just like she did at Jefferson. Olive Oyl skinniness. Shapeless dress. Knee socks. Thin hair pulled back in a ponytail with a plastic hair band. Too-large glasses.

"Well," says Oona, "you always did like archeological stuff."

Oona is referring to his social studies project, "Funeral Customs of the World"—little pyres made of matchsticks, cardboard sarcophaguses, seven plaster of Paris Towers, even a plastic vulture from an old Dungeons and Dragons board game. It might have won too, but on the way into the building a sudden cloudburst drenched everything. In a matter of seconds the plaster of Paris melted into unrecognizable lumps, Magic Marker ran down Virgil's arms and dyed his shirt, and the glue in the meticulously authentic funeral pyres dissolved, and the pyres turned into the ordinary piles of match sticks they were. One foot off the bus and *wham*, like a little cloud just for Virgil, following him all morning, waiting for the right moment.

"I'm at LSU now," says Oona. "I'm studying Poly-Sci and sociology."

Virgil blinks. He remembers now. Oona had been a smarty. Beta Club and all.

"Say," says Oona. "You *do* remember that social studies fair, don't you? Tenth grade? You know you would have won it if it hadn't been for the rain. I saw it on the bus. I always thought of that blue ribbon as yours."

Virgil doesn't know what to say. He is touched.

"Well, gotta go. Hey—You remember Lyle?"

Lyle. Lyle.

"Lyle Johnston? He was four years older than me? He's at LSU. Pre-med." Oona drops her eyes. "We're engaged."

"Oh, yeah. Lyle Johnson," lies Virgil. It is his day for lies. "That's great."

"John-ston. Good to see you, Virgil. I gotta go meet Lyle." Oona takes her hair band off and rakes it back on again. "Say Virgil. I always wondered what happened to you."

Virgil watches her go. Oona Willard. Well, that is nice of her. He thinks of the Social Studies fair ribbon tacked up somewhere in old Oona's room. It had been a good project. Virgil gets up to go, too.

Outside, in the clear hot summer day a cloudburst has descended and managed to compress the temperature and moisture to where it is almost like a steam bath. Virgil pauses on the top step and sees Oona getting into a late model red Nissan. He sees her scoot up real close to the driver, who has fuzzy hair and who looks just as skinny as Oona. They kiss. Oona and Lyle will have tall, emaciated children with awful hair. They will live in a big doctor's house and be happy. Virgil's breath aches with envy.

Virgil goes right into the rain. As he walks home, he can feel the bathtub temperature water run down his collar, and melt the torn shirt underneath. It rains on him good all the way home.

Eighteen

Daisy has reason to believe that it is been her perfect contempt for beauty contests that helped her win them, and two in one year, no less. Daisy beat out blondes, brunettes, college-bound girls, girls who had nose jobs, and girls who had cut their teeth on baby grand piano legs. Daisy beat out all those piano playing perfect noses with her garage sale accordion and her repertoire of imitations: Lauren Bacall, Loretta Young, Katherine Hepburn, Myrna Loy, Grace Kelly. But she has no doubt that it is her complete disgust for the whole process that gave her the edge: the others had been so sweet, eager-to-please, and so nervous that Daisy had stood out from all the rest of those meek mice. All those shy, downcast eyes. Don't tell her, real men don't want something more than packaging. She has tried to explain all this to Lorna Jean when she came up after her two years later, but she never listened. And Lorna Jean is always a runner-up, never a queen.

Especially did she always keep the edge with her talent for body language. Daisy learned body language long ago from *The Big Sleep*. Lauren Bacall was one person who believed in a lot of hard core eye to eye contact and letting it all hang out sexpot stuff.

Daisy enters contests with a mercenary eye. On a personal level she has no use for them. The prize for MISS CHICKEN OF TOMORROW was a VCR and the prize for MISS POKE SALAT was a CD player and a hundred-dollar gift certificate at Laverne's Sound Warehouse.

Former Miss Chicken-Poke-Salat did a lot of things for sound, practical, monetary reasons. Right now though, Daisy, devoid of any avarice at all, is walking up Owen's steps to where he is waiting inside. She won't have to knock. Owen is the kind of guy who never locks his house.

Daisy loves thick-aired summer nights, sweet cut grass aromaed, cricket-voiced. She loves filmic situations. Take one, thinks Daisy. Enter Daisy. Slow pan to Owen. Close up of Owen's eyes, looking at her looking at him. Quick cut to: A June bug careens through the door from Owen's porch light. It dive bombs Daisy and tangles in her hair.

"Durn," smiles Daisy, going into the kitchen. She pulls on the bug gently. She hates the feel of one crushing.

Owen's kitchen is its usual unusually tidy place. The oilcloth on the table is wiped clean and the old double-unit porcelain sink is empty. A dishrag hangs neatly and humbly on its divider.

"What?" says Owen, watching her pull on her hair.

"Bug."

Owen takes the strand Daisy is working on and gently extracts the thing. They look at it under the naked kitchen bulb that hangs over the table. The June bug climbs up Owen's finger and opens the cases over its neatly folded wings. It stretches them out, thin, clear skins, spread over tiny struts.

Owen scoops it up with his other hand and Daisy opens the door. Owen holds his hand up to the outside light and gives it a shake to make it fly.

Owen pulls her to him. He is the first man in Daisy's life who never used cologne. He smells like Lava soap and tobacco and WD-40. He kisses her some more.

Owen's bedroom is just as neat as his kitchen. He has a good bed but not much furniture. He keeps his clothes and stuff in a couple of cardboard boxes beside his desk. His desk is made out of a door laid across two chairs. It is stacked with old *Mechanics Illustrated.*

Owen picks up, what looks like to Daisy, a long rug off the bed.

He throws it on the floor.

Daisy looks at it. It is gray and pink Aztec print with a wide fringe.

"That's a horse blanket," Owen explains. "It's new. I got it in a garage sale across the street."

"I'm glad you didn't get the horse with it," says Daisy. She puts her purse on the upside down Tide carton that is Owen's nightstand. Then she sits down on the bed and sloughs off her Ropers while Owen goes to get the drinks. Daisy swings her feet up and snuggles them in the horse blanket, satisfied as hell. She leans over, takes out four already rolled joints from her purse and lines them up on the carton.

Owen comes back carrying two super-full drinks walking carefully like he is holding lighted candles. He looks atDaisy in bed. "Whoa," he says.

Owen sets his drink down and goes into the bathroom. She hears him pissing and the toilet flush. Then the sound of water running into a drainpipe. A good thing about movies is that you can cut all this stuff. Daisy giggles.

Owen comes out of the bathroom and starts taking his shirt off. He has a little beer belly and his skin is too pale but he has nice muscles on his arms and back. Daisy stands up and pulls off her blouse. Used too, she always liked to be the first undressed. In fact she used to get turned on by snuggling up naked to men who were fully dressed. Now though, it doesn't seem like the thing to do.

Owen pulls back the bedspread and they get in and pull his silk sheet up to their chins and sip their drinks.

"I always like these sheets," says Daisy, wiggling her toe into a hole.

"They kinda old."

"What possessed you to buy silk sheets?"

"I like the way they feel. And they were cheap. I bought them in a—"

"Garage sale," Daisy finishes for him.

"They was almost new," says Owen.

They don't look at each other. The house is quiet. Owen puts his drink down on his Tide carton and takes Daisy's out of her hand and sets it next to his. The only light, that from the bathroom.

"That light bother you?

"Never has."

"I always sleep with a light on." Owen turns to her and runs his fingers down her face. "It runs in the family. My daddy sleeps with the light on because once he stepped into a dirty diaper pail. My grandpa slept with a light on because he was a bootlegger and had to get up in a minute's notice and move the still."

Daisy runs her hand down Owen's back. Underneath the skin, in a few places, are the bumpy scars he picked up in Vietnam.

Owen pulls closer. Daisy sneaks a look at the bumps by the light from the bathroom. They are three moon-shaped ridges. For some reason they turn Daisy on.

"Jesus, you're a delicious boy," says Lauren Bacall.

Afterwards Daisy snuggles up against him and Owen puts his arms around her and holds her tight. He hugs her. When has she ever been hugged before Owen? Making it, yes. Kissing clutches. But hugging?

"We can fuck all night," says Owen, "if we have a mind to. I'm so glad you off work. What did you tell your folks?"

"All night film extravaganza. Centenary College. Shreveport." Daisy is still turned on and sleepy at the same time. She snuggles down deeper in Owen's bed. She feels Granma Lilah whirling in her grave. She feels Granma Bee giving her the high sign. The room, the walls, the thin light, begin to fade out with a slow even tilt to it like the end of a good film, getting ready for the titles and credits.

∞

The next day, Owen and Daisy sit on the porch waiting for Duran Duran, Owen's big yellow tomcat, to come home and devour probably his zillionth can of Nine Lives. It is 5:00 and they have long had lunch, hot dogs split with cheese wrapped in bacon, and after that, love in the afternoon. And now a cigarette. It is really too hot to sit on the porch and smoke like this, but they are too lazy to go back in.

"So what have you found out about Speed Maxwell?" Owen is saying. "Has any of your snooping paid off?"

"No," says Daisy. "We keep hoping Virgil will tell us something, but he's so spacey. If something happens under his nose, he'd probably miss it. At least we know it's not women, which was the main thing Lorna Jean was worried about."

"Virgil," says Owen. "He's a funny guy. Looks like the type of person that would jump out of his skin if you said "boo" to him and here he works in the funeral home and all."

"Yeah," says Daisy. "I think he's probably cracking up, though." Daisy studies the ashes of her cigarette. "He's got the hots for my cousin, but she doesn't know he exists. She's a little nuts herself. She's hooked up with the biggest sleaze ball in town and she doesn't even know it."

"So why don't you tell her?" says Owen. "You keep talking about how awful it is and all. Just lay it on the line."

"Oh, maybe she knows," says Daisy. "She just doesn't want to admit it." Daisy eases the ash off her cigarette. Even if she gave Lorna Jean a little heart to heart, Lorna Jean will never believe her. And the only way she will think Daisy is a credible source will be for Daisy to admit to sleeping with old Speed. What Lorna Jean is going to have to do is find out some big old awful thing about Speed. Proof. Thrown in her face.

Daisy sails the cigarette, half-smoked, over the railing. If she doesn't fill her lungs up with anything she is able to smell honeysuckle. Old Miz Holly next door, old nosy thing, always glaring at them over the boxwood, has some kind of garden. From the porch, she can see hydrangeas, mock banana, azaleas coming on, and day lilies. You can eat those day lily pods if you had a mind to.

"Jimmy Lee," somebody yells from down the street. "Come on!"

There is a smack of a ball and bat and a few subdued shouts. Everything seems lazy and drenched with summer.

"So you haven't found out exactly what this Speed Maxwell is up to?" says Owen. He rubs the back of his head like he always does when he is thinking.

"Huh? Oh, Speed. Well, the other night, about eleven-thirty we followed him to the funeral home again. He parks his Bronco, and then goes in. In a little while he comes out, drives off in one of Harvey's trucks, it's one Douglas drives some time, with a load of Porta-potties. We couldn't follow him, of course, because he knows our cars and everything. That's it."

"Maybe he's just delivering Porta-potties for Harvey."

"He's never done an honest day's living—that I've ever heard."
Daisy never told Owen either that she'd had a few dates with Speed in
the remote dark past. "Besides, why would he need to deliver the pots at
night? And why doesn't he tell Lorna Jean what he's doing? Why doesn't
Virgil know? Virgil has swore he never knew Harvey to have Porta-potties
delivered at night!"

"Maybe Virgil is in on whatever they doing," Owen says. "Maybe
he's not so wimpy as we think."

"No," says Daisy, "all he thinks about is Lorna Jean. Besides he's
so honest it's a crime."

"Virgil!" Owen laughs a little. "I saw him at the Food Lion the
other day. He opened an egg carton, and was just staring like a loon at
the eggs. For the longest time."

"Probably thinking they need a decent burial," Daisy says. "One
time he started collecting road kill and freezing the stuff. His Meemaw
told Mom, and I told a few people. Then at school everybody called him
"Road Kill Matthews.""

"What was he trying to do?"

"Don't know. He's just hung up on dead stuff and all."

Then Daisy says, "Lorna Jean's my cousin. I always looked out
for her since we were little. If I could just show her what a jerk Speed
Maxwell is, we could probably go off to school with a peaceful mind—
you going with me, of course. But she's always flying off the handle. If I
just told her, she would accuse me of wanting Speed or something."
Owen has already decided to go with Daisy when she heads out to
California. It is good practice to keep reminding him, though.

"So what are you going to do?"

Daisy puts her cards on the table. "We thought about you
following him one time, and see where he goes. We can't do it because of
course, he'd recognize us."

"Aw, Daisy," says Owen. "I don't know..."

"You can use Laurene Tinsley's car. He won't know her Mustang,
and he won't know you."

Daisy figures Owen should like to do this, use his Vietnam
skills in trailing somebody, and all. But you never can tell about Owen.

Just then a leaf moves, and Duran Duran hops up on the porch.

"Duran Duran!" says Owen. "You old heart breaker, you." Duran Duran has been gone for a few days and Owen has been worried. "Heartache, nothing but heartache," says Owen, reaching over and scratching behind Duran Duran's little cat ears.

Daisy looks at Owen. He sits back and pulls on his cigarette thoughtfully, staring out into the yard, and stroking Duran Duran in his lap. Tough as he looks, he loves that stupid cat.

"I forgot to mow under that forsythia bush," Owen says.

Just then Lorna Jean drives up in her Ford Escort and hops out. "Hey, you two," she says. She is wearing a pair of Daisy's red short shorts loose in the leg and that rides up over the bottom of her buns. Pee Wee made Daisy get rid of them.

Just then there is another smack on a ball. "Jim-meee," yells a voice. "Second base!"

Owen cocks his head. "Well, hey, Lorna Jean," he says, more like he is listening to the ball game.

Lorna Jean looks at Daisy and raises her eyebrows.

"He's thinking about it," Daisy says.

"Aw," says Owen. "A conspiracy."

Daisy goes into the house and brings out some wine coolers. "Did you wear that to work?"

"Heavens, no," says Lorna Jean. "We can't even wear jeans to work. I stopped off and changed. It's so hot and everything, I took off a little early, because Mr. Swanger's supposed to be at the chiropractor's and all."

"How's that car run?" says Owen. He changed the oil for Lorna Jean last week.

Lorna Jean shrugs. "All right, I guess."

"Sounds like it's missing."

"Probably is," says Lorna Jean. "Beings it's not even paid for."

"Bring it around some time," says Owen.

"Thanks. I will. Oh, by the way. Laurene says we can use her car. She has finally quit being mad at us."

"How come she's so nice to you?" Daisy says.

"Laurene?" says Lorna Jean, taking a swig of her cooler. The wine foams up and runs down her glass. "Laurene and Mr. Swanger are getting it on. I cover for them all the time. They were gone this whole afternoon."

Daisy wonders what Laurene sees in Mr. Swanger. He looks like Mr. Rogers with a mustache.

Lorna Jean stays for supper with them. She and Daisy and Owen move around the kitchen making tacos. Owen washes the dirty dishes scummed with the hot dog cheese from lunch. Lorna Jean chops tomatoes and lettuce. Daisy stirs the meat and the taco kit seasonings together.

"Speed and me never do anything like this," Lorna Jean says, turning the Bee Gees up a little on the radio. "Can I find another station?" The Oldies But Goldies DJ says, "Now for your next Oldie but Goldie." Harry Chapin is about to come on with "Cats in the Cradle." Lorna Jean knows nothing of the classics.

After supper, Daisy is a little embarrassed when Owen turns on the TV to watch *Mystery Science Theater 3000*. They are getting like an old married couple. Owen gets up and brings in more Nachos with whole jalapeño peppers thrown on top and more wine coolers and sets them down on his utility wire spindle coffee table.

Owen says, "Well, I guess I could see what old Speed Maxwell's been up to. It might even be kind of inter-resting."

"Thanks, Owen," says Lorna Jean. Daisy can't help noticing, she smiles a little teensy bit like Carole Lombard in *To Be Or Not To Be* when Benny outwitted the Nazis during World War II.

Daisy chomps down on a jalapeño pepper. She has industrial strength taste buds. Then Daisy put the jalapeño stem on the floor for curious old Duran Duran, the heartbreaker, just to be mean.

Nineteen

"OK. OK," hisses Douglas through the double doors. "Listen up. We got nine customers coming in from Dubach. Train and a pick-up accident. Clear out that end drawer on the bottom next to the wall. Y'all need to quit keeping y'all's Cokes in there, anyway—that'll give us exactly nine to use."

Virgil jumps, almost knocking his kidney bowl off the cart. They have seven free drawers, the Coke drawer—and Rock's.

"Come on, son. Hustle. Bring the—" Douglas stops, stares at Virgil, then lunges at him. He grabs Virgil's hand, the one with the trocar in it, and twists it up into the air, holds it, and stares with maniac eyes into Virgil's. "Closed casket, right?"

"Ow," says Virgil.

What is it with Douglas, Virgil mutters to himself, rubbing his wrist as Douglas claims the Beloved One Virgil has been working on. Every day it is, "I got it, I got it," when a closed casket is checked on the clipboard. Like he is catching a baseball or something. And Virgil gets stuck with all the intricacies of open caskets or the autopsies and their tons of discreet little stitches and synthetic stuffing. That is what is behind it! Douglas hates stitching. He hates aspirating. In fact, Virgil has a feeling Douglas is not aspirating at all—dang! He almost forgets Rock!

A few minutes later Virgil is beating it down the hall Rock wrapped in an old morgue sheet. Around the corner, he almost bumps into a Bereaved One and has to duck into the laundry room until it is clear again. This is getting old. Yesterday only by luck had he overheard that a too-early blanket of flowers—Harvey hates those because they cover up the beautiful casket that everybody can admire—should keep overnight in Rock's drawer and Virgil has just enough time to sneak Rock back in with Mr. McDavid and then return him after the funeral. Now here he is again. Virgil believes he is getting a hernia just from carrying this dog around. Over a hundred pounds of frozen dog.

Downstairs, holding Rock like an overgrown infant, Virgil switches on the light with his shoulder. There is plenty of room, but no hiding place. He drops Rock heavily into the corner and turns him around so that his tail is more toward the wall. Virgil pauses by the door for a split second—he is so out of breath he thinks he is having a cardiac arrest himself—and glances at Mr. McDavid's body bag. "Sorry," he feels compelled to say. If and when Mr. McDavid is ever revived through cryonics, Virgil, who is feeling kind of like they know each other, will have a lot to tell him. Then he switches off the light and runs.

∞

"Lorna?" whispers Virgil into the phone.

"Yes?" says Lorna Jean Gibson.

"It's Virgil."

"Virgil?"

"Yeah."

"Oh."

"I'm calling about Rock."

"Is he OK? I mean, is he still—secret?"

"Uh, yeah. But I keep having to move him and—"

"But you still have him?"

"Yeah. But—you have to tell. I can't keep him much longer."

"Oh, Virgil." Lorna Jean sounds genuinely distressed. "I can't. I just can't. I try and then I think how Speed's going to look. What he's going to say. Can't you just wait a little longer? He really thinks the dog is going to come back. That he's just off breeding something or that maybe some of those boys from Oak Ridge have kidnapped him—just until after the Holiday in Dixie Trials—They did that to him and Buddy Ray Snuggs' hound last year remember? It was in the paper? He went over to Long Ridge yesterday and rattled some cages, and of course they hadn't done a thing—but they teasing him. They won't say *yes*, they won't say *no*. He's worried, but he's not crazy. Besides, him going around looking all the time is helping me keep up with him. Can't you wait until we're married?"

Virgil takes a deep breath. "When—when?"

"Soon?"

Absolutely no. Impossible.

"Please. Virgil? This, this would mess up everything." Sniffing. "He'll quit looking soon. We'll get married. Then I—I'll confess. I can't take a chance now."

No way, thinks Virgil. This is the end of the line. All over. Can't be done. But he hears himself say, "Ok, Lorna Jean. OK."

ဢ

"She (chomp) hasn't told him, yet," says Daisy, chewing something in his ear. "Because she's scared of him, I think (chomp, chomp)."

Virgil moves the phone to the other ear and looks over his shoulder. "I keep having to move him around," he says. "It's getting dangerous."

"Well—" Daisy pauses and makes noises like she is licking something off her fingers, "(squitch) if you want, call and tell her she needs to tell Speed, *now* (squitch, squitch)."

"I already did. I mean I already tried."

"She's just trying to get married. After she's married, she thinks she can get Speed to do anything. She thinks she's going to train him or something. She's dreaming. This is a man who pays for an abortion as a birthday present."

Virgil is floored. He can hardly talk. He wishes Daisy was more...delicate, or something with the facts. "Whuhhh-whuh-why don't you tell her?"

"What?"

"That he's a jerk." Virgil blurts out. Why can't Daisy see she needed to do something? "That he tried to fool around with you," he adds, steeling himself.

"Do you really think she'd care?"

Virgil doesn't say anything. Of course, Daisy knows more about these things than him. But—

"Tell her. You tell her. That he's a jerk. Tell her that dog business is ridiculous. Besides Speed's spending more money on finding him than he ever did on any woman. He's got posters from here to Morgan City. You know what he did yesterday? Drove over to Long Ridge and almost got his ass licked. Messing with those boys across the river. They kept hinting stuff. Like they did it—like last year. Tell Lorna Jean you through."

"Naw, I don't know..." says Virgil.

"Chicken?"

"Naw!"

"HMMMmmm," says Daisy. Then she says, "Is it better to have loved and lost than never loved at all, folks? Only Virgil knows."

"Good-bye." Virgil hangs up. He is horrified. Daisy is too damn smart. Virgil feels about a ca-jillion years old.

"VIRGUHLLLLLL!"

Austin.

"CUSTOMERS! Come on!"

80

Benjamin Franklin, who predicted humans would one day live to be 1,000 years old, once said he would prefer to live one year every 100 years, so that he could peek into future centuries, even millennia.

Virgil looks at his watch. This afternoon the lobby is full of Bereaved Ones. A family of five skids off the interstate into an overpass and Virgil has to return the flat, stunned stares of the next-of-kin as he sets up an appointment for a Beautiful Memory Conference for tomorrow.

Virgil looks back down at his magazine article. He loves his breaks. Used to, lunch hours, breaks, they made him nervous. Used to, he didn't know what to do after he ate his Spaghetti-O's. He knows what to do now: hide out as long as he can.

Modern-day cryonics may eventually fulfill that fantasy, and the United States, home of the world's most prominent cryonics facilities, is in the vanguard of this emerging science—investigating suspended animation to enable sick humans to hibernate at sub-zero temperatures for decades, even centuries, without damage to the cellular structures, and to be awakened when cures are found for them.

Virgil stops reading and stretches a minute. He can hear Austin and somebody bumping around in the preparation room, but he has a good ten minutes left. Let Austin handle everything by himself for a while. Really, they had been swamped yesterday and today.

Since 1968, when the first human was cryonically suspended, the number has been steadily growing. There are now some 20 people worldwide in suspended animation, and hundreds have signed up.

Virgil pauses. Someone hollering. He reads on. *But the technology of cryonics has not yet been perfected. Patients who are frozen with today's techniques cannot be thawed out and revived. The cryonic suspension procedure involves the lowering of body temperature to -196 degrees C, after having perfused protective chemicals through the circulatory system.* Virgil stops reading and stares into space a minute.

"It's not going to work." Douglas bangs through the door. He is carrying a bucket of Kentucky Fried Chicken and a giant Icee. Austin is heavy on his heels.

"We outta stuffing. We outta paper towels," he says.

"Tough," says Douglas.

Virgil goes back to his magazine. He doesn't want to talk to either of them.

All experts agree that at liquid nitrogen's temperature of -196 degrees C, molecular motion is extremely slow and decay is essentially nonexistent. At this cold temperature, degeneration that would take one second at normal temperature would take 30 trillion years.

"You got any ideas?"

"Well, hell, I don't know. What is in the lost and found right now?

"Down jacket—nerdy. Umbrella, busted. Galoshes. City map."

"Hey, Virgil. Want some chicken?"

"Naw," says Virgil. *But the process also causes freeze damage. In fact, no vertebrate has ever been or can presently be revived after deep freezing and thawing. So although cold can preserve, it can also destroy. At -20 degrees C most of the fluids in cells are frozen, causing the formation of ice crystals and possibly substantial damage.*

"And I think somebody's left a CD, a couple of paperback books."

"What's the CD?"

"Rod Stewart."

"Bring everything. Well, hell. Go on. You always in such a big hurry."

...death is not a moment but a progressive pathophysiological process of systems shutting down...it occurs over time. A patient is declared dead after his heart stops beating and the coordination of his body is absent.

"Hey, Virgil. Through with that Spaghetti-O's can?"

Virgil looks up. He sighs. He hates it when they are out of stuff to pack with. "Yeah," he says. "Take it." He glances at Douglas' Icee for a second. He looks down. He blinks as the words on the page. *Thus, true death occurs when a person is pronounced dead and left at room temperature, causing the cells to deteriorate. Burial then permits the total destruction of the organism.*

∞

Virgil unzips the body bag.

Mr. McDaniel's eyes are sunk so far into his head they look like holes. His face is an awful vermilion and his hair is plastered so tight against his skin it looks like a black paint smear brushed across his forehead. His cheeks appear swelled, and though Virgil does not know how he looked before he died, they appear sunk in in the wrong spots and puffed up in other spots, the skin pulled by gravity into odd depressions and arrested in frozen, billowing bumps, with pulled tight leather skin outlining the bony ridges of his skull. The eye sockets, the nose, the gums, all about a trillion years old-looking. Virgil bends closer. He studies Mr. McDaniel's glacial lips, his mouth like an oblong piece of weathered rubber. All what must be the effect of the ice crystals on the cells, like tiny overstuffed monsters, stretching, tearing the tissue.

෨

Virgil stares down at the table on which lies a Beloved One whose face, he notes idly, resembles Pope John Paul's, and whose heart attack early this morning on the fourteenth hole at the City Golf Course has brought him to this particular stainless steel moment. The Beloved One has been duotronically injected, aspirated, and sewn up. Usually by this time, Virgil has developed a kind of affinity with the Beloved One, as though they have come through a great battle together or something. Now, though, this Beloved One seems to be staring reproachfully at Virgil—and at the Beyond. And why shouldn't he?

Virgil pulls up his rubber gloves, but his heart is just not in his job. He suddenly hates the next step, constructing the Semblance of a Smile, not a real smile, not even a faint smile, but the faint suggestion of a Smile. "As though Life was a pleasant memory, but the Hereafter is even better," is the way Harvey put it when Virgil first started as an apprentice.

Virgil's head feels heavy, his whole body, heavy as the Beloved One's. The Beloved One's color has not completely lost its bronzeness from the duotronic injection. He needs war paint. Virgil touches a cheek, and feels the marble cold coming through his glove. He pushes tentatively. Then using both hands he moves the Beloved One's face.

Virgil steps back. He looks at his work. What has he done? The expression now is less of reproach, more of horror, at this final card life has dealt. This will never do!

Putting his fingers on the Beloved One's face again, Virgil closes his own eyes for a second, then opens them and lets his fingers move. But the Beloved One won't cooperate! When he is finished the Beloved One looks disgusted!

Virgil hesitates, and then he adjusts the left eyebrow and smoothes the eye cusps to make sure they are stuck good. Then he pulls up the sheet and leaves it.

⸏

It is after midnight. Virgil picks up his scalpel thoughtfully. Outside, a summer shower's lightening brightens the Lorna Jean Window for a second. It causes a large bear-like shadow to be thrown on the opposite wall.

Rocky lies on the table in his heavy cringed position, in that twilight stage before completely returning to room temperature. Beside him lies *Volume 8* of Virgil's mail order taxidermy course.

Twenty

When she was twenty years old and lived in Plain Dealing, Meemaw had been one of the first people to have a car. Papaw bought her one, and Meemaw learned how to drive by practicing in the cow pasture until she was good. One day, under the delusion that it was a guide, she lined the radiator cap up with the yellow line in the middle of the new highway and drove to town, cars and pick-ups flying out of her way left and right. Meemaw never learned reverse—how to back up. Before Shelby quit letting her drive, she always parked in a way that allowed her to make a big circle wherever she went. In fact, Virgil had never known Meemaw to reverse on anything. She just made big circles, while people flew left and right.

"No way, José," she is saying right now. She looks out from underneath the flop of her sunbonnet at the deliveryman from Purina Feed and Seed. She has been planting late peas so that they will climb the old satellite dish Shelby hauled home but never fixed up. Now she crumples up the empty bag and hollers, "Virgil! Man needs to pick up some feed." Meemaw has discovered a new feed store, Evergreen, with cheaper chicken feed and she called Purina right there on the spot to come get their corn chops and Gro-start back. The deliveryman has been under the impression he was delivering an order.

Then the guy looks at her like he is remembering something.

Meemaw didn't buy enough feed to have delivered free in the first place, but somehow, a long time ago, she badgered the Purina people into not only delivering but also not charging her a delivery fee.

The man follows Virgil into the little shed where Meemaw keeps her feed.

"So this is the white lady with the little bitty old order every month," Virgil hears him muttering behind him.

After Virgil shows him where the feed is, he starts back to the chicken house. All morning Virgil has been cleaning out the chicken house, a job he hates, while Meemaw keeps a running commentary on everything he does because everything he does is too slow or not good enough for her. "Now he's washing roosts without taking them down," she says. "Now he's finally remembering the coal oil to disinfect." "Now he's looking for the lime 'cause he didn't put it back where he found it last time he used it." "Now he's found the lime and—"

Shelby calls from the patio, "Virgil. I need you to hold something while I drill."

"Now he's taking a break," Meemaw says, coming around the house with sack of fertilizer and a hoe.

Virgil doesn't even know what Shelby is asking him to hold. The contraption has two short PVC pipes sticking out of an old hair dryer hood and he is drilling a hole for a third with his old-fashioned bit and drill that looks like a big eggbeater.

Mike Hammer is busy digging in the new sweet potato slips. "Is oo helping Meemaw?" says Meemaw.

It is just the kind of scene Virgil thinks later he would have hated anyone to see: The delivery guy, hotly gunning the Purina truck out of the driveway; Meemaw, baby talking Mike Hammer, who was flinging up knee high size dirt storms; and Shelby, choosing just that moment to set the hair dryer hood on his head, gaze upward thoughtfully, and adjust the PVC pipes.

And there she is. Lorna Jean. Coming with Daisy through the honeysuckle. He hasn't seen her since the middle of summer.

"Yip! Yip-yip-yip-yip," hollers Mike Hammer.

"Hey!" says Daisy, leaving Lorna Jean treed by the satellite, and coming over to him and Shelby. "Shelby!" she says, knocking on his hair dryer. "Ho! Good grief! Anybody home?"

"Howdy. Howdy, girls!" says Shelby. "Virgil! Do we have any machine oil?" He wanders toward the back door like an addled Martian.

"Mind my clean kitchen floor!" bellows Meemaw after him. Then she turns to Lorna Jean, "You! Girl! Take two giant steps forward!"

Lorna Jean jumps forward three giant steps and keeps going, followed by Mike Hammer, suddenly quiet, bird-dogging her ankles.

"You was standing in my compost," Meemaw says maliciously.

"Well, Virgil," Daisy says. "Lorna Jean needs to get you know what. Like maybe not tomorrow, but the next day. Virgil? Virgil? Are you listening—"

Virgil is watching Lorna Jean move toward them. "Whuh—" he says. It is a wonder Lorna Jean doesn't run from this crazy place. He can feel his neck burning, his face, his arms.

"Well, hey Virgil," says Lorna Jean. The summer sun has turned her into a tawny angel. "How's it going?" And then without waiting for him to say anything back, "I can get Rock back, now. We're going to do it! Speed's going to Texas tonight, Monday we get married, and then he finds Rock."

The raw August sunshine suddenly frees itself from their giant old oak tree and blazes up the whole back yard. Virgil blinks. *Finds* Rock? "Lorna Jean," he says. Then he thinks of her married to awful Speed, himself depressed forever. "No hurry. Rock's fine where he is. He's not a problem anymore."

"Well, hey, little guy," says Daisy, bending down to scratch Mike Hammer who turns with frank amorous interest from Lorna Jean's to her ankle. She straightens up. "You so crazy, Lorna Jean!" she says. "She's not going to confess, Virgil. She's going to try to make it look like she had nothing to do with it at all!"

Lorna Jean says, "Do you think, Virgil...Do you think you could put him somewhere? Like maybe on the doorstep? Number 10 Raintree Apartments? Then when we get back, we can get that all over with, and it won't look like I had anything to do at all with it. Could you start thawing him out for Tuesday? And put him out about midnight?"

"Well, I don't know," says Virgil. He is floored. He never told Lorna Jean or Daisy about Rock's new state of preservation. He didn't know Lorna Jean wanted Speed to get back a seemingly fresh dead dog.

And what was he supposed to have done for a whole summer? "Er, maybe that'd be all right..." he says slowly. "But..." he hears his voice trail off. Maybe when Lorna Jean sees how nice Rocky looks, she will see the beauty of it all.

"You still have him?" says Lorna Jean quickly.

"Well, yeah. But—"

"Virgil!" Shelby yells from the back door. "Harvey on the phone!"

"Tuesday, then."

"Well, I guess it's OK..." says Virgil.

"You'll do it?" says Lorna Jean, frowning. "And why wouldn't it be OK?"

"Yeah. Sure." says Virgil, ignoring the second question.

"Virgulllll!" hollers Shelby.

"I got to go," says Virgil, edging toward the back door.

"HEEEY!" yells Daisy at Mike Hammer.

"See ya," says Lorna Jean. But before anyone can move good, Meemaw reaches down and turns on her sprinklers, the sprinklers Shelby this summer has souped up to beat all hell.

"YIIIIII," the girls scream, stampeding under the bullets of water.

Virgil cringes under the jet spray and ducks toward the door. He wants to die.

"Haw, haw, haw," says Meemaw.

&

Virgil eases up on the clutch but the funeral coach lunges forward so strongly he has to slam on the brakes. Then he gives it too much gas again, and he ends up lurching and braking, lurching again out the driveway. As he turns onto the street, the right rear tire rolls up over the curb.

Yesterday, when Harvey called him, Virgil neglected to tell him that, outside of driver's ed, he'd only driven about five or six times completely by himself. Long ago, at the beginning of the summer, he'd also neglected to tell Harvey not only does he not have a chauffeur's license, he does not have a regular license either. He just checked the box "no" on his application when he first started work, and when Harvey told him to drive today and he had not mentioned anything about that. He must not have noticed. Virgil had left his license in his school locker a long time ago and it disappeared, along with his math book and an old braided friendship bracelet he'd found in the library once and didn't care about anyway. Virgil hadn't gotten another license because he had been afraid the license bureau would make him take another driving test. Virgil wants to be seen as little as possible in Shelby's Hyundai with the cockroach on the roof and its derby hat.

The problem with Harvey is that he just assumes too much—assumes Virgil knows how to hook up the electrical system of a microphone, assumes Virgil knows how to drive a coach. Assumes Virgil knows his way around the backwoods of Webster parish.

Virgil eases up to the light on Stoner Drive and stops. In the back of the coach is a member of one of those backwoods communities who is to be buried today, Mrs. Harriet Higginbotham, 91, who Virgil has been entrusted to drop off at the Longview Community across the river. "Drop off," as Douglas puts it.

Normally on a call like this Virgil could have used the van. But the Higginbotham family insisted on the coach for effect. He is supposed to drive Mrs. Higginbotham to the church and arrive a few minutes before the service. Virgil looks at his watch. The funeral is at three. The trip to Longview Community takes forty-five minutes according to Douglas. Well, he has exactly forty-seven minutes to get there. Virgil knows how to get to the Bayou Macon. He knows to turn left at a country store but then what next? What road does he take after that?

A horn behind Virgil honks impatiently and he realizes the light has changed. He pulls off too fast, then he slows down to a creep and after he turns onto the boulevard, the driver of the car that honked at him, an elderly man in a new BMW, passes him, and without looking over, serenely shoots him the bird.

Virgil inwardly groans. It looks like a tough afternoon ahead of him. He tries to remember what he knows of the area he is going to. Near the Longview community are the clay pits where the wild kids at school had beer parties. Daisy!

Daisy went to those parties. She would know how to get to Longview. If only he'd thought to call her! Virgil remembers once how

Pee Wee grounded Daisy one summer and she climbed out of her window down a mimosa tree. Virgil was mowing the yard with a push mower that Shelby rigged up with an old Maytag washing machine motor and it kept quitting on him. He was leaning over, trying to decide if he'd left the choke on and flooded it or not and he looked up to see Daisy dropping out of the mimosa like a cat. She said, "Wanna go to the clay pits?" as if she dropped out of mimosas every day and invited whoever was in the yard. And of course Virgil said, "No". Back then he'd found Daisy even more upsetting than now—now, he is even getting used to her. Virgil has often wondered what would have happened to him if he had gone with Daisy that day. If he just left the stalled Maytag out in the yard, hopped into her bug like a regular person would have, and gone. Would he have been part of some kind of crowd after that? Would he have come out OK? He and Booger, despite all Booger's bullshit and big talk of doing it, and dope, had after all been, both of them, geeks.

A nervous lump comes up in the back of Virgil's throat. Why, oh why, hadn't he told Harvey he couldn't remember his directions? Asked him to go over the directions again, or write them down, or draw him a map, even. Then half a block from Burger King, Virgil thinks to look in the parking lot, and sure enough, there is Daisy's yellow bug parked in one of the spaces toward the rear. On impulse, he turns in. He will just pull up to the drive-in window, ask for Daisy, get directions, be on his way.

The line doesn't look long. A car in front of him is all there is. The kids in the back of it stop punching each other, hang over the back seat, and stare at him. A young woman with a desperate look on her face leans out of the driver's window and talks into the microphone.

Virgil drums his fingers on the steering wheel. His watch says two-thirty. Finally the car with the kids pulls away to the pick-up window. It occurs to Virgil that he should order something so as not to cause Daisy any trouble. The tinny voice coming out of the speaker is not Daisy's. "May I take your order," it demands.

"Uh, Coke please," says Virgil.

"One large Coke," says the speaker back to him. "Would you like some fries with that, sir?"

"Naw." Virgil thinks of asking for Daisy then decides against it. Ahead of him the woman in the car full of kids is being handed Happy

196

Meal after Happy Meal through her window. Then there is some kind of discussion and one of the boxes comes back. Come on, Virgil breathes. He notices people, getting out of their cars to eat inside, are looking at him.

Finally Virgil pulls up by the window. He can see Daisy in the background at a cash register. The girl at the window hands him a sack and a straw and takes his money. "Is that all, sir?" She leans over slightly and takes in the rest of the coach.

"Could I ask Daisy Wade something?" says Virgil.

"Huh?" she says. She leans over some more.

"Daisy," says Virgil. "Daisy Wade." The girl straightens up and pushes away the speaker thing, which begins to talk, "Y'all still have that Pocahontas glassware?"

The girl didn't take her eyes off Virgil. "Daisy! Hey, Daisy!" She calls over her shoulder without turning around.

Daisy shuts the drawer of something and walks over. "Good Lord," she says. "Virgil."

"How do you get to the Longview community once you're past the bridge?" says Virgil quickly. He did not have time for explanations.

"Take the first three black tops, all lefts, after the store," says Daisy. For once the cocky look is wiped off her face. Then she adds, unnecessarily thought Virgil, "You have actually driven a hearse to the Burger King."

"Lord," says the other girl, "is that what that is?"

"Good-bye," says Virgil, letting off on the clutch.

"Hello?" says the thing. "Hello?"

Virgil heads toward Highway 141 out of Harrisonville, Coke sloshing between his knees. He looks at his watch. It is two-thirty already. But he thinks he can make it. Daisy's instructions have been simple enough.

Out on the highway the coach is easier to handle. After the houses thin out, Virgil rolls down his window and throws out his Coke. He needs both his hands. Virgil hates a straight stick because in driver's ed, the student learner car had been automatic. But on the highway, he grinds around until he finds fourth gear and concentrates on relaxing. He puts his hands at ten o'clock and four o'clock and leans his head back a little. The old Chrysler is so well cared for its engine noise is barely audible. When he started it up back at the funeral home, Virgil had thought the engine had died on him. But it was just running quiet and smooth. The V-8 engine has power, too. The interior is real leather and shines dully. The floor is spotless, criss-crossed with vacuum cleaner marks on it. Virgil relaxes more, and begins to feel cool. He pretends he is driving a Lamborghini. Then he pretends that he is flying a B-16. He feels sealed up and invulnerable in a cockpit.

The funeral is at Bethel Rose of Sharon Primitive Baptist Church—there cannot be too many churches by that name in the community. He can do it! Virgil picks up a little speed. He is a better driver than he remembers.

The last time Virgil drove a car was eons ago when he headed toward the new shopping center east of town to look for new shoes. He never got his shoes that day. On the four lane that runs past the car dealerships and motels where the traffic is the worst and fastest, he saw a crazy thing. A box turtle wandered into the lanes and actually made it halfway across the street. Virgil recklessly careened around it, and then he looked into the rear view mirror and saw the little head sticking out of the shell, gamely plugging along like Mr. Magoo as cars whizzed by it, inches from the shell. Then Virgil stopped, pulled over, and—what made him do it?—stuck one leg out of the car to go back—he was going to actually carry it across—and he almost died. The box turtle went under a truck, emerged completely unharmed, and then missed a city bus by inches. Then the next car, a Trans Am with flames painted on the hood, with plenty of room to miss, suddenly veered off its track and squashed the turtle deliberately. It was a curious thing. Virgil was in a strange mood that day, anyway.

He'd just gotten fired from his job at the Conley's Poultry and Egg Company. He had this job culling eggs all day, separating the good eggs from the blemished eggs by putting the good eggs in cartons to sell and the bad eggs on a conveyer belt that went into the incubators. Virgil was too slow on the job. If the egg had blemishes or too many bumps on the shell it was supposed to be culled, put in a box for the hatchery. If the egg was smooth and the right color, it was supposed to go into the carton for the store. It was like deciding life and death. Virgil did not like being emotionally involved in those kinds of decisions. And how many was too many? Three, four? Finally Virgil decided on five blemishes. He thought his system was working out well, but Mr. Wesley, the supervisor had thought he was just too slow.

So Virgil was in an unusual state of mind when he saw the turtle. He'd been missing Booger too, or maybe just the idea of Booger, and the boring, safe monotony of high school. Normally, he wouldn't care about turtles that much. Stopping to save a turtle had been one of those things he'd never do with Booger around. After the car mashed the turtle, it honked at Shelby's cockroach as it sped by. The Trans Am had a bumper sticker on the rear that said, "Shit Happens." Then Virgil got this even weirder feeling, like he forgot how to drive or something. He stared at the D1, D2, R, and P and couldn't move. He sat there like an idiot, parked on the side of the road, until finally the feeling passed. He started off driving slowly toward the shopping center but something happened to the car. The car was slow-acting and the tires started to make scary noises. He smelled burning. So he turned around as soon as he could find a good wide parking lot—like Meemaw he tried to avoid reverse as much as possible—and went home. Shelby figured it out. What happened was that he forgot when he stopped that he put the emergency brake on and all his driving had burned it up.

When Booger joined the Navy, that just floored Virgil. Booger just came over to the house one day and announced it. Not that Booger had not mentioned a million times that he was going to do it. It's just that he also announced a million times that he was going hitch to across the United States and start a casino in Nevada. And go to New Orleans to be a stockbroker. And go to Alaska and run a salmon cannery. It never occurred to Virgil that Booger would do anything but live with his parents and spend his allowance. Virgil, to be perfectly honest, had never even, deep down, liked Booger. Booger was too braggy. He also had smelly breath and never washed his hair that Virgil could tell. But after Booger left, Virgil missed him. He almost wished for a while he'd gone into the Navy with him. Except that crowds, or just people doing the same thing together in general bothered him for some reason. There was just something wrong with those situations. Even school buses crowded with kids made him uneasy.

A horn sounds behind the coach that almost makes Virgil rise up out of his seat. It is one of those horns like the Dukes of Hazzard had on the General Lee. He looks in the rear view mirror and sees that it is a pick-up truck with those big tires like they have at truck races. Virgil speeds up slightly, and then decides to slow down, hoping it will pass him. The awful horn sounds again. Then the truck gets so close to him Virgil can see plainly in his mirror the people in the cab. Three youngish guys, wearing caps. The one on the side by the window sticks his head and shoulder out and bangs the side of the truck. "EEEEEEEEEEEEeeeeeeeeehaaaaa," he yells. Virgil groans. The truck pulls up even with him and doesn't seem to want to pass.

"Hey, Frankenstein," yells the one hanging out of the window. "Wanna drag?"

Virgil can see them all braying with laughter. He picks up his quivering knee and touches the brake so that for a few minutes they surge ahead. Then they pull over into his lane and slow to a crawl. Virgil slams on his brakes and hears Mrs. Higginbotham slide forward from the back of the hearse. He must have forgotten to strap the gurney in. "Sorry," he calls over his shoulder for some reason. His heart suddenly suffuses with blood, and excitement, dread, dizziness. Something in his head begins a faint roaring, buzzing.

The truck slows down so much the coach is almost at a standstill. But when Virgil timidly edges into the other lane to pass, the pick-up speeds ahead.

PAH-pah-pah-pah-pah-pah-pop-pah-pah PAH! Virgil slows down again, but he hits the brake too hard and he almost skids off into the ditch. When he comes back into his lane his elbow hits something hard, and he realizes it is Mrs. Higginbotham. He gives her a push backward with his shoulder. Then he sits up straight and leans forward while all the muscles in his face twang tight and hard. He suddenly becomes aware his vision blurring, his eyes burn.

When he drops behind, the truck predictably slows down. He can see the three whooping their heads off and the two boys on the passenger's side are actually falling around and against each other they are laughing so hard.

Virgil bends forward over the wheel and he can feel for a split second his blood rush up his neck. Then he makes his decision. He just does it--when they speed up, he speeds up too. The sides of the country outside the coach dissolve into green and blue and brown as he and the hearse and Mrs. Higginbotham are propelled at some tremendous speed.

The sounds from the truck become deafening, the shouts, the General Lee horn, the wind. Somewhere he can hear Booger's voice—there's a lot of chicken in you, huh, boy, and he shakes it off around eighty-five miles per hour, and then he lays the accelerator flat against the floor mat. He clenches his teeth. A sign whizzes past—*Trucks Use Low Gear.* The stretch is double-lined, the hills, curves blind. His eyes flood. The truck, the hearse, the wind, all neck and neck. Incredibly, a thrill springs out of Virgil's fear as they top one hill, unkilled, and down the next, accelerating faster and faster, and for one wild second faces seem to observe him, faces forced to admire, to marvel. Booger. Booger's cousin Wilfred. Boys pause in the can at Harrisonville High, their joints halfway to their mouths. Phil Martin. Dewayne Newton. Then Daisy's face. Douglas.' Speed's. And Lorna Jean's—different than he's ever seen it.

Then the truck is behind him and the river bridge looms in front of him. It is an old one lane. He straddles the centerline. A semi-trailer, parked on the shoulder of the road at the bottom of the bridge blurs into nothing. Then he hits the bridge, going up, up, like a jet. On the apex of the bridge he can see clouds, the sun, and coming down, cattle, spotted horses grazing beside and flowing into the river. Then he is sea level, effortlessly, like a B-16 re-entering gravity.

At the first pot-hole, which bounces Mrs. Higginbotham up into the air, Virgil takes his foot off the gas and coasts at breakneck speed. The road curves narrower and narrower and he concentrates on staying between the ditches, enduring the potholes' wild jarring. The coach begins to slow and Virgil picks up his foot and lightly tests the brakes. He presses a little once, twice, then, as the world outside slows a bit, he presses harder. He doesn't want to skid into the river. The trees along the other side slowly begin to lose their dizzy shapes. On the river side, the water steadily unblurs.

By the time the wild flight is over and Virgil's brain stops spinning, he realizes, peering out, that he doesn't even know where he is. He does not remember passing roads to the right, or roads at all. He does not remember a country store.

He drives along, glancing in the rear view, fighting a hot pain in his chest, which is heaving up and down. His knees quiver like other beings.

Virgil strains his eyes, not only for landmarks, but also to draw some kind of soberness from the trees and occasional shack, the fences. Virgil stares at the pastureland and white-faced cows, barbed wire fencing, sucking in the colors and objects to convince his brain he is really still alive. Then he glances into the back of the coach, and the casket, plain and pine, gleams at him from the back. Mrs. Higginbotham is safe.

The coach hums along as if it is used to suddenly being raced from time to time with pick-ups and screaming good old boys. Virgil looks at his watch. It is already three-thirty, past the time of the service! Harvey is simply going to kill him. He knows that. The road loses its divided lines and begins to get narrower. Virgil decides to go over the next rise and if there is not a black top to the right, he will turn around and go back the way he came.

There is nothing over the rise but more pastures, and barbed wire. Virgil stops at the first gate that he comes to and turns in. He bumps over the cattle gap, then wastes a few minutes until he finds reverse. Three white-faced cows raise their heads to watch him. Two of them suddenly turn and gallop away, but the third, one with a yoke made out of a forked tree branch, stretches out her neck and bawls at Virgil.

As he backs up, Virgil notices a gathering shadow rise and fall over the stretch of pastureland behind her until it touches the dark woods. At that moment the dull red ball of a sun sinks out of sight, leaving a line in the sky like pink ribbon hanging over the treetops. Officially late afternoon. Virgil feels like opening his mouth too, for a long, lonesome bawl.

He heads back in the direction of the bridge. If he meets those country boys, he'll just have to outrun them again, if he can keep his wits together. He can say one thing, his driving skills have been improving in the last hour. If he can at least find the store, he can ask directions. But according to Daisy it is the first right after the store, then another right. So he must have gone past the first road while he was still excited. Maybe he can still find it. He hates the thought of asking directions of anybody, especially in these parts. What he hates even worse is being so scared, and shy, and stupid acting.

That is why he gets stuck with so many jobs that he doesn't want to do. Or couldn't do. Wait until Harvey finds out about all this. Of course, Virgil is already in so much trouble with Lorna Jean and Speed and Daisy, though, one more mad person doesn't really matter.

After several miles the bridge looms up murkily in the sky. He still has not seen the country store. He looks at the piers of the bridge and shivers. He expects to see the pick-up come roaring down the bridge on the trumpet of the General Lee.

He has to turn around. He finds a gravely spot with burned timbers and trash but that is plenty wide enough to make a circle. Forget reverse. His rear tire spins dangerously in a horrible softness for a second, but he makes it. Virgil drives down the road retracing his route.

After a long hill, a couple of kids step out of the woods carrying fishing poles. Virgil is so glad to see such young, harmless humans, that just the sight of them makes his eyes tear up again. He slows down.

When Virgil pulls up even to the kids, he sticks his head out of the window. One of the kids has a string of bream, still alive and flapping slightly against his jeans. Their scales catch in the mulberry light of the sunset. "Hey," says Virgil, hoping he doesn't sound desperate. "Y'all know where Bethel Rose of Sharon Primitive Baptist Church is around here?"

They keep walking, not even turning their heads. "Naw," says the bigger one. Then they walk faster.

"You sure?" says Virgil driving along beside them. "It's an old church. It's got a cemetery around it?"

The boys don't say.

"Do you know where a store is then?" says Virgil. "One after the bridge?"

"Burned down," the boy who is doing the only talking said and gives him a quick reflexive glance. Then as if on some kind of invisible cue, they both start running.

The burned-out place he turned around in is the store then, and the road to the right has to be up ahead somewhere. He should have never stopped and turned.

Virgil passes the boys, still running, the fish dancing and flapping between them.

After a while it is good and dark on the river basin. Virgil peers at the panel in front of him and flicks a switch. The windshield wipers come on. He tries another and hits the lights. Then Virgil feels the big motor sputter a few times. But after that it goes smoothly enough. He just about decides he imagined it, when the motor coughs. Oh, hell.

Please God, no car trouble, Virgil prays. He hits a gentle downhill curve and the coach picks up speed and stops coughing. But as the road levels out and he presses the gas harder, the accelerator goes completely lifeless under his foot. He looks at the gas gauge. "Oh, no," he says to the dashboard. "Oh, no, no, no, no." He is supposed to check the gauge every time he gets into the coach. That is the rule. How could he have forgotten?

He coasts as far as he could, then pulls off the road. Virgil locks the doors and turns off the lights. This weird calmness descends upon him. He has a stupid feeling like he knew this was going to happen. He takes his hands off the steering wheel and hugs himself. Now he doesn't have to worry about being late. Now he would probably never get there.

Should he get out and walk until he comes to a house--hasn't he seen one a few miles back? But he can't move. He is afraid to leave Mrs. Higginbotham. And what if he meets those old boys in the pick-up before he finds the house? And who is he going to call?

Virgil is definitely going to lose his job. He is going to get fired again, like the time he got canned because he couldn't cull eggs fast enough. Only this is far more serious. To get lost with a Beloved One, when somewhere, at some backwoods church, Mrs. Higginbotham's family is probably worried out of their minds.

Virgil lies down on the oily leather seat. Through the window he can hear night sounds, crickets mostly. A bullfrog. He can't help it, he starts crying. He's failed at his dreams. What can he try next? Taxidermy? Is there even any use? He did a pretty good job on old Rocky if he did say so himself. He is preserved for the ages. And can be stored anywhere without refrigeration. Will Lorna Jean marry a taxidermist? Why is he always worrying about her marrying him, when he knows she probably won't even go out on a date with him. And now, he has to worry about how she is going to react to Rocky. Why has she been saving him, anyway, if not for sentimental reasons? Why this strange plan to leave Rocky on Speed's doorstep? He will just have to call and tell her before she leaves for Texas. If she is getting married, it is all over anyway. His whole life. Virgil looks at his watch again. If only the coach has a cell phone in it. Daisy's Volkswagen has a cell phone in it and a Fuzz Buster. A Fuzz Buster in a Volkswagen. That is pretty crazy. She will only need it if she is going downhill, and the wind is with her probably. But the wind is always with her.

Right now Daisy is more than likely over at her boyfriend, Owen's. And Lorna Jean is packing to go to Marshall.

Virgil sinks deeper into the leather. He feels a gathering craziness in his stomach. The leather feels like a greasy, tough, warty old alligator hide. He lets his hand drop to the carpet. There he feels something sticking out from under the seat. He pulls on it. A package that feels like cellophane. He peers at it in the darkness and sniffs. It is a package of Oreos. Some driver kept emergency rations in the coach.

He is hungry though. Virgil has one survival instinct that never fails. He can be worried out of his mind and still eat. Sometimes he thinks he is really depressed, but after he eats he knows he wasn't depressed at all. He had just been hungry. He opens the package and bites into an Oreo. He eats it and another one. And another one. Nope. He's depressed, all right. He wishes he had the Coke he dumped. His throat feels dry and choky.

He has a visual image of Owen and Daisy sitting down to dinner. He sees Oona and Lyle driving around Baton Rouge together. He sees Lorna Jean and Speed doing it.

Lorna Jean! What she is doing, is probably having a mushy goodbye with Speed, the sleaze, before he takes his last business trip before he gets married. Then he comes back. Marshall. And Lorna Jean and him set up house. Virgil tries to get that picture out of his mind. He can't handle that now. Even Shelby and Meemaw are probably sitting down to supper together. Probably wondering where he is by now.

When he left for work this morning, Meemaw stood on the porch, the old timey bibbed apron almost swallowing her up and screamed, "Light bubs, boy! Bring us some light bubs!" She knows better than to ask Shelby to bring them home. He always forgets everything. Little does she know she may never see Virgil again. He may die here. Starve after the Oreos give out. Be brutally beaten by the old General Lee boys. And Shelby—he would probably forget to look for Virgil, even after he realizes he is missing.

Once when Virgil was ten, Shelby made him go to Little League way out on Fraser Road, and then after dropping him off, he simply forgot to pick him back up. Shelby went back to work, then at five, home. When he sat down to supper, and Virgil didn't appear, it came back to him to him where Virgil was. Virgil had stood out on the edge of the Little League Field, like a dope, after everybody else had gone home.

It had been a thoroughly horrible day. First he got assigned right field. Everybody knew that meant you were a dud. He hadn't even wanted to play baseball in the first place. The coach was a tobacco-spitting drill sergeant type whose personality permanently scared Virgil in the first ten seconds of practice so that he was hardly concentrating on the balls anyway. In right field so few balls came by that he was lulled into a kind of daze so that when once in a million years one did pop over, it had been so surprising, he'd dropped it. After the game, after refusing several rides, thinking Shelby was about to appear, Virgil stood by a lone pine tree on the edge of the field and watched the stars come out, and a sad, white, gibbous moon. He has that same awful abandoned feeling now, come to think of it, only ten times worse. Because nobody will ever come.

To make up for forgetting him, Shelby took him on a camping trip the next weekend, another disaster. Their tent, designed by Shelby, was one that was supposed to fling into place with the tap of a toe on a lever, but the poles and lines all mixed up and Shelby and Virgil spent hours unsnarling everything. By then it was dark and Virgil had to beg Shelby to make a fire because he had a portable Sterno rigged somehow to actually bake TV dinners and didn't see the need of something that primitive. The fire was good, though. Shelby—Virgil didn't know he had it in him—made Virgil peer into the blaze, and the burning sticks and pieces of charcoal turned into villages and little cities and people that Shelby made stories up about. The Fire People. During the night, though, after they went to sleep, Shelby's mosquito zapper blew the battery out in the truck, and came close to killing them both.

Suddenly the inside of the coach splits with light. Virgil sits up as sheets of rain rattle down on the hood and roof. Great. What next? The rain is so hard what little light there has been of the evening is squeezed out, except for the lightning which comes again in a few seconds. The noise is stunning. Meemaw would have said, like a cow pissing on a flat rock. The rain gives Virgil a blind, helpless feeling. He could be anywhere. On the moon. He is like a rat in a hole. Maybe this is the way Owen felt in a foxhole in Vietnam. If they had foxholes in Vietnam. No wonder he is strange and Daisy had to cure him with psychology books.

Virgil peers into the darkness outside the coach. The rain begins to slack off. Obviously nobody is going to come down the road and save him. He thinks if he locks the doors good, he may be OK to leave Mrs. Higginbotham for a little while. Perhaps he can walk down the road a little piece, just to see if he can spot a house. He switches on the lights a second to get his bearings. They shine down the rain-greased blacktop. He must be on a back road to end all back roads. He is beginning to worry about the people in the Rose o' Sharon church *finding* him now. He wants help, but they are weird people. Mrs. Higginbotham's people were loud and rude at the wake. They brought in food and sandwiches and their gathering seemed more like a party. The men wore overalls and slapped each other on the back and laughed loudly. The women sat, fiercely impassive, watching the men. And nobody cried over the Beloved One. Harvey rolled his eyes and explained to Virgil that a customer was a customer. But he was not been too happy with those customers.

Virgil opens the door of the coach and gets out. He walks around and checks all the doors. The rain hasn't completely slacked off. The drizzle comes out of the dark and down his collar. The moisture and the blackness make him feel like he is moving inside a wet bag. Then off in the woods, he thinks he sees a light. But before he can really decide how far away it is, it disappears. It doesn't seem to be a light on the road, or in some yard, but a light way off in the trees. Then he sees it again. It almost as quickly disappears again.

"Jeeze," he moans. Maybe he has imagined it. He peers steadily, holding his hand over his eyes to hold off the misting. A wind or something must have lifted up some branch and there is the light for a few seconds again. Must be a house down there in the woods and the wind is blowing the trees. But there is no driveway that he can tell. Just trees rising like tall monuments in the dark. He steps off the road. He realizes he is holding the Oreo bag. He drops it and takes a step off deeper into the dark. Bushes, scratchy things embrace him. He works his shirt loose from something.

To his surprise, the next step he sinks in mud up to his ankles. Then his feet fly out from under him and he falls, sliding several yards down in wet sticks, mud, scratchy stuff. "Oh, shit, oh shit," he moans out loud. Then he thinks, Snakes! and then, I'm dead. Something catches him, a mess of bushes, like a giant net, and he gives up and doesn't move for a minute. Then without even thinking about it, without trying not to, he starts crying. He can feel the hot tears fill his eyes and run down, but his cheeks are numb. He puts up his hand to his face. He must have three inches of mud on his skin. "Quit sniveling," he says to himself, like his Meemaw used to say to him when he was little and started crying. But that makes him feel worse. Then Virgil hears a sound that raises the hair on his head straight up. It is the General Lee's horn, faintly wafting from the highway, getting louder. "Oh lord," he moans, pulling himself up. He yanks, tears his clothes from the brush.

He starts running, falling, sliding, picking himself up and running again. He hits trees and bushes. Snakes, he thinks again. A branch grabs him by the hair and traps him as neatly as a strong hand. He twists loose and runs on. He thinks he's lost the light completely but he is wrong. It winks at him through the dark, like a tease. The light looms closer and closer. Finally he is at a clearing. It is a floodlight, like a security light in town, for Christ's sake. A homemade security light in the woods. Above a little clearing and a cabin. Another light glows from the cabin's window.

He finds a good strong tree and clings to it. He is shaking so hard he can't make himself stop. He is totally out of breath.

The thought of going up to the cabin to knock on the door makes him want to throw up. Lord knows who lives there! Then he thinks he should sneak up to the window and see what he is getting into.

He tucks his head and runs. His shoes are so heavy with mud and water he feels like he is wearing weights.

He makes it to the side of the house but he stumbles into something hard. He reaches out and touches wet wood. A woodpile under the window keeps him from getting close. He squats down in standing water.

A million little darts of pain hit his neck. He grabs at it and a busy, cheerful noise fills his ears. Mosquitoes! He falls forward on his knees and crawls until he is out of the woodpile. He is right up next to the front of the house now. He looks around. Across the yard, right under the eerie glow of the light, an old, what looks like rusty Chevy truck was parked. It seems to be enveloped in some kind of misty mass.

Just then a door opens. Virgil stiffens and sucks in his breath. He hears a high child's voice say, "I knowed I laid it here, Daddy."

The door's opening cast a wedge-sized shape of light in the muddy slush. The door creaks and the light enlarges.

"Heah," a deep voice says, "take my hand. Yuh gonna slip in this here water. Huhhhhhhh, look what a rain we done got. Here, boy, I said hold my hand."

"Yes, sir."

Virgil lets out his breath. A feeling of relief crawls up his spine. They sound like civilized people!

Then the child's voice says, "Where'd them star go? Wouldja look at that? Black's a bitch."

"Black's pitch, son."

"Pitch, then. Lass night you said, here's Cassie-o-peea. This here the North Star. Where'd they go?"

"Them's clouds over them stars. They don't go nowhere."

"How come? Can a space ship go out there? Where the sun now? Can you see the North Star from the moon—

"I don't know, Tim. I don't read them funny books. Hey! Looks like you done forgot where you left your old forklift. You got to have 'at toy tonight?"

"Yessir."

"Heh, heh, heh," the daddy laughs. "As if I don't know the answer to that. Look there, now. See that mist over by the pickup? That's where the ground's warmer than the air gettin' cooler all of a sudden."

"Look like a ghost, daddy."

"Ain't no ghost."

"Look like one."

"Ain't."

Silence. Virgil squints at the mist.

"Didn't I see you over by the spreader with that dump truck today?"

"Fork lift."

"Fork lift, then. You was playing over there this afternoon.

"Oh, yeah."

Silence.

"You go with me."

"Nawwww."

"Please, daddy."

"You a man. You go."

"Please."

"Ain't got my shoes on."

Silence.

Virgil huddles in the dark. He wants to move but he gets this stupid feeling that he doesn't want to interrupt them.

On the other hand, he has another second feeling he wanted to get to know them better. Suddenly his eyes tear up again.

"Lemme get my shoes. You beat everything, you know that?"

"I know," says the kid in a pleased voice.

The door creaks.

Virgil hears the kid say, "That old mist not scarin' me." Then Virgil hears him chant, "Angel Devil. Life and death. Devil Angel. Leave my breath."

Virgil knows just how he felt. He stands up. He walks into the light. "Hey," he says as softly as he could.

The kid is a skinny boy about seven in overalls. He takes one look at Virgil, backs up against the screen, throws back his head, and starts screaming.

"Daddeee," he yells and without a breath--"there's-a-man-Help!-Here's-somebody-bad-Yiiiiii!"

Virgil is horrified. "I'm not bad," he croaks in somebody else's voice. "I just need help." Too late he thinks of how he must look, his muddy face, his clothes full of sticks and leaves. The door opens in the next second and a tall, bearded guy in overalls stands in the light.

"Miller!" a woman's voice screams behind him. His arm reaches down and in one swoop he pulls the kid out of sight. "Who are you? What do you want?" he yells in a voice completely different than the one he used a few moments ago.

Before Virgil can open his mouth, the woman screams again, "Here's your rifle, Miller!"

Virgil sees the flash of a thin barrel and he turns and leaps for the woods.

"Hey!" the man's voice shouts. "Hey! Get out of here! You!"

Virgil hits the underbrush and plows in. Snakes, he thinks as he falls and rolls. He jumps up. He pauses, then starts running back the way he thinks he's come. A blast and a whine reverberate over his head. Virgil veers to the left. After about fifty yards of thorns, he begins to cut right. Almost immediately he hits something solid with his knees and does a perfect somersault over it and lands in a pool of water. He feels himself squish down in the muddy bottom. He gives up then. Let Miller kill him. Let the old boys come. He doesn't move. He thinks he'll never move.

He is going to die here and it is a good thing. A good, good thing. Funny he always thought he would never be prepared. Then he faintly hears his name. He is being called, he guessed.

"Virgilllll!" in the wind.

He *is* really dying. It sounds like Daisy. He wonders, as he lies dying, why he is imagining Daisy's voice and not Lorna Jean's. Even in his last hallucinations, Lorna Jean is rejecting him.

"Virrrrjullll!"

Virgil closes his eyes tight. Then he hears crackling in the underbrush. He figures it is either the pick-up boys without benefit of their General Lee horn, or Miller, who knows about the stars and totes a gun. He opens his eyes. A light grows up out of the mud and water and comes toward him. It crawls along the ground then flashes full in his face and blinds him. He squeezes his eyes shut.

"Hey," says the Daisy voice. "Here he is."

Virgil opens his eyes and behind a dancing light from a flashlight sees a dark blur. The blur bends toward him. "Virgil?" its voice says. "Virgil."

He blinks. Mud and water cling to his lids and lashes and under their weight Virgil sees a figure. The person is a woman and it does favor Daisy.

"You dufus."

It is Daisy all right.

Behind her Owen's face appears, chiseled by shadow and light.

"Jesus Christ," he says.

"How-how—" Virgil croaks.

"Let's get him up." Daisy reaches down and Owen reaches down. They pull on him.

"How-how—" Virgil tries again.

"Let's get him back to the cars," says Owen. "Jee-sus Kuh-rist, son."

Twenty-one

Virgil sits in the back of Daisy's Volkswagen and rubs the mud off his face with a chamois cloth. Outside Owen, wearing Daisy's yellow slicker on his head, is siphoning gas out of the VW. The rain has picked up again.

"Then I thought," Daisy is saying, "well, hell, he must be lost. I told Shelby on the phone, 'He must have got turned around.' I went right over and Harvey was still there talking to Meemaw and Shelby. Shelby said he was going to look for you—but talk about the blind leading the blind. He had taken his spark plugs out anyway and was soaking them, and he had to do all that, so I said, 'I know the way. I'll go'. And Shelby said, 'OK, we'll take your car,' but then I said, 'Hmmm, I'll take a friend of mine who knows about fixing hearses and you stay by the phone.' And he just blinked and didn't say anything and I went on and got Owen. The storm slowed us down a little."

"Harvey?" Virgil says. He's gotten stuck on a mental picture of Harvey's frown, and his usual accompanying "Ssss." Trouble. He is in deep.

"Oh, he was worried—about the hearse and the business. He thought to call the police, but I talked him out of that real easy. I said, give'em a few hours. He's just lost. Then I told him about you coming by

Burger King and you didn't know where you were going. I said, we'll find him."

Virgil puts the chamois on the back of his neck where the mosquitoes have bit him. He puts his nose up to the window. From where he sits the coach looks OK. Through the downpour, the top of Mrs. Higginbotham's casket is barely visible from its rear window.

"When we saw the hearse, these jerks had stopped and were looking in the windows. Real punks! Three old boys in Caterpillar caps. But they took off when we drove up."

Lord, Virgil thinks. He buries his face in the chamois.

Owen looks up from where he is holding a hose he has stuck in the VW. He gives them the high sign. Then he pulls the hose out and walks over to them. Daisy rolls down the window. "Need help?"

"Naw," says Owen. "I just hope it ain't flooded. Hand me something. Paper, something. I got gas all over my hands."

Virgil hands him his chamois. "Now we're cooking," says Owen. "This should be enough to get us to the church. They better sho have some gas there though."

A few minutes later Virgil is in the coach following Daisy's taillights down the highway. Owen is sitting beside him. He smells like gas, and Virgil sees that he is almost as muddy as Virgil is. Virgil stares at the VW's rear lights as he follows it as close as he can down the road. Suddenly he feels lightheaded and sleepy. His eyes begin to ache. "Take your foot off the clutch, son," he hears Owen say. He takes his foot off.

"How'd you find me in the woods?" he thinks to ask.

Owen says, "Daisy shone the light around and we saw the Oreos by the side of the road, and then we saw the brush all broke up. We followed your tracks. What a mess."

Daisy flashes the interior lights on for a second, then she gives them the high sign. How, thinks Virgil, how does one person in life wind up in one car, all smart, and half-way together, and another wind up in a funeral coach flying down the road being chased by a load of old boys? Good old Daisy! And he thinks nobody would look for him.

Lorna Jean! He hopes she never finds out. Jesus Christ! He has to have her. He has to have something, some destiny. Life can't keep getting worse and worse. Every day, even at the funeral home, even preparing, the white walls closing in like icebergs, she stays somewhere in his mind. And somewhere, there is always a ghost of him, pacing, wringing his hands, worrying about everything, wanting, plotting to get Lorna Jean. This other Virgil, the panicked one, wants to run out every minute and find her. And now, in a few hours, she will be married. And in a few days, she will know about Rock.

Daisy's right blinker comes on. Virgil turns his on. Then he follows the VW onto a smaller, badly paved road. Daisy starts weaving crazily from one lane to the other, and Virgil catches on to what she is doing when the coach's front right tire drops into what must have been a two-foot pothole. KA-Blam! It sounds like the front end goes out. He glances in the rear view. The casket is staying put. He's strapped it, like he was supposed to in the beginning.

"Slow down," says Owen. "Don't try to keep up with her. If she loses us, she'll just have to find us."

It occurs to Virgil that eventually he will have to face Mrs. Higginbotham's people. He knows these swamp people could be tough. At the wake, when Mrs. Higginbotham's Bereaved Ones brought in their orange Kool-Aid, and cans of Pringles and sandwiches, Harvey said, "Let them," not so much as the customer is always right but that maybe they kind of unnerved even Harvey. "Just be glad they didn't bring their snake handlers," Harvey said.

Finally, around a dark bend, the lights of a building greet them. Bethel Rose o' Sharon Primitive Baptist church. A few old cars are parked in front of it. Some pickups, but Virgil notes with relief, none of them familiar. In one of the pale lights gleaming through one of the windows, a shadow materializes a second and disappears

Virgil turns the coach into the churchyard and stops in front of the double doors. He looks at Owen. Owen looks over at him. "Stay cool," says Owen.

Virgil gets out of the coach and goes to the rear. He opens the door and gets a square of Visquine lying on the floor and puts it over the casket to protect it from the rain. He thinks crazily for a minute how useless that is, protecting it for a few seconds of rain, when he knows where it is going, what is going to happen to it.

Owen appears beside him. The light from the interior of the coach that has come on when the door is opened lit up his face. He looks calm. Virgil takes a breath. Then Owen takes one set of handles and helps Virgil heave the casket out of the coach.

Virgil and Owen carry the casket toward the light.

The rain starts with new force and makes them half blind. The casket feels as though it has gained weight since Virgil and Douglas put it in the coach that afternoon. The rain drenches them, baptizes them.

Inside, they walk down the aisle, their wet shoes squeaking. A dull light is made by rows of candles before an altar. Virgil looks closely before easing the casket into place. The altar is a row of old fashioned wooden Coke cases with a wide board over their tops.

Virgil straightens up and looks around. Three of what look like identically dressed women gather in the aisle. Their long dresses remind him of Meemaw's but more faded. Their hair is thin and tired, and all pinned back in the same way. The tallest of them steps up to Virgil. She has a man's nose, a man's jaw.

"He had car trouble, Ma'am," says Owen.

The woman stares at him with an impersonal, weary look. Behind her children are lying asleep on the church pews. One, a girl, with jaundiced-colored hair moves, turns over, and flings an arm off the side of the pew. The room seems intensely still, but at the same time not really quiet. Some sound, a humming, from another room, over the rain, comes in a continuous flow, like a delicate flutter. Then Virgil hears a low peal of laughter.

Virgil clears his throat. "I ran out of gas," he finds himself saying. "I got lost."

The woman's eyes bore into him and take on a slight, reptilian quality. Her lips move. Her throat seems to swell.

Virgil feels himself take a step back. The child on the pew squirms and is now at a precarious angle. The woman's lips move again. Virgil realizes she is talking to him.

"Ma'am?" he says.

The woman looks like she is trying to swallow something awful. "Ahhh," she says. Then she stops.

"Ma'am?" Virgil says.

"Ahhh," she says. "Ahhhh. Open it."

She looks at Virgil with a kind of careful detachment. She nods her head at the casket. Behind her the girl sighs and falls off the pew. The humming from the other room stops. Then, as clearly as if Virgil were sitting in Booger Beall's TV room back in Harrisonville, he hears the tinkly, buffoon music of the Super Mario Brothers. On the other side of the wall, a man's voice whoops.

Virgil takes a deep breath like he is bottom side in a pond and is about to fight his way to the surface. What if she has gotten all askew with his wild racing around. What if she is all mushed up or something.

"Open it. We havin' open casket."

Virgil turns and fumbles at the latches. Mrs. Higginbotham lies in her timeless sleep, her face bone white and rapt, her lips stretched into the Smile. She lies in her repose, oblivious to rain, and guns, and monster tires on noisy pick-ups, and to her daughter's soft breathed word, "Mama."

Virgil feels the breath easing out of him. He gives thanks for the powers of *rigor mortis.*

"Men is out looking," Mrs. Higginbotham's daughter says Men is out looking, Mrs. Higginbotham's daughter says. Didn't know what happened. Didn't know if you a body snatcher. People talk about such." Her eyes have a battered look but they stare at Virgil steadily.

Owen says, "Anywhere we can get gas around here, ma'am?"

"Store burned down," says the woman. "Got some lawn mower gas in the back."

"Have oil mixed in it?" says Owen.

The woman looks at Owen. Then she says, "Naw." She walks to a door that when opened releases its Super Mario theme to full swing.

"Cecil!" the woman yelps in a voice louder than Virgil thinks she is capable of. "Get me all them gasoline cans under the shed."

"Doo-DOO-Do-Doot!" follows her words into the room. Owen is staring at Virgil. His eyes are hard in disbelief. Then his face relaxes and he shakes his head slightly at Virgil and slowly winks.

Without warning, one of the women in the aisle begins singing, "There is a splendor in my lord..."

∞

"I been in the arm service," says Cecil. "I been all over the State of Georgia. I took the bus one time clear to Los Angeles." He holds a flashlight as Owen fills the tank.

"One thing I would like to do is git married. That's one thing I ain't done. That and get to the Warp III in the Mario Brothers."

Owen fills the coach with everything in the can. He picks up another can and empties it too. Then he pulls out a handful of bills and change from his pocket. He hands it to Cecil.

Cecil stuffs the wad into his pocket. "I live at home now," he says. "But I want to get me a wife." He hunches his shoulders slightly like some rain has run down his neck. "Y'all come back." Then he nods, turns, and sprints back into the church.

Then Owen says, "Daisy can run on her reserve for a long while. You might have enough to make it to town. Stick close to us, not too close to stop." He put his hand on Virgil's arm. "You was tailgating a while ago, son."

"Sorry," says Virgil.

He gets into the coach. One last leg of the journey. He starts the engine. Daisy beeps her horn and pulls off.

Virgil puts his hands at nine o'clock and three o'clock and follows her. When the VW's light catches a gaunt tree by the side of the black top, Virgil counts two seconds to check how many car lengths he is behind like he learned in driver's education. Lord. He is going to make it!

The road curves sharply and Virgil watches for potholes every time he sees the VW swerve. He concentrates with everything he has left. He mostly fights his impulse to get as close as he can to Daisy and Owen and his feeling that the little pod-shaped car may at any moment sweep out of sight into the dark.

When they round the next curve he sees a row of lights floating along the side, the sight of which stays in his mind for a long time. A line of men with torches, the kind made of sticks and burning rags or something like in an old monster movie, pause, and turn their faces to them with stiff interest. Virgil looks at them as they flash by. He shivers.

Twenty-two

W hen Virgil pulls the coach into Harrisonville, he can see the fierce rain he was in out in the country was only the tail end of something. The streets slop wet, and under the apple-green night sky, pine cones, felled trees, and stray shingles litter the dark. Long stringy whiskers of Spanish moss, sucked out of the same swamp he'd been in today, have beat him to town and draped the still swinging power lines.

At the funeral home the first thing Virgil sees is Harvey, his long black raincoat whipping around his legs as he waits for him under the overhang. The parking lot is covered with pine needles and broken branches.

Weary, so weary he doesn't care, Virgil gets out of the coach to be fired. But Harvey says, "Virgil. I need you to stay overnight. Austin's flat quit. Also, the power's real iffy right now." Behind him the security lights flicker.

Virgil groans under his breath and follows Harvey. He is glad he is not fired, but he is bone tired, and fed up with the funeral business.

Inside, Harvey says. "Here's some candles. If you need them. Here's a flashlight." He looks at Virgil's torn, muddy clothes. "SSSsss," he says. "You made your delivery?"

Virgil nods.

"SSSsss," says Harvey.

Daisy opens the door to the funeral home for them.

"Miss Wade!" says Harvey. "I want to thank you, little lady. Thank you for finding him."

"He was all right," says Daisy. She says that like she doesn't like Harvey.

Then Lorna Jean appears. "Well, there you all are," she says. "Virgil! What have you been doing?"

Virgil just stares at Lorna Jean. He is just stumped for a reply.

"You got mud all over you!"

"No duhhhhhh," says Daisy.

Harvey looks at Lorna Jean for a second. Then he says, "Virgil. Hold down the fort." Then he leaves.

"Virgil!" says Lorna Jean. "Have you got Rocky out?"

"Shhhhhh," says Daisy and Virgil together. Then Virgil sticks the candles and flashlight in his pockets and locks the doors. He turns around, "Lorna Jean," he says. "I..."

Lorna Jean says, "Speed didn't go because of the storm. Everything's delayed twenty-four hours—"

"Lorna Jean!" says Virgil.

"Yeah?"

"Look," says Virgil. He doesn't know what to say next. They both stare at him. He takes a breath. "I got something to show you both. Come with me." He wants to get this all over with.

Behind him Daisy warns, "Owen's in the car. I don't have all night."

He leads them to the storage room. Several large Cavicide cartons take up one end of the room. Virgil starts moving them around. Behind the last one is a crawl space for plumbers and electricians. He opens the door and turns to them.

Lorna Jean is looking around, wide-eyed. Daisy is staring at the nude Beloved One calendar. She says, "Good grief."

"I couldn't keep him refrigerated for so long," Virgil begins to explain. They both look at him, hard. "I had to do something. So. I just...I just..."

Virgil reaches in the crawl space and grabs Rocky's paw. He

rolls him out—the wheels make the moving easy—"fixed him," he finishes lamely.

Lorna Jean and Daisy look at Rocky. They stare, their stares gradually becoming incredulous. Finally Daisy takes a step closer and says, in a funny voice, "He's....stuffed."

And then Lorna Jean starts screaming. It is a long scary, horrible, disturbed scream, a scream that Virgil will remember for the rest of his life. At that instance the light stops flickering, stays on, remains low and dim, and Virgil's back erupts in pile-ups of goose bumps. He puts one hand on the wall to keep from fainting.

"Shut up," says Daisy in a horrible voice.

Lorna Jean shuts up. The silence is even more ghastly. They both seem hypnotized by Rocky—Rocky in his classic grizzly bear rearing-up pose—Virgil's only volume on large animals—it was either that or a woodchuck or something. To get Rocky up on his hind legs, paws extended, took seventeen-and-a-half hours, five full nights, three trips to Wayne's Taxidermy Equipment and Supply, and over a hundred feet of non-putrefying thread.

In the weak light, all Virgil's hard work stands out in super big relief. Virgil has transformed Rocky's cringed expression to an out-and-out snarl. His teeth, which Virgil painstakingly polished with Bon Ami, glint dangerously. One extended paw swipes at something imaginary, and his fur glistens with mineral oil. His glass eyes glitter supernaturally and his rearing pose makes him seem tall, bigger than he had been, even, in life. Before, Virgil thought it was an interesting transformation, from something looking scared to something more... well, savage. Now, though, he can see that it was too big, far too big of a change.

"What... the fuck.... have you...done...Virgil," says Daisy, like she is making a gigantic effort.

"I...I...thought she wanted him kept," Virgil tries to explain. "I thought she wanted him... saved, I mean preserved..."

"Saved!" Lorna Jean comes out of her trance. Her beautiful voice squeaks, "Saved for the insurance! That damn dog had a $3000 accidental death policy. His daddy was a Holiday in Dixie three times Champion. And you're— you've stuffed him!"

Virgil's legs buckle. He sinks down cross-legged onto the floor. The light is dimming even more, like a power plant somewhere is rapidly giving out.

Lorna Jean bursts into tears. "God! Speed is going to kill me." She runs for the door and stops. Her eyes fizz at Virgil. Then she says something awful, something so awful that it feels like a giant trocar stabbing Virgil all the way to his living heart, "You so weird, Virgil Matthews. You so weird."

On her heels, Daisy hollers, "Nobody's going to give you a vet's certificate for a stuffed bear!"

Virgil puts his head in his hands. "I didn't know. I didn't know," he mutters to the floor.

Daisy must have paused at the door. Her voice hammers Virgil, "Why oh why, Shit-For-Brains, would anybody *ever* want to keep anything dead around unless they could make money off of it?"

Twenty-three

Lorna Jean is acting just wild. Daisy follows her to her car, which she parked in front of the T.C. Haynes building in case Speed showed up. "I'm just dead," Lorna Jean wails. "There is absolutely nothing I can do but tell Speed the truth. Oh, God!"

"Maybe he won't care," Daisy says, thinking, *fat chance*. "Maybe it won't be as bad as you think."

"Oh, sure!" says Lorna Jean. She gets in her Escort and looks up at Daisy. "I'm dead, cuz. Dead." She cranks up.

"If Speed gives a damn about you, he'll come around."

Lorna Jean stares at Daisy a second. "That is an absolutely stupid thing to say," she says. She races her motor twice, and roars off.

Daisy beats it back across the street, breaks into a run when she passes under the live oaks, still swaying with the last of the hurricane winds.

The parking lot is deserted, looking severe and dark as a frozen lake.

"Owen," Daisy yells.

The wind picks up his name and smashes it back in her face. A light has come on behind the cyclone fence where Harvey's Porta-potties are enclosed. Daisy hops up on the porch and trots between the columns.

On the other side of the funeral home, outside the gate, two men sway against each other in the back of a pick up truck full of Porta-potties.

Daisy goes closer, presses herself against a column, and peers at them.

"I tell you you making a big mistake, boy." It is Speed, and Owen has him in a clinch.

"I said, talk!"

The wind lifts their words.

"I don't have all night, man," Owen says. "I ain't a narc, I ain't with the FBI. I ain't the police. I'm a crazed 'Nam vet and I need to know what you think you doing."

"I'm just going to deliver these pots, man. I didn't know anything was in them," Speed says and then, "OW!" Owen obviously wasn't satisfied with his answer. Daisy snorts. Then she crouches down to make herself littler, and duck walks around the side of the column.

"Ow!" Owen must have increased pressure on something.

"It—it's all legal, man. I got the consent forms from the relatives. All these people are going to science. Haven't you heard of biotechnology companies? And the new, uh market? It's all legal, man."

What? Daisy squints at their shadows. Why would Porta-potties go to biotechnology companies?

"Well, how come you going in the dark then, with them in toilets, if it's all so legal, man?" Then Speed folds in two as Owen hits him in the stomach. Still doubled up, Speed jumps, half falls off the truck, and goes stumbling up the drive, then up the steps to the door of the funeral home.

Daisy flattens herself against the column as Speed flies by her, and then she stands up and hops off the porch. She runs up to the cyclone wire.

"Owen!"

"Daisy!" says Owen. "Stay where you are."

In a minute he is beside her. "Let's go!"

"What the hell is going on?"

"I'll tell you in the car."

"No! Tell me now! I'm not budging until you tell me what that was all about."

Owen sighs. Then he puts his hand under Daisy's chin and

turns it toward the truck with the Porta-potties lined up in it like ancient stones. "See that?" he says. "There's dead people in those things. And body parts. Look hard. See that mist? It's dry ice."

"What! You crazy—"

"Naw, now listen. I saw Speed spooking around back here. See that door on the potty that's open? I jumped him and made him open up. There was a body bag inside. I made him unzip it. There's this lady, Daisy. It's weird. She's all smoky covered, from the ice, and dressed up, with auburn hair and little pointy shoes. They stealing bodies for something. Probably selling them somewhere."

The wind pushes Owen's hair up off his head, like in a cartoon when someone gets frightened. It is warm out, the air sticky with hurricane smells, but Daisy shivers, hard. "How? How? Is it legal? He said something about papers, didn't he?"

"Bullshit. All bullshit. If he has any papers, they probably forged."

"Jeesusss," says Daisy. "What do we do now? Just leave them?"

"What else can we do? Call the police? Oh, sure! With all that stuff you have in your purse? And with the goods we got right now at home, Daisy? Come on. Let's go." Owen finishes abruptly, catching her arm. "This is all too weird."

But Daisy pulls her arm back. She stares at the toilet coffins in the back of the pick-up where the auburn lady waits for a fast ride to nowhere. For a wild second she sees Granmaw Bee in her purple flowered funeral dress, her little pearls, and hand crocheted sweater she was wearing the last time Daisy saw her. "Jesus! I have to tell Lorna Jean! I got to find her now! Speed could be dangerous."

"Naw," says Owen. "He's just a little wimp underneath. He probably ain't dangerous. All coward. He was scared to death of me. We'll go tell her though."

Daisy takes two steps and then comes to a full stop. "Virgil! He's just going to die!"

⁊

The candles make the rest of the darkness worse somehow. Their flickering distorts the shadows of things around him into elongated, jittery shapes. Virgil sits in the light cast from the candles, and his throat closes on him so that he can barely breathe. Horror—not of the darkness, not of the fact that he is entrusted, alone, to guard the Beloved Ones through the night—but of the inescapable, eternal disfavor of Lorna Jean Gibson.

Virgil flattens down on the couch and closes his eyes. He keeps seeing her face, the shock growing in her eyes. The way she pauses, aims, "You weird, Virgil Matthews."

True, oh true, he groans out loud. He can see in that one second how he looks to her. His job. His stupid job. What an idiot he is. Always thinking, doing the wrong things. Believing the stuffed carcass of a dog would be important to anyone. Virgil sinks deeper into the couch. Lorna Jean! So innocent. Innocent! They are as far apart as any two people can get. As if she is shut away in a glass case. Where he can never touch her. Like Sleeping Beauty. Glass casket! Her untouched by him or by the way things can disappear on you, return viciousness and loneliness for just being born. Virgil shudders, thinking of Rocky. Why did he think he did such a good job? After they left, he could see the stitches he thought he hid by fur, the hide like one of Meemaw's patchwork quilts, the ears uneven, the fur burned in places where a chemical leaked. And that pose. An accident to tell the truth. Virgil was going to make him on all fours, but he kept going along, going along, following the instructions to the letter, and then suddenly, it was too late. Virgil had created a grizzly bear, standing up, pawing the air! But he hadn't known how awful it was, how *weird* it looked for somebody to try to keep something from going away. He remembers how Meemaw made him dump all the animals from her freezer—suspended glacial beings omitted from the world...*It is awful. He doesn't want anything to really go away. Forever. He thought that was how Lorna Jean felt about Rocky. But it hadn't been.*

And then Virgil feels himself drift into a half sleep where everything that happened that day appears and jumbles together, starting with Daisy and Burger King and Mrs. Higginbotham, all the way to Rock careening from the shadows on his wheels, and Daisy's and Lorna Jean's faces. Lorna Jean's face.

The candles on the floor waver, then send some smoke up behind that last image, like the white cloud fingers of crematory smoke he avoided all summer, and all the faces, all kinds of faces of all the Bereaved Virgil has ever known fill his mind: the fearful faces, grieved faces, bored faces, those stingy, those grateful for skill—no matter how fractional, unfinished. They zoom in and out silently, each waiting their turn to fill his brain for a second. Virgil pulls his legs up on the couch and finally sleep comes down over him, pitched and dreamless.

ဢ

Mutters. Breath blown out. Swishes.

Virgil opens his eyes. The five candles, almost gone, still gutter against the dark. What woke him? He sits up, panic rising in his throat. Then he hears it. Voices. Upstairs, he thinks.

Naw. They are probably outside. Fixing the utility pole, or something. He strains. Nothing.

Virgil lies back down. His eyes feel like a couple of heavy stones. His skull pounds and a taste like a shot cap pistol scorches his tongue. He closes his eyes. It is too painful to stay awake. But he isn't sleepy anymore.

Then he hears it again. Arguing. Inside the funeral home.

Virgil gets up, reaches for Harvey's flashlight, and goes to the door. He opens it and stands there. Then he turns it on and lets the beam wash down the hall. The voice again. Douglas! Aw. Virgil's back caves in relief. Is a Beloved One arriving? And why hasn't he heard the phone ring? The van cranking up? But what is Douglas doing here? Virgil should have got that call.

Virgil edges into the hall. His legs creak with each step like they belong to an old, old man. He is so stiff he almost has to move sideways. He stops. Everything so damn creepy.

But he guesses he should go see. Strange that Douglas is here. Does Harvey think Virgil can't handle even staying overnight? Then he hears Speed Maxwell say, plain as daylight, "Aw, shit."

Virgil walks toward, almost goes to, the elevator. Stupid. Electricity off. He goes into the stairwell. The long shadows around his flashlight beam almost put him off. What does he care though? After what happened with Lorna Jean, how bad can anything get? He starts up the stairs. For some reason, he tiptoes.

At the top of the stairwell, he hesitates a second. He doesn't hear anything now. He switches off Harvey's flashlight.

He edges into the hall and feels along the wall for the door of Preparation. Something shroudish swishes against his hands. Virgil gasps, but before he really freaks out, he remembers the bunch of old Masonic and American flags standing in the hall that Harvey has culled. Which Austin was supposed to take down to Storage, because the new ones Harvey ordered have come. Virgil makes his way around them to the door. He pauses. All quiet. He cracks it open a little. Inside are a pale light and a gurney. The light is coming from somebody's electric lantern. On the gurney is some newly dead person.

Why would anyone prepare this late at night? If Virgil goes in there and Douglas finds him, he might get stuck with doing something. But then Virgil thinks about returning to his couch and the candles.

"Hey," he calls, suddenly reckless.

Nothing.

Virgil waits. He opens the door wider. "Hey."

Virgil goes in. Nobody alive is there. He looks at the newly dead in the dim glow of the lantern. Virgil moves closer. He looks hard. He squeezes his eyes shut, and then he opens them. The Beloved One is still there. And he is not newly dead. He is Mr. Barney T. Walters. Buried at eight o'clock yesterday morning. Virgil lets out his breath. Dreaming. Bad dream.

Behind the gurney, on the floor, is a body bag. And another. Virgil walks closer, treads, like he is moving in water. He bends down and grasps the zipper. At first, he is paralyzed, can't make himself pull...then setting his teeth, he slowly unzips the bag one inch, then another, finally to the face... of Mrs. Arnez Nelson. Services 11:00 am yesterday. Virgil feels himself in his bad dream floating, pulled to the next.

Third zipper. Mr. Edward Stevenson. From yesterday. Dreaming, dreaming, bad dreaming. Somewhere, downstairs, a door starts being pounded on.

Virgil moves in a cloud of lantern vapor. The walls glisten and waver as he makes his way out and back to the stairwell and stumbles down the steps like a drunk person.

The pounding is nonstop, important. Someone who does not have a key is hammering big time, hell-bent to get to him. He drags open the door, lifts up the flashlight to a face.

"Jesus Christ, Virgil. Listen." It is Daisy, throwing up a hand. "Get that light out of my eyes!" In the dark that comes on when he snaps off the flashlight, behind her, the cottonwoods bow with the wind, expose the moon hanging like a naked light bulb above the trees by the crematory.

"Speed and Douglas are stealing bodies from you all!" she shouts. "They selling them."

Virgil stares at Daisy. Everyone has gone insane. Including himself. He feels an electric prickle run up his spine and meet the one running down his spine. Maybe, somehow early, early this morning, he died and has simply gone to hell. That is it. Yeah. That explains everything that happened today. In that case, Daisy is a figment.

"Do you hear me, Virgil? I don't have time to fool around with you, now! I've got to go find Lorna Jean." Daisy grabs Virgil by the arms and brings her face up close to his. "Come on with me. They could be crazy. They could be dangerous." Up close, the skin on Daisy's face is made of fine white and gray shadows. Virgil has this weird feeling that they, he and Daisy, are about to dance.

"Virgil! Virgil! Are you nuts or something! Get a pulse, Virgil! You need to go home."

Then Virgil, like he always does, in a decision between the living and the dead, chooses the dead. "Naw," he whispers.

"Crazy!" hisses Daisy, and she darts off.

Virgil shuts the door, and leans on it a second, feeling the sweat springing from every pore, running down his arms and legs.

80

He makes his way back to the room where the unburied are. He pushes open the door.

Something grabs his arms from behind, shoves him into the room, and shakes him, hard. "You little shit. You little shit," says a voice he knows real well.

"Aaargh," Virgil gasps.

"Aw, Virgil," Douglas says. "What you doing here? We thought you was asleep."

Speed keeps holding onto Virgil, digging holes in his arm. A chair is shoved up and they push him into it. Then both of them lean over and look him in the face with awful eyes—tribunal eyes. Speed's face so close to Virgil's he could see a row of little blue pimples on the edge of his nose. He smells Speed's scalp smell, Tic Tac breath over cigarette smell, and a wave of dizziness hits him so that if he hadn't been held so hard, he would have fallen over.

"Well, this just about makes a perfect afternoon. First, this damn storm, a psycho in the parking lot, and now this weirdo comes into the picture."

Weirdo. *Weird.* If two people say it, it must be true. He opens his mouth, but nothing comes out.

"Maxwell! Shut up!" says Douglas. "We've got to think what to do."

"Do! If it was up to me, I'd be delivering one damn fresh corpse tonight!" Speed yells then.

"Listen," says Douglas. Dreamily, Virgil sees his jaw muscles spring out on the side of his face like the day of the Fat Lady. "You just wait one damn minute."

"How you expect me to get off with a delivery and then have to deal with all this shit?"

"Can it, you!"

Virgil finally finds his voice. He croaks, "Whuh. Whuh's— Whuh's Mrs.—"

"Shut up!" They both yell at him.

"We just got to talk him into being quiet," Douglas goes on like it is only the two of them, him and Speed, in the room.

"Oh, Jesus Christ!" Virgil's chair shudders with a kick. "Well, go ahead. Be my almighty guest."

They stare at each other like they are about to start slugging.

"Listen, son," Douglas says to Speed, running his fingers through his James Dean hair so that it stands straight up. "We in a mess now but you need to shut up here, and let's up figure out what to do." He straightens up. "Jesus, I'm sweating bullets. He gave me a start!" He punches Speed on the arm. "Let go of him! He's not going anywhere."

Speed lets go of Virgil, moves in front of him, and puts his hands on his hips like he is fixing to do karate. His nostrils flare in and out with each breath. He looks scarier, then, than all the risen Beloved Ones behind him.

Douglas puts his face up close to Virgil's. "Now Virgil, we need you to think about something important," he says in his best casket-selling voice.

Then the terrific feeling of terror in the pit of Virgil's stomach is joined by an equally terrific doomed feeling. He stares at Douglas, and feels the Icy Hand on his own neck. None of this is a dream. And he isn't in hell. He isn't mercifully dead. This is real.

"See, son," says Douglas. "All these bodies are going to medical science, you can be assured of that, but we need your complete silence. And trust. Can we count on that, Virgil?"

"Oh, right," says Speed, glumly. "Silence is right."

Douglas looks at him. "Be quiet, please," he says, meanly. He stares at Speed a second longer then he turns back to Virgil. "We just need you to keep quiet."

Virgil's throat scalds. "Waugh ah..." he whispers a word unintelligible even to himself.

We don't want to hurt you." Douglas looks at Speed. "Don't say it. Don't say nothing!"

"Naw," says Virgil, shaking his head. "Naw, naw, naw." He is dizzy, so dizzy, a black border edges his vision. Like he's going to faint. Body sellers! It's true. True. All his work. All Virgil's beautiful work, making everybody look nice, making sure everything was—

"We going to have to ask you to just listen to us a minute," says Douglas, now in his preachy voice he used to teach Virgil preparation.

Virgil becomes aware of a great pain in his chest. He is holding his breath. He opens his mouth wide to breathe and starts to yell instead.

"Oh, Jesus, quit screaming, you wimp," says Speed, disgustedly, whacking him on the side of the head. "Shitttttt, we in a fine fix now."

Douglas puts his hands on Virgil's mouth and shoves his head back against the top of the chair. Virgil shuts up. Then Douglas straightens up and incredibly smiles at Virgil again. "Naw, now, " he says, pleasantly, like he is trying to get Virgil to come to the Lipstick with them or something, "Old Virgil here'll come around in a minute. You goan be quiet now? " Virgil nods. "You sure?" He moves his hands.

"Body snatchers!" Virgil hollers. "I know what you up to. You selling them!"

Somebody's fist knocks him into a galaxy of stars.

After a stunned minute, he tries to start up to run, but blood mysteriously mixed with formaldehyde from somewhere suddenly begins to beat through his arteries, sticks at his heart, and quick-freezes his whole nervous system. His butt sticks to the chair, his legs, paralyzed. *Rigor mortis* sets in.

"Now Virgil, just listen. Just hear me out, OK? And then if you don't like what we say, and I believe you will when we tell you the part where we cut you in, and how much money you can make, and how much we doing for science, you can just leave, OK? Just listen for a little minute."

Virgil squints up like he is looking through shattered plate glass. The electric lantern light shivers, an old, unreal harvest moon, a Halloween moon over death mask, and tricksters.

Douglas leans over Virgil again. "Ready to listen, son?" he says, in a deadly voice.

Behind Douglas Virgil can see the blur that is Mr. Stevenson. Fifty-nine. Brain tumor. Two children. A wife. Mole, right shoulder. Appendectomy scar. He knows him as well as he knows anyone. Which, of course, is not at all. A heaviness pervades his body. Tired, so tired. If he could just rest a minute. "OK," he whispers.

"Now, that's more like it," says Douglas in a fake, heartily nice voice. "Let's just all sit down like business men and let us catch you up. Sit down, Mr. Speed. We all friends here."

They pull up chairs. Speed sits. Douglas sits.

"You got to understand, Virgil, first, what a incredible age we live in. There are a whole lot of people out there who need well, they need dead folks. No shit! Hard as it is to believe. Now, just listen. All I'm asking is you right now is to listen. OK?

"Now, you got your pharmaceutical companies. You got your scientists. Lord, you got artists doing plastination, and folks doing what they call biocollectin'. They patenting genes now, Virgil. They using DNA to run computers—it's better and cheaper and holds more stuff than anything else they got.

"There is eye banks, Virgil, that will pay more for one eyeball than you make in a month! One eyeball, boy! The North Carolina Eye Bank will pay that! There is calls for spleens, and livers, and kidneys. Listen! One company grinds up bones, makes a powder they sprinkle on broken bones, and it makes them heal! They take discs and put them in people whose backs are shot. There are thousands of biotechnology companies developin' products from body tissue. There is thousands of funeral homes all over the country, morgues that are in on this. We are in on it. We are entrepreneurs, son. And, naturally, you can be a part of it."

Virgil's brain swims up from some deeper current. "Ill," he breathes. "Ill. Eagle." He tries again. "Illegal!"

"No, boy! It ain't illegal. That's the beauty of it. None of the laws has kept up with the technology. The human body is not considered property. Yet. The most they could get us for is transporting human remains without benefit of a public health permit! That's just a misdemeanor!"

"Families. Families? Families!" Virgil musters.

"What they don't know, boy. What they don't know, huh?

"We just doing mankind a great deed. And we at the apex of the market. We got calls for Alzheimer folks. The North Carolina Biological Supply Company! Heart disease folks. The Kissimmee Tissue Bank! Brain tumor folks—and folks with certain genes. Remember Mr. Fishbein? He's what you call a descendant of an Ashkenazi Jew! Perfect genes for Canavan disease. Whatever the hell that is! He don't even have to have the disease! He went for $5000! The Genome Project has opened the doors to the best thing that ever happened to us poor slobs in the funeral business. Are you with us, son? Are you with us?"

Then Virgil leaps up, fueled by some secret strength he didn't know he has. Adrenaline pushes out the formaldehyde, surges through him, kicking his whole being up a jillion notches. Harvey!

"Harvey! I'll—I'll tell Harvey!" he shouts.

Incredibly, Douglas throws back his head and laughs. Virgil stares. Douglas laughs and laughs.

"Hot dang! Harvey! He's the one who cut us in."

"Liars!" Virgil yells. The effort makes him dizzy, his pulse rustles in his ears, and a knifelike pain streaks through the soppy space between his shoulder blades.

"Naw, Virgil," says Douglas. "Remember what Austin did? Caught without being suited up? Doctor who tested him reported Harvey. Now Harvey's got a fine from OSHA of $300,000. You think he'd pass up a buck anyway? He was born with dollar signs in his eyes. Do you know, Virgil, what one human body is worth if you sold all the parts off it? All together, if we could sell everything a body has to offer, it's worth over five hundred thousand dollars!"

Virgil's jaws fall open. A huge sigh escapes him like a body being aspirated.

"Well," says Speed. "This obviously ain't working. You might as well give up on this one."

"I ain't giving up. Once Virgil here believes Harvey has started this whole extra business, he'll come around. He'd follow Harvey to hell."

"Liars!" Virgil falls, jumps up then, stumbles, and bolts for the door.

"Let him go," he hears Douglas holler. "Speed! I said let him go!"

At the same second Virgil throws open the door, an ungodly crack of thunder, then a giant slice of lightning sends enough energy into the hall to light up a stadium, to completely illuminate every thread, every shining wet hair, every biological molecule of Harvey L. Sloane, who stands there, his coat thrown around him like a cape, his face like a sacristan.

"Sssso, Virgil, you disscovered our sssecret?"

Virgil leaps blindly down the hall. It's true!

"Get that boy! Sssssss!"

He can hear one of them behind him as he heads for Storage, as he flings open the door and lunges in the dark direction of the desk and the phone. He grabs, knocking the phone over, making it jingle, and scrambles for the receiver. *Number! Number! Think! Think!*

The door opens and the lights burst on, almost blinding him.

"Hold it, you little fucker!" Speed lunges through the air. Virgil rolls over the desk and stumbles into the shelves. He grabs something in front of him, and throws it. Speed roars when it narrowly misses his head and explodes as a box of eye cusps on the wall behind him. Virgil grabs something else, pitching wildly and Lyf-Lyk tint packages splatter the wall. He grabs objects blindly and swings: eye cement—one after the other, a box of denture replacers, a Gordan Leak-Proof Earth Dispenser—all splat against the wall between Speed's ducking. Virgil's fingers close on one more last weapon and he winds up like a baseball pitcher. The something whizzes through the air, takes shape as a rubber positioning block, ricochets back, smacking Virgil full in the face.

"Lousy pitch, Virgil," says Speed, circling. He dives for Virgil, and Virgil dives for the Cavicide cartons. He scrambles behind them, but his face hits the floor, his spine whips, as Speed catches his foot and jerks. Virgil kicks, frees himself, clutching at the crawlspace door. He pulls and falls in onto a huge furry shadow. Rocky. Virgil grabs at him like he is a lifeboat.

"Pitch this," he yells, rolling Rocky out on his wheels and slamming him with all his might toward Speed in mid-lunge. Rocky hits Speed broadside and topples over on him.

At first, Speed must have just not known what it was. Just a scary, brown animal. "Aahhhhh," he screams a screams so frightened, so unsettling that Virgil turns back. Speed is clawing Rocky away. Then he stops suddenly. He raises himself half up from the floor. His face turns the color of margarine.

Speed stares and stares. His chest moves in and out. His breath rages in soft, scraping sounds.

Then Speed reaches out a hand, slowly, and touches Rocky with one finger on his snarl. "Huhhhhhh?" he whispers. "Huhnnnnn..." Speed leans his head to one side. He leans his head to the other like he is calculating distance. "My God!"

As Virgil watches, Speed sits on the floor and feels the dog's stiff head, his face, his now exposed fangs, and all down his chest, his paws, his wide, stiff tail. After that, he sits back. For a long second he doesn't move. Then he puts his head in his hands. His shoulders heave. Speed rocks back and forth and Virgil hears strange, muffled sounds coming from him.

Jesus Christ on roller-skates! Speed is crying!

Suddenly Virgil feels like somehow he has got connected to Speed's brain. And what he is connected with is that the thing he is seeing is not Rock, but some wounded, mutilated, tied-together hide.

That will never be Rock again. And this fact is so final, so awful that nothing can change it. Virgil's heart beats dangerously. He drags himself the rest of the way into the crawlspace. After he swings the door to, there is nothing but the dark.

இ

Virgil crawls, his head bumping air ducts, peeling through layers of dust, dust choking him, his clothes snagging on invisible things. He doesn't stop until he comes to a square of light and air from a vent. He lies there, listening to his own breath, harsh, arrhythmic.

Virgil feels weightless, like in the last several hours he has lost dozens of pounds. In fact, he feels light as the Wicker Man mummy—Virgil Matthews, the original Wicker Man, straight from the peaty bogs of Scotland, his brain, heart, freeze dried to weightlessness.

He forces himself to slow his breathing, to take the air slower. Mixed in with the smell of dust are fainter smells of old formaldehyde, pesticide. A heavy, decaying kind of smell on top of everything. And oddly, something weird, out-of-place, that reminds Virgil of fresh dirt.

The minutes stretch and buckle by him.

Then he hears their voices as close as if they were in the crawl space with him. He must have crawled so far he is next to the Preparation room.

Virgil puts his head between his arms, shudders, and shuts his eyes so tight pinprick points of light float in his brain, like glimpses of dizzy neon fish, chasm dwellers.

"Where you been, man? What's the matter? You look like you seen a spook."

"Rock—Rocky!" Speed, out of breath.

"What? What?"

"Rocky's downstairs, stuff—stuffed. Somebody killed Rocky and stuffed him. Where's Harvey?"

"He's in his office. What do you mean, stuffed?"

"Stuffed, stuffed—you know like a deer head or something."

"Virgil! Virgil! Where is Virgil?" yells Douglas.

Speed shouts, "I tell you there's a dead, stuffed dog down there. My dog! Rock's Royal Rexford! What—what kind of crazy, damn place is this?"

"Well, never mind, boy. Whatever you talking about. We got other problems. Where is he? Virgil?"

"I think he got away. Ran in a crawl space. Somebody killed my dog though. And I'm going to kill him—"

"Well, shit. We better buzz Harvey. First the crazy guy in the parking lot. Then Virgil. Then a, a what? A stuffed dog."

Virgil catches his breath and opens his eyes. Inside his crawlspace, the dark thickens. He can hear his heart clutch, double thump. His lungs expand tissue, like something losing gills. The dark itself breathes, observant.

"Harvey? Douglas."..."Yeah, I know."... "He couldn't find him. The little son of a bitch has stuffed a dog downstairs. Dog! Dog! Huh?...I know you thought—" "Speed has a problem with a dog..." "No! We didn't catch him. He's still around here some place. Yeah. Right. But the storm—"..."Well. We got room for another one tonight... Since Virgil is spooking around somewhere and we don't know where—Yeah, OK. We'll do that first."

The receiver clunks. "Boy, is he ticked. He's coming down. He said to find the little pisser. Pissssser, he said."

Virgil covers his head with his arms. Harvey! Oh, Harvey. The chief tribunal! The Heart of Anubis. Art. Science. The shrine! Honoring of the bones! Virgil falls halfway between the quick and the dead then, pancaked with all his knowledge. He feels his skin changing from pink and green shadow to yellow and purple. He feels his blood stop circulating, gravity pulling his flesh down. His nose sharpens, his cheekbones collapse. His temperature drops terminally. He closes his eyes, begins his dying without so much of a whisper of pre-need plans.

"What did he say about Rock?" Speed's whine, following Virgil into his flesh coffin.

"Dog! Dog!" The voices of the living, so far, far away. "Who cares about a damn dog, man! We shot our wad anyway. We got a crazy kid running around, screaming, 'I'm goan tell! I'm goan tell!' and you're saying *dog* to me? You let yourself get attacked by some weirdo in the parking lot where you spill everything. You go running in here like you crazy yourself, leaving the door to Mrs. Ferguson's potty open and scare me to fucking death when I drive up. And you're saying *dog* to me? SHADDUP!"

"HEY! You shut up—"

"Now! Stop a minute—" Speed's voice changes, Virgil notices weakly, amid his final throes. "Less not fight. LEGGO! Listen now. I was working on it while you were chasing Virgil. We *got* all we need. If you so hell bent for another cadaver—What about that stiff down there in the cooler? You know I told you about him? In the basement? Been here for years because his bill ain't been paid. Let's get him and go, and leave Harvey to take care of Virgil, and the Feds, or whatever trouble Virgil's going to cause."

Virgil opens his eyes.

"The frozen guy?"

"Yeah."

"Well, I don't know...What kind of condition is he in?"

"Who cares? He's got stem cells, don't he? He's got frontal lobes, don't he? He's got twenty-three chromosomes! This is got to be our last run, anyway. There's too many people who know. Too damn many. Besides, Virgil is nuts. And there's somebody else running around Harrisonville right now who knows everything, thanks to you. Let's just pick up this McDavid, the McDavid guy."

Mr. McDavid! Virgil sits straight up and almost knocks himself out on the ceiling. He drops to his chest and lies there stunned.

The square of criss-crossed light darkens with shadows. "Virgil? You in there? Hell! He's right in here!"

Virgil starts crashing wildly back the way he came, towards the door. Behind him the crawlspace echoes with the sound of the metal vent being pounded and pryed and Speed's and Douglas' shouts. Then he is at the exit, and out, up on his feet, barreling through Storage, on the stairs, running, half-falling.

As Virgil zooms down the hall, he brushes through the flags like sentinels outside the place Douglas and Speed give up on the crawl vent and start to clatter toward the doors. Virgil screeches to a halt, grabs a flag and dives, flinging his weight against the Preparation doors just beginning to explode open—and wrestling the surprised bump back— shoves the flag between the double handles. The thing has been made for the job.

Virgil leans against the wall, and takes a deep breath like a swimmer about to go underwater. Then he sprints towards the basement as his coworkers call after him, "Hey, you!" "Son of bitch!" "Virgil!" "Shit!"

In the basement, Virgil pushes open the door to Mr. McDavid's room. The iced down air envelops him, and suddenly a rat the size of Harvey's van runs over Virgil's grave.

Shivering wildly, he picks up the body bag—and staggers to one knee beneath what feels like a ton of granite. Virgil swings Mr. McDavid up on his shoulder, weaving like a drunk for a second before he gets his balance. But when he tries to move out, he falls flat, and Mr. McDavid crashes to the floor like a giant shattery ice cube. He heaves again, but the stiffness, the unwieldy cold of it win out. He bends over Mr. McDavid on the floor then, grabs his bag, and begins dragging him, hustling as good as he can out and down the hall. Finally getting a weak rhythm, Virgil Matthews breaks into a stumbling lope, turning his back on the gods.

⁊

Outside, the sky is a raw charcoal with red streaks—Maisie's #10's—fading at the horizon into flesh tones, the color of webby tissue. Virgil's breath comes hard. He pushes the Glide Easy Casket carriage with the Bronze Metallic Classic Beauty across the driveway and down the shell-covered path to the crematory. At the door, he fumbles for his keys.

Inside, Virgil touches the button that connects the spark plug to the gas, the button that makes the retort instantly 1750 degrees.

The white tile walls blaze with the reflection of the giant flames. The whole place wavers with silent, profound motion and Virgil, at the window of the retort, almost faints at his first good gander at the secret hideous show. His heart stalls, he can't move, and then he is mesmerized by his own gaze, by the flames intricate as dancers' steps. Debris from the last cremation simmer and release jets which shoot up spirally like joyous whirlybirds, and the bottom of the retort heaves, melts, and remelts into scarlet and blue and brilliant orange.

Virgil stares at the flames like an Early Human. As if he has never seen fire before, or anything like it. How clean it looks after the dusty dark of his crawlspace. How pure. Purifying.

Virgil's eyes blur and he sways and has to put his hand on the wall to keep from falling. He blinks his eyes as hard as he can, and stares and stares at the conflagration.

The gauge is beside the belt. He reaches over to turn it up. Babies have to be burned slowly, he knows. A healthy adult is easier. It takes two-and-a-half hours. A frozen body, mutilated by the cold, and the fear of the living, he does not know about. He turns the gauge as far as it will go.

Then he hefts and slides the Bronze Metallic Classic Beauty onto the belt. He opens the outer doors and pulls the steel one up. The fresh heat slaps him in the face and singes his eyebrows, blows up the memory of feathers and Saturday mornings. Then he stops. Something old and familiar twists in his stomach. For a second, he forgets why he is here.

Then Daisy's voice: *Why oh why, Shit For Brains, would anybody want to keep a dead thing around unless they could make money off of it?*

Virgil flips the switch.

The Bronze Metallic Classic Beauty glides silently into the retort. Its sides blaze with color. It is not really bronze. It is fiberboard, painted bronze, the glittery metallic kind, the kind that shines in the dark. It is made to burn.

When Mr. McDavid is safe inside, feet east towards Paradise, Virgil pulls the steel door down and bolts the lock into place.

Virgil looks through the window one last time. He watches the fake bronze melt under Mr. McDavid's element. He watches Mr. McDavid start to go back to what he came from.

∽

Outside, in the west, a pale Delta moon is fading into sky. Sunlight is melting the last stray strands of black from the horizon, a gray-green light gleams off the trunks of the pines, and everything seems to be floating, or made of water. Virgil moves with ice-clean motion, transparent and light as vapor.

Behind him, in the retort, the Bronze Metallic Classic Beauty burns away. The rapid oxidation liberates a heat and light higher than the old retort has ever known. Tissue and ice blaze around Mr. McDavid's gelid heart, eat greedily toward his pacemaker. The soft alkali in its battery, the lightest of all metals, ruptures then, colors the compounds of the flame one bright volcanic red. The brick walls buckle and crack. The intense heat gives birth to gargantuan fireworks and whirls its human shrapnel into nothingness, a split second before leveling all things in that place.

Virgil stumbles slightly from the tremor under his feet, but he does not turn around. He walks on into the elements. Fire! Wind! Water! Air! They have been there all the time.

Twenty-four

Virgil is sleeping and dreaming under his pillow and his football pennant bedspread. He dreams he is driving a coach down a long stretch of river road. *He comes to a church, the yard awash in pine needles and sunlight. He can hear people singing from inside.*

*Virgil gets out of the coach and opens the rear. He drags the casket on the gurney out, the wheels pop down, and he starts pushing it toward the church. When he gets to the door, he pushes on the handle. Stuck. He tries jiggling it. Real stuck. He stands back. Then, without warning, it opens from inside. The sanctuary is filled with people sitting on rough-hewn, bare pews. The singing gets louder. A tall, bearded man in a white robe, a lady in a big hat, and a little boy in overalls are standing at the front, waving Virgil down the aisle. Virgil pushes the gurney through the singing people. In the front of the sanctuary are dozens of homemade crosses and Stars of David hung on the wall, lit up by a bright, bare light bulb dangling from the ceiling. Under the crosses and Stars is a small square door. Virgil steps up into the sanctuary and unbolts the door. Behind the door is a retort. Virgil stares at the flames. Inside, the coals shift and glow. They tumble around to form patterns and shapes—like houses, little cities, and beautiful villages. St. Helena. Pompeii at its most important moment in history. Christa McAuliffe and **The***

Challenger zooming upward, magnificently and irretrievably. Then within the molten coals, turning, and bending, and waving, Shelby's Fire People appear, whole cultures of them taking shape and lining themselves up. Lining themselves in front of a huge super highway leading away from earth. They tumble onto the highway, a huge mess of souls tumbling forward soundlessly. There are all races and kinds of people. They are laughing, and singing, and waving their hands. Soundlessly, they are calling for the earth to cover them. And fire. And to be cast into the sea. A whole history of humans moving and living...and dying...all marching to become Beloved Ones, to be buried, burnt, cured, salted, put into the sea, delivered into sand, into the air. Their Bereaved Ones call for their preservation—by quicklime, bog states, mummifying, shrinking, formaldehyde, pickling. Those Beloved Ones fall, writhing, again and again, to rise, to be prepared again and again by the sorrows of the Bereaved. But there are those returned to earth, to fire, water, air. They disappear before Virgil's eyes, each tiny flume whirling into invisibility. The Bereaved around those Beloved Ones appear to Virgil, of which he seems one of now, less bereaved; the Beloved Ones, safer than the others, safer from...not the worms, not decay, obliteration by mold, or desiccation, but safer from the living and all the things the living do, not to be scared. The singing behind him gathers. Virgil lifts the Beloved One's casket onto the belt. The belt moves, and after the flame has received the casket, he bolts the door. From the back of the congregation, he hears someone call, "Good-bye, Ma." Virgil starts back down the aisle. He sings too. "There's a land beyond the river." He sits down in an empty seat. At the piano, Mrs. Charles Montgomery changes the tempo— Garth Brooks' number "Rope In The Wind." Virgil hums along. He doesn't know the words, but he sounds good. The congregation snaps their fingers.

Then Virgil is standing in Daisy's yard. The stars are coming out. Lorna Jean, wearing her tightrope walking costume, climbs down the crepe myrtle and sits underneath it. She calls, "Come here, you old thing." Rocky runs up. He wags his tail and barks. His fur shines in the moonlight. Lorna Jean, as usual, doesn't notice Virgil. Virgil looks up at the nighttime. For once the stars, the constellations look the way he always wants them to look—like the constellations in books, each one outlined like the dots have been connected. Cassiopeia in a chair. The Sea Goat. On the Great Bear's left, the Charioteer, and on the right, Perseus, carrying the Medusa by her snakey locks. Next, Daisy climbs down the crepe myrtle. She snaps her fingers. "Up, Rock. Up," she says. Rocky barks, and with a burst of fire and air leaps up into the sky to become Sirius, the Dog Star. Oona Williams is next. She is trailing Virgil's ribbon, the one he almost won in the Social Studies Fair. She slides down the tree as if it were greased. "See Virgil?" she says. "You may already be a winner."

Then he is walking down a ragged slope churned with footprints and littered with bottles and paper and cans. The slope leads to a river where a tree has had a sign hung on it, "NO TRASH DUMPING." All the litter on the slope is sliding towards the river. Virgil moves some of a mess of litter with his foot. Underneath is his briefcase. The lock is torn off. Inside is a silky rucked lining, torn and coming away from the sides. Behind a tree, something moves. A boy, waving his arms, sits on a tree root and preaches a sermon about seven loaves of bread. His thin, high child's voice rises over the river. Above the boy's head, vultures sit in the highest limbs and hide their heads from the sun. "Well, hey, Virgil," the child says, suddenly looking at him like a small bird or animal would—nervous, and distrustful. "What are you doing here?"

"I was just leaving," says Virgil. Under the circumstances, it is the only thing he felt he can say.

∞

The sun deepens into acid orange, slides through Virgil's window, and wakes him up. Virgil moves around stiffly and feels the mud falling off his face and arms and onto his sheets that Meemaw keeps bleached and white. As he looks around his room, squinting at the odd color of the light, he hears Braxton Bragg start crowing his loud, old sheet-metal crow that he likes to do every morning to get everybody up and moving.

Shelby pokes his head in Virgil's door. His lips are shiny with butter. "Virgil! You waked up yet? We got eggs and sausage! We got hot biscuits!" His daddy comes in, jostles the foot of Virgil's bed to help him get moving.

"Oh." Virgil blinks his eyes. He blinks hard. "OK. All right," he says, sitting up, arising.

Epilogue

Dear Daisy,

I am so glad you called last night since I hadn't heard from you
all in weeks and even though you acted like you were in a such a big
hurry. I had some more to say that I didn't get in edgewise last night
thanks to Daddy acting like collect calls cost a million dollars a minute
the way he always does. Hon, Daddy and me are so proud you are
finally in college. Hard to believe a year has passed since you all left!
Hope you will like your new college life and as I told Daddy even though
it is not the University of Mississippi, UCLA is probably a very nice
college. Mrs. Doyle asked about you the other day at the A&P—the
nosy old thing. I do wish you and Lorna Jean were able to afford an
apartment by yourselves. I really have to watch what I say to everybody.
It's too bad that rent is so expensive out there that you have to make do,
but am glad you found a four bedroom house and that the rent is split. I
just wish you and Lorna Jean was living with two other nice girls instead
of those men. Your Aunt Mattie has just had a hissy fit all year and is
back on Prozac. Tell Lorna Jean to call her mother, once in a while, Hon.
You did say four bedrooms, didn't you?

I was floored when Virgil Matthews ended up going with you

all. Did you say he was working in a pet cemetery? They have pet cemeteries out there? What will they think of next? When you all packed up and left after that fire at the funeral home and was on your way to California, well, people was wondering why he left. And wouldn't talk to anybody much before he left. But nothing came of it. They said the fire was natural causes. Always was a good boy, but a little quiet and peculiar. Don't tell him I said that. Addie and Shelby were <u>real</u> floored, though. Naturally, Addie is having to do everything by herself, and, frankly, her tomatoes aren't so good this year but probably because WE HAVE HAD NO RAIN!!!! Has your friend Owen found a job yet, Hon?

Well, here is the big news I didn't get a chance to tell you last night. Janice and R.C. are going to Europe! They will start off in London for a six-week tour! Janice was up to run Junior League again, but she doesn't care! She ran her last benefit dinner Friday night. (Aids, or some such thing.) Main course was BBQ Shrimp on Pineapple Planks, with Go Anywhere Garlic Green Beans (your Grandma Bee's recipe) and for the dessert and the high point of the evening was a Clove-laced Watermelon Cooler she found in one of her cooking magazines. Hon, it was just like squeezing a whole watermelon in a parfait dish. I can't tell you how good it was. It's that clove and brown sugar mix that does it.

Sister, I think you should know Crystal has gained fifteen pounds after Dr. Davis took her off Phen-Fen. I told her go ahead, live! Eat! Don't worry! But she is real concerned and trying this over the counter diet pill that she has to take two pills three times a day prior to a eating occasion. She is just not herself, lately. Kindly like she was before when she and R.C. was having a little trouble? You remember? Maybe you could call her some time and be real sweet.

If Lorna Jean doesn't like working for Kelly Girls I do hope she will find something more to her liking soon. She would be surprised if she knew that old boyfriend of hers is doing so well. Yep! Mattie has had to eat her words that Speed Maxwell will never amount to anything. After Harvey probably got all the insurance, I guess, from the fire thing, he bought two more facilities—remember the McCoy plantation house? And also that huge old thing they filmed that movie at when you were in high school over by the new Super Wal-Mart? Well, they are Harvey's new funeral homes! Imagine, owning three funeral homes! I was in the one of them at Brother Shackleford's funeral. (Prostrate cancer, poor old thing!). It is all remodeled and looks like a Hollywood mansion. I kept looking for a swimming pool! Well, anyway, Speed runs one of them. And his friend, Douglas Something runs the other. Do you remember him, Hon? I believe he is from Wisner. Maybe you shouldn't tell Lorna Jean all this. That Speed Maxwell went on to make something of himself and all. Fact is, we saw him the other day driving what Daddy called a Land Rover. He also has a big new house over at Ellerbe Estates. I guess the funeral business pays real well! I say they deserve it, all of them! Having to do such a tacky job that nobody else would want! Bless 'em, I say.

Now Daisy, please be careful out there. You need to watch out for the earthquakes and Lord knows what else. Daddy and I worry about you every minute and we love you so much and we hope one day you'll finish your education and come back home. Tell Lorna Jean, hey!!! And Virgil! And Owen.

Love, Mama

About the Author

Dorie LaRue was educated at Louisiana Tech University and at the University of Southwestern Louisiana, where, in 1986, she obtained her Ph.D. in Creative Writing and American Literature while studying with Ernest J. Gaines. She has taught at Grambling State University and LSU in Baton Rouge, and currently teaches Creative Writing and Composition at LSU in Shreveport. In 1992, she attended the Breadloaf Writer's Conference, where she studied with Linda Pastan and Camille Hukes. She attended the Squaw Valley Community of Writers' Conference, where she studied with Ed Barber, Mark Childress, and Al Young. She has published short stories, poetry, book reviews, interviews, and scholarly articles in such journals as the *Southern Review, The American Poetry Review*, the *Massachusetts Review*, the *Kentucky Poetry Review*, the *Maryland Poetry Review*, the *Southern Quarterly, Manoa,* The *Chattahoochee Review*, and many others. Dorie LaRue has published two books of poems: *The Private Frenzy* (University of Nebraska Press, 1992) and *Seeking the Monsters*, (New Spirit Press, Kew Gardens, NY, 1993). She is the recipient of four grants from the Louisiana Endowment for the Humanities. She was Poetry Editor of the *Quarterly Review of Ideology* for three years. In 1993 she was awarded the Outstanding Faculty Member in Teaching Award, and was recently awarded the Shreveport Regional Arts Council Fellowship and an LEH teaching institute for the summer of 1999 in autobiography. She has also been awarded a Division of the Arts mini-grant, as well as a Division of the Arts fellowship for her unpublished poetry manuscript. *Resurrecting Virgil* is her first published novel.